BEYOND TH

STEVE TURLEY

ISBN: 978-1-906628-40-6
Published by CheckPoint Press, Ireland
www.checkpointpress.com

CheckPoint Press
Quality Fiction - Quality Reading

Cover image courtesy of Valentina Cucciara, Liquid Jungle productions,
www.liquidjungle.tv

BEYOND THE LIGHT ZONE

BY STEVE TURLEY

Hope you enjoy it
Nigel.
Best Wishes

STEVE

CheckPoint
Press

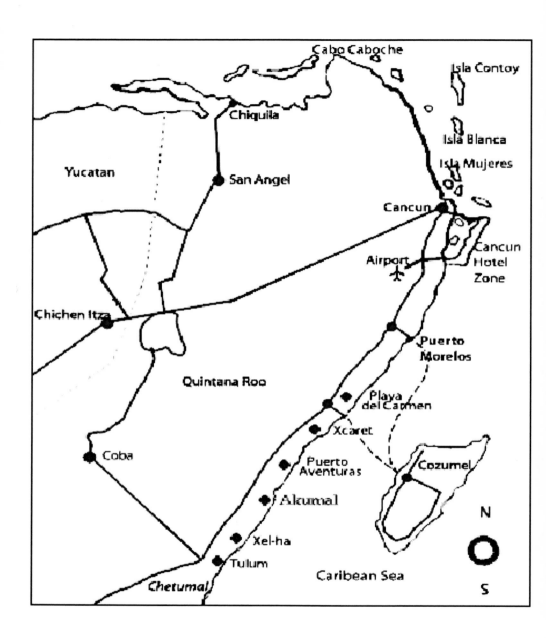

Cabo Caboche

Isla Contoy

Chiquila

Isla Blanca

Isla Mujeres

Yucatan

San Angel

Cancun

Cancun Hotel Zone

Airport

Chichen Itza

Puerto Morelos

Quintana Roo

Playa del Carmen

Xcaret

Coba

Puerto Aventuras

Cozumel

Akumal

N

Xel-ha

Tulum

Caribbean Sea

Chetumal

S

PROLOGUE

YUCATAN PENINSULA, MEXICO

There was an oppressive stillness in the air the day that Ramón found the body.

The dry forests of the lowlands can be an unforgiving place. What little rain falls during the wet season is quickly soaked away into the bedrock of limestone leaving the sun to burn away any trace of moisture which remains. The conditions in the forest are harsh and unrelenting and yet there are enough resources hidden both above and below the ground to satisfy the needs of those determined enough to make it their home.

Ramón Del Castillo had lived there all his life, eking out a meagre existence from the smallholding which he'd inherited from his father. There was maize to make tortillas, black turtle beans and avocado to fill them, but livestock was a valuable commodity and hardly worth sacrificing when there was game to be had just a short walk from the village.

Ramón had struck out along the hunting trail that day as he did most days, with his old ranch hat pulled down against the glare of the afternoon sun, a Model 12 Winchester slung casually over his shoulder and his faithful fox terrier Dudo trotting obediently beside him.

Soon he was immersed in the sights and sounds of the forest, following the raised remains of one of the ancient stone flagged routes which once connected the great centres of Mayan culture. He moved stealthily, his footfall almost silent on the fallen leaves and his keen eyes alert to the slightest movement. There were quail to be found on the forest floor and he'd confidently promised his wife a brace of them.

As he approached the deepest part of the forest, where deer, peccary and wild turkey roamed freely, Dudo suddenly became agitated, twisting back and forth while sniffing the air with excited jerking movements of his slender snout. A distant screech echoed through the trees and Ramón tightened his grip on the rifle stock, searching for movement in the shadows. Beside him, Dudo gave a sudden low growl and ignoring Ramón's remonstrations bolted into the dense undergrowth bordering the trail. Ramón cursed and gave chase, conscious of the dangers which might lie in wait for a small domesticated dog whose courage far outstripped its instinct for self-preservation.

'*Venga Dudo! ¿Qué haces?* - Come back Dudo! What's got into you?' Ramón hissed as he struggled to follow the agile hunting dog through the thorny scrub. His troubled eyes flicked skyward as an explosion of dark birds took to the wing, thrashing the sea of leaves which formed the fragmented canopy above. He lifted the Winchester from his shoulder, charged the chamber and followed the sound of Dudo's insistent yapping. The overpowering stench of rotting flesh suddenly reached his nostrils and he gagged, pulling his neck-scarf up around his face. He threaded his way through a thicket of huano palm, emerging into a small clearing where he finally caught up with Dudo to find him leaping into the air and snapping in frustration at a yellow-headed vulture, perched defiantly in the lower branches of a tall kapok tree. A cloud of buzzing flies swarmed around a cadaver that was lying at its base and Ramón approached, holding his breath against the putrefying stench. The menacing cries of the vultures intensified as he drew closer and seemed to reach a mocking crescendo when he finally registered the full horror of his discovery. Crossing himself vigorously he stared in revulsion at the partially stripped flesh and decaying features of what was unmistakably a human corpse.

The gnawed skin which remained on the body was black, or at least Ramón assumed it to be skin until he noticed patches of white lettering on it. He gently prodded the rotting flesh with the barrel of his Winchester and the troubled lines of his leathery face deepened when he realised that what he'd taken for skin was in fact a wetsuit.

If the presence of a diver so far from the coast was a mystery to Ramón, the same could not be said about the cause of death. The left side of the ribcage had been cleaved open, and behind it lay a bloody, gaping hole.

CITY OF THE DAWN, YUCATAN PENINSULA, MEXICO 1527

The three Spanish prisoners glanced around in terrified awe as they were forced to their knees before their captor. They had heard many accounts of the magnificent cities which were to be found in the new world, but nothing could have prepared them for the sight which now met their eyes.

Zamá, City of the Dawn, was a coastal fortress, perched high above limestone cliffs with a commanding view over the turquoise waters of the Mexican Caribbean. Enclosed within its seven metre thick walls, intricately carved temples with tiered colonnades stood imposingly around a central plaza, some painted in astonishing tones of red, white and blue. Layers of sweeping steps tapered upwards towards high platforms crowned with magnificent shrines, and on the seaward watchtower a ceremonial fire burned fiercely; a warning to all who dared to approach.

From the main platform at the summit of a steep flight of carved stone steps, the three young soldiers had an unparalleled view of the complex, and their gaping eyes captured every vivid detail of it in the dire knowledge that it would almost certainly be the last thing that they witnessed on this earth. For Kenich, the chieftain who now stood before them, his reptilian eyes staring down at them with impunity, was known to them through the harrowing accounts of Geronimo de Aguilar, a survivor of a party of ten Spaniards who'd arrived shipwrecked on the coast of Yucatan some sixteen years previously.

After falling into the hands of the evil Kenich, half of them were promptly sacrificed in honour of the Mayan gods and served up as a feast to his people. Left to fatten, de Aguilar and the others managed to break free of their prison and sought refuge with a more moderate chieftain, but eight years would pass and three more would perish before de Aguilar finally escaped by canoe to join the forces of General Hernan Cortés, after learning of his arrival on the island of Cozumel.

If any of the three young captives had thought de Alguilar's disturbing accounts to be exaggerated, the hatred expressed in the venomous stare of the tyrant Kenich and the fresh blood stains on the statue of the serpent headed jaguar which now towered above them, poised as if ready to strike, must have left them with no further doubt. They could only pray that their passage to the next world would be swift.

Kenich stepped forward and struck the ground violently with the base of his sceptre.

'Why do you return here?' he bellowed, the silver amulets rattling in his ears and nose.

With no knowledge of the Mayat'an language, the three Spanish captives could give no reply.

Sensing the Chieftain's growing frustration, an elaborately dressed official stepped forward. His skin was brightly painted and decorated with intricate tattoos, a skirt of silver plates hung from his waist and he was crowned with a magnificent head-dress of gold, jade and exotic plumage.

As Chilán, interpreter of the responses of the demon, he felt compelled to address his leader.

'They come in increasing numbers and with greater determination, my Lord,' he said with great concern in his elderly, bloodshot eyes. 'Our warriors overcame these men at Pole, but they were just a small part of a much greater army travelling north. The signs are there for all to see...and I feel that it is my duty once more to remind you of the demon's warning.'

The Chilán paused uncertainly as the Chieftain's eyes locked with his.

'They spoke of the arrival of a foreign race that would come to rule over us - who would preach a new god and the virtue of an uplifted tree, of great power against our protectors. The great white Toltec king Quetzalcoátl himself prophesised that he would one day return from the direction of the rising sun and is it not true that these men share his likeness? The great city of Tenochtitlán has fallen, the lands of the Toltec are defeated and now the white men turn their attention toward our lands. I ask how we can defend ourselves when the armies of the Xiús and the Cocoms are bitter enemies, the smaller tribes bicker and fight amongst themselves and even we people of the Ecab cannot live in peace with one another. The Sun Jaguar will never desert us in battle, there is no doubt of that, but even his great powers cannot shield us from the white men's spears of thunder.'

The chieftain Kenich scowled and paced the ceremonial platform as he considered the Chilán's words. The corner of his mouth began to tremble and his eyes suddenly flashed towards the three captives kneeling at his feet. Without warning he snatched a sickle from the guard to his left and with a powerful sweeping motion of the arm, severed the head of the nearest of them with a single blow. There was a cheer from the gathering crowd below as the head bounced down the stone steps towards them, spraying the air with a mist of scarlet droplets.

Staring mockingly into the eyes of the two remaining captives, who were now struggling to keep their dignity as the headless body of their compatriot slumped to the ground before them, Kenich wiped a splatter of blood from his forearm and licked it from his finger.

'See how they quake with fear,' he sneered. 'These men have no divine power. Why should we not vanquish them?'

'They are not immortal, as you have rightly demonstrated, but we have seen that they can each take the lives of many brave warriors before they are slain. We can wage war with them, certainly, and we will perhaps slaughter many, but others will come to take their place. However valiantly we fight, our end will inevitably come when our last warrior falls.'

Kenich let his eyes sweep across the crowds gathered in the plaza of the great walled city.

'Is there no hope for us then Chilán?'

'Perhaps there is a way,' the Chilán replied, deep in thought. 'We might implore the favour of Chaac. His divine protection would of course incur a great debt of human sacrifice...and we would be forced to abandon the City of the Dawn forever.'

Keniche stared at the Chilán, a look of hardened resolve gradually returning to his cruel face.

'Leave? Never! We will fight until we have destroyed our enemies or until we face annihilation ourselves...and only then will I consider deserting this great city,' he said, making a broad sweeping motion of the arm.

In the silence that followed, the Chieftain's blazing eyes fell on the two remaining captives and deep lines spread across his pockmarked face.

'But you are right. We must be prepared for the worst. And if Chaac requires blood in exchange for his favour, then blood he shall have. Take these white skinned wretches and let the contents of their veins serve a more gainful purpose.'

○ ○

Utila, Bay Islands, Honduras

There was a note of uncertainty in Mike Summer's eyes as he inserted the dart that he was about to fire at the world's largest shark into the slot of a powerful speargun.

'Have you ever used one of these before?' asked Alistair Stapleton, Director of Field Operations for the Shark Research Institute.

'I can't honestly say that I have,' admitted Mike, his brow tense with concentration as he examined the firing mechanism of the modified weapon. 'I've never really been keen on spear fishing.'

'That's not a problem,' replied Alistair, his warm, brown eyes glinting, 'Most conservationists have reservations about using an instrument which is designed to kill, but you just need to think of it as the best tool for the job. Rifles are excellent for tranquilising lions, spearguns are the most effective way to dart sharks.'

'It makes sense I guess,' agreed Mike, checking that the speargun's safety catch was activated. 'These darts look pretty mean though. Can they do any permanent damage?'

'They're a lot less invasive than you might imagine,' said Beth Draper, lecturer in marine biology for the Scripps Institute of Oceanography in San Diego. 'As long as you pick the right spot, the dart will only pierce the shark's thick epidermal layer and as a result it won't cause the host any discomfort at all. The tags create minimal drag in the water and have been designed in such a way that they will be expulsed naturally over time. There's also little if any risk of infection because sharks have very effective immune systems.'

'Let's hope I don't fire wide of the mark then' said Mike, smiling as he stared into Beth's striking blue-grey eyes.

'We have absolute confidence in you,' said Alistair, rubbing the dark stubble on his chin. 'The trick is to keep your arm perfectly straight and get as close to your target as possible before you pull the trigger. The ideal place to implant the tag is between the dorsal fin and the first lateral ridge. For anyone with good diving skills it's a relatively simple task. That's why we usually get the participating dive centre instructor to do it. You guys have the greatest control, mobility and awareness under water and usually the best breath-holding ability.'

'Yeah, well that all depends on what I was up to the night before,' said Mike, with a discreet glance at Beth, who flushed and took a sudden interest in the satellite transmitter tag.

'Well I hope that you're on top form today,' said Alistair, 'because we might only have one chance to get it right.'

'Don't worry; once that water hits my skin, I'll be like a sprinter out of the blocks.'

'I'm sure you will Mike,' said Alistair, glancing at his watch. 'Right, is there anything else which you need to know before I go and brief the project participants?'

'Everything is crystal clear Al. You guys go and spread the good word.'

'OK. If you're happy, then so am I,' he said, clapping Mike on the shoulder. 'You ready Beth?'

'I'll be with you in a moment.'

Alistair inclined his head and went to join the student volunteers on the upper deck of the Sea Wisp, a 40 foot converted sport fishing boat.

When Beth was alone with Mike, she turned and glared at him icily.

'I could have killed you for making that comment.'

'Comment? What comment?' said Mike innocently.

'You know very well what I mean.'

Mike grinned.

'Al was none the wiser,' he said with a shrug.

'You'd better hope so, because those little nightly privileges you enjoy can easily be taken away.'

Mike sucked in his cheeks.

'I guess it was a little unfair,' he conceded.

'It was more than unfair. It was idiotic.'

'OK. Point taken,' he said with a sigh. 'How can I make it up to you?'

Beth's eyes narrowed.

'You could start by taking me to dinner.'

Mike rocked his head in playful contemplation.

'OK. It's a deal.'

'Good. And as for hitting the spot, I think performance anxiety is the least of your worries.'

'Now you're going to make *me* blush.'

'I doubt that very much.'

Mike's eyes traced the smooth curves of Beth's slender figure as she rose to her feet, flicking back smoky locks of shoulder length hair. As she was turning to leave, he raised the speargun and pointed it at her behind.

'Hey Beth, maybe this transmitter tag would be a good way for us to keep in touch,' he said with a glint in his eye.

'Don't you dare!' Beth squealed, hurrying out of the cabin and into the warmth of the bright Honduran sun.

Mike chuckled to himself as he recovered the dart from the floor by his feet. When Beth was out of sight, he flipped off the speargun's safety catch, aimed at the cabin wall and felt a satisfying jolt run through his arm as he fired at an imaginary target. After a couple more practice shots, he put the speargun to one side and went to join the rest of the team on the upper deck. Avoiding Beth's reproachful stare, he skirted around the seated students and went to join the skipper at the helm.

'You see anything yet Bill?'

'Not yet,' the Captain replied in the guttural Caribbean drawl of the island's English speaking community. 'A couple o seabirds on the move...thass about it.'

In his leathery European features and lank red-brown hair, Mike sometimes thought he caught glimpses of the pirates from which the majority of the white skinned islanders were descended.

'Do the conditions look right?' pressed Mike, his unruly mop of sun streaked hair blowing in the breeze.

'Pretty good...but y'aint never sure.'

Mike nodded. No one knew the sea around here like Bill. He'd fished it, dived it and explored it since he was a small boy and he'd learned to read every subtle detail of its shifting moods, as if deciphering an enormous blueprint.

'I'm gonna take a look round the north wess. If they's here, thass where we'll likely find em.'

'Whatever you think is best Bill,' said Mike, scratching the stubble on his broad chin. He swung around as Alistair began to address the assembled students, introducing them to the Shark Research Institute's current programme and providing background on their origin and aims. When the formalities were over, Alistair introduced Beth as a guest speaker and leading expert on the study of whale shark behaviour. There was a round of applause as she stepped forward to speak and Mike's over zealous whistles earned him another reproving look. He flashed a mischievous smile and gave her the thumbs up as she turned to face her captive audience.

'First of all I would like to thank you all for taking part in this important conservation project,' she began. 'Our greatest tool in the fight to protect endangered species is without doubt knowledge, and today you will be helping to expand what we know about whale shark behaviour by adding your observations to the data that we have already recorded. Although whale sharks are by far the largest living fish in the sea, we still know surprisingly little about their basic biology, population size, migration and breeding patterns. They are benign, slow moving filter-feeders which spend most of the 100-150 years of their natural lives in solitude, calmly sifting plankton from the surface of the warm oceans of the world. They can reach lengths of around 12 metres and weigh anything up to 34 tons when fully grown and as a consequence they have few natural predators in the wild. But over the last few years, the increasing demand for shark fin soup from the Asian food market has put enormous pressure on the whale shark population by making them a prime target for fishermen. Part of the problem is that they don't reach sexual maturity until they're around 25 years old, by which time they are close to 9 metres in length, a tempting proposition for shark fin hunters. Sadly, the culling of immature adults from the population has seriously undermined their overall ability to reproduce and this has led to such an alarming decline in numbers that the World Conservation Union now lists them as being vulnerable to extinction. There is still hope however. The SRI is actively involved in campaigns around the globe to convince fishing communities in the developing world that whale sharks are a viable, sustainable tourist attraction and infinitely more valuable to them alive than dead. Bringing people like yourselves to an area such as this generates income for the local people, raises awareness of the whale shark's plight and encourages conservation practices for the future. It also gives researchers like Alistair and I a fantastic opportunity to increase our knowledge of whale shark migration patterns so that we can better understand what triggers their movements and target other areas where they might be at risk. In the past these movements have been monitored through telemetry; the electronic tracking of individuals using tethered satellite tags, and although this method has revealed some surprising results, the overall migration picture remains inconclusive because the satellite tags have a nasty habit of breaking loose before they have fully served their purpose. Biopsy samples have gone some way to helping us determine the range of breeding pools and overall genetic diversity, but the major breakthrough in tracking movements has come from a totally unexpected source. As you probably know, whale sharks are covered in white dots when seen from above and the arrangement of these dots is totally unique to each individual. When the Hubble Space Telescope was developed, software was designed which could log the relative positions of small groups of stars so that they could be quickly identified and distinguished from the millions of other constellations in the universe. That same technology has now been successfully applied to the identification of individual whale sharks by recording the unique arrangement of white dots which can be found in the area just behind the gill slits. A simple digital photograph uploaded to our database is now all that is necessary to instantly check if a whale shark has been referenced, pull up its details and record its current geographical position. The system is so simple to use that we can now rely on the general public to add to the immense amount of data that we have already accumulated. Of course, you have to find a whale shark in the first place, and that would be an enormous problem if it wasn't for the fact that they have an incredible ability to travel thousands of miles, guided mostly by a highly developed sense of smell and arrive bang on time just when the ocean is about to serve up one of its rare seasonal bounties. This could be anything from plankton blooms, ocean upwellings, mass hatchings and even periodic crab and coral spawning. A whale shark is attracted to these events because it has a huge biomass to maintain and to do so it must optimise the amount of food which it can filter from the 6000 or so litres of seawater which pass over its gills every hour. Of course, being seasonal, these ocean feasts have a limited duration and when there is no longer enough food to sustain the huge appetite of the visiting whale sharks, they simply flick their tails and head off to more promising pastures. So timing and location are obviously the factors which determine the most advantageous opportunities for whale shark study and that brings me to the reason why we now find ourselves on the island of Utila…because on the surface of the deep waters of the Caribbean which lie to the north of this island, one of these exceptional seasonal events is presently taking place.'

'She's good isn't she?' said Mike, drawing close to Alistair.

Alistair turned and nodded.

'She's incredibly knowledgeable and she really knows how to inspire enthusiasm for the subject,' he said, keeping his voice low. 'We're very lucky to have her with us on this trip.'

'How did you manage to prise her away from San Diego?'

'She volunteered actually. She was due some leave and I think that this was a way for her to take a break while still being involved with what she loves doing.'

'Now that's dedication.'

'It certainly is. I've rarely seen such passion.'

'Me neither,' agreed Mike, fighting to keep a straight face.

'I see something!' Bill suddenly called out behind them. Mike excused himself and went to join Bill at the helm.

'Where's that?' he said, pushing his shades onto his forehead and using a hand to shield his eyes from the sun.

'Bout ten degrees to port.'

Mike's keen eyes played back and forth along the line of the horizon for almost a minute before he finally saw a faint white line appear, an almost imperceptible disturbance on the surface.

'You've got one hell of a pair of eyes there Bill.'

Bill gave the slightest inclination of his head in acknowledgement.

'You see it Mike?' asked Alistair, arriving beside him.

'I think so,' Mike replied, reaching for a pair of binoculars and pressing the lenses to his face.

Alistair drew near, eager to hear his verdict.

'Yep, that's a feeding frenzy alright. Let's hope the big boys have come for lunch too.'

'Fingers crossed,' said Alistair. 'Right, I'm going to cut in on Beth and give our volunteers a quick briefing. Go get yourself ready Mike. I'll see you on the dive deck in five minutes.'

'No problem.'

Mike returned to the cabin below and pulled off his tee-shirt, exposing his broad sun-bronzed shoulders and the stylish Polynesian tattoo that encircled his right bicep; a souvenir from a trip to Vanuatu.

Stripped down to his board shorts, he picked up the speargun and walked out onto the dive deck, his skin tingling with anticipation. He retrieved his long skin-diving fins from under a bench, slipped them on and pulled a mask onto his forehead. Behind him, the project participants were descending and fanning out around the deck, their excitement palpable as they rushed to put on their snorkelling equipment.

'Ah see one!' came a shout from the bridge.

Mike carefully lifted his fins onto the side deck and stood upright, grasping a rail to hold himself steady. Fifty metres ahead, a patch of sea the size of a tennis court was boiling with activity. Mike watched a bait fish leap high into the air pursued by a living missile, a sleek metallic blue striped bonito, which traced a neat parabola and crashed back into the foaming chaos, continuing its relentless hunting spree below the surface.

In the midst of this astonishing arena where the hunter and the hunted fought out a frantic battle for survival, the apex predators showed no mercy for the weak. Mike saw the dorsal fin of a small shark break through the turmoil and then another towards the outer edge, slowly meandering from side to side. On closer investigation he noticed that it was darker, its movement much slower than the first and the regular sweeping pattern which it made was instantly recognisable to the trained eye. A smile crept across Mike's face, knowing that Bill too had spotted the tip of the upper lobe of the whale shark's huge tail sweeping the surface. Staring deep into the seething mass, he could now see a huge dark shape looming into view, creeping slowly and silently towards centre stage.

'Can you see anything?' asked Beth, appearing by his side.

'Oh, it's there all right,' replied Mike. 'A big one by the looks of it.'

'Yes!' squealed Beth, pumping the air with her fist.

The boat glided to a halt with the engines idling.

'Ah see another!' Bill shouted from above.

'Now we're talking,' said Mike. 'Pass me the speargun Beth.'

Beth held it out to him, her eyes alive with excitement.

'Make darned sure that you don't come back with this,' she said, pointing to the satellite tag.

'That's the idea,' replied Mike, flashing her a grin as he pulled his mask over his face.

'OK get ready!' shouted Bill. 'Starboard side!'

'We're going in Alistair!' Mike yelled. 'It's now or never.'

'Time to hit the water guys,' said Alistair, urging the volunteers to sit along the rail beside Mike.

A momentary burst of throttle pushed the Sea Wisp forward then Bill slipped the engines into idle, letting her glide towards the centre of the turbulent patch of sea. The overwhelming sound of frenzied splashing met their ears, like bacon frying in a pan.

The first Mike saw of the whale shark was its huge mouth, an elongated gaping cavern lying just below the surface. Alistair had explained to Mike that in these particular waters, the whale shark's behaviour was unique in that they assumed a vertical upright position close to the centre of the feeding frenzy and opened their huge mouths to trick the desperate bait fish into using it as a refuge. Once inside the whale shark's huge jaws, they were safe from the marauding bonito, but doomed to conclude their role in the food chain none-the-less.

Bill knew what they were doing too, and he'd had enough encounters in these waters to know that the best chance of getting close to a whale shark was when they'd assumed the upright position.

'OK Mike, jump!' he shouted from the bridge.

Mike anticipated the forward momentum of the Sea Wisp and timed his leap to perfection, one hand pressing his mask to his face and the other holding the speargun aloft. Beneath the water a silvery blue missile streaked past him, leaving a vapour trail of tiny bubbles in its wake. To his right Mike spotted the shadow of a black tip shark skirting the edge of the bait ball and slipping silently into the background. He tore his eyes away and stared ahead, where barely two metres in front of him was a sight which made him catch his breath in awe. The whale shark's massive body rolled a fraction, the white polka dots on its grey back shimmering under the penetrating Caribbean sun. As its mouth began to close on its prey, a small dark eye, oddly out of proportion with the rest of the gigantic body, began to study him with unhurried curiosity. In the midst of the frenzied activity that was taking place all around, Mike was struck by the whale shark's calmness and apparent lack of urgency, every movement executed with near perfect economy. Overcome by the uniqueness of the moment, he floated motionless, watching his target begin to sink slowly into the depths with only the slightest sweep of its massive tail. The sound of the student volunteers splashing and hollering in the water close by broke the spell and Mike tightened his grip on the speargun, reminding himself of his mission. He took two deep breaths in succession and then a third, filling his lungs to capacity before plunging his head below the surface and lifting his long freediving fins into the air. Now he was slipping down through the columns of refracted light, powerful scissor kicks sending him ever deeper, chasing after the plummeting giant below. Five metres passed and he gripped his nose, blowing hard against it to relieve the mounting pressure on his eardrums. Ten metres passed and he eased back, trying to conserve the oxygen in his body. Fifteen metres passed and the gap between him and his target was steadily growing. He pushed harder, past the twenty metre mark, momentarily gaining ground, but at twenty five metres his advantage slipped back and he realised that he would be unable to maintain the pace. He watched in frustration as the white spots below began to fade and disappear into the obscurity of the seemingly bottomless depths. There was a telltale cramping sensation in his diaphragm and he flipped his body upright, ready to kick back towards the surface. He became acutely aware of the added weight of the speargun and a sliver of doubt ruffled his concentration as he stared up at the collection of tiny bodies which were treading water, the equivalent of a seven storey building above him. He steeled himself and started the long, slow climb back towards the surface, biting back sentiments of failure.

At ten metres, he was pacing himself for the final push when to his astonishment, a huge form appeared from the gloom to his right and a cloud of white dots began to flash across his path. He quickly changed his position in the water, determined not to let a second opportunity pass him by. With his eyes trained on the whale shark's huge dorsal fin, he made three powerful fin kicks to keep pace with it, while rising to within perfect firing range. Gripping the speargun stock tightly, he stretched his arm out, picked his spot and gently squeezed the trigger. Thunk! The whale shark's huge body shivered and to Mike's great relief he saw that the tethered tag had been firmly implanted into its flank. Thunk! Again the whale shark's body twitched and a silver shaft was pulled from its flesh before it disappeared into the shadows. Mike looked up in surprise to see Beth just above him, her hair floating mermaid-like in the water and a speargun grasped firmly in her hand. She smiled and gave him the thumb touching fingertip OK sign before reeling in her line and retrieving the attached biopsy probe. Mike shook his head and grinned as he followed her back to the surface, the aching in his lungs momentarily forgotten in his glowing sense of triumph.

○ ○ ○

SEVILLE, SPAIN

Arturo Mendoza opened his eyes and immediately wished that he hadn't. The searing pain in his temples was worse than ever and his stomach felt like it had been washed in bleach. He reached over and grasped a half full tumbler of water, downing it quickly, before the nausea returned. The watch on the bedside table told him that it was close to 10am, just six hours after he'd turned in. He'd been to a party at a friend's house the night before and although it had been quite an eventful evening, he couldn't remember drinking that much. Maybe he was just suffering from dehydration.

He smoked a cigarette and thought about the girl in the black dress. She was a real peach. Unfortunately, she was also Juan Garcia's girlfriend, but from the way that she'd been looking at him all evening, he had a feeling that she wouldn't be for very long. His lips curled into a smile that transformed into a grimace when a sharp pain tore into his abdomen. He cursed and threw back the bed sheets, planting his feet on the floor and holding his head in his hands. It had never been as bad as this before. Maybe he ought to go and see a doctor...but then they'd probably want to do a blood test and who knows where that would lead? He picked up his discarded jeans and reached into a pocket, pulling out a small paper wrap. It was a little early, even by his standards, but right now it was about the only thing which could offer him any relief. He pulled a fifty euro note from his wallet and then padded unsteadily into the bathroom. A queasy feeling came over him and he fell to his knees, vomiting into the toilet. Streaks of crimson slid down the white ceramic bowl along with the meagre contents of his stomach. The sight of it made him recoil and he quickly pushed himself to his feet. He stood in front of the washbasin, staring at his reflection in the gilt framed mirror. His cheeks were sunken, his skin had taken on a yellow hue and his eyes were puffy and bloodshot. He opened the small paper wrap, carefully poured the contents onto the side of the washbasin and used a credit card to separate the fine white crystals into parallel lines. It was slowly destroying him, he knew, but it was harder than ever to give up. The stuff that had hit the streets recently was of the highest quality and the price per gram had almost halved.

He rolled the fifty euro note into a tube and used it to snort the white powder into each of his nostrils. He sniffed and let his head fall back, waiting for his strength to return as the active chemical entered his bloodstream. Within ten minutes, he felt ready to face the world again. He took a shower, dressed, drank a strong cup of coffee and picked up his college notes, ready for afternoon lectures. He closed the door on the well appointed apartment that was rented under the name of his influential father and began to make his way down the wide, spiralling stairwell. He made it no further than the first floor.

* * * *

'Do we have a signal yet?' asked Mike as he sat beside Beth in her room at the lodge, watching her input data into a laptop.

'I'm just about to find out.'

Beth pulled up a file, tapped in a command and sat motionless, staring intently at the screen as a stream of telemetric data began to upload.

'Awesome,' she breathed reverently as one by one, three dotted lines appeared on a graphic representation of the Honduran Coastline. 'I think that's the best haul we've ever had.'

'Look, this one's already on the move,' said Mike pointing.

Beth nodded.

'Most of them seem to go north from here. We've managed to track them as far as Belize and the Mexican Basin, but where they go after that is anyone's guess.'

'Don't worry, my tags will soon solve the mystery,' said Mike.

'Yes, I'm sure they will,' said Beth, rolling her eyes.

'What about the photos? Any matches?'

'I haven't checked yet, but from what I saw on the boat, there's at least one image which I can use. Let's have a look on the database.'

Beth connected to the SRI website, uploaded a digital photograph taken by one of the project participants and began to map out the arrangement of dots behind the gill slits. When she'd finished, she hit the return button and waited for the computer to search the electronic archives. Shortly afterwards the words – '*no match found*' - appeared on screen.

'Looks like we got ourselves a new specimen,' trilled Beth. 'Alistair will be delighted.'

'Excellent. Do we get to name it?'

'A name? Like what?'

'I dunno...what about Dotty?'

'It had claspers Mike, so it's obviously a male. Anyway I think maybe we should just stick with a standard reference, don't you?' Beth said, raising a perfectly plucked eyebrow.

'You academics are no fun.'

Beth gave Mike a sideways glance, then without a word stood up, threw a slender leg over his thighs and slid down onto his lap.

'No fun did you say?'

'Oh! Hello Alistair!' said Mike, turning his head towards the open door.

Beth jumped up smartly, pushing herself away. She glanced around anticipating the surprised look of her host, but all she saw was an empty door frame.

Mike chuckled and attempted to scurry away across the bed, but Beth's reaction was swift. She cut him off and leapt on top of him, gripping him around the neck and wrestling him to the floor.

'Ouch that hurts!' protested Mike as several well aimed blows rained down on him.

'Good, you deserve it. It may not look that way, but I know how to handle myself; I grew up in ranch country.'

'OK, OK, for God's sake don't get the branding iron out.'

'I can do much better than that. I've castrated bulls before now.'

Mike instinctively clenched his thighs, a pained expression washing across his face. It softened to an amused smirk when his cell phone began to ring. Beth pursed her lips, her eyes narrowing.

'Count yourself lucky,' she said, as she lifted her weight from him.

'You'll be punished for this later,' said Mike rolling to his feet, reaching for his phone and directing a reproving glance at her.

Beth scoffed, shaking her head.

'Hello, Mike Summers ...shark hunter, adventurer and *bon vivant*.'

'Mike? It's me...Ken,' said the voice at the other end of the line.

'Ken? This is...unexpected,' said Mike, his mood quickly sobering. He shot a glance at Beth and stepped out onto the balcony.

'Yeah, well things are a little *unusual* around here at the moment to say the least.'

'Frankly, I'm surprised to hear from you after what was said the last time we spoke.'

'Oh...yeah. Look, I'm real sorry about that Mike. The guy was a senator for Chrissake. I had to take his side while we were face to face, but you were right...he was an asshole and I was a jerk for not defending you.'

'He should never have been allowed to dive in the first place. A let's forget about that now. Why are you calling?'

'How are things going over there?'

'Great....look, let's not beat around the bush Ken, you didn't call just to ask after my health. What do you want?'

'Um, well there's no easy way of putting this Mike, so I guess I'll just come out with it straight. I'm desperate for a cave diving instructor at the moment and I was hoping that you might consider coming back to help me out...and before you start mouthing off at me, I'll pay your airfare and give you a 500 dollar bonus.'

'Jeez Ken, you really must be desperate...but I'm still not interested; things are going well for me here. Why can't Frank do it anyway?'

There was a pause.

'I guess word didn't get to you then?'

'About what?'

'Frank. He's dead Mike. They found his body out in the jungle four days ago.'

SEVILLE, SPAIN

Professor Miguel Velásquez was staring fixedly out of the third floor windows of the *Instituto Nacional de Toxicología y Ciencias Forenses* when *Inspector jefe de la Policía Local*, Antonio Dominguez, walked into his office unannounced.

'*Buenos dias Profesor. ¿Cómo está hoy?* – Good Morning Professor. How are you today?'

'*Bien gracias. ¿Y usted?* – Fine thank you, and yourself?'

'*Bien tambien.* – I'm fine also.'

The Inspector hovered.

'*Siéntese por favor.* – Please take a seat.'

Inspector Dominguez pulled up a chair, observing the dark half moons below Professor Velásquez's small brown eyes. It looked as if he'd had little sleep in the last 24 hours, but then it was hard to tell. The deep worry lines that were permanently etched into his forehead and the unkempt appearance of the tufts of dark hair that nestled resolutely above his tiny ears gave him a permanently haggard appearance.

'So what news do you have for me?'

Professor Velásquez glanced into the dark penetrative eyes of the stocky Inspector, beads of sweat glistening on his exposed scalp as he nervously rearranged the notes on his desk. He'd never quite felt comfortable in the presence of Inspector Dominguez, despite the fact that they'd worked together for years. The Chief Inspector's overbearing presence and aggressive questioning techniques always made him feel more like he was under interrogation rather than being consulted for his forensic expertise. He dabbed the perspiration from his brow with an embroidered handkerchief and breathed a sigh.

'I'm afraid that you're not going to like what I have to tell you Inspector Dominguez.'

'And why is that?' asked the Inspector, the carefully trimmed moustache above his fleshy upper lip jerking sideways in disapproval.

'The death of the Governor's son cannot be directly attributed to the use of recreational drugs as we first thought. Certainly there were traces of cocaine in his bloodstream, but not nearly enough to have caused a fatal reaction. And besides, even prolonged cocaine use could not explain all the medical conditions which we found during the autopsy.'

'Medical conditions?' asked the Inspector, a raised eyebrow prompting a more detailed explanation.

'Gastrointestinal inflammation, renal complications, malignant growths, chronic iron deficiency; a real mess. His collapse and death were undoubtedly the result of multiple organ failure.'

'So what was it? Some kind of drug related disease? Hepatitis? AIDS?'

asked the Inspector, his snarling lip betraying his revulsion.

'No, nothing like that. These conditions were not caused by disease,' said the professor, confidently shaking his head.

'Then what?'

'He was poisoned.'

'Poisoned?' said the inspector in alarm. 'You mean he was murdered?'

'That is something which I cannot yet say for sure. You see this is far from being an isolated case. We've had dozens of similar incidents all over the country recently.'

'But how is that possible Professor?'

'Well, we've explored several avenues. At first we thought that we were dealing with accidental poisonings, the active chemicals, mostly cyanogenic glycosides and alkaloids being naturally present in several commonly available foodstuffs. These types of poisonings are quite rare of course, since few people are inclined to eat raw, unripe tomatoes, potatoes and beans in any quantity, especially over a prolonged period of time. So when several of these cases appeared over a relatively short time frame, we began to realise that we could be faced with the accidental or deliberate contamination of processed food products.'

'Deliberate contamination?' said the inspector, frowning.

'It would not be the first time,' continued the Professor. 'Typhoid and Botulism were both accidentally introduced into cans of Argentinean corned beef in the 1960's and early 1980's, and in 1989 extortionists deliberately contaminated products from the Heinz food conglomerate. Of course, given the present climate of unrest, it would be foolish to ignore the very real possibility that these incidents are part of a terrorist campaign.'

The Inspector's expression hardened.

'Let me get this right. Are you saying that the Governor's son may have been killed as part of a terrorist plot Professor?'

'It remains a possibility. Naturally, we were reluctant to announce our findings until we had identified the source of the poisoning and unfortunately that proved to be far more difficult than we'd anticipated. The problem was that we found no contaminated foodstuffs in the houses of those who'd been poisoned and we couldn't identify any particular eating habit which was common to all of them.'

'And now?' prompted the Chief Inspector.

'We'd only assumed that the poison had been administered through a food source, but when we found no reliable evidence to support that theory, we re-evaluated the situation, conducted some more tests and finally discovered a habit which linked all of the victims - a habit which the Governor's son clearly shared.'

For once Professor Velásquez held the Chief Inspectors stare, prompting him to make the connection.

'Cocaine?'

The professor spread his hands in silent affirmation.

'*Puta!*' swore the Chief Inspector, bringing his fist down hard onto the professor's desk. 'This is going to be a nightmare. An absolute nightmare. Impossible to control. How in God's name are we supposed to track these sons of bitches down if they are hiding in the shadows of the illegal drugs trade?'

'I sympathise with you Inspector. If they are operating high up the distribution network, it may prove difficult, if not impossible to flush them out.'

The inspector's silent scowl left the Professor wondering if he had spoken out of turn. He frowned, cleared his throat and stared at his notes for a moment.

'Perhaps there is a way in which we can refine our search,' he said finally.

'How?' asked the inspector, his patience thinning.

'We found a few intact plant cells in the contaminated cocaine samples from which we should be able to extract DNA. It may be a long shot, but genetic fingerprinting can sometimes yield surprising results.'

○ ○ ○ ○

AKUMAL, YUCATAN PENINSULA, MEXICO

Mike wasn't sure whether it was the quesadilla which he'd bought from a street side vendor in Cancun, the tiresome flight connections or the disturbing circumstances surrounding his return which were responsible for the queasy feeling in his gut. On reflection, he decided that it was probably a combination of all three.

From the dusty window of the old American school bus, which was spending its final years ferrying passengers up and down the Costa Maya, Mike spotted the sign for the small town of Akumal and slipped a half read, dog eared novel back into his bag. He made his way towards the front of the bus and when it pulled into a dusty lay-by, he stepped out into the jostling crowd of passengers, touts and vendors which had been eagerly awaiting its arrival. His travel scarred backpack and diving equipment were unceremoniously dumped onto the dusty ground and after fending off the solicitations of a sly looking baggage tout, he hailed a battered Chevrolet taxi and threw his luggage into the trunk.

'*Plaza Ukana por favor*,' he instructed, slumping back into the dubious comforts of a sagging, leather rear seat. The squat driver nodded wordlessly and pulled away, narrowly missing a reversing truck.

Mike guided the driver through the centre of Akumal and past a succession of small eateries, bars and gift shops that catered for the seasonal influx of tourists. A confusion of emotions were swirling in his head as he motioned to the driver to pull over beside the familiar façade of the dive shop where he'd once worked.

For the most part Mike had been happy at CavePro, but he'd left on bad terms six months ago and never expected to return. He wasn't doing this as a favour to the owner. Ken could go screw himself as far as Mike was concerned, but Frank was a different matter. He'd been a great friend, a remarkable instructor and an absolute pleasure to work with. Everybody loved Frank and Mike couldn't think of a single reason why anyone would want him dead. But there was something Frank had mentioned to him a couple of weeks ago that had put a niggling doubt into his mind.

Hauling the heavy bags onto his shoulder, Mike handed a few crumpled notes to the cab driver and walked into the dive shop to find Ken behind the counter, busily tapping away at a computer keyboard.

'Hey Mike. It's great to see you again!' trilled Ken with his lilting South Carolina drawl.

Mike dropped his luggage to the floor and accepted the owner's outstretched hand. Ken's coiled mop of red-blonde hair and goatee beard gave him something of a comic appearance, but Mike had rarely found him to be anything but intense.

'Yeah, well I'd rather be here for happier reasons,' he said flatly.

'Of course,' said Ken, conscious that Mike was still sore at him, 'but thanks for helping me out just the same. I can't tell you how much I appreciate it.'

Mike nodded and glanced around, noticing the numerous spaces between the wetsuits, regulators and buoyancy jackets which hung from the surrounding rails.

'I take it you're pretty busy then?'

'It's peak season Mike. It really couldn't have come at a worse time,' Ken said, shaking his head.

'So how much do you know about what happened?'

Ken frowned and breathed a sigh.

'Not a great deal I'm afraid Mike. Frank went diving with Pablo on his day off. He said something about exploring some new cave system or other....probably thought it would bring him glory. I told him he was nuts diving on his day off, but he just laughed. You know how he is...I mean *was*,' he said, screwing up his face. 'Next thing I know Pablo calls me all freaked out to say Frank's gone missing. He says they'd finished their dive and then Frank went to take a piss in the bushes. Never came back.'

'Where were they diving?'

'A place I've never been before. Out near Chalchén. We got a search team together and went out there, checked every damn blade of grass, but we couldn't find a trace. A few days later they found his body in the jungle a couple of miles away, all beat up and mutilated. The police wanted to keep it hushed up cause they were afraid to scare the tourists away, but hell, you can't keep a thing like that under wraps. He had his heart cut out for crissakes. Anyway, as soon as Pablo found out what happened, he made off as fast as his legs could carry him and I aint seen him since. Can't say I blame him either. Somebody was going to go down and Pablo was first in the firing line. In the end they found some poor peasant fucker to pin the blame on...said they found a knife in his hut, covered in blood.' Ken shook his head. 'Who knows what happened Mike? There's plenty crazy motherfuckers around this place.'

'That's for sure,' agreed Mike, rubbing the two day old stubble on his chin. 'The worrying thing is, it could quite easily have been me out there with Frank.'

'Huh? Howdya figure that?' asked Ken, pulling a face.

'He told me he'd found a new cave system a couple of weeks back. In fact he wanted me to come back and map it out with him. I was tempted too. I mean, everyone wants to discover something new; go someplace where no one else has ever been before, right?'

'I guess,' Ken shrugged.

'Well I was getting plenty of excitement where I was anyway and I figured the cave wasn't going to disappear anytime soon. What I couldn't have known was that Frank might not be around when I eventually came round to the idea.'

'If it's any consolation Mike, you didn't miss a thing. We searched the system extensively when we couldn't find Frank. After a quarter of a mile all the tributaries narrow into corridors as tight as a lawyer's wallet.'

Mike sighed and shook his head.

'So much for his shot at glory.'

'They say that fame is fickle,' said Ken, scanning the rows of equipment with an air of resignation.'

'Well I guess I'm going to need somewhere to stay,' said Mike. 'You got any ideas?'

'Your old place is empty now Frank's gone. I'm not sure how you feel bout that. The owner said she'd hold it for you if you're interested.'

'I am...and I don't have a problem with it,' replied Mike.

Ken nodded.

'His stuff has been moved anyways. The police took a few things away and his family shipped out the rest.'

'OK, I'd better go up and see her right away. Can I leave my gear here?'

'Sure, help yourself. I think your locker's still free over there.'

'Thanks.'

Mike dragged his bag towards the row of wooden lockers at the rear of the shop. A local bar promotion sticker with Mike's name on it was plastered onto the door of one of them. It triggered a memory which brought a smile to his face. He opened the vented wooden door and stood back in surprise to see one of Frank's old wetsuits hanging inside. On the top shelf was a heavy instructor manual and when Mike pulled it free a small notebook dropped to the floor. He hoisted the manual up onto the top of the locker, bent down to pick up the notebook and through curiosity began to leaf through it. Inside he found a pencil drawing of a diving figure, a sketched diagram of a cave system, and an arrow pointing to the small town of Yalché at a distance of two kilometers. He frowned and turned towards Ken.

'How exactly did Frank find out about this cave system Ken?'

'I'm not sure. He was hanging out with a guy called Fabrizio; a scientist type who's doing some kind of research in the area. I think it might have been him who put Frank onto it.'

'Any idea where I might find him?'

'He's Italian,' he said with a shrug, 'they'll probably know him in the Dolce Vita.'

'And where did you say that cave system was again?'

'Chalchén.'

'Chalchén? That's a good distance from Yalché right?'

'About 15 miles I guess. Why?'

LABORATORIO DI GENETICA MOLECOLARE, INSTITUTO GASLINI — GENOVA

Professori Massimo Benedettia was puzzled. To receive a recently discovered plant species for genetic analysis was not particularly uncommon, but to be sent a DNA sequence for identification from a totally separate source and which proved to originate from the same plant was a quite extraordinary coincidence.

There was absolutely no doubt about it though, he told himself, as he squinted through half moon spectacles at the columns of statistics on his computer screen; the variable repeating sequences identified the two profiles as being not only of the same subspecies, but of almost identical parentage.

If he'd had to make an informed guess, he would have said that the source plants had been specially bred from a hybrid in a laboratory, but why that would be, he had no idea. The pharmaceutical company which sent him the original sample had clearly thought that the plant tissues might have medicinal properties, but there was no discernible difference between its active compounds and those of any other member of the *manihot* genus, except perhaps for a marked concentration of deadly alkaloids and cyanogenic glycosides. Of course, once flushed with water and cooked, *Manihot Esculenta*, or cassava as it is better known, could be safely ingested and Professor Benedettia was well aware that the starchy root was an important basic food source in many African and South American countries. Yet if this species had been specifically bred for consumption, it would have seemed logical to select its beneficial properties rather than those which were harmful. The more that Professor Benedettia thought about it, the more likely it seemed that the toxins themselves were the desired end-product. And that might have seemed odd, had the plant not been found in Mesoamerica, where naturally occurring poisons were sometimes used for hunting and fishing purposes.

While Professor Benedettia was concluding his notes, a familiar proverb sprang to mind.

One man's food is another man's poison.

A wry smile lit up his face as he entered his observations into the database. With his work concluded, he glanced up at the chrome clock on the wall opposite his desk and realised to his annoyance that he should have been home over an hour ago. With a sigh, he pushed his reading glasses onto his forehead, rubbed his bloodshot eyes and pulled the urgent dossier from the *Instituto Nacional de Toxicología y Ciencias Forenses* towards him. The pharmaceutical company would no doubt be disappointed with his findings, but at least he had good news for Professor Velásquez in Seville.

SOMEWHERE IN THE SKIES ABOVE BRAZIL

A small burst of cold hydrazine gas corrected the angle of the KH-11 Keyhole series surveillance satellite, orbiting 22,300 miles above the surface of the earth. A servo whirred into action, minutely adjusting the infrared reconnaissance camera lens, allowing the ground controller to continue to monitor his target. It was far from being a difficult task, since the exhaust outlets of the 25 metre power launch were radiating heat like lava vents.

In the highly secretive U.S. Photographic Interpretation Center in Washington DC, Larry Kruger released the toggle on his control panel and continued to stuff the contents of a carton of stir-fry noodles into his gaping mouth, the grease glistening on his fleshy lips.

'They're definitely heading towards the coast,' he muttered, still chomping through a mouthful of the gelatinous strands.

'You know it's just as well my ear is trained to interpret garbled information,' his colleague said, watching him wipe his mouth with the back of his hand.

'You can't beat Chinese food,' said Larry, swilling down the masticated remnants with a diet cola. 'You think they're gonna refuel again and make their way north?'

'I doubt it. They made it all the way to Belize without refuelling, so my guess is they'd have enough reserves to reach the Keys or the Bahamas if that was their intention.'

'We'd better speak to the NDIC. They seemed pretty keen for us to report any movements along this coast. Who've we got on the ground?'

'One of the Drug Enforcement Agency's men. He was alerted two hours ago so he should be operational by now.'

'Let's get him on the line.'

Thousands of miles to the south, Special Agent Rafael Rodriguez was tearing along Highway 307 with a Red Hot Chilli Peppers track blaring out of the speakers of his black four wheel drive Chevrolet Tahoe. He scowled and plucked a plump Cuban cigar from his lips as a hand-held satellite phone began to ring on the passenger seat to his right. Holding the steering wheel with one hand, the cigar still protruding from his fist, he blew a dense stream of smoke against the dashboard and reached over to answer it.

'This better be good. I left a hot date and half a bottle of tequila behind in Playa del Carmen for you schmucks.'

There was a pause.

'Agent Rodriguez, this is Larry Kruger of the National Reconnaissance Office. I'm sorry if we spoiled your evening's entertainment, but me and my colleague here have been sat watching a tiny red dot move across a featureless expanse of ocean for the last five days for the benefit of your department.'

'I'm sure my boss will be eternally grateful to you. What's the deal?'

Rafael heard Larry Kruger exhale through gritted teeth.

'We've got a runner in your sector. Looks like he's headed for a quiet stretch of coastline just south of a place called Chacalal.'

'You mean Chalacal.'

'Yeah...whatever. I really don't give a damn what the godforsaken place is called. What's your current position?'

'I'm on Highway 307, heading south, just beyond *Xel Ha,*' he said, exaggerating the pronunciation.

'OK, put your infrared light on.

'You could at least say please,' said Rafael huffily. He reached over to flip a switch on the dashboard which activated a locating beacon on the roof of the Chevrolet. Back in Washington, Kruger saw a distinct greenish white glow appear on his screen. He touched a joystick and zoomed in on it.

'You shouldn't be smoking while driving Rodriguez,' he said smugly.

Rafael began to look in all directions, trying to spot the hidden camera.

'How the hell did you know that? Are you snooping on me?'

'What do you think we're paid to do? We've got a billion dollars worth of equipment following your ass, so you'd better watch your step.'

'Great. I always thought there was an angel watching over me, but it turns out it was just some bored government agent with bad breath. Now that aint verifiable, I know, but *I'm* paid to use my intuition.'

Kruger glared at his colleague, who was trying unsuccessfully to hide his amusement.

'OK wise guy, let's cut the crap. I want you to continue past the town of Chacalaca, or whatever the damned place is called, and take the first turning on your left. It's a minor road which leads to the coast.'

'I'll be there in five.'

'We know. Keep the line open.'

Rafael tossed the phone back onto the passenger seat and broke into a smile, cranking the music up as loud as he could bear it. After a few minutes he left Highway 307 and began to head east towards the coast. He lowered the volume and then picked up the phone once more.

'You still there?'

'Affirmative. Half deaf from that shit you're playing, but still here. OK, when you reach the junction at the end of the road, take the unsurfaced track to the right. You'll reach a dead end. Park up there and report back.'

'Your wish is my command.'

Rafael found the turning more through luck than judgement and continued along an increasingly bumpy road until it came to an abrupt end.

'OK, I've gone as far as I can go. What now?'

'You're approximately 800 yards north of the point where they'll reach the shoreline if they maintain their present heading. Proceed on foot in a southerly direction and find a place to observe. No flashlights.'

'Hey, you're talking to a professional.'

'You could have fooled us.'

'Yeah? Well, any half wit could do that.'

Rafael reached into the glove compartment of the Chevrolet and pulled out a pair of night vision binoculars. He stepped out onto the road and took a last puff on his cigar while listening to the sound of surf crashing against a rocky shoreline.

'*Adios mi amigo*,' he said, letting the cigar fall to the ground before crushing it firmly beneath the heel of his boot. He set off along the narrow path which continued where the track ended, a quick glance at a digital compass confirming that it led south, following the line of the coast. The dark bordering scrub and rutted earth hardly made for perfect conditions, but with the help of the night vision binoculars and some shrewd navigation, he managed to forge a way through.

After a 15 minute hike, he headed east and emerged unscathed above an 8 metre high cliff from where he had a clear view out to sea. In the moist, tropical air, the gentle throb of the boat's diesel engines reached his ears a good few minutes before he picked out the bright hull against the darkness. Through the image enhancing binoculars, he watched the launch gradually advance towards the coast, its deck and cabin lights extinguished. He hunkered down and edged his way along the top of the cliff, the stars providing enough light for him to see a crewmember leave the cabin and

41

step out on deck. There was a splash as an anchor was dropped and the launch began to swing around to face the incoming swell, settling just a few hundred yards from shore. Rafael dropped to his stomach and pulled out the satellite phone, taking care to mask the LED display with his thumb.

'OK, I'm in position,' he whispered. 'The boat is anchored and I see someone out on deck.'

'We also have a visual. Try to move a little further south.'

Rafael glanced up at the night sky, as if he might catch a glimpse of the surveillance satellite which now had its powerful telescope trained on him. It was an eerie feeling being watched from outer space.

'I hope you sickos aren't staring at my ass.'

'Don't flatter yourself.'

Rafael edged his way along the cliff top, repositioned himself and scanned the fractured coastline from north to south.

'You see any movement shoreside?'

'Negative. We see no sign of any persons or vehicles in the immediate vicinity.'

'Great. So I guess that means I'll be spending the whole evening lying here with rocks sticking in my ribs.'

'I feel for you.'

'Sure you do.'

Rafael muttered a silent curse as he stared at the motor launch snatching at its anchor like a tethered beast. After a while he noticed that a patch of interference had appeared in the foreground and he adjusted the contrast of the night vision binoculars in an attempt to compensate for it. When it had no effect, he pulled the binoculars from his face and was astonished to see that the aberration was still there, visible to the naked eye.

'Hey wait a second. D'you guys see anything in the water?'

'Like what?'

'Dunno. I can see like a faint green glow moving towards the boat.'

'We have nothing here. You sure you didn't hit the Tequila bottle a little too hard?'

'Switch to low light surveillance.'

Kruger picked a strand of chicken from his teeth and reached over to flick a switch on his console. After a few seconds the glowing thermal imagery on his screen was replaced by enhanced shades of light and dark.

'What the fuck is that?' he suddenly yelled, seeing what could only be described as a cloud of light moving towards the white hulled vessel.

'Could be divers,' said Rafael, 'but they'd have to be moving fast.'

'That's impossible. We'd have picked up traces of their body heat well before they entered the water. Did you see anything thrown over the side of the boat?'

'No, but then the merchandise could be attached to the hull.'

'Well I'll be damned. Looks like they're stopping right beneath it.'

'Yeah, and you can bet your ass they'll go back the way they came.'

'Then we'll track them when they leave the water.'

'You won't get a chance.'

'What makes you say that?'

'Because they came from a place where even your multi-million dollar technology can't follow. They entered the sea directly from the base of the cliff.'

NATIONAL SECURITY COUNCIL, MADRID

The rapidly assembled crisis management team studied their hastily typed briefs while exchanging concerned glances. They'd worked through some difficult situations in their time and had to stand firm against the demands of such notorious terrorist organisations as Al Qaida and ETA, but this present crisis was unlike anything else they'd ever encountered. For some unknown reason their Government was being targeted by an organisation which had no face, no clear objective, no principles and a total disregard for human life. It had always been the policy of the Spanish authorities to refuse to negotiate with terrorists, but the message which that was meant to convey became futile when there was clearly no one to negotiate with.

The sound of scraping chairs announced the entrance of the Prime Minister, a middle-aged, silver haired man with a meticulously trimmed moustache, hooked nose and steely eyes. He urged the members of the emergency council to regain their seats and took his place at the foot of the long conference table, scanning the familiar faces of his trusted advisors.

'Buenos Dias Señors y Señoras.'

'Buenos Dias Presidente,' the assembly replied in chorus.

'I am sorry to have convened this meeting at such short notice, but I am sure by now that you are fully aware of the crisis which is facing our nation. The number of fatalities which have been directly attributed to the use of contaminated cocaine has now reached an alarming level and the public are demanding that we take immediate action. There are people dying all over Europe; important people. Forty deaths at the last count and hundreds more in a critical condition. The majority of those poisonings have occurred in Spain, with the remainder taking place primarily within bordering countries and we now believe that this pattern is no coincidence. Recent evidence suggests that we as a nation are being specifically targeted by a terrorist or criminal organisation. Why that would be we have no real idea, but yesterday our fears were confirmed when we received an anonymous call demanding that we pay one hundred million euros into a company account in Panama or face the prospect of an accelerated campaign of attacks. The company, you will not be surprised to learn, is bogus and the directors fictitious. Our aggressors have warned that any attempt to block or manipulate the account will result in immediate reprisals. They have given us just seven days to comply with their demands.'

There were muted murmurs around the room.

'I have spoken to the King this morning and he is now fully aware of the situation which we are facing and he has given me his full backing to use whatever resources, military or otherwise, are deemed necessary to track these criminals down and bring them to justice. We have recently enlisted the help of our European and American allies after a potentially vital clue was unearthed by one of our most eminent scientists, Professor Miguel Velásquez of the *Instituto Nacional de Toxicología y Ciencias Forenses* in Seville. The discovery of a link with the Americas has given us some cause for optimism, but our investigation is in its infancy and we have only a limited amount of time in which to act. If we are to prevent further loss of life, we may yet be forced to consider negotiating some kind of settlement. It is far from being an ideal solution, but as always, I am open to your suggestions.'

The Minister for Internal Affairs, a mature brunette wearing a dark wool suit, a white silk blouse and bright red reading glasses raised her hand. The Prime Minister acknowledged her with a nod.

'Señor Presidente. Since the victims are all cocaine addicts, would it not be simpler to launch a major publicity campaign warning them of the danger of contaminated drugs?'

The Health Minister, a small man with slicked back hair and a thin moustache, replied in the Prime Minister's place.

'Señora Diaz, I am afraid that you do not fully appreciate the compulsions which drive a drug addict's behaviour. They are ill people; desperate people, who sometimes cannot choose between what is good for them and what is bad. Uncontaminated cocaine is in itself detrimental to health and has the potential to kill, yet every addict is perfectly aware of that fact and continues to expose themselves to its dangers. Even if these people are informed of an increased risk, they still may not be able to control their cravings. Try to imagine what it would be like if you were suffering from extreme thirst and someone gave you a bottle of water that had been exposed to a high level of radiation. Would you be able to resist the desire to drink from it?'

'I see your point Señor Gomez, but what if we set up temporary clinics where addicts could be assured of finding uncontaminated cocaine; anonymously of course.'

'On the surface that may seem like a good idea,' replied the Health Minister, 'but in practice it would work only for those who are unashamed of their habit. There are many people who would have a great deal to lose if their drug problems were exposed; lawyers, bankers, doctors, media entertainers, politicians even,' he said spreading his hands wide. 'There would be such a fear of being recognised, discredited and vilified that these

46

respected people would probably continue to feed their habits through illicit channels.'

'You have a very valid point Señor Gomez,' said the Prime Minister,' and besides, from a moral standpoint I am not sure that we could be seen to facilitate or encourage the sale and use of illegal drugs.'

'It would probably prove to be a mere inconvenience to the extortionists even if we did choose to go down that line,' said the Chancellor, a stocky man with a receding hairline and heavy jowls. 'Cocaine is just one of several drugs which could be successfully contaminated and there is no guarantee that they will not switch to other narcotics if we circumvent their supply. Then we would be faced with the prospect of becoming our country's principal drug distributor.'

'Yes, I think that we can safely discount that idea. So what other options are open to us?'

The members of the emergency council leafed through their notes, tinkered with their pens, and tried not to communicate their growing sense of unease. There were no easy solutions after all. The illegal drugs trade would never be completely eradicated and determined terrorists would always be a thorn in the side of established powers. Everyone sitting around that table knew that the Spanish Government could not afford to show any sign of weakness. The settlement would at first be refused, and as a consequence many more people would die. There was a sentiment amongst some of the council members that the unfortunate victims of this show of strength would only have themselves to blame. But behind their self-righteous assurance lay the unsettling doubt that their own family and friends might also harbour secret vices.

* * * *

There was barely any light inside the cave, even though the water which flooded it was crystal clear. The diver who was gliding through the natural corridor, its floor and ceiling sprouting enormous stalactites and stalagmites, like the teeth of a snarling wolf, retraced the nylon cave line on which her survival might depend. Her fingers were looped lightly around it to guard against straying from her intended path or mistakenly turning around and following the line deeper into the system; a frighteningly simple and seemingly innocuous error which had led to numerous premature deaths.

Her fin movements were calm, measured and amphibian-like; especially adapted to suit the cave environment, where downdraughts of water could easily stir up fine silt and rapidly reduce the visibility to zero.

Suddenly an unforeseen problem arose. The diver could no longer draw air from one of her primary cylinders. Controlling her rising anxiety, she drew on her training and switched regulators, all the while maintaining contact with the line. The air tasted sweet, invigorating. It was so easily taken for granted. For a while her calm returned and she settled back into a gentle rhythm, but then to her surprise the second regulator became difficult to breathe from and promptly stopped delivering its vital supply altogether. With no further back-up to hand, she was now in a potentially life threatening situation. Drawing on her training, she kept her composure and tried to think the problem through. There was a staged emergency cylinder tied into the line just a short distance ahead and right now it appeared to be her only option. She forged ahead, determined to find the physical and mental strength to reach it. Time seemed to stretch exponentially, the passing seconds dragging their heels until they felt more like minutes. As she fought the instinct to bolt wildly into the darkness, a phrase from her training repeated in her head like a mantra.

The line can save your life, whatever you do, don't lose contact with the line.

Finally, through the gloom, her eyes fixed on the emergency cylinder, lying in the sand where she'd positioned it earlier. She rammed the regulator into her mouth, opened the valve with feverish hands and drew in huge lungfuls of the blessed gas. Never had air tasted so good. Once her breathing was under control, she freed the cylinder from the line and attached it to the clips of her harness. Within seconds she was moving away again, passing through a narrow chamber where a dull greyish light began to filter through the darkness. She rounded a dogleg and entered a straight corridor, the far end of which was illuminated by a glowing aura of blue. Her spirits were lifted by the sight of daylight and she increased her pace, weaving through the long tree roots which reached down from the cavern ceiling to tap into the precious reservoir which lay beneath the forest floor.

Now the sky was above her. A large blue circle surrounded by dancing images of grey-white rock and leafy vegetation. The circle widened as she rose towards the surface and as if passing through a looking glass she broke the surface of a small pool, sending concentric ripples racing towards the edges. Another head emerged beside her and then a third. Regulators and masks were removed. Smiles lit up faces.

'Congratulations. You are now a certified cave diver,' said a smiling Mike Summers.

'Oh my God, I was so nervous,' admitted the young female student. 'I was trying so hard to stay calm. The worse part is that you know what's coming - you just don't know when.'

The young girl pulled off her wetsuit hood and threw her head back into the water. Her strawberry blonde hair flattened against her scalp as she lifted it clear and she raked the wet strands behind her ears with her fingers.

'You did an excellent job Gail. In fact both of you have been excellent students, said Mike, turning to face the third diver; a handsome, bronze-skinned man with long dark hair, pulled back into a neat pony tail.

'I think you did quite well too Mike, if you don't mind me saying so' said Rafael Rodriguez, who Mike knew simply as Rod. 'I think you need to work on your technique a little bit, but given time you'll soon look as stylish in the water as me.'

'Is that so?' said Mike, raising an amused eyebrow. 'Well you didn't look particularly stylish during that last exercise when you couldn't find your back up regulator.'

'It was just temporarily misplaced; no big problem,' he said with a shrug. 'I was in total control of the situation.'

'Yeah? I'd hate to see you when you're in real trouble then.'

'Oh, I've been in trouble many times. Usually through a combination of women and tequila,' he said grinning. 'Do you like tequila Gail?'

'Yeah, I like tequila,' she said, a thin smile on her lips, 'and so does my boyfriend.'

'Does he like diving too?' asked Rafael.

'No, he's actually more of a beach person.'

'Shame. It's important to have things in common. To share your passion. You and I, for example, would make perfect companions,' he said with a teasing smile.

Gail rolled her eyes and turned towards Mike.

'Please don't leave me alone with this man for a second. He's far more dangerous than any cave.'

'Yes, I think you might be right about that.'

'All I want to do is spread a little love,' said Rafael with a shrug of innocence.

'Yes I'm sure you do,' said Mike. 'OK, time's moving on and we need to get going. We'll strip our equipment down by the truck, pack it into bags and then stow it with the mats and cylinders. Make sure you don't leave anything behind because we won't be coming back. I'll fill out your dive logs and sign all the paperwork when we get back to the centre. OK?'

Mike led his two students up the rocky bank which surrounded the pool and supervised the dismantling of the equipment. Soon the gear was lashed into place and they were bouncing their way along a rough forest track which snaked around a dry river bed and finally emerged onto a partially surfaced road. After a forty minute drive they were back at the dive centre in Akumal. Mike unloaded the truck, passing the cylinders to Chicho, a young Mexican boy who helped out in the workshop. While the compressor was throbbing away in the rear, Mike filled out the certifications of his two students.

'There you go guys. Well done to both of you. Now that you're certified I would strongly suggest that you practice the skills you've learned whenever you get the occasion. Of course, you can now join us on any of the cave excursions which we run from the centre. Just come in or call us beforehand to check that we have a trip running and then we'll book you in. So thanks again for taking part in the course guys and I hope we'll see you again soon.'

'You can count on that,' said Rafael.

'I'd definitely like to do another dive,' said Gail, 'but I'll have to check back with you in a few days.'

'No problem.'

'You'll be joining us for a celebration drink tonight though won't you Gail?' asked Rafael.

'I'm afraid I'm going to have to pass on that.'

'But why? You can bring your boyfriend along if you wish.'

'That's very generous of you Rod,' she said, with more than a hint of sarcasm, 'but the answer is still no.'

'I see,' said Rafael nodding. 'Well I guess everybody has to live with their decisions.'

Gail rolled her eyes, much to Rafael's amusement.

'Well, looks like it's just you and me then,' Rafael said, turning towards Mike with a shrug. 'And don't *you* try to give me any excuses. After what you've put me through these last few days, I think you owe me.'

'Er, there was actually something important that I needed to do tonight Rod...but I suppose it could wait a day.'

'Now that's what I like to hear,' said Rafael, clapping Mike on the shoulder. 'And you can rest assured, my friend, that if we end up in any more dark and dangerous places before the day is over, I will be on hand to guide you safely towards the exit.'

'Hmm, I'm not sure I like the sound of that. You sure you don't want to tag along too Gail?' he asked with an air of supplication.

'I'm afraid you're on your own there Mike. Much as I'd like to hang out with you guys...well, one of you anyway,' she said with a sideways glance at Rafael. 'I'm afraid that I've got other commitments. Maybe we'll catch up later in the week.'

'Fair enough. Have a great evening anyway.'

'Thanks. You too. Adios guys,' she trilled, raising her hand in salute as she turned to leave.

'What a sweet young thing,' said Rafael, tilting his head in admiration as he watched her walk away.

'She's cute alright,' agreed Mike, nodding.

'Her loyalty is admirable...and yet somehow regrettable,' said Rafael with a shrug. '*Que lastima!* So what's the venue tonight Mike?'

'The venue? I guess we could go to the *Buena Onda*. It's a bar just down on the beach here.'

'Do they have tequila and pretty women?'

'They did the last time I was there.'

'Then it sounds like a perfect choice. Shall we meet there at eight?'

'Eight's fine by me.'

'*Bueno!* See you there.'

Rafael lifted a bag onto his shoulder, winked and took his leave. Mike was not long to follow. His lodgings were a ten minute walk away, near a run down resort tucked away on the edge of town. Just a couple of rooms in a flat roofed building with a crumbling, rust coloured, stucco façade that was shaded by a couple of tall palms. Inside, the minor comforts included a small kitchen, a simple, white tiled shower, a lounge cum bedroom and an outside terrace, strung with colourful hammocks.

After a quick shower, Mike put on fresh clothes, checked his mail and an hour later was stepping out into a fragrant spring evening. The sounds of laughter and the rhythmic beat of a Rumba spilled out into the street from a local *comedor*. An emaciated dog lowered its ears and scurried out of Mike's way as he crossed its path.

He picked up a tortilla filled with spicy grilled beef from a street vendor and made his way south along the coast road. The sky was turning a dark shade of pink by the time he reached the beach and it was reflected in the gently rolling breakers which raced out of the sea to greet him. The fine, perfectly white sand squeaked beneath his feet like fresh snow, the rhythm of his footfall competing with the gentle hiss of waves, the rising drone of crickets and the sounds of a distant mariachi band. Beyond the small, pineapple shaped palms which lined the head of the beach, the bright neon signs of the bars and restaurants were lighting up, flickering away in vibrant symphony.

The *Buena Onda* bar was located almost directly on the beach and the low thudding cadence of its external speaker system reached Mike's ears well before he could see it. It was an oval shaped *Palapa*; a wall-less, thatch-roofed canopy supported by thick wooden columns which enclosed a huge, 'O' shaped bar. Mike strolled towards it and climbed into one of the high wooden stools that were supported by stakes driven deep into the sand. He quickly scanned the faces around him, but saw no sign of Rod. A pretty waitress came to take his order. He leafed through the drinks menu and settled for a Tecate beer, letting his eyes linger on the young waitress as he placed his order. She had dark, medium-length hair, soft almond eyes, finely sculpted cheekbones and rose petal lips, the kind that begged to be kissed. Mike watched her graceful movements as she turned and crouched to open a glass fronted cooler, her light cotton dress hugging the curves of her slim figure. There was something about her that fascinated him and he found it hard to take his eyes off her as she placed the ice cold beer in front of him.

'Twenty Pesos.'

'I haven't seen you here before,' he said, pulling a few bills from his wallet.

The girl shrugged.

'I've been working here for six months.'

'I used to come here quite often,' said Mike by way of explanation, 'but then I've been away for a while. May I ask your name?'

'Gabriela.'

'Pleased to meet you Gabriela,' he said, stretching out his hand. 'My name's Mike. I work at CavePro just around the corner.'

'Oh,' she said with a brief nod of recognition.

'Perhaps you know some of the other guys from there?'

'Maybe,' she said with a shrug. 'Pablo works there doesn't he?'

'Yeah, that's right. Pablo's been working there for a while.'

'I know Pablo...and I think the owner came here a couple of times too.'

'Ken? Not exactly the life and soul of the party is he?'

'He seemed OK to me. He was polite anyway.'

'Yeah, he's not a bad guy,' conceded Mike, wiping the condensation from his bottle. 'I hear that Pablo left town.'

'I heard that too.'

'Nasty business. Did you meet Frank at all?'

'Frank? Maybe,' she said, lowering her eyes. 'I see so many people come and go here.'

'He worked at CavePro too. He was about my age, dark hair...'

'Look, I'm afraid I really need to get back to my work if you don't mind sir,' she said, cutting him short.

'Oh...yeah, sure.'

'Here's your change.'

'Thanks Gabriela,' he said as she turned to walk away.

He frowned, took a swig from his beer and nearly spat it out again when a hand fell on his shoulder.

'Nice place. Who's the hot waitress?'

Mike swung around to see the grinning face of Rafael.

'First time I saw her,' he said with a shrug.

'Sweet little ass,' said Rafael, admiringly. 'You trying to hit on her?'

'Not with any great deal of success.'

'Well, they say that success comes to those who persevere.'

'Yeah. Either that or a jail sentence for stalking.'

Rafael chuckled as he installed himself on an adjacent stool. He shot a critical eye at the bottle of Tecate that was standing on the bar.

'What's that you're drinking?'

'You've never seen beer before?'

'Of course, but you should only drink beer when you're thirsty, and we're here to celebrate.'

He pulled out his wallet and slapped it on the counter.

'*Senorita, por favor,*' he called out to Gabriela. '*Dos tequilas añejos.*'

Gabriela, who was at that moment serving a middle-aged American couple, turned, gave Rafael a blank stare and nodded curtly.

'She's pretty, huh?' he said.

'Stunning,' agreed Mike.

'And feisty too. Maybe I should put a word in for you.'

'I'd rather you didn't, thanks all the same.'

Rafael shrugged, a smile playing on his lips.

When Gabriela had finished serving the American couple, she brought a bottle of amber coloured spirit and two tall shot glasses over to where Mike and Rafael were sitting. She presented the label of the bottle to Rafael, and after he'd nodded his approval, she poured a golden measure of tequila into each glass.

'*Cuarenta y ocho Pesos.*'

Rafael pulled out a 500 Peso bill and drew Gabriela in close so that he could whisper in her ear. When he withdrew his lips, she directed a concerned glance at Mike.

'What did you just say to her?' Mike demanded after she'd left.

'Oh, nothing. I just told her that you thought she was pretty.'

'Oh great! Thanks Rod. Did you see the look she gave me? She'll probably avoid me for the rest of the evening now.'

'No she won't,' he countered. 'She's flattered Mike. Who wouldn't be? And what do you stand to lose?'

'Look Rafael. I just like to do things my own way OK?' he replied firmly.

'Hey, don't be so sensitive; we're here to have fun,' Rafael said, waving away Mike's protest. 'I presume you like tequila?'

'Yeah, I like tequila,' he shrugged.

'But do you know a good tequila from a cheap one?'

'I've drunk plenty of tequila, but I don't profess to be an expert.'

'Then this is the perfect time to learn. The first thing you need to know is no salt or lime.'

'But it's always served with salt and lime.'

'A poor quality tequila is served with salt and lime,' Rafael corrected, tutting. 'Good tequila was never meant to be drunk quickly, or with any additions. It's a noble spirit which should be savoured as it is, pure and unadulterated. The practice of adding salt and lime became popular in the thirties when American tourists started to spend their vacations in Mexico. The wily Mexicans managed to convince them that the accepted way to drink tequila was with the addition of salt and lime, when in fact its real purpose was to disguise the taste of a poor quality tequila.'

'You're kidding?'

'I'm deadly serious. And the worm in the bottle goes even further.'

'The worm? Why? What's the idea behind it?'

'None. It's a gimmick; designed purely for export sales...and it's really quite a sick joke if you ask me. The worm in the bottle is actually a parasite which feeds on the agave plant, its very presence suggesting that the crop used to produce the tequila was suffering from an infestation. And astonishingly, while the evidence for the inferior nature of the ingredients is on unashamed display, the parasite itself has somehow become associated with authenticity.'

'Now that is some powerful marketing,' said Mike, shaking his head and grinning.

'It's quite a feat isn't it?' agreed Rafael. 'They say that ignorance is bliss, but it's equally true that knowledge is power, and personally I like to know when I'm being made a fool of.'

'I'll drink to that,' said Mike. '*Salud*!'

'*Salud*!'

They raised their *Caballito* glasses, brought them briefly together and then sipped at the golden liquid, letting the subtle flavours fill their mouths and flow tantalizingly over their tongues. Mike nodded appreciatively, as the delicately spiced vapours rose into his nostrils.

'Wow, I have to say that's by far the best tequila I've ever tasted. Thanks Rod.'

'My pleasure. *Tequila añejo* is the equivalent of a single malt whisky. It's made exclusively from the blue agave plant and matured in oak barrels for a minimum of one year, which gives it its smoothness, rich colour and delicate flavour.'

'I have a feeling that I'm being surreptitiously converted into a tequila snob.'

'Then my evening has already been a success,' declared Rafael.

'I'm a little disappointed about one thing though,' said Mike regretfully.

'What's that?'

'The salt and lime is a hell of a lot of fun when you're doing body shots.'

Rafael nodded ponderously.

'Yes, well one should always embrace progress Mike and tourism has certainly brought some interesting ideas. I guess the occasion can sometimes dictate the quality of the tequila...and if you're planning on drinking it from the skin of one of those drunken women who make fools of themselves in the tourist bars of Cozumel, a cheap tequila would seem to be perfectly adequate.'

Mike laughed, tapping his glass against Rafael's. He took a lingering sip and then set the glass down again, rolling the base along the dark wood surface of the counter.

'You're not from Mexico are you Rod?'

'No, I grew up in Puerto Rico, so really I'm American.'

'Do you still have family over there?'

'In Puerto Rico? Just aunts and uncles. My father died when I was young and my mother took us all to live in Miami. It wasn't a good move on the whole. We found it hard to settle there and it was the worst possible environment for my younger brother. He got heavily involved in the local drugs scene and sadly, one night he was gunned down just a few blocks from home.'

'That must have been a tough time.'

'It was hard to accept, but that's the way of the street Mike. There were plenty more kids waiting to take his place. I might have gone the same way if it wasn't for my mother. Luckily I managed to keep out of trouble until I was old enough to sign up for the Marines.'

'So what do you do now?'

'I work in the security services.'

'What...like a bodyguard or something?'

'Let's just say that I look after people. So what about yourself; what brought you here?'

'The diving mostly...and the history of course. I've been travelling around from place to place for some time now; ever since I learned to dive in fact. The main reason I came to the Yucatan was because it has some of the best cave diving in the world. If you want to master the disciplines and techniques of underwater cave exploration then this is the place to be.'

'Sounds like you've found your nirvana.'

'Well, a temporary one at least.'

Mike drained the last drop of tequila from his *Caballito* as Gabriela was passing by.

'Hey, Gabriela, could we have two more of these please,' he asked.

'Sure, I'll be with you in a moment,' she replied.

'Already on first name terms I see,' remarked Rafael.

Mike smiled and shrugged.

'If you want to catch fish, you have to go fishing.'

'Better not let that one get away then.'

Gabriela returned shortly afterwards and replaced their empty glasses with full ones.

'Thanks Gabriela,' said Mike, his confidence now buoyed by the tequila, 'and while you're here may I just apologise for my friend, who for some reason feels that he has the right to speak in my place. Having said that, he's quite right; I do think that you're very pretty.'

'Well that's very nice of you to say so,' replied Gabriela, looking to Rafael for an explanation, 'but I'm not sure that he said what you think he said.'

The composure drained from Mike's face as he turned towards Rafael.

'What exactly *did* you say Rod?' he demanded, his eyes narrowing.

'I was er...just trying to act in your best interests,' replied Rafael.

'Tell me something Mike,' said Gabriela, her eyebrows raised, 'is it true that you just split up with your girlfriend?'

'No. I don't even have a girlfriend,' Mike replied exasperated.

Rafael grinned and looked away.

'Then maybe you should be more careful who you choose as a friend,' she said, glancing at Rafael.

'Thank you. I think I will.'

'This is what you get when you try to help someone,' said Rafael, folding his arms sulkily.

'I could do without your kind of help, thanks.'

'Suit yourself.'

'Forty eight Pesos,' prompted Gabriela, a smile creeping across her face.

'Charge him the double,' muttered Rafael.

Mike was just reaching into his wallet when his eyes fell upon a newspaper clipping. It was the report of Frank's murder which Ken had given to him a few days earlier. He took it out and carefully unfolded it, staring at the photograph of Frank below the bleak headline.

'Hey Gabriela, the guy I was asking you about earlier, Frank, this is him here,' he said, showing her the grainy photograph. 'He died recently; it's been in all the newspapers. Surely you must have heard something about it?'

A wiry waiter with leathery skin, flattened nose and eyes half hidden behind drooping eyelids overheard the conversation and came to stand next to Gabriela.

'No, I'm sorry I don't think I recognise him,' Gabriela was saying.

'Are you an investigator?' asked the flat nosed waiter, staring at the newspaper clipping.

'No...nothing like that. The guy who was killed was a friend of mine.'

'I'm sorry to hear that, but the police found the murderer,' said the waiter.

'Yes, I know.'

'Then I don't understand. What more do you need to know?'

'I just...I'm just trying to piece together what happened I guess.'

'I see. Well you'll forgive me for saying so, but it was a very unpleasant event and most of us here just want to forget about what happened...and we'd greatly appreciate it if you could avoid alarming the other tourists.'

'Sure...I understand. I'm sorry if I've upset either of you.'

'There's no need to apologise. Please continue to enjoy your evening.'

'Keep the change,' said Mike, as Gabriela took the 60 Pesos which he'd left on the counter.

She smiled weakly and followed the flat nosed waiter to the cash register.

'May I see that?' asked Rafael, as Mike was about to put the news clipping away.

'Sure,' said Mike, handing it over. 'It doesn't make pleasant reading though.'

'Murder never does,' said Rafael as he began to scan through the report. 'She was lying you know.'

'Who was lying?'

'The waitress; Gabriela. She knew who you were talking about.'

'How do you know that?'

'Her body-language mostly. Things we pick up in training.'

'But why would she lie? She's got nothing to gain from it.'

'I've no idea. All I can tell you is what I saw.'

Mike glanced to his right and saw Gabriela at the far end of the bar in heated conversation with the flat nosed waiter. When he made eye contact with her, she averted her eyes.

'This sounds like some kind of ritualistic murder,' said Rafael. 'Did your friend have any dealings with organised crime?'

'Not that I'm aware of.'

'And the cave system he was exploring, did it have any physical connection with the coast?'

'No, it was fully explored after the murder. It's an inland system; like the one we dived today.'

Rafael pursed his lips and frowned.

'Is there any chance that your friend could have had some involvement with the movement of narcotics?'

'I doubt that very much. This is a small community and you get to know people's business. Besides, he never seemed to have much money; he was always complaining to Ken that we weren't being paid enough.'

'Well, this is a very unusual case, and I find it hard to believe that such a complex murder was the work of one man,' said Rafael, handing back the newspaper clipping.

'I have my doubts too. I could be wrong, but I've got a feeling the police just wanted to find someone to pin the blame on. After all, murder is bad news for a place like this.'

'Very true,' agreed Rafael. 'And if, as I suspect, you intend to do a little private detective work on the side, may I suggest that you tread very carefully. Whether right or wrong, a line has been drawn through this incident and no one will appreciate it rearing its ugly head again.'

'I'm starting to realise that,'

Rafael picked up his glass and tapped it against Mike's.

'To absent friends.'

'To absent friends,' echoed Mike.

They drank in silence for a moment, each taking the time to reflect on what they had just learned from one another. Rafael was the first to stir, draining the last few drops from the bottom of his glass before ordering two more. He pulled a stout Cohiba cigar from the inside of his powder blue dress jacket and rolled it admiringly between his fingers.

'Do you mind if I smoke Mike?'

'Not at all.'

'Good, that'll save me having to sit at the other side of the bar from where I would have to shout at you.'

'You could always offer me one.'

'Do you know how much these things cost? Believe me, I'll be doing you a favour by not introducing you to such an expensive habit. In fact I'm secretly hoping that they'll kill me before I'm declared bankrupt.'

'Cheapskate!' taunted Mike.

Rafael grinned.

Gabriela appeared at that moment and placed two *Caballitos* in front of them.

'These are on the house gentlemen.'

'Wow! That's most generous,' said Mike. 'Thanks Gabriela.'

'You're welcome,' she replied. 'Please enjoy them.'

She flicked her pretty almond eyes from Mike to Rafael and then back again, a teasing smile playing across her lips.

'Did I just imagine that?' said Mike as she turned to walk away.

Rafael shrugged.

'I often have that effect on women.'

'You're such a dork Rod,' said Mike, shaking his head.

He watched Rafael dip the butt of his cigar into the tequila, bite off the end and light the tip over a gently swaying match flame.

'We all have our faults Mike,' he said, curls of dense smoke drifting away from his parted lips, 'but under the circumstances I'll forgive you your jealousy.'

'Yeah? And I'll forgive you your narcissistic delusions.'

Rafael began to laugh, spluttering clouds of cigar smoke into the evening air. Mike was soon laughing along with him.

As the evening progressed and more tequila passed their lips, they found themselves exchanging tales of adventure and amorous encounter with the ease of old friends. Their good humour spilled out into their surrounds and before long Rafael had attracted the attentions of a pretty young Norwegian girl who introduced herself as Silje. She was tall and delicately proportioned, her ice-blue eyes and dark chestnut hair making a striking combination. Mike admired Rafael's ability to bring her smoothly into the conversation, his gentle teasing and cajoling quickly putting her at her ease. He seemed to have a natural charm which he could adapt to suit his audience, encouraging people to speak and listening attentively while subtly controlling the course of the exchange.

Mike was no match for it, he knew, but what he lacked in technique, he more than made up for with his cheerful disposition, rugged good looks and calm confidence. It wasn't unusual for him to receive attention from unexpected quarters, but even he was surprised at the sudden interest which Gabriela was showing towards him after their earlier impasse. It seemed that whenever she had a moment spare, she would find an excuse to drop by and exchange a few light-hearted words of conversation. And with Rafael's attention now taken with Silje, Mike had her mostly to himself. As the barriers between them were lowered, Mike tried to find out more about her. At first she was reluctant to speak about herself and seemed more interested in talking about him, but as the night wore on, he gradually managed to coax a few details out of her.

'So where did you live as a child?'

'I grew up in a village a few miles from here.'

'On the coast?'

'No, inland. A very small community. Just a few huts and houses really.'

'Is that where your family is from?'

'More or less. My father was from the neighbouring village, but he died when I was very young. My mother still lives there. I don't think she'll ever move.'

'Any brothers or sisters?'

'A brother, but he no longer lives there. No one from my generation wants to stay and work in the fields anymore. It's not a life for young people. We all work in the tourist areas now. Hotels, bars, restaurants; that kind of thing. Some of us even work in diving, like your friend Pablo.'

'How long have you known him?'

'Pablo? I've known him since he was a child,' she said with a shrug. 'He's from the next village. I remember he was a real handful when he was young; always getting into trouble.'

'That sounds like the Pablo I know,' said Mike, smiling.

Gabriela drew closer and lowered her voice.

'Listen Mike, this friend of yours that you were asking about. I think that I met him once...with Pablo.'

Mike looked up in surprise.

'When you showed me the picture in the newspaper I wasn't sure, but now I think it's the person I saw him with. They were here just a few days before he went missing; getting drunk. I think they were celebrating something.'

'Celebrating? Do you know why? Did you hear anything they said?'

'I overheard one or two things, but first tell me what you're hoping to find out. Don't you believe what the newspapers say?'

'I'm not convinced,' said Mike, frowning. 'There are some things about the whole story which just don't add up.'

'Such as?'

'I can't say right now because I don't have all the facts. I'm just asking around at the moment in the hope that I might be able to piece things together...so any information you could give me would be greatly appreciated.'

'Look, you have to understand that this is a very delicate subject. You saw how my colleague reacted earlier. I'd like to help you if I can, but this is not the right place. If you can wait 30 minutes until I get off work we could take a walk along the beach or something.'

'Yeah, that would be great. I don't think we have any immediate plans to leave,' said Mike, glancing over at Rafael and Silje, who looked to be just moments away from tearing each other's clothes off.

'*Muy Bien*. Look, I have to go now,' she said, glancing towards a stern looking customer who was holding up his empty glass expectantly. 'We'll speak later OK?'

'For sure, thanks Gabriela.'

After she left, Mike stared at his untouched tequila, deep in thought. He took a sip and then reconsidered, attempting to pour half of it into Rafael's glass.'

'You had enough already?'

Startled, Mike swivelled in his seat, to find Rafael grinning at him.

'Does nothing escape you?'

'Not if I can help it.'

'Yeah, I've noticed. I'm just trying to keep a clear head that's all.'

'I guess that's understandable seeing as things seem to be going well between you and our pretty hostess. You wouldn't want to fall at the last hurdle now would you,' he said with a smirk. 'You got plans?'

'Gabriela said she'll be finishing her shift shortly. We were thinking of taking a walk along the beach. Wanna join us?'

Rafael looked enquiringly at Silje, who appeared to have developed a lopsided grin.

'You want to tag along with these wierdos?'

'Yeah! Let's go to the beach,' she said a little too excitedly. 'We could go for a moonlight swim.'

'I guess we'll be joining you then,' said Rafael, with a shrug. 'I think maybe we'll put the swim on hold though.'

'Oh don't be so boring,' said Silje, a hiccough punctuating her speech. 'I'm on holiday. I want to have fun.'

Mike was amused to see Rafael blowing out his cheeks.

'Yes, don't be a bore Rod. It's a perfect night for a swim,' he teased.

'Oh, well if everyone's going to do it, then I'm all for it,' said Rafael. 'Have you mentioned this to Gabriela at all Mike? Perhaps we should ask her too.'

He motioned as if to call her over, but Mike quickly intervened.

'No, let's just surprise her instead.'

'Are you sure Mike? It would only take a second to ask.'

'Yes, you've made your point Rod. Let's just play it by ear shall we?'

'As you wish,' he replied with a knowing smile.

As soon as Gabriela had finished her shift, she slipped on a jacket, passed through a hinged opening in the oval bar and came to join Mike, brushing down her skirt and preening her lightly coiled hair.

'You look even prettier close up,' Mike said as she climbed into the seat next to him.

'Thank you,' she said, her cheeks flushing. 'Have you finished your drink?'

'Yes,' said Mike, looking at his empty glass, 'I'm good to go. I hope you don't mind, but I invited Rod and Silje along too.'

Gabriela looked up in surprise.

'I thought we'd be alone?'

'Don't worry, we won't be bothering you for long,' said Rafael, who'd been listening in to their conversation. 'We'll just get a bit of fresh air and then we'll be leaving you in peace,' he said motioning towards Silje, who now seemed to be having trouble staying awake.

Gabriela took a look at Silje and nodded.

'OK, but I'd like to go soon.'

'We're ready when you are,' said Rafael, with a glance in Mike's direction. 'The sooner the better.'

He stood up and helped Silje down from her stool, supporting her as she landed in the soft sand.

Mike and Gabriela went ahead, strolling along the shoreline with Rafael and Silje trailing a short distance behind. The cool sea breeze tugged at Gabriela's hair, sweeping wayward strands across her face, which she teased back and swept over her shoulder with her fingers. With her slender nose and high cheek bones powdered by the soft moonlight, Mike thought she looked like a tragic heroine from some old black and white movie.

'You look as if you're deep in thought,' he said, seeing the distant look in her eyes.

'Do I? I wasn't really thinking about anything.'

'Not even questioning why you're walking along the beach at night with a total stranger.'

'Well, that of course,' she said with a half smile. 'Should I be concerned?'

'You're in the safest of hands.'

Gabriela bit her lip and looked away.

'Hey Mike!' came a sudden shout from behind. They turned in unison to see Rafael kneeling next to Silje, who was now lying spread-eagled on the sand, giggling and staring up at the star studded sky.

'You two go on ahead!' yelled Rafael, his hands spread wide in apology. 'I think this is about as far as we're going.'

'OK. Best of luck,' said Mike laughing. 'We'll catch you later.'

'*Hasta luego*,' Rafael replied with a casual salute.

Gabriela led Mike further along the beach, away from the light of the hotels and restaurants and up into the cover of palms. When she judged that they were safe from prying ears, she stopped abruptly and turned to face him.

'OK Mike I guess we can talk here. I'm sorry to have to be the one to tell you this, but the truth is that your friend Frank got involved in things which he should have left well alone. He upset some very dangerous people.'

'What? Hey wait a minute, how do you know all this? You told me that you barely knew Frank.'

'I had to say that. Look, I'm putting myself in danger just by speaking to you about this, so please just be quiet and listen. You have to stop asking questions about your friend, because if you don't you're going to end up just like him. You have no idea what you're getting yourself into. My advice to you is to take the next bus out of this place and never come back.'

'But that's crazy. Frank wouldn't hurt a fly. I've never known him to be in any kind of trouble.'

'It wasn't his intention to upset anyone, he just happened to be in the wrong place at....'

Gabriela fell silent and stared into the darkness, her eyes suddenly wide with fear.

'Mike, get out of here...now!' she said, pushing him away.

Mike hesitated, spinning around wildly when he spotted silhouettes flashing through the surrounding palms. Before he had time to react, figures wearing dark hoods leapt out at him and tried to knock him to the ground. Through the heavy blows that rained down on him, he saw two men grab Gabriela by the wrists and drag her protesting towards a waiting car. A rage overtook him and he kicked out, breaking free and running to her aid, but he was tripped and stumbled forwards, his face pounding hard into the sand. Before he could drag himself to his feet, there was a flash of white behind his eyes and he felt a sharp explosion of pain in his skull. Dazed and with the fight knocked out of him, he tried to crawl away, but was quickly seized and rolled onto his back. He saw the night sky above him and the heads of two hooded men as they stooped down, pinning his arms to the ground. There was a squeal of tyres as the car was driven away and Mike's fear turned to terror as a third man appeared, stepping over him and pulling a long bladed knife from his jacket.

Was this it? Was he going to die like Frank? Scared, alone and far from home?

The prospect of imminent death brought sharpness to his muddled senses and he kicked upwards with all his might. The knifeman cried out as he was struck in the groin, the force enough to lift him from the ground. There was a grunt as he stumbled forwards, colliding with the man holding Mike's left arm and using the confusion to his advantage, Mike raised both legs towards his chest and flicked them forwards, springing to his feet. His left arm was pulled clear and he rolled forward to free his right, but he landed awkwardly and lost his footing in the soft sand. A hand reached out and seized his ankle before he could scramble free and in desperation he kicked out in a vain attempt to shake off the hold. The knifeman was now back on his feet again and Mike grimaced when he saw moonlight reflecting from the long blade that was grasped in his fist. A torrent of unintelligible words came from behind the man's gritted teeth as the knife was raised into the air, ready to strike the blow that would end Mike's life. Then, just as his arm reached the apex of its swing, he was suddenly pitched forward as if struck from behind by a speeding car. Mike watched bewildered as the knifeman went flying through the air, his arms flailing wildly as he went head over heels and pitched into the sand with a heavy thud. A boot swept through the air just inches from Mike's nose and crashed into the temple of the man holding his ankle. As soon as Mike felt the grip slacken, he burst into action, pulling his leg free and rolling forward, wrenching the elbow of the man to his right and making him cry out in pain. Filled with a sudden fury, he silenced his assailant with a straight punch to the jaw. There was a sudden flurry of movement behind and anticipating another attack Mike threw himself to one side. He rolled swiftly to his feet ready to defend himself, but all he saw was a dagger flying through the air, a whirlwind of kicks, thrusts and punches and the jerking body of the hooded knifeman bucking and collapsing unconscious into a ragged heap on the sand. Incredulous, Mike dropped to his knees.

'Do I have any blood on me?' asked Rafael, pulling at his clothes. 'If these assholes have ruined my jacket I swear I will cut their balls off.'

Mike, still reeling from shock, took a moment to speak.

'I nearly just got killed and you're worried about your jacket?'

'You're being a little over-dramatic Mike. And besides I'm very fond of this jacket. I had it specially made in Bolivia. Where's Gabriela?'

'Gabriela? I...don't know. They took her away.'

'That's a pity. I would've liked to have slapped her around a little.'

'What? Are you completely crazy? She's just been abducted. For all we know she could be dead by now.'

'You have a lot to learn my friend. It was her that led these men to you.'

'Oh yeah? And how do you know that?' Mike challenged.

'Think about it. Who did you speak to about your friend Frank apart from me, Gabriela and that ugly waiter?'

Mike stared at the twisted body of the knifeman.

'Then it must have been the waiter,' he said. 'I don't believe that Gabriela would do this.'

'Ha! It's amazing how easily logic can be distorted by a man's ego. Don't you realise that women have been used to lure men into danger since the dawn of time?'

'But she tried to warn me. She told me that Frank had got into some kind of trouble...and that I should stop asking questions or I'd end up just like him.'

'OK, but as you've just proved, she lied to you back there in the bar...and if you want my opinion, all that sudden attention which she gave you was just an excuse to win you over and draw you away from the crowds. If I hadn't seen these sly fuckers stalking you along the beach, I probably wouldn't have made the connection myself.'

Mike shook his head.

'I don't know Rod. Maybe you're right, but I swear she was genuinely surprised when these men turned up...and it's not as if she went with them voluntarily.'

'Then the chances are that she was being played Mike. Someone probably persuaded her to meet you here on some pretext or other so that they could use the situation to their advantage.'

'Now *that* would make more sense,' agreed Mike nodding.

There was a muffled groan from one of the downed men.

'Come on, let's get out of here. We're not going to learn anything by hanging around,' said Rafael. 'Silje's waiting for me in a taxi up ahead. She's probably fast asleep in the back by now.'

Mike dusted himself down and followed Rafael back along the head of the beach, never taking his eyes from the shadows.

'I suppose I should thank you for saving my life,' he said.

Rafael grinned, pulled out a cigar and wrapped his arm around Mike's shoulder.

'Didn't I tell you we'd have fun tonight?'

CARTAGENA, COLOMBIA

Julio Morales pushed his black BMW 5-series through the outskirts of Cartagena as fast he dared. He sped along the desolate coastline to the south, blaring his horn as he tore past a procession of trucks, beaten up cars and horse-drawn carts, leaving them enveloped in thick clouds of dust. After an hour's drive he left the main road and continued along a woodland track which terminated at the gates of a private estate. Wiping away the sweat that was pouring from his thinning temples, he leaned out of the window and pressed an intercom button.

'*¿Quien es?* – Who is it?' asked a crackling voice.

'*Julio. Abre!* – Julio. Open up!'

There was a humming sound as the remotely operated wrought-iron gates swung open. Julio gunned the BMW through and sped along a pristine drive, bordered by tall palms and meticulously tended lawns. He reached a security post, stopped and lowered the darkened, bullet-proof windows, waiting for the surly security guard with the semi-automatic rifle to make his inspection. When the guard saw fit to raise the barrier, Julio passed beneath a stone archway into a wide courtyard that was enclosed by neat ornamental gardens, the ancient walls of which were covered with colourful swathes of bougainvillea.

He tore around an ancient well, which had once served the needs of a monastic order, screeched to a halt besides two imposing blacked out Hummers and climbed up a short flight of steps towards a pair of solid oak doors. A metal screen was pulled aside as he reached for the doorbell and a pair of dark eyes scrutinised him closely. Heavy bolts were pulled free and the steel reinforced doors creaked open with arthritic reluctance.

'Está arriba – He's upstairs,' the man standing behind the door informed him.

Julio nodded curtly and made his way through the marble tiled reception hall. He climbed the sweeping staircase, past displays of antique weaponry, priceless ceramics and works of renaissance art which had once graced the finest galleries of Europe.

A maid bowed her head respectfully as they passed on the upper landing and the sound of children's voices briefly reached his ears when a door was opened and closed just behind him. He reached the end of a wide hallway and paused behind a plain panelled door, smoothing his dark moustache as he stared into the lens of the security camera built into the wall to his left. The door opened a fraction, and a stern eye set into a dark-skinned face made a last sweeping check before Julio was finally allowed to enter the inner sanctum.

'I came here as soon as I could liberate myself,' he said, bursting forwards and striding towards the owner of the property, who was seated behind a desk carefully positioned to take advantage of the spectacular panoramic views of the Colombian coastline below.

Ángel Batista marked a pause before turning to face his brother-in-law, his elbows resting on the arms of a leather chair and his thumb and finger tips touching lightly as if in prayer. Julio felt his gut tighten as he peered into those familiar yet distant eyes, never entirely certain whether Ángel considered him to be anything other than a subservient member of his notorious cartel.

'I take it that there has been a problem of some kind?'

'Problem is not an adequate word for it,' said Ángel, the inflection in his voice indicating the anger that was silently raging behind his calm expression. Without further explanation, he picked up a console that was lying on the desk in front of him and pressed a button which operated a concealed panel in the wall. It opened with a hum, revealing a giant flat screen monitor which immediately flickered into life.

'Sit down Julio,' said Ángel, motioning towards a reclining leather chair. 'Carlos...the lights!'

Blinds silently began to descend in front of the huge floor to ceiling windows and Julio had barely made himself comfortable when a pre-recorded news bulletin began to play on the panoramic screen. He sat back in the leather chair and listened in astonished silence as a journalist relayed news of the chaos that had gripped Europe following the hundreds of cases of cocaine related poisonings that were sweeping through the continent. For the first time he learned of the audacious attempt by an unknown terrorist group to blackmail the Spanish authorities and the extraordinary measures that were being put in place to try to disrupt the international drug distribution networks. Finally, there was footage of combined American and Colombian military forces laying waste to a coca plantation in the high plateau and Julio watched in silent horror as one of Ángel's most fierce competitors was dragged out of his lavish family home in handcuffs.

When the report switched to news of the kidnap and murder of a prominent local banker, Ángel turned off the monitor with a derisory snort.

Julio took a moment to speak.

'I can't understand why anyone would do that,' he said finally as the blinds began to lift, flooding the room with sunlight once more. 'If you can move that much coke, you're going to be rich anyway, so why would you want to blackmail a government? It just doesn't make sense.'

'They're probably political idealists,' said Ángel with contempt in his voice, 'but I have no interest in trying to understand their motives. All I care about is stopping them from threatening my business.'

'But what can we do? Nobody seems to have any idea who these people are.'

'As yet,' countered Ángel. 'In this business we normally consider our competitors to be our enemies, but when a crisis like this hits the industry, we find a way to work together. All the major cocaine producers have been in consultation recently and we have each agreed to run checks on our largest clients to find out if they are in any way involved in the deliberate contamination of our produce. Unless these lunatics have access to clandestine resources, they must be buying in volume from a major supplier, and if they are, then we should be able to track them down. Of course, such a sensitive information gathering exercise could arouse suspicion and resentment from our respective clients if discovered. It is therefore essential that our enquiries are carried out in the most discreet and professional manner. I cannot afford to risk losing the confidence of any of my major partners, especially under the present circumstances.'

'Naturally Ángel. So what is your plan?'

'I'm putting you in charge of the operation Julio. Right now our biggest buyer is Señor Pacal from Mexico who, you may recall, you introduced to our organisation just over a year ago.'

Julio felt the hairs prickle on the back of his neck.

'Y-yes. Of course,' he said, loosening his shirt collar.

'Señor Pacal's last few orders were quite substantial, which normally would have delighted me, but under the present circumstances, it makes me deeply suspicious.'

'I understand Ángel, but how can I find him? We know virtually nothing about him.'

'We know enough. I doubt if he'd be careless enough to use his real name, but we know what he looks like, which flights he uses and the rough area where he bases his operations. I want you to go to Mexico with a couple of my men, ask around, grease a few palms, find out who his contacts are and more importantly, where his business interest lie. I'll give you whatever resources you need, but I want answers and you can forget about coming back here until you have them. Is that clear?'

'Yes, of course Ángel. So when do we leave?'

'Tomorrow.'

'Tomorrow? But Ángel, that's impossible, you have to understand that I_'

'Can I count on you or not Julio?'

Ángel's measured stare was a warning, and Julio did not dare contemplate the consequences of ignoring it.

'Of course Ángel.'

'Good. Here are your plane tickets. You'll fly first thing in the morning.'

* * * *

The dive centre was already busy by the time that Mike arrived. He checked the planner, went straight through to the back of the shop and began to gather together the equipment that he would need for the group of divers he was allocated that morning. While he was busily sifting through a pile of lead weights, Ken came to stop him.

'Hey Mike, you can leave that; I've got something else planned for you today.'

'Uh? What's that?'

'One of your students rang first thing this morning and booked you as a private guide. You'll need to put together a set of cave gear.'

'One of my students?' asked Mike, surprised.

'The big guy with the ponytail.'

'You mean Rod?'

'Yeah, he's here in the shop. He just walked through the door.'

Mike walked out to see Rafael standing barefoot in the shop clutching a large carton of coffee in one hand while studying a selection of sleek, wrist mounted computers in a display cabinet. He was wearing a blue flowered Hawaiian shirt, board shorts and silver wraparound shades.

'And there's me thinking I'd seen the last of you,' said Mike, shaking his head.

Rafael turned towards him and grinned.

'Yeah, me too, but just my luck, all the best instructors have been taken.'

'Very funny. So what's this all about?'

'I want to do some exploring.'

'And you're prepared to pay for a private guide?'

'For where I want to go, absolutely.'

'And where's that?'

'I'll let you know when we get there,' said Rafael, much to Mike's confusion. 'I've got the Chevy outside, so we can throw all the gear in the back and head off just as soon as you're ready.'

Mike frowned and turned towards Ken

'Are you happy to go along with this?'

'Why not?' said Ken with a shrug. 'He's paid over the odds, so take him wherever the hell he wants. Just make darned sure you bring him and my equipment back in one piece.'

Ken walked away leaving Mike staring at Rafael in disbelief.

'What's the matter? Don't you like surprises?' Rafael asked, smirking.

'Not if they're anything like the surprises I had last night. My head still feels like it's in a vice.'

'Ah, you live such a sheltered life Mike. You need to take a walk on the wild side from time to time.'

'And you need to take a walk on the *sane* side.'

'Now where would be the fun in that?' Rafael chuckled.

'Well, since I'm stuck with you, I suppose I'd better go get us some gear.'

'I'll give you a hand,' offered Rafael.

They loaded the gear into the back of the Chevrolet and drove out of town, heading southwards along the coast to the sounds of Pink Floyd's *Wish you Were Here*. After a few miles, Rafael slowed and turned into the walled entrance of a five star hotel complex.

'Did you forget something?' asked Mike.

'No.'

'I take it you're staying here?'

'Yeah. Nice place huh?'

'So are we picking up Silje or something?'

'Silje? No, I dropped her off at her hotel this morning.'

'Then would it be foolish of me to press you for the reason why we *are* here?' asked Mike, as they drove on towards the waterfront.

'See that boat over there? said Rafael, pointing towards an 8 metre Boston Whaler that was moored up alongside the hotel's private jetty.

'Yeah.'

'That's the reason we're here. I've hired it for the day.'

'We're taking a boat? But there aren't any cave systems along the coast. At least, none that I'm aware of.'

'I'm not entirely certain that there are either,' said Rafael.

'So what are we doing? Just diving in and exploring random spots, hoping for the best?' Mike asked, exasperated.

'No Mike. I've got something particular in mind, but I don't know what to expect so you'll just have to bear with me for the moment. I know this is a little out of the ordinary for you, but you're here for two reasons; firstly because I trust you and secondly because I may need your expertise.'

Mike pursed his lips.

'OK Rod. Whatever you want, I'll go along with it, just as long as whatever you're planning doesn't put either of us in danger. And by that I mean danger as I see it, not as *you* see it.'

'That's fair enough,' said Rod.

'Right. Let's get this equipment loaded onto the boat.'

A short while later they were making their way south, the long fibreglass hull of the Boston Whaler powering smoothly through the incoming swell with its 90 horse-power Mercury engine leaving a widening swathe of foaming water in its wake.

Rafael consulted a handheld GPS and ran a course close to shore. He sped past the town of Chacalal and eased back on the throttle as the target waypoint drew near. Soon the limestone cliffs which had served as his surveillance post a few days earlier came into view. From his seaward perspective he could now see two bright white patches painted high up the rock face, clearly serving as transit markers to guide small boats in at night. The GPS alarm sounded, confirming that he was within metres of the spot where he'd taken the reading. He glanced over the side of the boat, went to the bow and dropped the anchor.

'OK, this will do fine. Let's kit up and see what we can find at the base of those cliffs.'

'Whatever floats your boat,' replied Mike, unconvinced.

Without further debate they strapped on their twin cylinder cave rigs, clipped emergency sling tanks, reels and back-up lights to their harnesses and pulled on their masks and fins. After making methodical safety checks, they gave each other a final nod, slipped over the side of the boat and plunged into the warm embrace of the Caribbean.

Shoals of yellow tail snapper darted around as Mike and Rafael took turns to rotate, checking their equipment for leaks. A curious French angelfish came to investigate, turning back and forth on itself and flashing its gold flecked scales as it accompanied the strange intruders towards the cliff face. Pink soft corals, reached up vertically towards them from the sea bed, like stretched chewing gum swaying back and forth in the swell. Soon they were following the base of the cliff, gliding over the remnants of the fallen rock face, where reddish brown hard corals flourished on the exposed surfaces. Patrolling them were the ever-present butterfly fish, bird wrasse and parrot fish, never passing an opportunity to feed on tender, living coral polyps.

Mike watched their activity with detached curiosity, but Rafael had other things on his mind. He was busily scanning the area in all directions, determined to solve the mystery which had been plaguing him since he'd seen the motor yacht anchored there the previous week. As the minutes ticked by, he began to wonder if he'd let his imagination run away with him, but when a faint line of disturbed sand came into view up ahead, running perpendicular to the cliff face, he knew that he'd been right to trust his instincts. As they drew closer, he traced the line back towards the coast and uttered a muted cry of triumph when he saw it disappear into a dark opening at the base of the cliff. He beckoned Mike over and made it clear that he wanted to investigate further. Mike agreed to follow him, but as they approached the cave entrance, the clarity of the water changed and everything around them became hazy and distorted. Their progress became laboured and Mike realised that they were swimming against an outflow of fresh water. He was about to point out to Rafael the futility of proceeding when he noticed that the line of disturbance on the sea bed was caused by the links of a thin chain, partially buried beneath the sand. He took a hold of it to steady himself and then urged Rafael to do the same. Now that they had a point of anchorage, they began to pull themselves hand over hand against the current into the mouth of the cave. When the natural light began to recede, they switched on their wrist mounted flashlights to guide them, but their progress came to a sudden halt when they found a submerged gate barring their way. Mike shone his light beam beyond it and saw a vast air pocket in the distance with the white hulls of two small craft floating above.

Intrigued, he rattled the vertical bars of the gate, studied the groove which held it in place against the walls of the cave and then probed the sand beneath it with his fingers. Knowing that it was impossible to go any further without the right equipment, he signalled to Rafael to retreat. Ten minutes later they were back on the boat.

'OK Rod, I've got an idea how I might be able to get past that gate, but first I want a few straight answers.'

Rafael sucked his cheeks in.

'OK Mike. What do you need to know?'

'You're not here just for fun are you? There's something unusual going on in that cave and you have some idea what it is.'

'I guess that would be difficult to deny,' said Rafael with a shrug.

'Right,' said Mike, nodding irritatedly. 'So before we go any further, I'd like you to explain to me just what it is we're doing here and then I want to know what your intentions are.'

Rafael slowly scanned the cliffs behind him and then leaned in close.

'I'm a drug enforcement agent.'

Mike snorted, waiting for the punchline, but Rafael's face remained impassive.

'Christ, you're not kidding are you?'

Rafael held Mike's gaze and slowly shook his head.

'I've been assigned to investigate a ring of drug traffickers who are operating in this area and I have good reason to believe that they're using that cave down there as a means to smuggle their consignments inland.'

'Drug smugglers?' said Mike, astounded.

'Please keep your voice down,' cautioned Rafael. 'Well you wanted the facts and now you have them,' he said bluntly, 'so what do you want to do?'

'Tell me something first,' said Mike, still digesting the information. 'Did that attack on me the other night have anything to do with all this?'

'As far as I know, absolutely nothing,' said Rafael shaking his head emphatically, 'although I have to admit that at one point I wondered if your friend's death might have some connection to what's going on here.'

'Frank?' said Mike, bemused. 'Why would you think that?'

'Because the guys who move the stuff around are divers...and considering the circumstances surrounding your friend's death_' he said, raising his eyebrows.

'Frank was not that kind of guy,' said Mike, his eyes brimming with emotion. 'He would never have got involved in anything like that.'

'I'm sure you're right,' said Rafael, keen to reassure him 'and anyway the facts didn't seem to fit.'

Mike frowned and stared out to sea.

'You've been stringing me along from the beginning haven't you?' he said resentfully. 'I'll bet Rod isn't even your real name.'

'I haven't lied to you once Mike. And Rod is actually my nickname,' he said with an apologetic smile. 'That's what they used to call me in the Corps and I guess it stuck.'

Mike looked down at his equipment and let out a sigh.

'So to carry out your investigation you need to take a look inside this cave, right?'

'If that's not too much to ask,' said Rafael, with a shrug. 'Otherwise I'll have to try to get by on my own.'

'It needs two people,' said Mike. 'And anyway, I don't fancy hanging around on the surface if there's a chance that one of the gang will turn up unannounced.'

'Looks like we're a team again then,' said Rafael, the smile returning to his face.

'We've got some work to do first.'

Mike worked quickly, stripping the backplate from his buoyancy wings, and clipping a single sling tank to the 'D' rings of the harness. While Rafael was putting his equipment back on, Mike jumped into the water to check his buoyancy. The small, steel cylinder provided enough ballast for him to sink without the need for a weight belt. As soon as Rafael had joined him, they descended and returned to the cave entrance.

Mike reached the gate first and immediately started to scoop away the sand beneath the vertical bars with a baler. Once he'd dug a trench deep enough for his body to pass beneath them, he unclipped the sling cylinder from his harness and slipped it through the gap so that it lay on the other side. With the regulator still held firmly in his mouth, he rolled onto his back and wriggled head first under the gate, using the bars to push his way through. Soon he was safely on the other side, clipping the sling tank back into place and giving Rafael a triumphant thumb touching fingertip OK sign.

With a single flashlight strapped to his wrist, he turned and began to pull himself deeper into the blackness of the cave. The beam of the flashlight illuminated the underside of the two small craft that were moored in the air pocket above and Mike used the chain to pull himself up as far as an iron ring that was bolted into a narrow quay. He pulled himself clear of the water, climbed onto the quay and used his flashlight beam to trace a cable which ran along the wall behind it. The cable passed behind a row of lockers and then entered a plain white control box. Mike opened the cover to find a row of fuses, a lever and a switch. He threw the switch and a series of lights were turned on along the inner wall of the cavern, lighting it along its whole length. It was an astonishing natural passageway that had been painstakingly enlarged by hand. Moored beside the stone quay on which he was standing, Mike could now see a sled transport system for divers and a jetski. He turned to open one of the four standing lockers and was not surprised to discover that they contained diving equipment. Returning his attention to the control box, he raised the lever to the left of the switch and heard a whirring sound as a winch mounted on a concrete platform began to haul in cable. As he'd suspected, it lifted the gate which barred the entrance from the submerged passageway and soon Rafael was able to rise up the chain to join him.

'Very impressive,' said Rafael, his voice reverberating along the passageway as he began to release himself from his equipment. 'These people are obviously no amateurs.'

'Looks like someone's pretty determined,' agreed Mike, helping to haul Rafael's equipment onto the quayside. 'What do you think they use the sled for?'

'From what I saw they use it to pick up contraband from boats which moor up beneath the cliffs at night. The chain we saw buried in the sand probably serves as a guide, leading the divers from the cave entrance to the drop off point and back.'

'Ingenious.'

Rafael nodded.

'They need to be pretty inventive in order to beat our sophisticated surveillance systems.'

'So what do we do now?'

'Well I could call the boys in, wait for the next drop off and then set up a trap, but we have absolutely no idea when the next consignment will arrive...and unfortunately there's a time element involved here. I take it you've heard about the poisoned cocaine that's hit Europe recently?'

'Yes, I saw something about it on TV.'

'Then you'll understand how serious the problem is. There are agents like me working along the whole coast of Central and South America at the moment, trying to find out where this cocaine is coming from and more importantly who's adding poison to it. I wish that meant that the responsibility was equally distributed between all of us, but guess what? Some scientist type has worked out that the poison actually comes from an area which falls right here on my patch. How he worked that out, God only knows, but now I've got the big chief at the DEA breathing down my neck because he's got some schmuck from Washington breathing down his. From what I've heard, the whole of Europe is knocking on the President's door right now.'

'So, nothing much for you to worry about then?'

'What?' asked Rafael, bemused.

'Forget it. English cynicism,' said Mike. 'So I take it you want to find out where this tunnel leads?'

'That's the plan. You happy to tag along?'

'Well I'm guessing we're alone down here, since the lights were off when

I arrived.'

'That's a fair assumption, but we can't rule out the possibility of it being remotely monitored or even booby trapped.'

'Do you think that's likely?'

'I doubt it,' said Rafael, pursing his lips and shaking his head.

'That was a lie wasn't it?'

'You catch on quick,' grinned Rafael.

'Oh well, I guess it all adds to the excitement,' said Mike with a cavalier shrug. 'Shall we take a spin on the jetski?'

'Be my guest.'

Mike threw his leg over the jetski, fired up the engine and cast off the thin line that secured it to a metal mooring ring. As soon as Rafael was seated behind him, Mike twisted the throttle and felt the small craft pull away sharply against the gentle current. The deafening high pitched whine of the petrol engine reverberated around the walls of the narrow cave as they advanced, echoing into its furthest reaches.

After half a kilometre, the tunnel-like passageway suddenly began to open up and then terminated abruptly in a huge bowl shaped cavern with a large circular pool lying at its centre. There were two more jetskis tied up alongside a wooden jetty at the edge of the pool and beyond them a flight of wooden steps which spiralled up towards the roof of the cave. Mike crabbed his way towards the jetty against the eddying upwelling that was gushing from an unseen subterranean source. While he was making fast, Rafael stepped onto the bare rock platform beside the jetty and scanned the chamber in all directions. He quickly spotted a fixed surveillance camera mounted high on a metal bracket and his jaw tightened when he saw the red light flashing. Without waiting for Mike, he ran up the spiralling flight of steps and found himself staring up a vertical access shaft. He climbed the steel ladder that was fixed to one side of it and reached a closed hatch at the top. Within seconds he'd released the catches and pushed it open, emerging into the bright light of the forest. Conscious that time was against him, he quickly scanned the area, noted the presence of a rough vehicle track leading away and then consulted a device that was strapped to his forearm. By the time that Mike had stuck his head out of the hatch, Rafael had finished what he set out to do.

'Get back down Mike. It's time to retrace our steps.'

'What? But I only just_'

'Don't argue with me Mike. Just trust me on this one. It's time to leave.'

'OK,' said Mike, exasperated.

Rafael waited for Mike to descend and then lowered himself down into the shaft. Just as he was about to close the hatch, he heard the roar of a powerful engine and the rumbling scream of car tyres sliding to a halt.

* * * *

They'd been working tirelessly since their arrival in Cancun, making enquiries in all the bars and restaurants along the east coast of the peninsula, from Chetumal in the south as far as the busy resort of Playa del Carmen in the north. Given the scant information at his disposal, Julio had been prepared for a protracted and laborious campaign. Even his middle-man in Belize, who'd introduced him to Pacal in the first place, had no real idea of his whereabouts, but then Julio would have been suspicious if he did. Most of the big players liked to operate discreetly, and if they didn't then that was a good reason to keep them at arms length.

As it happened, Pacal proved far easier to track down than he could ever have imagined. Barely 50 kilometres from the point where Ángel's organisation had been instructed to make their drops, the grainy photographs of their illusive client, taken from the security cameras at the José María Córdova International Airport, brought a string of positive identifications. As Ángel had suspected, Pacal - or Luis Meléndez as Julio now knew him to be called, was a man of influence. And people who coveted power rarely remained inconspicuous.

Of course, locating him was only half the problem. The point of the exercise was to find out if he was in any way involved in the contaminated cocaine that was threatening to destroy their international markets. And that would take a little more time and thought.

He began by researching the companies and organisations to which Meléndez's name was associated. After eliminating the likelihood that any of his interests in the tourism industry were being used as a front for trafficking, he investigated a joint directorship of a company called Solaco, based in the elegant town of San Cristóbal de las Casas, close to the border with Guatemala. Solaco was a well established refrigerator manufacturer with export links to several European countries and when Julio discovered that it had its own freight service, which travelled the length of Central America, he knew that he was on the right track.

After making a quick call to Colombia to seek Ángel's approval, he and his small team took an overnight bus to San Cristóbal. They arrived in the early hours of the morning, continuing by taxi to a large industrial estate on the outskirts of town. Following the address which Julio had given him, the driver stopped outside a large, modern looking factory with *Solaco* written in large white letters above the main entrance. Since Julio's face was known to Pacal, he sent the youngest member of his team to make enquiries posing as a salesman, but the slick haired man returned shortly afterwards with a shrug of defeat.

'*¿Qué ha pasado?* - What happened?'

'I couldn't get past the gate,' the man replied dourly, studying the dirt on his patent leather ankle boots with annoyance. 'No entrance without an appointment and they're very particular about which companies they deal with.'

'Now why would that be?' said Julio, narrowing his eyes. 'Do you think there's a possibility that we could break in?'

'It would be a suicide mission,' the young man replied shaking his head. 'They have security cameras, double razor fencing, dog patrols and heavily armed guards. I doubt if they'd worry too much about shooting anyone either, so if you're thinking of trying your luck, count me out.'

Julio scowled and kicked a stone along the ground in frustration. He was just considering what to do next when he glanced up and saw a couple of workers exiting through the main gate.

'Maybe we won't have to break in after all,' he said, watching the men sling their bags over their shoulders and head towards a bus stop on the main road. 'Get in the car.'

* * * *

'Start up the engine,' Rafael shouted, while bounding down the wooden steps three at a time. From the urgency in his voice Mike knew that they were in trouble. He ran towards the jetski, untied it and was starting the engine as Rafael leapt onto the seat behind him. Within seconds they were accelerating away, churning the dark water beneath them to an oily froth and sending waves shooting up the walls of the passageway in their wake. The noise was deafening as Mike cranked up the speed, tearing down the tunnel as fast as he dared, just feet away from solid rock walls. Suddenly they were plunged into total darkness and Mike's heart leapt as they careered blindly into the void, anticipating the sickening impact that threatened to come at any moment. It seemed to take an eternity for the jetski to stop and when it did the chasing waves overtook them and toppled them into the water. Disoriented and fighting for the surface, Mike reached for the back-up flashlight that was still strapped to his wrist. He flicked it on and found himself in a blurred tumult of swirling bubbles. The white hull of the jetski loomed to his left, the engine still idling and he reached out to it, using it to pull himself clear of the water.

'Rod, where are you?' he shouted, as he remounted.

'Over here,' came the answer, from somewhere in the darkness to his left. Mike heard the distant whine of an approaching craft as he picked out

Rafael's ashen face in the darkness. Even in the poor light, he could see that there was a stream of blood pouring from his brow.

'Hang on, I'm coming!' Mike yelled, twisting the jetski's throttle and bringing the nose sharply around. As he drew near, he reached out an arm and Rafael grasped it, using it to pull himself smartly up onto the rail.

'Go Mike, go!' Rafael shouted, falling heavily onto the seat. Mike needed no encouragement. A powerful light was now piercing the darkness behind them. He gunned the jetski into the middle of the passageway and opened up the throttle, his flashlight beam jarring as it picked out the carved rock walls that were hurtling by on either side. The darkness began to recede as their pursuers closed in, but the end of the tunnel was now in sight and Mike kept the power on until they reached the quay. At the last second Mike released the throttle and he and Rafael leapt from the jetski while it was still in motion.

'Take my cylinder Rod,' shouted Mike. 'I'll take the twins.'

Rafael knew better than to argue. He put on his mask and fins, quickly strapped on the harness and rammed the regulator of the sling tank into his mouth.

'Just go!' said Mike, heaving the twin cylinders towards the edge of the quay. A burst of gunfire sent a spray of water arcing into the air right in front of them and it spurred Rafael to jump over the side and disappear into the swirling darkness. The next burst of fire was closer, sending rock splinters and water spray flying through the air. There was a loud clang as a bullet ricocheted off one of the aluminium cylinders and Mike quickly pushed the regulator into his mouth, heaved the twin set over the edge of the quay and held onto it as it fell through the water.

He was dragged down beneath the surface just seconds before a jetski burst from the tunnel and swerved to a halt above him. There were flashes and dull percussive sounds as bullets drilled down after him, forming searing diagonal lines in the water. Counting on the semi-darkness and the refraction of the water to confuse his pursuers, he finned as hard as he could, the current helping to push him away from danger. The cylinders crashed into the sand at the base of the tunnel and Mike pumped air into the buoyancy wings to lift them free again. Now kicking with all his might, he began to advance swiftly, but the submerged gate suddenly began to descend in front of him like a port cullis. He pushed harder, aiming for the rapidly receding gap, but he was not fast enough. It dropped down into the sand, separating him from Rafael, who was waiting helplessly at the other side. For a moment they came face to face and Mike saw the mounting anxiety in Rafael's eyes. He tried to reassure him with an OK signal then quickly set to work, purging the air from the buoyancy wings so that the twin cylinders would lie flat on the sand. Keeping the regulator in his mouth, he inverted his body and slipped into the trench which he'd dug earlier. Rafael was ready to share air with him as he wriggled free and it was fortunate that he was close by because as Mike's head cleared the gap, a diver appeared behind him and a knife was thrust through the bars of the gate. Rafael reacted swiftly, sweeping his arm across in time to push the blade away and prevent it from being planted into his friend's neck. A slight jarring was all that Mike felt as the point of the knife tore through his wetsuit and nicked his shoulder. He turned to see Rafael snap the forearm of the diver between the bars, pull the knife from his limp hand and let if fall to the ground out of reach. Mike squeezed Rafael's arm in thanks and then reminded him that he was still in need of air. Rafael nodded and pulled the regulator from his mouth. As he was handing it over, Mike checked the needle of Raphael's pressure gauge and saw that it was hovering dangerously close to the zero mark. He took a half breath and then handed it straight back, drawing Rafael's attention to the danger and urging him to leave the cave immediately. As soon as he'd begun to move away, Mike stole a quick breath from his abandoned regulator under the nose of the wounded diver and then swam the last few metres which separated him from the cave exit while holding his breath. He reached the surface to find Rafael white faced from sucking on an empty tank.

'Christ, you must have been born with gills,' gasped Rafael.

'No time for chatting,' replied Mike. 'There are more people back there and if they suit up and launch the sled we'll be sitting ducks.'

'Good point, let's high tail it back to the boat.'

Mike swam swiftly across the surface, reaching the Whaler a few seconds in advance of Rafael. He leapt aboard, started the outboard engine and was busily hauling in the anchor when a distant whine reached his ears.

'I think we've got company,' he shouted, seeing a powerful RIB crashing through the surf towards them.

'Yeah I see it,' said Rafael, rushing towards the helm. 'Hold on tight!'

Mike grabbed the rail to steady himself as Rafael rammed the throttle forward, the engine screaming as the bow lifted into the air. He dived for cover as a burst of automatic machine gun fire suddenly rained down on them from the cliff tops above, but the Whaler soon picked up speed, taking them out of range. When the boat levelled out, Mike got a chance to see what they were up against. The sleek RIB in their wake had three armed men on board and its powerful twin outboards were gradually eating away at the couple of hundred meters advance which they had over them.

'They're gaining on us Rod!' he shouted over the drone of the engines.

Rafael cursed and reached inside a locker, pulling out a handgun.

'OK Mike, you'd better take the helm and keep a steady course. And for Christ's sake keep your head down when the slugs start flying!'

Mike checked his rising anxiety and did as Rafael asked. This was no time for weak hearts. He braced his legs against the slamming of the waves and winced as a bullet went searing through the air to his right. When Rafael returned an immediate volley of fire, the surprise caused Mike to temporarily lose control of the helm.

'Keep a straight course damnit!'

'Sorry!'

Two more shots rang out and there was a loud cracking thud as a bullet struck the hull.

Mike ducked again, but this time he kept his hands firmly gripped on the helm. Rafael took aim and fired off a single shot.

'Got you, you little fucker!' he said in triumph, as the helmsman recoiled, clutching his shoulder. 'That'll slow them down a bit. OK Mike, when I say go I want you to turn hard to starboard and then head out to sea; understand?'

'Yeah!' shouted Mike, recoiling as a burst of automatic fire peppered the sea around them.

'OK. Ready.....Go!'

Mike turned sharply and heard Rafael fire off three steady shots in succession as he cut across the bow of the pursuing RIB. From the corner of his eye he saw one of the gunmen fall backwards and stumble overboard clutching his chest. One of the bullets had pierced the air filled sponson surrounding the base of the RIB and it was now flapping about limply in the waves.

'That should evens things up a bit,' said Rafael with a nod of satisfaction.

'Do I keep heading out to sea?'

'No, you can return to your original course. I'm low on ammo now so just do whatever you can to stay ahead and keep them from taking aim.'

Mike grit his teeth, wondering just how long they could keep going before the fuel ran dry. There was still a third of a tank left, but at the speed they were doing it was draining fast.

More shots rang out and a quick glance over his shoulder told Mike that they were still not pulling away. He cast his eye along the coastline, trying to think of a place where they might be able to ditch the boat and make a run for it. A familiar dive spot came into view at the next headland and as Mike was considering his options, he had a sudden idea. He veered away and headed for its most distinctive feature; a gap between the headland and a leaning sea stack. As he neared it, he eased off the throttle so that the pursuing RIB would close in on him.

'What are you doing? They're gaining on us!' shouted Rafael in alarm.

'Don't worry, I've got a plan,' said Mike.

'Well it'd better be a damn good one, otherwise were gonna be fish food.'

Undeterred Mike eased the throttle forwards again and began to slalom towards the gap. The two men in the RIB gave chase and encouraged by their sudden advantage, began to spray the sea with automatic fire. Mike held his nerve and began to run a straight course allowing the RIB to draw closer still, then just as they were about to pass through the gap, he suddenly turned hard to starboard and pressed the switch which raised the outboard engine. There was a sharp bump as the hull grazed something beneath the water and then a rumbling vibration as it slid briefly over a hard surface before finally drifting free again. Rafael whipped around in time to see the chasing RIB come to a sudden crunching halt as the outboard engines were ripped from their mountings, sending the two occupants cart-wheeling through the air and crashing helplessly into the sea ahead. Mike pulled back the throttle of the Whaler, lowered the outboard and came to join Rafael at the stern.

'How the hell did you do that?'

'It's a popular dive site,' said Mike with a shrug. 'I know the underwater formations there like the back of my hand.'

'No shit!' said Rafael shaking his head. 'I knew there was a good reason why I brought you along.'

'Yeah? Well I'd have kept well clear if I'd known what I was getting myself into.'

'Can't say I would have blamed you,' said Rafael with a grin.

'So what now? You wanna to pick these guys up?' said Mike, motioning towards the two men, who were now standing in waist high water.

'There's not much point. Neither of them will talk...and besides I don't want to get blood all over the boat.'

Mike stared at Rafael aghast until he saw a wry smile appear at the corner of his mouth.

'Shouldn't we turn them in though?'

'It would be more trouble than its worth…and besides I don't want to scare them into hiding.'

'So what do you plan to do?'

'Follow them,' said Rafael taking out his phone.

'Follow them?' asked Mike, bemused.

'That's right.'

Rafael winked, pulled out a satellite phone and keyed in the number of the Photographic Interpretation Center. After a short delay a gruff voice answered.

'Is that you Kruger?'

'Ah, Rodriguez. Nice to hear from you again. You whored away your budget yet?'

'No, I've still got a couple of pesos left…and it should last me a while yet because unlike you, I don't have to pay to get laid.'

Kruger's face went puce, and darkened further when he caught his colleague sniggering.

'Always the wise guy Rodriguez. What do you want now?'

'Did you pick up my beacon?'

Rafael heard a sigh, followed by the sound of fingers tapping on a computer keyboard.

'Yeah, we got it. What is it? Some transvestite bar where you like to hang out?'

'Just put the numbers in and take a look.'

Kruger resentfully tapped in the coordinates. The powerful telescope built into the geostationary surveillance satellite that was orbiting the equator responded to the command and centred in on its assigned target.

'OK Rodriguez, this looks to me like the place where you were a few days ago and all I see is trees.'

'Beneath them is the entrance to an underground passageway that leads all the way to the coast. You can't see it because it's camouflaged.'

'Now that's one I aint heard before. What you been smoking in those cigars of yours?'

'Just trust me on this one. Now pan out a fraction and see if you can see a four wheel drive vehicle nearby.'

More keyboard tapping.

'I see something down there. It's obscured by the tree canopy, but yeah, it's definitely a vehicle of some sort.'

'Good. Now I want you to track its movements for the next 24 hours.'

'Any particular reason for doing that?'

'I'm hoping it'll lead us to the viper's den.'

SAN CRISTÓBAL DE LAS CASAS, CHIAPAS, MEXICO

Julio thanked the two workers for their assistance and slipped them a hundred pesos each for their trouble.

Illiterate peasants, he thought to himself as they returned toothless grins. The poor were always easy to intimidate and exploit, which is probably why Solaco had hired them in the first place. If there *was* a cocaine smuggling operation taking place within Solaco's walls, then those two were definitely unaware of it, and that was fortunate because they had been fooled into divulging sensitive information. To them a shipment of products was just the end result of a week's hard labour; an event which had no significance other than that it served as a regular marker in the tedious cycle of drudgery which ruled their lives. But to an entrepreneur, the shipment was the culmination of a complex organisational process that would ultimately lead to reward. Even more so if that person was a criminal, using his business as a cover for a lucrative drug smuggling operation. The downside for a middleman like Meléndez was that it was also the weakest link in the chain, the point at which all control was at some point relinquished to fate, and Julio intended to take full advantage of that weakness.

He stepped out of the taxi and walked over to a piece of waste ground with a phone pressed to his ear, pacing up and down until his call was connected.

'Ángel? It's me, Julio.'

'Julio! So...what news do you have for me?'

'We found Meléndez's company. It's a refrigeration factory on the outskirts of San Cristóbal, built like a fortress.'

'Did you get a look inside?'

'Not a chance. I sent Diego, but they turned him away at the gate. Security is tight and its 24 hours.'

'So what you gonna do? Just sit around and wait for someone to come out and tell you what's going on in there?'

'No, I've got a better idea. There's a regular shipment which goes out by truck twice a week...and the next one leaves this evening. I'm pretty sure that's how they're moving the coke.'

'Where does it go?'

'Panama, straight down the Pan-American Highway.'

'You sure of that?'

'There's no doubt. I spoke to people who know the truck drivers. The company exports to Europe by container ship from Panama. It's a classic run.'

Julio heard Ángel drumming his fingers on his desk.

'So what's your plan?'

'We use our connections to intercept it.'

There was a pause.

'OK...but you'd better be right about this Julio, cause it's gonna cost me big bucks to set up.'

* * * *

It took several hundred dollar bills to persuade the hotel manager to overlook the fact that there were now three bullet holes driven into the otherwise pristine hull of his boat. Once he'd agreed not to report the incident to the authorities, Rafael handed him a conciliatory cigar, shook his hand and climbed behind the wheel of the Chevrolet.

'I trust you'll appreciate that I have to ask you to keep quiet about what you saw today,' he said to Mike, as they drove back to the dive shop.

'That goes without saying Rod, but what do I tell Ken?'

'Just tell him we went for a dive along the coast somewhere.'

'I was thinking more along the lines of what happened to his kit.'

'Oh yeah. Er...tell him I lost it over the side.'

'He's not going to be happy about that Rod. You can be sure he'll charge you for it.'

'It's no big deal Mike; just stick it on the bill.'

'He'll probably make you pay over the odds.'

'That's fine.'

'You sure?'

'Absolutely. I have a generous expense allowance for this assignment. I might have some problems explaining all the huge bar bills that I've built up, but for the other stuff, they won't blink an eye.'

'Really? That must be nice.'

'One of the perks of the job Mike,' said Rafael with a wink.

'So I guess you won't be needing my help anymore then?' said Mike, watching a young boy riding a rickety cart that was being pulled along by an equally dishevelled looking donkey.

'Probably not,' replied Rafael with a shrug. 'I really appreciate all that you've done, but at this point I need to call in a team of professionals. We're obviously dealing with some very dangerous people here and I can't risk you getting involved any further.'

'I wasn't necessarily offering my services Rod. Sure it was exciting and everything, but when people start trying to kill me, I tend to draw the line.'

'That's perhaps just as well.'

Rafael pulled up outside the dive centre and helped Mike to unload the gear. Once he'd settled his bill, refunded the cost of the missing equipment and calmed Ken with a generous tip, he took Mike aside.

'Listen, thanks for everything,' he said, slipping two hundred dollar bills into Mike's hand. 'I'll be away for a few days now, but once the assignment has concluded, I'd be happy to do anything within my power to help you find out what happened to your friend.'

'Thanks Rod. I'd appreciate that, but this really isn't necessary you know,' he said, holding the bills uncertainly.

'Just think of it as a reward from the US Government,' Rafael said with a wink.

'Yeah? Well in that case, I'll make certain that it goes towards a worthy cause...like helping to support the Mexican economy.'

Rafael smiled.

'I've heard that the tequila industry is in dire need of investment.'

'Then I consider it my duty to help in any way that I can,' grinned Mike.

* * * *

Fabrizio Germini was a great adventurer and explorer, although he was mostly oblivious to the fact. He'd spent most of his life seeking out the more remote and desolate areas of the planet, not out of curiosity, egotism, or any particular desire to see what wonders the world had to offer. His life was dedicated to the discovery and study of new plant species, especially those which had the power to heal.

He was a botanist, and the multi-million dollar pharmaceutical company which employed him, understood the value of herbal medicines. The industry as a whole owed its existence to them and even now was dependant on the natural or synthesized plant compounds from which ninety percent of its modern products were derived.

Among the industry's greatest triumphs were treatments for cancer, malaria, leukaemia and multiple sclerosis; miraculous plant derived compounds which routinely saved millions of lives. Their complex organic chemicals gave hope to millions of sufferers of illness and disease while injecting massive profits into the coffers of those pharmaceutical companies which produced and marketed them. In the quest to unearth the next revolutionary drug and guarantee lasting notoriety and profitability for many years to come, researchers like Fabrizio were worth their weight in gold. And Farmáciazona Industries considered themselves fortunate to have him on their payroll.

When he was not scrambling through the damp undergrowth on his hands and knees, searching for shoots, leaves and roots to send back to Genova for analysis in the laboratories of Farmáciazona, Fabrizio could generally be found indulging in his other passion; the gastronomy of his homeland. The jungle satisfied most of his basic needs, and if necessary he could easily survive on its natural resources for many months at a time, but eating roots and bitter fruits was certainly no substitute for a delicious *Pollo Pastorella* or a bottle of finest Barolo.

And so it was that after a hard day spent gathering samples from the mangrove swamps and dry forests of lowland Yucatan, Fabrizio was seated at his preferred table in Akumal's finest Italian restaurant, the *Dolce Vita*. As he was happily twisting his fork into a delicious mound of *Linguine ai Frutti di Mare*, a young man entered the restaurant and approached the manager. Fabrizio took little notice of the intrusion until to his surprise he heard his name being called.

'Hey, Fabrizio! *Hai visite!* – you have a visitor!'

'*Un ospite?* – a visitor?' replied Fabrizio, a fork hovering between the plate and his mouth.

He watched in bewilderment as a young man approached his table and greeted him with a nod.

'I'm sorry, I didn't wish to disturb you while you were eating. Could I maybe arrange to come back and speak to you later?'

Fabrizio picked up a serviette and wiped the corners of his mouth. His blue-green eyes squinted from behind his silver, wire-rimmed spectacles, forming crow's feet at the sides of his freckled face.

'What ees it exactly you wish to speak to me about? I'm sorry, I've no idea who you are.'

'My name's Mike Summers,' said Mike, extending his hand. 'I'm a friend of...or rather *was* a friend of Frank Pearce. I believe you met him.'

Fabrizio shook Mike's hand, frowned and then pressed the serviette to his lips once more.

'Yes I knew Frank,' he nodded. 'A good man.'

He took a thoughtful sip of crisp Vermentino wine and gestured to the seat opposite him.

'Why don't you join me... did you eat yet?'

'No, but I'd be honoured...if you're sure that you don't mind.'

'Of course not; I would be pleased to have your company. You like pasta?'

'Sure.'

'Then I recommend the *spaghetti alla vongole*. Clams, garlic, white wine...ees the house speciality.'

'Sounds perfect.'

'Excellent. *Claudio! Una Vongola e un'altra bottiglia di Vermentino per favore.*'

'*Con piacere* – my pleasure,' came the reply.

Mike watched Fabrizio toy with his food, his thinning sandy coloured hair sticking to the beads of perspiration that were forming at his temples.

'So, you were a close friend of Frank?'

'We worked together. I only knew him for a relatively short time, but we became friends almost from our first meeting. He was just one of those truly selfless people who you're instantly drawn to.'

'Yes, I ad that impression too,' said Fabrizio, dabbing the perspiration from his brow. 'He was a kind man, and did not deserve...what happened. The sad thing ees that in some way I feel responsible for it.'

'Responsible for Frank's death? Why?'

'Because I showed him the caves where he was killed.'

'Well maybe you did, but there's no way that you could have foreseen what would happen.'

'Of course; but it still plays on the mind. What if this happened? What if that happened?' he said, shaking his head.

Mike nodded his understanding.

'How did you first meet Frank Fabrizio?'

'With Claudio,' he said pointing his chin towards the tall, red cheeked manager, who was just bringing a steaming plate of pasta to their table. Mike paused to watch Claudio place the *spaghetti alla vongole* before him with reverence.

'*Buon appetito!*'

'*Grazie,*' replied Mike, uncertain of his pronunciation.

'*Prego* – You're welcome,' came the reply.

'Claudio, this ees Mike, he was a friend of Frank,' explained Fabrizio.

A pained expression flickered across Claudio's face.

'A friend of Frank? Then you are also a friend of mine,' he said with great solemnity, 'and please...your meal is offered on the house.'

Mike attempted to protest, but Claudio held up his hand.

'It is the least I can do,' he said firmly before excusing himself and taking his leave.

'Frank was Claudio's diving instructor,' explained Fabrizio when Claudio had returned to the kitchen, 'and Frank sometimes came here to eat. That's how we met in fact.'

'Oh I see. And do you dive yourself Fabrizio?'

'Me? *Mamma mia*...no! I'm not comfortable in water,' he said with a look of horror. 'Taking a shower is about as far under the water as I will go.'

Mike laughed.

'So what is it that you do Fabrizio?'

'For work you mean?'

'Yes.'

'I'm a botanist. I travel round the world looking for plants...medicinal plants...and when I find something interesting, I send it to my company...for research.'

'That sounds like a very interesting job.'

'Finding the plants...yes, but spending hours in the jungle with spiders, snakes, leeches, flies and ticks...ees not for everyone.'

'I see what you mean,' said Mike, pulling a face. 'And this cave system you found. Did you come across it while you were working?'

Fabrizio nodded.

'I told Claudio, Claudio told Frank and then Frank...he ask me to take him there,' he said with a shrug.

'So where exactly are these caves?'

'West of here,' he said waving his hand, 'near a place called Yalché.'

Mike's eyes flicked open.

'The newspapers said that the cave where Frank went missing was in Chalchén.'

'Yes...strange, but I think maybe they make a mistake. Or Frank found another place to dive.'

'Could be I suppose,' said Mike nodding. 'There's only one person who really knows for sure and unfortunately *he* hasn't been seen since.'

'You have some suspicion about what happened?'

'I didn't until I found some notes belonging to Frank. There was a sketch he made of a large cave system about two kilometres from Yalché and a drawing of some kind of figure.'

'That sounds like the cave I showed to him,' said Fabrizio, 'but I don't

103

know anything about the drawing.'

'Is there just the one cave?'

'No, there are others and there is a sink hole....a cenoté.'

'A cenoté? Do you know whether Frank explored it?'

'I have no idea. I just showed him what he ask,' said Fabrizio with a shrug. 'He said he would need a lot of equipment to explore it, but I don't know if he tried anything.'

'I see,' said Mike, nodding. 'So how long was it after you showed Frank the caves that he went missing?'

Fabrizio exhaled and rocked his head from side to side.

'A week...maybe two.'

'Two weeks? It could take months to explore a cave system like that,' said Mike, shaking his head. 'The organisation itself would be a major undertaking. So why would he just suddenly abandon the project and go and take a look at a minor cave system somewhere else?'

'I'm afraid I can't help you there.'

'Maybe you can.'

'How?'

'Would you be prepared to show *me* the caves?'

'Ees possible,' he said with a shrug.

'Good. When can we go?' asked Mike, keen to push things forward.

'Well...any time...tomorrow if you like.'

'I'll have to rearrange a few things, but sure, tomorrow it is.'

'*D'accordo* - OK,' said Fabrizio, nodding.

After washing down his *spaghetti alla vongole* with a half glass of Vermentino, Mike exchanged phone numbers with Fabrizio and arranged to meet him at 8am the following morning. He left the *Dolce Vita* with his throat still burning from the tumbler of grappa which Claudio had insisted he drink and made his way over to the beach. He went straight to the *Buena Onda* bar and approached the oval serving counter, hoping to find Gabriela. She was nowhere to be seen and fearing the worst, he called over the flat-nosed barman.'

'Excuse me. Do you happen to know where Gabriela is?' he asked.

'Gabriela?' enquired the barman, a blank look in his eyes.

'The girl who was working behind the bar yesterday,' he prompted.

'She no longer works here,' said the barman flatly. 'She handed in her notice this morning.'

GRAN BAHIA, AKUMAL

Rafael awoke at 2am and checked out of his hotel. He threw a soft leather suitcase into the back of the black Chevrolet, drove to the main entrance and joined the highway going south. Two hours later he reached the small town of Muyil and headed north along an unmarked road. After a mile or so he reached a partially cleared section of forest and when his GPS confirmed that he was in the correct position, he came to a stop, leaned back in his seat and lit a cigar. Fifteen minutes later he heard the low fluttering beat of rotor blades, phasing in and out as the sound carried over the damp night air.

He jumped out of the car clutching four red hand flares and set one off while striding across the clearing. The sound of the rotors grew louder. He dropped the lit flare, ignited another and walked away, counting thirty paces. After dropping the second flare he turned ninety degrees and walked another thirty paces, repeating the process until he'd marked out a square on the flat terrain. A UH-60 Black Hawk helicopter appeared in the night sky, circling noisily above. Rafael returned to the Chevrolet, flashed the hazard lights twice in succession and then extinguished them altogether.

The Black Hawk hovered over the marks and began to descend, sending streaks of red smoke whipping outwards in all directions. Rafael remained shielded behind the wheel of the Chevrolet as flying dust and dry grass filled the air. The chopper had barely touched down, when a side door flew open, and three soldiers in combat gear leapt out and came running hunched over towards him. Rafael flashed the hazard lights once more and the soldiers converged on the Chevrolet, using it to protect themselves from the downdraught as the power to the Black Hawk's rotors was increased.

Once the night bird had lifted clear of the surrounding trees to make its return journey, Rafael opened the door of the Chevrolet and the interior light illuminated the faces of the three crouching soldiers.

'Welcome to Mexico boys,' he said, handing them an open bottle of tequila.

'Hey Rodriguez, looks like you put on some weight,' said a rugged-faced man with a blonde crew-cut.

'I could still kick your ass any day of the week Spicer,' replied Rafael.

'Yeah, that's if you can still run fast enough to catch him,' said a young African-American, grinning.

'Try not to choke on my tequila Zach.'

'Still as cheerful as ever,' said Zach, taking another swig from the bottle. 'You already met Shy Wolf huh?'

'Look, can we just drop the Shy Wolf shit?' said the third man, an American-Indian with greying temples. 'My name's Dan OK?'

'Whatever you say *Chief*,' said Zach, before bursting into fits of laughter.

'It's good to see you again Dan,' said Rafael. 'I hope these two kids didn't annoy you too much on the way over.'

'I can handle myself,' said Dan coolly. He stared at Zach and casually pulled a gold necklace from beneath his shirt.

'How d' ya like my new chain?'

Zach immediately put his hand to his throat.

'Jesus, how'd you get that?' he demanded.

Rafael began to laugh.

'I've been wearing it ever since we took off,' said Dan, lifting it over his head and returning it to its rightful owner.

'You should be careful who you mess with Zach,' said Rafael, grinning. 'Dan could creep into your tent at night and cut you out of your sleeping sack without you knowing.'

'Holy shit dude!' said Spicer. 'The man's a genuine Witch Doctor. You'd better watch your ass Zach.'

'Yeah, I'm gonna watch my black ass real close if Indian Joe's gonna start prowling around creeping into tents at night.'

'Don't worry I'll be real gentle,' said Dan, touching Zach's arm and winking suggestively.

Rafael, Spicer and Dan burst into laughter as Zach pulled his arm away cursing.

'OK boys, time to make a move,' said Rafael. 'Who's got my kit?'

'It's all here,' said Spicer, tapping a canvas sack, 'and Dan brought along your weapon of choice, an M16A4 with close combat optic.

'Good work guys. Now throw your gear in the trunk and sit your ugly asses down in the snug leather seats of my Chevrolet. It's going to be the last bit of comfort you'll see for a while.'

*　*　*　*

Mike awoke early. He pulled on a pair of jeans, walking boots and a long sleeved sweatshirt, slung a bag over his shoulder and stepped outside. A brief overnight shower had given rise to a damp earthy smell and pockets of cool air were being buffeted around by the breeze. As he was heading towards town, Mike saw a car pull over by the kerb just ahead and when he drew level with it, the driver's window opened with a barely audible hum.

'Excuse me sir.'

Mike stopped and stared at the driver; a well dressed local with a dark angular face and lank black hair, cut in a straight fringe. There was an ugly scar that looked like chewing gum just beneath his jaw, which vied for attention with the gold cross he wore around his neck.

'Can I help you?' said Mike.

'I'm here to give you some advice...Mr. Summers,' came the reply.

'Advice? Who are you...and how do you know my name?' Mike asked, trying to make out the eyes that were concealed behind a pair of dark wraparound shades.

'Who I am is of no interest to you,' said the man, 'but for your own good it's important that you listen. Now do I have your full attention?'

'I guess so,' said Mike with a shrug.

'Good. I'm afraid that you have upset some important people Mr. Summers; people who do not take kindly to being inconvenienced...and if you continue to make a nuisance of yourself and put your nose into places where it is not wanted, you will not have a pleasant stay in Mexico. Am I making myself clear?'

'I don't know what you're talking about.'

'Please don't waste my time Mr. Summers,' said the man, fixing him with an icy glare. 'You know perfectly well what I'm talking about. We know everything about you and we see everything that you do, so don't try to play games with us. You are just a visitor in this country and we can easily arrange for your work permit to be rescinded and your stay to be cut short. And if that doesn't persuade you, then think about this. A lot of accidents happen in Mexico; on the road, in the home, sometimes just walking down the street. I'd hate for you to become another statistic, but these things do happen. Now have a nice day Mr. Summers and think very carefully about what you want from life...while you still can.'

Mike could only stand and stare in bewilderment as the car pulled away and drove off into the distance. For a moment he was unsure what to make of the encounter. If this was something to do with Rafael's investigation, he could count himself lucky to still be alive and fortunate that he would have no further involvement. But if it was a consequence of his enquiries into Frank's death then he would have to carefully reconsider his methods.

Deep in thought, he walked on towards the town centre and by the time that he reached the Dolce Vita, he'd made a decision.

'*Buongiorno* Mike, so good to see you again,' trilled Claudio, busily serving one of his clients on the small outside terrace.

'Morning Claudio. *Tutto va bene?*'

'*Va bene* Mike. *Va bene, grazie,*' Claudio replied with a smile. 'Fabrizio hasn't arrived yet, but I'm sure he won't be long, can I get you a coffee or something?'

'No thank you Claudio, I need to go and pick up something from the dive centre. When Fabrizio gets here, could you ask him to wait five minutes and then meet me outside the general store?'

'You mean Raoul's shop?'

'Yeah, that's the one.'

'Sure, whatever you want,' said Claudio with a shrug.

'Thanks Claudio. Have a good day.'

'You too.'

Mike walked the short distance to CavePro, entered and nodded to Ken as he passed.

'Hey Mike, I thought you weren't coming in today,' Ken said, tetchily.

'I'm not; I've just come to fetch something,' Mike replied, continuing straight into the compressor room. Ken shook his head and returned his attention to his computer screen.

'Hey Chicho, do you mind if I take these two slings?' asked Mike, eyeing a pair of slim diving cylinders standing in a rack.

'Help yourself,' replied Chicho. 'For you only five dollars.'

Mike grinned.

'You'll make a great businessman one day,' he said. 'I'll get you a *quesadilla* next time OK?'

'And a Coke too?'

'It's a deal.'

Mike slipped the two slings into a mesh equipment sack along with a short wetsuit, a buoyancy jacket, two small underwater lights, an emergency breathing canister and his mask and fins.

'Right Chico, you didn't see what happens next, OK?' said Mike as he put his arms into the straps of the equipment sack.

'Whatever you say Mike,' said Chicho with a shrug.

'Thanks bud.'

Mike strode out into the back yard, upturned a plastic water barrel and used it to climb onto the surrounding wall. Within seconds, he'd lowered his equipment bag over the side and jumped down next to it, landing in a patch of wasteland which afforded access to the road beyond. The general store was directly opposite and Mike remained out of sight, waiting for Fabrizio to make an appearance. Soon a Toyota Landcruiser pulled up outside and Mike spotted Fabrizio's unmistakable strawberry-blonde hair through the open window. He checked both sides of the road and then bolted towards the waiting car.

'Hi Fabrizio,' he said in passing, as he wrenched open the passenger door and leapt into the back seat. Fabrizio turned in bemusement to see him placing his equipment in the trunk.

'Are you in a hurry?' he asked, unimpressed.

'Sorry Fabrizio, didn't mean to be rude. I just saw someone I'm trying to avoid.'

'Oh, I see. A girl perhaps?' said Fabrizio, his frown now transforming into a smile.

'Yes that's it. You know what it's like. Is it OK if I stay back here until we're out of town?'

'As you want. S'no problem for me,' replied Fabrizio. 'Did you bring water?'

'A little.'

'You should take plenty. There's more in the back if you need.'

Mike turned to see six large bottles of water surrounded by a collection of cutting, digging and measuring tools, bottles of yellow liquid, an ice box, camping stove, sleeping bag and a box of files.

'Looks like you're prepared for a full scale expedition here.'

'Sometimes I stay out for a few days,' said Fabrizio, pulling away from the kerb, 'especially if I am going to a remote place. Ees better than a lot of travelling back and forward.'

'I suppose it is,' said Mike, peering through the rear window to make sure that they weren't being followed. 'How long will it take us to get to the caves?'

'About an hour.'

'That's what I figured.'

Mike sat back and watched the town gradually give way to open fields. After a quick glance at the road behind, he climbed over to join Fabrizio in the front.

'I think I should be safe now.'

'Oh, you're never safe from women,' said Fabrizio. 'Even the good ones will make you run in the end.'

'Yeah, you're probably right,' said Mike, feeling a little guilty at his deception. 'Are you married Fabrizio?'

'I was married a couple of times, but with a job like thees...,' he said with a shrug. 'Now I work only for six months of the year. The rest I spend in Salerno, on the west coast of Italy. You know it?'

'I'm afraid I don't.'

'A beautiful place. I have a house there overlooking the sea, with a large garden and two nurseries where I cultivate rare plants. I send many of them to collectors; to places all over the world.'

'Sounds like a nice little set up.'

'I'm happy with things.'

'Good for you,' said Mike nodding. 'So tell me Fabrizio, about these caves you found. Did you speak to anyone else other than Frank and Claudio about them?'

'I don't think so. No.'

'What about the police? Did you tell them anything?'

'The police? They never spoke to me and I never spoke to them. I don't think they knew anything about me.'

'I see. So the chances are that no one apart from me and Claudio know that it was *you* who found the caves and not Frank.'

'That can be I suppose, yes. Why?'

'I think it may have saved you a lot of...inconvenience shall we say? So have you been back to the area since?'

'No, I finished working there at the time I met Frank. I'm working further to the north now.'

'That might be just as well.'

Fabrizio shot Mike an inquisitive glance. It went ignored.

They travelled south down highway 307 and after a while turned north-west, heading towards the ancient town of Coba. The narrow, dusty road took them past small villages bordered by fields of maize, avocados, beans and pineapple, their vibrant fertility in sharp contrast to the long stretches of drab, low lying forest which lay between.

After a good forty minute drive Fabrizio pulled off onto a dirt track that plunged deep into the heart of the forest and a world which had remained unchanged for millions of years. Their progress was slow and laboured over the rough terrain, but after twenty minutes of jostling and bouncing, they finally caught glimpses of a fractured escarpment dissected by a series of narrow gorges. Soon the trees which surrounded them were no longer greyish, gnarled and dull. They grew taller, with fleshy leaves, creating a pleasantly cool and humid space beneath their thriving emerald canopy.

'Thees is about as far as we can go by car,' said Fabrizio, drawing to a halt as the track petered out.

'Yeah, I can see that,' said Mike, staring into the densely packed undergrowth which surrounded them. 'It's more like jungle here.'

'Yes,' agreed Fabrizio, nodding. 'Ees an unusually fertile area, fed by springs from the escarpment. That's also where the caves are. There's a path here in front of us which will take us to them. You must take care though, there are thorns and leaves which irritate the skin, and there may be tarantulas and snakes on the ground.'

'And there's me thinking we were going for a pleasant hike. I'll let you go first if that's OK?'

'S'no problem.'

They jumped out of the Landcruiser and collected their bags from the trunk. Fabrizio tucked the legs of his khaki safari suit into calf length boots and then sprayed insect repellent on his cheek, neck and forearms.

'You'll need this,' he said, passing the bottle to Mike.

'Hmm, I'm beginning to understand why people rarely come this way,' said Mike, eying the bottle warily.

'It's quite an isolated place,' agreed Fabrizio. 'Even the indigenous people don't come here often. Maybe it has something to do with the cenoté. In Mayan mythology they are believed to be gateways to the underworld.'

'I can understand why they'd think that,' said Mike as he sprayed his skin with insect repellent. 'After all, the cenotés were always closely associated with death.'

'That's true,' agreed Fabrizio, his eyes drifting towards the mesh equipment bag that was lying at Mike's feet. 'Are you going to take all this stuff with you?'

'I'd like to if possible.'

'S'up to you,' said Fabrizio, shrugging, 'but we need to walk for about half a kilometre, and it will not always be flat.'

'I'll live with it. We're not in a rush are we?'

'I suppose not.'

Fabrizio threw a water canister over his shoulder, picked up a large machete and slipped it into a leather holder on his belt.

'Ready?'

Mike pulled on a small backpack and threw the mesh equipment bag over his shoulder.

'I'm good. Let's go.'

They set off walking along a small footpath, a barely recognisable trail along the forest floor that was traversed here and there by black lines of marching ants. Fabrizio used the machete to clear leafy shoots while keeping a running commentary on the trees and plants which they passed.

'That's a Ceiba, good for healing wounds...thees one is spurge, can be used to cure eye disease...thees is horsetail, used in the treatment of dysentery and some venereal disease...ah look, that is golden aster, which you perhaps know as arnica, good for bruising and swelling...and there beside it is wild yam. An amazing plant. Did you know that it was responsible for the sexual revolution of the 1960's?'

'Why? Is it an aphrodisiac?'

'No,' said Fabrizio, laughing. 'It was used to synthesize the female birth control pill.'

'What? You mean a vegetable was responsible for the swinging sixties? For Woodstock?'

'In many ways yes,' said Fabrizio, with a shrug. 'Almost everything you see growing here has uses which extend far beyond the forest.'

'Well if you see anything that's good for fatigue, let me know' said Mike, struggling with the weight of his equipment. 'I'm bushed.'

'No problem. If I find some *talauma mexicana* we can make tea from the bark.'

'Hmm, on second thoughts, maybe I'll just wait till we stumble across a Starbucks.'

A little further along the trail, Fabrizio paused to examine a small clump of vegetation. While he waited, Mike dropped his equipment bag onto the ground and sat down heavily on a fallen log.

'*Molto interessante,*' Fabrizio was mumbling to himself as he pulled a leather bound notebook from his breast pocket and began to take notes. While Mike was watching him take a clipping with the blade of his machete, he heard a sudden rustling movement beside the log and leapt to his feet when he saw a long, black and green striped tail disappearing into the undergrowth.

'Jesus, what was that?' he cried in alarm

Fabrizio glanced around, his face impassive.

'It was probably just an iguana, resting inside that log you're sitting on.'

'Holy crap, I thought it was a coral snake,' said Mike... 'and shit, I'm covered in giant ants,' he said, dancing around and slapping his legs. 'Can't even sit down for two minutes without being attacked,' he grumbled. 'Are you going to be much longer?'

'I've nearly finished,' said Fabrizio, a glimmer of amusement on his face.

'Good, let's keep moving.'

They continued along the path until they reached a neat green patch of cultivated land, its regularity at striking odds with the sprawling vegetation surrounding it. Fabrizio wore a puzzled expression as he examined it.

'What's this?' Mike asked.

'Ees *manihot esculenta*....cassava, or at least a variation of it. Ees a very unusual breed; in fact I sent a sample back to my company for analysis quite recently. The strange thing is that they called me later to ask me where exactly I find it. For some reason they think it could be important in solving a crime.'

'What sort of crime?'

'I have no idea. They didn't give me details. All I can tell you is that cassava is a common source of food here, but when incorrectly prepared it is highly toxic.'

'Interesting. Are there other plots like this?'

'Yes. I've seen one or two_.'

Fabrizio was interrupted by a sudden commotion. Piercing squeals cut through the relative quiet of the forest and Mike glanced up in alarm to see dark shapes moving swiftly through the tree canopy. Beside him Fabrizio tightened his grip on the handle of the machete only to release it again when the hooting and crashing sounds receded into the distance.

'*Cazzo*, what a fright,' he said, shaking his head. 'Spider monkeys!'

Mike stared at him blankly for a second and then burst into nervous laughter. Fabrizio followed suit.

They pressed on shortly afterwards, continuing along the trail until they reached a fork at the base of a steeply rising limestone escarpment. Fabrizio slowed to a halt and took a long slug of water from his canteen.

'Thees ees where the caves start,' he said, wiping his mouth with the back of his hand. 'There's a small one along here to the right which Frank thought would be good for diving and a second one higher up the ridge which is a leetle more challenging. The path which leads to the second cave also leads up to the plateau where you can find the cenoté. Which you want to see first?'

'Let's go take a look at the second cave and the cenoté. I'll leave my equipment down here for now.'

'Yes, I theenk that would be better,' agreed Fabrizio.

'Good, let's crack on then.'

Mike pulled a flashlight and a reel from his equipment bag and then stashed it behind a prominent patch of scarlet-bush. Once he'd transferred the items to his backpack, Fabrizio led him along the base of the ridge and up a narrow walking track.

The incessant buzz of jungle cicadas and the screech of lored parrots gradually began to recede as they emerged above the dense canopy and soon the only sound to be heard was the deafening hiss of cascading water. Midway up the limestone ridge, they encountered the source of the noise; a huge cave which spewed water out over a rocky ledge and down into the lush, green jungle below. Fabrizio led Mike into the cave's cathedral-like entrance, scrambling over the huge fallen boulders which littered its floor.

When the natural light began to fall away, Mike pulled the flashlight from his backpack and under its pale yellow beam they picked their way along the fractured cave floor until they reached a rising vertical wall of rock, worn smooth by the surging curtain of water which cascaded over it into a dark plunge pool.

'Thees is about as far as we can go without a ladder and ropes.'

'It certainly looks that way,' agreed Mike as he played his flashlight over the gently undulating surface of the ochre limestone face. 'Nice formations though.'

'Yes, and there are probably more. The cave goes much deeper,' said Fabrizio cupping a hand to his ear. 'Can you hear?'

Mike listened intently, and through the reverberating hiss and rumble of cascading water, he could just make out the echoing high pitched squeaks of the cave's secretive residents. Bats.

'It would be interesting to come back here with the right equipment and explore this system properly,' said Mike.

'Yes, I'm sure it would be worth it,' agreed Fabrizio.

'Not much we can do now though.'

'No, unfortunately,' agreed Fabrizio with a shrug.

'Better move on then.'

They backtracked towards the cave entrance, carefully clambering over the huge wet boulders that choked the river bed, conscious that an awkward fall could have serious consequences in such a remote and inhospitable location.

Soon the cool humidity of the cave was left behind and they emerged into the glowing warmth of the morning sun. Fabrizio led them further up the narrow trail, the drop to the jungle below growing more vertiginous with each step. After negotiating the roots of gnarled trees, shimmying along narrow ledges and carefully picking their way around precarious rock falls, they finally arrived unscathed at the top of the escarpment. A short walk through the dryer forest which covered the high plateau brought them in sight of an ancient stone flagged route, overgrown in places, but still recognisable as one of the original communication routes of the Maya Indians. Fabrizio stepped up onto it and with Mike following close behind, he headed south, slashing at the thin vines which reached down like tentacles from the higher branches of the overhanging trees. After a short hike through dense foliage, they reached a sudden break in the canopy, the sky opened up and to his astonishment Mike found himself standing at the edge of a precipice. His heart quickened as he edged his way to the very end of the causeway and leaned over to peer down an enormous vertical shaft, almost perfectly cylindrical, that disappeared into darkness over fifty feet below.

'Wow, that's incredible,' he said, shaking his head. 'I've never seen anything like that before. It looks almost as if the jungle has been sucked down a huge drain.'

'Ees amazing isn't it?' agreed Fabrizio. 'You can understand why these places were so special for the Maya. The cenoté are an important source of fresh water in such a dry area, but surprisingly some of them were reserved exclusively for sacred rituals and never used for drinking water.'

'I read that the Maya threw people down them as offerings to the gods in times of drought,' said Mike. 'I guess that might put you off drinking the water down there.'

'That's true, but the bodies were not the reason. They believed that the water at the bottom of the cenoté was special because it was the home of the rain god Chaac. The sacrifices were made so that he would bring relief from the drought.'

'I guess that would explain why objects of value have been found at the bottom of many of them.'

'Yes, certainly,' agreed Fabrizio, nodding.

'Frank must have been tempted to explore the pool, knowing that there might be priceless artefacts down there.'

'But it would be a difficult operation. No?'

'Oh yeah! It would be a major undertaking. You'd need to set up a gantry with a wire and cradle that was strong enough to support a diver with full cave equipment and of course you'd have to get it all here through the jungle in the first place. It could be done though, and there's certainly plenty of incentive. The thing is that if Frank was serious about doing it, he would have had to recruit a team of people he could trust. And if word got out about the find, there would have been plenty of people wanting to muscle in on a piece of the action.'

'So you think this could have been the reason for his murder?'

'Maybe. It's as good a reason as any.'

Mike was still staring pensively into the depths of the cenoté when he suddenly heard the sound of running feet behind him. Before he had time to realise what was happening, he felt two hands strike him in the small of the back and send him tumbling helplessly into the gaping chasm.

* * * *

Dan tapped Spicer on the shoulder and gave an urgent signal to take cover. Following Dan's lead, Spicer plunged into the bordering foliage and joined him behind a thicket of thorn scrub, their arrival startling a pair of macaws which took off, cackling noisily into the air. Dan winced and pulled Spicer down low, calling for silence by pressing a finger firmly to his lips. They listened to the distant sound of drumming feet, soft and irregular, but growing steadily in intensity.

Dan peered through a gap in the bushes as a group of men flashed past, some carrying old carbines and others with simple wooden bows and quivers of arrows slung over their shoulders. A man at the rear of the group slowed to a halt and brushed aside a leafy branch, sniffing the air as his eyes probed the undergrowth close to where they were hiding. Dan grabbed Spicer's collar to caution against making any kind of movement while carefully unsheathing his Bowie knife. He pulled it free and held the blade firmly between thumb and forefinger when the man reached back and plucked an arrow from his quiver. There was a flicker of movement nearby and from the corner of his eye Dan saw a whitetail deer emerge into a clearing to his left. The animal froze when it caught sight of the man raising his bow and Dan tightened his grip on Spicer's collar a fraction of a second before it bolted, leaping high into the air and bounding away noisily into the undergrowth. Still holding the blade of the knife firmly between his fingers, Dan watched the man lower his bow, take a last piercing look into the shadows and then leap back onto the stone flagged route to hurry after his companions. Spicer was keen to follow, but Dan held him back, having seen enough to convince him that they were in danger of exposing their presence.

When he gave the signal to move on, they followed a course which ran close to the route which the men had taken, using the cover of jungle to screen them from view. After a few minutes they pulled up short at the perimeter of a vast sinkhole. While they were discussing their options, they heard sudden shouts of anguish echoing eerily around the vast chamber followed by a double splashing impact. They exchanged concerned glances, unsure what to make of it. Dan moved closer to the edge of the sinkhole, trying to peer in, but he was forced to pull back when he heard approaching voices. Reluctantly he gave Spicer the order to retreat and they melted into the jungle, returning to the refuge of their temporary hideout shortly afterwards. Behind a screen of leafy branches, Spicer chewed reflectively on a sliver of beef jerky.

'Do all the people out here run around carrying bows and arrows?'

'I don't know,' replied Dan. 'It's not exactly the deep Amazon here, but then ammunition is expensive and arrows are free. Maybe they're like my people and they just prefer to live simply.'

'I guess,' conceded Spicer, 'but the guy who stopped; that was kinda weird. D'ya think he'd seen the deer?'

'No, at least not at first. He stopped because he sensed that *we* were there, or at least that something unusual was there.'

'What, you mean like telepathy?'

Dan smiled.

'No, not like telepathy. More like an intimate bond with nature. It's like tuning all your senses into your surroundings so that you can piece together the information and use it to create an impression. I learned similar techniques from my Grandfather when I was a boy.'

'No shit? So what d'ya think he picked up on?'

'It could be many things. The macaws flying off probably didn't help, but there must have been something in particular which alerted his senses. You're wearing aftershave right?'

'No way. Not when I'm on operations.'

'Hair gel then?'

'I use a little bit, yeah,' admitted Spicer bashfully.

'I thought so. It's perfumed; I can smell it from here. That guy was much further away of course, but then he can probably pick out the scent of a flowering fruit tree from a couple of hundred yards away.'

'That far?'

'Sure. It could have been something else of course, some disturbed vegetation or our boot prints for instance. Either way, I'm certain that if we hadn't stayed absolutely still when that deer bolted, he'd have spotted us. And that's the last thing I wanted to happen, because I'd have been forced to take him out.'

'With the knife?'

'Was there a better option?'

'No...I guess not,' replied Spicer, staring at the ground pensively. 'I'm not sure it's something I could do. I mean I've never killed anybody in a close combat situation before.'

'Well, you're a soldier and one day you may have to, so you'd better get used to the idea,' said Dan. 'Now before we go putting ourselves into any more situations like that, I think we'd better speak to the boss.'

YALCHÉ, YUCATAN INTERIOR

The rush of air was sickening as Mike hurtled downwards, fighting to right himself before the surface of the water dashed him like a swatted fly. His reactions were rapid and instinctive, fuelled by cold terror as a dark green carpet came rushing unstoppably towards him. He had only a fraction of a second to stiffen his body, lift his arms above his head and take a last breath before the inevitable stinging impact. The rapid deceleration caused his knees to buckle beneath him and there was a dull roar in his ears as he was plunged into the churning turmoil of an enormous washing machine. For a moment he felt dizzy, unsure which way was up or down and when the rollercoaster ride finally came to an end, he knew only that he was alive. He opened his eyes and saw a sombre green sheet above him, towards which small flakes of vegetation and streams of fine bubbles were slowly rising. His skin felt like it had been shredded from his body, but a gentle flexing of his arms and legs was enough to reassure him that he'd suffered no serious harm. He kicked out and rose swiftly through the three metres which separated him from the surface, emerging into a dark tunnel, the sound of dripping water and an agonised groan.

'Fabrizio! Is that you?'

The sound of his voice reverberated shrilly around the walls of the huge chamber.

'Over here,' came a pained reply.

Mike peered into the gloom and saw Fabrizio's pale face lit up eerily by the weak light which filtered down from the world above.

'Are you hurt?'

'I theenk I dislocated my shoulder. *Cazzo!*' he swore. 'Not that it makes any difference now. We're going to die down here anyway.'

'We're not dead yet,' said Mike, trying to convince himself as much as Fabrizio, 'but we *do* need to get out of this water as soon as possible.'

'And just how do you plan to do that?' demanded Fabrizio, raising his voice in frustration.

'I don't know,' admitted Mike, but it's no good treading water here until we die of hyperthermia. Can you wait here for a moment?'

'Is there anywhere else to go?' replied Fabrizio dourly.

Mike ignored his comment and began to swim around the perimeter of the pool, past huge stalagmites and stalactites, some forming rows of slender columns whose opposing tips had joined and fused countless years before.

He reached the opposite side of the pool and spied a fissure that rose from the surface of the water continuing high up the side of the cavern wall until it was obscured by the roots of a stunted tree. A few metres from the base of the fissure was a group of stalagmites which had formed across the entrance of a shallow cave, their counterpart stalactites hanging above them like the jaws of some giant predator. Mike used one of the stalagmites to lift himself clear of the water and saw, as he had hoped, that there was a dry ledge behind. He returned to share the news with Fabrizio and found him lying motionless on his back in the water.

'Hey Fabrizio! Are you OK?'

'No I'm not OK,' came the curt reply. 'My arm is dislocated, I'm trapped at the bottom of a dark cavern and I will be dead before anyone knows I'm missing.'

'Don't talk like that Fabrizio,' said Mike sternly. 'Admittedly our chances don't look good right now, but we're alive, we have plenty of water and even a little food. There's every reason to believe that we have a fighting chance.'

'Yes, there's plenty of water...plenty of facking water...*stronzo!*' said Fabrizio, cackling darkly before clasping his left shoulder and grimacing with pain.

'I'm going to get out of here,' said Mike with calm conviction, 'and if you're willing to give it a try, I'll get you out too. All I need from you is a bit of positivity and cooperation. But if you'd prefer to stay down here full of reproach and self pity, waiting to die all alone in the dark, then that's entirely up to you. I can't help you if you're not prepared to help yourself.'

The harsh reality of Mike's words had a calming effect on Fabrizio.

'I can't keep treading water for much longer,' he said weakly.

'I've found a dry ledge on the other side of the pool. If you just lie back in the water I'll tow you towards it.'

Fabrizio nodded and did as he was asked. Mike reached down to grip the collar of his bush jacket and began to swim backwards, careful to avoid any contact with his wounded shoulder. Once they'd arrived below the mouth of the cave, Mike left Fabrizio clutching a stalagmite while he pulled himself clear of the water onto the ledge. He turned and sat down, straddling a pair of stalagmites that were close to the water's edge before extending an arm between them.

'OK Fabrizio, I want you to grab my hand with your good arm, use it to steady yourself and then start walking up the rock face.'

Fabrizio was not convinced, but left with little choice he reached up and grabbed Mike's wrist. Mike doubled the hold.

'Right I've got you. Now start walking.'

Fabrizio tentatively lifted his right foot onto the rock face until he found purchase on the uneven surface. Using Mike's support, he now lifted his left foot out of the water and placed it above his right. Mike began to pull with all his strength, and like a human fulcrum Fabrizio was lifted up out of the water until he was standing upright and able to step safely between the two stalagmites.

'Well that went better than expected,' said Mike as Fabrizio joined him on the sheltered ledge.

Fabrizio merely groaned and clutched his shoulder.

'We need to try and fix that. Have you dislocated that same shoulder before?'

'Yes...twice,' said Fabrizio through clenched teeth. 'You know what to do?'

'I've a good idea, and since you already have a weakness in that shoulder, there's every chance that it will be easy to fix. You'd better sit down.'

Fabrizio used the cavern wall to ease himself to a sitting position.

'OK, now I want you to straighten your back and try to relax. Think about...I don't know...a field of miraculous medicinal plants or something. Whatever does it for you.'

'I'd prefer to think of the beautiful girls from Salerno who lie on the beach in summer.'

'So you do have some red blood in there,' said Mike as he carefully placed Fabrizio's upper arm in line with his body and bent the elbow at a ninety degree angle.

'What you think? I'm a scientist, yes, but I'm also a man.'

'I don't doubt it for a second,' said Mike, pushing his forearm towards his stomach. 'And are the girls from Salerno pretty?' he asked, now easing it back in the opposite direction.

'They are the most beautiful girls in the whole of Italy,' replied Fabrizio, trying to mask the pain and if you ever…aaah….aaaarrrggh!' The cavern was filled with cries of agony as Fabrizio's joint was suddenly drawn back into the socket.

'*Cazzo!* Thank God that's over.'

'Well done Fabrizio,' said Mike, letting go of his wrist. 'If you don't feel any adverse affects, rotate your arm a few times to loosen the tendons and then just relax for a moment.'

'Thank you, it feels one hundred times better,' he said, bending his arm and slowly describing a circle with his elbow, 'but as for relaxing; it's not so easy when you're sitting on hard rock in cold, wet clothes.'

'You're right. We should get you stripped and dried off.'

Fabrizio nodded.

'You theenk they know we're alive down here?' he asked as he began to peel off his jacket.

'The guys who pushed us?' replied Mike, reflecting over what had just happened. 'If they didn't, they probably do now.'

'Did you see who they were?'

'No. It all happened too quickly.'

'Me neither,' said Fabrizio, shaking his head and pushing a strand of wet hair from his face.

'You think this could be what happened to Frank?'

'Who knows?' shrugged Mike. 'There's so much about all this that doesn't make sense.'

'Well it looks like somebody really wants to protect these caves,' said Fabrizio. 'And they must live close by because I'm sure nobody follow us here.'

Mike silently questioned whether that was true. Someone had been taking a close interest in his affairs ever since he'd met Rafael, and the cenoté might just have been a convenient place for them to put him out of the picture for good.

'That may be, but right now I'm more concerned about getting us out of here.'

He leaned out from the overhang and saw sunlight slowly creeping down one side of the cenoté.

'In a short while the sun is going to be almost directly above us and there'll be some light down here. You might have a brief opportunity to get warm. I'd make the most of it if I were you.'

'I will,' said Fabrizio, loosening his belt and letting his machete fall to the floor.

'I'm gonna need that,' said Mike, picking it up and pulling it from its sheath.

'What for?'

Mike pushed the blade of the machete into a narrow crack and bent it until it snapped in half.

'Are you crazy? We may need that!' protested Fabrizio.

'It's not going to be much use to us down here...and if we manage to get out then survival will be the least of our worries,' reasoned Mike. 'Now listen carefully. See that long crack in the cavern wall over there?'

'I see it,' said Fabrizio.

'I'm going to attempt to climb it. It peters out about half way up the cavern wall, but from what I can see there are long roots reaching down to it from the trees surrounding the rim of the crater.'

Fabrizio nodded.

'The trees in karst areas have extremely long root systems that help them to tap into the aquifer.'

'Do you think they would be strong enough to take my weight?'

'They're tough,' said Fabrizio with a shrug, 'but it's better not to put all your trust in a single filament.'

'I'll bear that in mind,' said Mike, easing the other half of the broken blade from the crack. 'Listen Fabrizio, I'd prefer not to leave you alone down here, but with your arm the way it is, I may not have much choice.'

Fabrizio frowned, nodding.

'I understand. I would only slow you down.'

'I shouldn't be gone for long anyway. If all goes to plan, I'll have a rescue team here by tomorrow morning.'

'I hope you're right,' said Fabrizio, retrieving his car keys from his jacket pocket. 'Here, I theenk you might need these.'

'Of course. Thanks Fabrizio.'

Mike slipped the keys into a zip sealed pocket and then pulled a plastic container from his backpack.

'Here, take my lunch. It'll be a bit soggy, but better than nothing when you're hungry.'

'You don't have a bottle of wine in there as well do you?' asked Fabrizio, his lips curling into a thin smile.

'I'll make sure I have a bottle of the best when I come back for you.'

'That would be nice. Thanks Mike and good luck,' said Fabrizio, clasping his hand firmly.

Mike winked, put on his backpack and with the handle of the broken machete gripped firmly in his hand, slipped back into the water.

A few strokes took him to the point where the fissure in the cavern wall emerged from the water. His eyes followed it as far as the stunted tree that was protruding from the rock face a good thirty feet above him. He reached up, slipped the broken blade of the machete into the crack and twisted it. When it was firmly lodged, he wedged a boot into a gap just below the waterline and used it to climb clear of the water. With his left hand he now reached higher into the fissure and balled a fist to hold himself steady. Another carefully placed boot supported him while he repositioned the machete higher up the rock face. By repeating the technique he was able to inch his way up the cavern wall, safe in the knowledge that the worse that could happen was that he would fall, take another dip and have to start all over again.

Within ten minutes he was within reach of the gnarled tree. The fissure was becoming too narrow to provide good holds, but by grasping the thick cord-like root filaments which dangled from the tree, he was able to haul himself up the last few feet and climb onto a ledge behind it. The sun was now almost directly above the opening of the cenoté and as Mike looked down he could see gaps in the carpet of lime green algae that floated on the surface of the pool. The water was crystal clear beneath it and he could see flashes of turquoise where the sun was reflected from pale limestone boulders several meters below the surface. Mike knew that there was a possibility that the network of submerged channels which fed the pool could offer an escape route, but without diving equipment, they might just as well have been sealed. He resignedly pulled his eyes away and lifted his head towards the crater, where the forest seemed to be falling in and slowly dripping down the cavern walls like candle wax.

The lip of the crater appeared much closer now and the challenge of reaching it, less daunting. While he was planning the next stage of his route, Mike noticed that the fissure continued for a short distance past the ledge and terminated a little higher, where it opened into a cave that was obscured by a curtain of long sinewy tree roots. He traced a clump of the fibrous filaments from their parent tree at the edge of the crater, down the side of the cavern wall to the pool of water over fifty feet below and as he was marvelling at their amazing adaptation to the testing environment, the seed of an idea began to grow in his mind. He reached out, cut six strands with the blade of the broken machete and then drew them up onto the ledge. Pairing them up so that he had three strands in all, he began to plait them, continuing until he had made up a short length of rope. To test the strength of it, he took a few turns on the trunk of the gnarled tree and pulled with all his might. The fibres squeaked as they worked against each other, but the makeshift rope performed admirably. Encouraged, he now set about in earnest, plaiting the remaining strands and winding in new ones until he had a coil of rope which could reach down to the pool some thirty feet below. To create a smooth surface for the rope to ride over, he used the machete to strip the bark from a drooping section of the gnarled tree. Next, he emptied his backpack, filled it with some boulders that he found on the ledge and then spliced it into one end of the rope. That finished, he tied a double loop at the other end and lowered it down to the surface of the water.

'Fabrizio! Can you hear me?' he shouted through cupped hands. The noise reverberated around the cavern for several seconds before he heard a reply.

'Yes! I could probably have heard you from Akumal!'

Mike grinned, pleased that Fabrizio hadn't lost his sense of humour.

'Can you see the rope that I just lowered down?'

There was a pause

'Yes, I see it! But....?'

'Good. Put everything in your backpack, swim over to it and attach it to one of the loops. I'm going to get you out of here.'

'There's no way I can climb with my shoulder like this!' replied Fabrizio in frustration.

'I'm not asking you to climb. I'm going to lift you up.'

Mike heard a distant outpouring of what he guessed to be Latin profanities. After they'd died down, he heard a splash and saw Fabrizio fully clothed and swimming as best he could towards the rope. Once his pack had been attached to the rope, Mike hauled it up, untied it and then lowered the looped end back down again.

'OK Fabrizio, now put one leg into each of the harness loops and hold the main line with your right hand.'

Mike held the rope steady while Fabrizio struggled into position, then pulled it up tight.

'Are you ready?'

'Yes. Ready to meet God!' came Fabrizio's caustic reply.

Mike carefully lowered the weighted backpack over the opposite side of the tree to create a counter-balance and then let go. The rope came under tension and Fabrizio was hoisted out of the water as far as his knees, but no further. Mike cursed, realising that he would need to add more weight.

'Just give me a minute,' he shouted down to Fabrizio.

A stream of mumbled obscenities came from below as Mike tried pulling on the rope. When he met with no success, he threw caution to the wind and climbed down onto the counterbalance. As soon as his weight was transferred, the rope began to slip and Mike found himself dropping back down towards the water. He tried to climb back to the ledge which he'd just abandoned, but the rope was moving faster than he was and he soon passed within inches of a surprised Fabrizio, going in the opposite direction. When the backpack finally plunged into the water, Mike's descent came to an abrupt halt and he looked up to see Fabrizio pinned against the gnarled tree above.

'Fabrizio, don't move!' he shouted. 'I need you to stay right where you are.'

'I can't move!' replied Fabrizio, anxiously. 'And this isn't comfortable.'

Mike quickly wrapped his legs around the rope and began to climb back towards the ledge. When he finally reached the tree, he realised that he had a problem.

'OK Fabrizio, you're going to have to hold the rope above my hands and take your own weight for a moment so that I can let go.'

Fabrizio shook his head, grit his teeth and did as he was asked. Mike quickly climbed up onto the ledge, grabbed the broken machete and cut both straps from Fabrizio's backpack. After knotting them together, he tied one end to the rope harness supporting Fabrizio's weight and the other to the trunk of the tree.

'OK, you can let go now.'

'Are you sure?'

'Ninety nine percent.'

Fabrizio slowly released his grasp and was relieved to find that he swung gently in towards the base of the tree. Mike immediately heaved up the counterbalance and when he had it safely on the ledge, he helped Fabrizio to climb up and join him. For a while, the only sound to be heard was laboured breathing as they lay exhausted on their backs, staring up at the newly appeared sun in a circular patch of sky.

'How's your shoulder?'

'It hurts like hell,' said Fabrizio, 'but I don't care if it falls off as long as we get out of this damned place.'

'The worst is over,' said Mike, propping himself up on an elbow. 'All I need to do now is climb to the rim, drop the rope down to you, lift up the boulders and set up another counterbalance. If all goes well, we'll be out of here in a couple of hours.'

'I hope you're right.'

'We'll be fine, don't you worry.'

Fabrizio stared up at the sun and saw that it was moving towards the opposite rim of the crater.

'You'd better not wait too long because we're going to lose the light again soon.'

'Yeah I see that,' said Mike, following his line of sight. Drawing a sharp breath, he stood up, untied the severed straps of the backpack and used them to fashion a rudimentary climbing harness.'

'Everything has more than one use huh?' remarked Fabrizio.

'It does when the chips are down,' said Mike, reaching for a canteen and taking a slug of water. He took a quick glance at the crater, stretched and shook the stiffness from his arms and legs.

'Right, I guess I'm ready to go again.'

'Mike, don't put yourself in danger for me,' said Fabrizio gravely. 'If ees better for you to leave to find help alone, I can stay here for the night. S'no problem.'

'I appreciate that Fabrizio, but don't worry, I'll get you out of here.'

'With some luck,' said Fabrizio, smiling.

Mike removed the heavy stones from his backpack, tied a coil of rope to it and then swung it onto his back. Turning towards the rock face, he raised his head, grasped a handful of root filaments and took a deep breath.

He began to climb, his arms pulling at the coarse, sinewy fibres and his feet searching for purchase on the uneven vertical walls. He rested briefly at the entrance to the cave and then pushed on, channelling his efforts into reaching the crater above.

As he neared the half way point his arms began to tire and he quickly tied the tail from his climbing harness around a bundle of root filaments, leaning back and breathing heavily with his feet planted firmly against the cavern wall. Once his strength had returned, he released the slip knot and continued climbing, never once looking down.

The sky was now opening up and the forest canopy was clearly visible above the rim of the crater. Encouraged, Mike began to climb harder, but just as it appeared that his ordeal might finally be over, there was a shout, a swooshing sound and a loud thwack as an arrow struck the rock face just inches from his head. Shaken, Mike watched the arrow fall away and go tumbling down into the depths of the cenoté below. He jerked his head towards the rim of the crater, now just a couple of body lengths away. He thought about making a dash for it, but when more arrows began to hammer into the rock around him and he heard voices approaching from above, he knew that his position was hopeless. For whatever reason, someone up there was determined to kill him and in the split second that it took him to make the decision to retreat into the safety of the cenoté, he was rocked by a sharp pain to his backside. Fearing for his life, he gritted his teeth and began to lower himself down the rock face as fast as he dared. He was surprised to feel the strength draining rapidly from his body and as his descent transformed into a controlled fall, he had to summon all his willpower to prevent himself from losing his grasp and falling to his death. He covered the last few feet to the ledge in a state of near collapse and fell into the waiting arms of Fabrizio who cushioned his fall as he stumbled to the ground.

'What happened?' asked Fabrizio, anxiously staring at the arrow that was embedded in Mike's flesh.

Mike tried to answer, but to his surprise, he was unable to move his lips. Despite his physical exhaustion, his breathing was getting shallower and he began to feel starved of air. He tried to will his lungs to relieve the growing agony in his chest, but to his horror he found that he no longer had any control over them. The suffering soon became unbearable and the concerned face of Fabrizio was the last thing that he saw before darkness clouded his vision and the cold hand of death closed its grip around his throat.

* * * *

From the lookout post which they'd set up in a ruined stable, Rafael and Zach watched the comings and goings of a small village, set deep in the forest. The dark blue Chrysler Aspen which the Photographic Interpretation Center had been monitoring on Rafael's behalf was parked just outside the village's sole attraction, a well-preserved colonial Catholic church.

'Any movement down there now Zach?'

'Nope. Since that hunting party went off into the forest it's been quiet. Just a couple of beat up dogs running around.

'Better keep your eyes peeled just the same.'

'Oh I will,' said Zach. 'And I'll be watching the ladies especially close, just in case any of them decide to go natural, like you see on the Discovery Channel.'

'I didn't see you as an anthropologist Zach, said Rafael smirking, 'but I reckon you'll be wasting your time. That's a Catholic church down there in case you hadn't noticed.'

'Damn those missionaries. Why'd they have to go around spoiling all the fun?'

Rafael was still chuckling to himself when he felt a vibration in the pocket of his flak jacket. He pulled out a satellite phone, glanced at the tiny screen and brought it swiftly to his ear.

'You found anything yet?'

'Affirmative,' said Dan, at the other end of the line. 'The coordinates on the satellite imagery were slightly out, but workable. We found two small plots with about a hundred to two hundred plants in each.'

'Do they match the photographs?'

'Oh yeah. There's no question. They have the same elongated leaves.'

'Good work Dan. You see anyone hanging around?'

'Yeah, strangely enough we did. Not sure if it's relevant to the investigation though.'

'Care to elaborate?'

'Well, this morning two white males turned up and stopped to study the plants. They were both non-Mexican and English speaking, although one of them had a marked accent. I'm not sure where they came from; they just seemed to walk right out of the jungle. We tracked them for a while, up a narrow path towards a high plateau and then everything went crazy. We had to hold back when a small group of native men appeared and ran past us, some with guns, some carrying bows and arrows. We nearly got eyeballed and had to backtrack deeper into the bush and then we just stumbled across this enormous hole in the middle of the forest, like a huge mining shaft.'

'That sounds like a cenoté,' said Rafael, 'a type of sinkhole. They're fairly common around here.'

'OK. Well we didn't see what happened next, but there must be water at the bottom cause we heard shouting and then a couple of splashes as if someone jumped or got pushed in. I can't say for sure, but I think it was the two white guys. The group of men who overtook us were closing in on them fast and from the looks on their faces I'd say they weren't planning a welcome party.'

'Did you check the cenoté afterwards?'

'Negative. I was about to climb an overhanging tree to get a look in, but then we heard people moving through the trees towards us and we had to pull out.'

'You did right,' said Rafael, deep in though. 'Tell me, this group of men you saw, were they by any chance wearing light coloured shirts, one in particular with a blue logo on the back?'

'Come to think of it, I'm pretty sure there was.'

Spicer nodded his confirmation.

'I thought so,' said Rafael. 'They came from the village. There was a bit of a commotion here about half an hour ago and a small party of men left shortly afterwards. It was as if someone raised an alarm.'

'You think the villagers are somehow involved in all of this?'

'At this moment in time I haven't a damned clue, but I'd certainly like to find out if they're in the habit of murdering people. Do you think there's any way you could get a look inside that sinkhole?'

'We could try later.'

'OK. Do it.'

*　*　*　*

Was it a heart attack? Fabrizio wondered as Mike's face began to turn blue, his life ebbing away by the second. Drawing on what he could remember from his survival training, he pressed two fingers against Mike's carotid artery. There was a pulse, but it was very weak. He stared at the arrow that was sticking into Mike's backside and with a sharp tug pulled it free. He examined the tip closely and then in sudden understanding, cursed and cast it aside. He quickly freed Mike from the burden of the backpack and began to give him the kiss of life. There was no immediate reaction, but Fabrizio persisted, checking regularly for signs of recovery. After almost ten minutes of ventilations he noticed that Mike's pulse was growing stronger and the colour gradually returning to his cheeks. Two more minutes passed and Fabrizio heard a gurgling sound as Mike's lungs struggled to work again. He sat back and let them regain their own rhythm, cradling Mike's head and watching the life gradually flow back into his inert body. A sudden intake of breath was the first sign that his senses were awakening and although Fabrizio had been expecting it, it still came as something of a surprise when Mike's eyes finally blinked open.

'Don't try to speak now. Just relax. You'll be OK,' he said reassuringly.

Under his knotted brow, Mike's eyes darted in all directions as if he'd awoken from a lucid dream.

'W-what happened?' he asked, his mouth struggling to form the words.

'I theenk that you were poisoned,' said Fabrizio, gently placing the backpack under his head.

'Poisoned?' said Mike, alarmed.

'Yes, but the effect is only temporary. You should feel well again soon.'

Mike frowned, his memory of the last few hours slowly returning.

'Was it the arrow?'

'Yes, I believe so. The point was coated in curare... an extract from the vine *Chondrodendron Tomentosum*. It has been used by the indigenous people of Central and South America to poison arrows for centuries.'

'So why am I still alive?'

There is an active chemical in curare which temporarily paralyses the muscles,' explained Fabrizio. 'In very small quantities ees an excellent remedy for complaints like epilepsy, muscular spasm and tetanus, but in strong doses it will stop all muscle activity, including those which control the lungs. Once curare has entered your blood you will die of suffocation, unless of course you have someone with you who can do the breathing for you.'

'So you saved my life?'

'I just helped you a leetle.'

'More than a little. I'd have been dead without you.'

Fabrizio shrugged.

'You should take a pee as soon as you can. It helps to get rid of the

138

poison.'

'I'll bear that in mind,' said Mike, slowly raising himself to a sitting position. 'That was by far the most terrifying thing that I've ever experienced in my life. I was fully conscious of everything that was happening to me, but there was just nothing that I could do about it. It was as if an enormous weight was pinning me to the ground.'

'It must have been orrible,' said Fabrizio, nodding, 'but ees finished now.'

'I'm afraid it's far from being over Fabrizio. For whatever reason, someone up there clearly doesn't want us to get out of here alive. With any luck they'll think that one of us is dead now, but I can't see them leaving the area until they're convinced they've killed us both.'

'Well maybe someone will realise we're missing and try to find us.'

'I'm afraid that no one knows where I am,' said Mike, 'and my phone died when I hit the water.'

'Then our only chance is Claudio...except he probably won't be surprised if I don't visit him for a few days.' Fabrizio thought for a second and then added solemnly, 'and unfortunately I never told him where to find the caves.'

Mike sighed and threw a stone off the ledge into the pool, watching the ripples expand into the green carpet of algae below. After a moment of reflection, he lifted his head and stared at the rim of the cenoté, wondering if he dared risk climbing at nightfall. As his eyes were retracing the route which he'd taken, they paused at the partially obscured cave a few feet above the ledge. He studied it in silence for a moment then stretched and carefully rose to his feet, flexing his muscles to see if they were free from the effects of the curare. When he felt no ill effects, he stepped away to empty his bladder and then reached up to wrap his hands around a bundle of tree roots. He lifted his weight from the ledge for a few seconds and then satisfied that his strength had fully returned, he tucked a flashlight into his back pocket.

'Wait here a moment, there's something I want to take a look at.'

'Don't tell me you're going to try to reach the top again?' asked Fabrizio alarmed.

'No, something a little closer.'

'Are you sure that you've recovered from the curare?'

'Let's hope so.'

Mike quickly scaled the steep incline which led to the mouth of the cave, pushed through the curtain of root filaments and stepped onto a solid rock floor. When he turned on his flashlight it revealed a narrow corridor that sloped gently downwards, disappearing far into the distance. He walked further into the cave, switched off the flashlight and paused to listen. There was the occasional ticking sound of water percolating down through the rock strata, the gentle hiss of a distant subterranean river and every now and then, echoing eerily around the dark passageways, the unmistakable high pitched shriek of bats. Deep in thought, he walked back towards the mouth of the cave and stared up at the circular rim of the cenoté, noting the place from which they'd been pushed in. From a glance at his watch and an observation of the angle of the retreating sun, he worked out the direction in which the cave system extended. It all seemed to tie in. Encouraged by what he'd found, he lowered himself back down to the ledge.

'Where did you disappear to?' asked Fabrizio.

'There's a cave up there, concealed behind those tree roots.'

'A cave?'

'Yep, and it seems to go back quite a distance. I was thinking that maybe we could explore it and see if it can offer us a way out of here.'

'I theenk I would prefer to die out here in the open rather than to get lost in the dark.'

'I'm fairly sure it runs back in the direction of the escarpment. And I heard bats in there too.'

'There are bats in most caves here,' said Fabrizio dismissively, 'and besides we only have one flashlight.'

'True, but it has fresh batteries in it. We can get two hours out of it at least and I've got a reel of line we could use for emergency back up. It's only got 50 metres on it admittedly, but we could extend that by tying some of these root filaments to it.'

'And how am I going to get up there in the first place?'

'I'll use the rope to support you as you climb. The rock face is not too steep here and there are plenty of good footholds.'

Fabrizio sighed.

'Well I suppose it's better than sitting on a rock ledge waiting for the vultures to find me.'

'Shall we give it a try then?'

'*Va bene* – OK.'

Mike discarded all but the most essential items to keep the weight in his backpack to a minimum. After helping Fabrizio into the harness he took the free end of the rope and climbed up to the cave. He walked backwards until he reached a huge flat slab of rock and then sat down at the opposite side with his feet prised against it. Once he'd pulled in the slack, he wrapped the rope around his waist and over his shoulder ready to take the strain. His whistle was the signal for Fabrizio to settle his weight onto the rope and begin to scramble up the incline. After much puffing and panting Mike finally saw Fabrizio's strawberry blonde mop rise above the cave entrance, like the morning sun climbing above a misty horizon.

'*Madonna!* If ever I get out of this place alive, I'm going to spend a whole month in a five star health spa,' vowed Fabrizio, clutching his injured shoulder.

'You and me both,' agreed Mike.

He rose to his feet, walked to the cave entrance and used the broken machete to cut a few fresh root filaments.

'This will be our only guide if the light fails,' said Mike as he knotted the roots together and wound them into a coil inside Fabrizio's strapless backpack. I would strongly suggest that you stay within an arms length of the lifeline at all times so that you'll be able to feel for it on the cave floor if we're suddenly plunged into darkness.'

Fabrizio nodded soberly.

Mike wound the last root filament into the backpack and then walked deeper into the cave. At the limit of the natural light, he tied one end to the base of a stalagmite.

'Well this is it Fabrizio. You can still back out if you want to.'

'No, I come with you,' he replied, struggling to keep the fear from his voice.

Mike gave him a reassuring clap on the shoulder, switched on the flashlight and began to walk deeper into the cave.

At first their progress was easy, but the roof of the passage soon began to descend and they were forced at times to crawl on their hands and knees. They traversed a series of larger chambers, each decorated with golden crystals and fine sugary needles, never before seen by human eyes. Thin lacelike columns lit up with a deep red glow when the flashlight played upon them and waves of ochre terraces glistened with a thin lacquer of moisture. The sound of rushing water grew steadily louder as they penetrated deeper into the system and helped to guide them through the labyrinth of interconnected chambers.

After a while they found themselves in an incredibly high and narrow passageway, so restricting that they were forced to walk sideways, squeezing their bodies through the narrowest of gaps. Fabrizio was struggling with the pain from his shoulder and Mike was beginning to wonder if it really would be possible to retrace their steps if the light failed. They'd been inside the cave for thirty minutes now and the last root filament had just come to an end. In the limited space Mike tied his reel line to the end of it, knowing that they could only advance for a further fifty metres before they would be forced to abandon and return the way they came. The sound of rushing water, now louder than ever, encouraged him to press on and after negotiating a tight bend he was rewarded when the passageway began to widen again. It fanned out much further than expected and he soon began to realise that they'd emerged into a massive underground cistern. Fabrizio joined him as he aimed his flashlight beam upwards picking out a swathe of writhing black bodies on the roof of the cavern, their twitching, rodent-like snouts emitting ear piercing shrieks. The stench of ammonia from the bat's guano reached his nostrils and the sharpness of the odour snapped his mind into focus. Conscious that the flashlight battery was draining by the second, he quickly played the beam across the cave floor and illuminated the channel of a swirling underground river which bubbled up from one side of the chamber and disappeared at the other, like a dark, glistening conveyor belt. Above it, at the far side of the cavern he noticed a faint glow and when he extinguished his flashlight he could see a dull greyish light illuminating the pitted surface of the rock where a high passageway connected it to the outside world. The natural opening clearly provided no challenge to the thousands of bats which used it to move in and out of their sanctuary each evening to forage, but to Mike and Fabrizio tired, injured and without even the most basic of climbing equipment, it represented a serious obstacle.

'There's no way I can climb up there,' said Fabrizio as Mike searched in vain for holds on the cavern walls.

'I doubt if either of us could get up there without a ladder,' said Mike resignedly. 'It's just not possible.'

'Should we try to make it back to the cenoté?'

Mike turned off the flashlight as he thought things through.

'Well, we could go back the way we came, but as things stand that probably wouldn't improve our chances of survival a great deal. From what I can see, there is one possible way out of here although something tells me you're not going to like it.'

'Why? What are you thinking about?'

'You're not too keen on water huh?

'No!' said Fabrizio. 'Especially after almost drowning in that *cazzo* cenoté.'

'Well I'm afraid that the only realistic way of getting out of here alive involves jumping into that river and hoping for the best.'

'*Madonna!* But how can you be sure it joins the outside?'

'Take a look.'

Fabrizio stared into the darkness and soon spotted a faint glow beneath the churning water.

'You see it? The river opens into daylight further down the tunnel. It's a sump.'

'If I go in there I will never come out alive,' said Fabrizio, sombrely.

'Nonsense, you just need a little guidance,' said Mike. 'The worst thing that could happen is that you panic, but with the force of the current you'll still come out the other end in one piece.'

'In one piece, but dead!'

'Even if you drown it's not necessarily the end. There's still a chance that I can bring you round. Return the favour if you like.'

'This is madness,' said Fabrizio, trembling in the darkness. 'I can't do it. Why in God's name didn't I just stay at home this morning?'

'You didn't, and you're here,' said Mike firmly. 'So now we have to stop feeling sorry for ourselves and concentrate on dealing with our present predicament. I'm going into that water because I think it's the best chance we've got. The idea of not making it scares me too, but I think there's a more than reasonable chance of getting through unscathed...and that's enough to convince me that it's worth taking the risk.'

'But, it's easier for you!'

'I guess that would be difficult to deny,' admitted Mike. 'Look, I can't force you to do something that you feel is beyond you, so if you're not coming with me, your only options are to wait it out here in the dark or try to make your way back to the cenoté alone.'

Fabrizio sighed and bowed his head.

'I don't think I could make it back there alone. And if I stay here I'll probably die of hypothermia. Explain to me what you plan to do.'

Mike sat him down in the darkness and went over his plan in detail. Once Fabrizio had started to come round to the idea, Mike taught him some basic relaxation, focus and breath holding techniques. After several exercises, a few dry runs and countless words of encouragement, Fabrizio finally declared himself ready to face his ordeal.

Keen to put his plan into action before Fabrizio changed his mind, Mike turned on the flashlight and went to lie down by the side of the river. He pulled on his dive mask, took a deep breath and plunged his head into the cool water. With the flashlight held at arm's length, he examined a previously unseen world.

The subterranean river was crystal clear, a good six feet deep and five wide. At the point where it met the wall of the chamber, Mike could see how the flowing water was diverted beneath the cavern wall, directly under the exit used by the bats. Deeper into the passageway, he saw faint traces of dappled light playing across the limestone rubble which was strewn along the river bed. Convinced that the sump offered a way out, he pulled his head from the water and stared at the half full reel of cave line.

'I'm going to have to cut this line further back. It'll partially sever our connection with the cenoté, but at this point I think we have to take the risk. I'll leave you the flashlight when I enter the water, so if you do change your mind about following me, you'll be able to find the guide line again.'

'I'm not going back,' said Fabrizio, determinedly.

'I'm glad to hear that. Here, you'd better hang onto this reel for a second.'

Fabrizio watched Mike's wavering flashlight beam retreat into the narrow corridor, illuminating the vertical slit like the eye of a cat. It transformed into a bobbing pinpoint of light as Mike turned around and retraced the line back towards him.

'Here, let's tie this loose end to your hand,' said Mike, holding the severed end of the cave line. Fabrizio held out his right wrist and allowed Mike to tie a loop around it. When he'd finished, they moved to the point where the river exited the chamber and Mike coiled the remainder of the loose line up on the ground.

'Well I guess this is it,' he said, shoving Fabrizio's backpack into his own and slipping it on. 'I think you might need these.'

Fabrizio took the mask and flashlight which Mike held out to him.

'Thank you, and Good luck,' said Fabrizio, gripping Mike's hand tightly.

'See you soon,' Mike replied, clutching the reel.

Fabrizio stood in silence watching Mike take a series of deep breaths before diving head first into the river and disappearing into its dark, gurgling embrace. The loose line uncoiled as it was pulled into the water, following Mike into a world which Fabrizio could barely contemplate. While waiting for his turn to come, he nervously pulled on the mask, weighing the horror of drowning in the bowels of some dark, watery hell against that of being abandoned in the cave system and trying to feel his way back to the cenoté alone.

He felt his heart beating in his chest as he watched the last loop of white, nylon line uncoil and disappear, like a strand of spaghetti being sucked from a bowl. The current pulled gently at the slack line tied to his wrist and for a moment he wondered whether Mike was still holding onto the reel at the other end. The answer came when he felt two distinct tugs on his wrist; Mike had made it and was waiting for him to follow.

Fighting to control his rising fear, Fabrizio closed his eyes, took in three stuttering breaths and crossed himself in preparation to face his demons. The shock of the cold water when he jumped was nearly enough to make him fall at the first hurdle. He forced himself to remain calm as the current took hold of him, sweeping him helplessly into the claustrophobic darkness of the submerged passageway.

Anxious and disoriented, his natural impulse would have been to claw at the water, but remembering Mike's instructions, he tried to will his body to go limp. The technique worked well until he felt a sudden sharp crack to the head and sucked in a mouthful of water, plunging him into a spiral of panic. The flashlight flew from his hand and water crept into his mask, cutting off his senses and fuelling his growing terror. The line was now pulling tighter and tighter on his wrist and in his confusion he became convinced that it was snagged somewhere, condemning him to certain death. Believing that he was beyond all hope, he kicked out wildly, trying to bite his way through the line. When the agony in his lungs became too much to bear, he breathed out and in again, expecting to choke and die. But to his surprise and confusion, he inhaled a lungful of fresh air, the line around his wrist slackened and he saw the dimly lit roof of a dry cave. A hand grabbed him firmly by the collar and he was unceremoniously hauled to his feet in time to prevent him from being swept towards the lip of a large pool and the precipitous drop which lay beyond.

'Are you alright?' Mike shouted over the sound of crashing water.

'Alright? I've never been so terrified in my life!'

'Well you're safe now,' said Mike, slipping off the mask and looping his arm through the strap.

The abandoned flashlight drifted past and Mike grabbed it before guiding Fabrizio away from the main current.

'Do you recognise this place?' he asked as they reached the calm water at the edge of the pool.

Fabrizio caught his breath and let his eyes drift around the spacious cavern. The surrounding features were strangely familiar to him and when he spied a distant exit that framed a patch of verdant jungle beyond, the realisation hit him like a thunderbolt.

'Oh thank God,' he stammered, the tension instantly melting from his face. 'Thank God we're out of that hell at last.'

'We're not out of it quite yet,' cautioned Mike. 'We've still got to get down the waterfall, but after what we've just been through, that should be a piece of cake.'

'I don't care what it takes. I just want to get out of here.'

'We will Fabrizio. Don't you worry about that.'

While Fabrizio rested, Mike fashioned a thin rope and harness out of the backpack straps and cave line. When he was sure that it would take Fabrizio's weight, he strapped him into it and gently lowered him down the calmest part of the waterfall. Soon Fabrizio was standing safely at the edge of the plunge pool with water up to his knees.

'Can you swim out towards the middle?' Mike shouted over the noise of the cascading water.

'You want me to go there?' asked Fabrizio, pointing to the base of the falls.

'Yeah. I want to know how deep it is.'

Fabrizio reluctantly waded into the water and was soon up to his shoulders and swimming.

'Ees deep here,' shouted Fabrizio, clearly keen to return to the edge of the pool. 'I can't touch the bottom.'

'OK, you can swim back to where you were.'

Fabrizio gladly returned to the edge of the pool and sat there looking up.

'I want you to pull the rest of the line in now,' shouted Mike.

'You want me to do wha...?'

Before Fabrizio could finish, Mike threw the reel down and launched himself after it. He hit the water below with a thudding splash and rose to the surface grinning from ear to ear.

'Are you crazy? You could have broken your legs,' said Fabrizio reprovingly.

'I knew it was deep enough, thanks to you and besides I don't want to lose the line.'

'Why? Surely we don't need it anymore?'

'You don't need it, but I do. I came here to dive that cave you showed to Frank, and that's exactly what I intend to do.'

'You want to do what?!'

Ignoring Fabrizio's protestations, Mike picked up his backpack and led them out of the cave entrance at a determined pace. They shielded their eyes as they emerged into bright daylight once more, in awe of the vastness of the forest after the claustrophobic conditions they'd been exposed to inside the caves.

At the base of the escarpment, Mike collected his equipment bag from behind the thicket of scarlet-bush and persuaded a reluctant Fabrizio to lead him along a thin game trail towards a small water filled depression, nestled at the base of the ridge.

In the shade of the surrounding trees Mike could see that the rock strewn bottom shelved down steeply and swept beneath the arch of a submerged entrance.

'Now this looks interesting,' said Mike, peeling off his tee-shirt.

'I'm staying right here,' Fabrizio stated firmly, sitting down in a small patch of sun with his back resting against a tree. 'I've seen enough water for one day.'

'You go right ahead,' said Mike, pulling out his equipment. 'There's nothing more you can do, except perhaps to keep an eye on the time. I should be out in forty minutes or so.'

As Mike was strapping the sling tanks together, he noticed a broken cable tie lying in the dust. After examining the area more closely, he spotted circular impressions made by the bases of diving cylinders in the soft earth. Someone had obviously been diving there before him.

He pulled on the rest of his equipment, grabbed his spare flashlight and recharged reel, then waded into the waterhole up to his waist. After a quick check of his gauges, he tied off the end of the line, eased himself into the water and slipped silently below the surface.

The worries of the world above seemed to disappear when Mike entered the water, as if his mind was temporarily disconnected from his body. It was a mildly intoxicating experience that sometimes invited complacency and in such a potentially dangerous environment, he had to remind himself to remain focused.

A straight corridor about a body length in width and height lay before him and he cautiously glided along it, watching blind shrimp and transparent cave fish, creeping silently along the cavern walls, their spidery whiskers sweeping the darkness before them. He marvelled at their ability to survive against the leanest of odds and it made him conscious of the fact that he was in a place where by all the rules of nature, he had no right to be. Without a flashlight his eyes were as useless as those of the shrimp, without a lifeline, he was in danger of becoming hopelessly lost, and without a reserve of air on his back, his existence would be limited to a matter of minutes. When pushing back the boundaries of nature, there was always an element of risk.

A prominent stalactite came into view and Mike paused to wind the safety line around it, pulling it taut so that it rested a few inches above the fine sediment. When he glanced up again, his flashlight picked out a cylindrical object lying flat in the silt ahead. A few gently executed frog kicks brought him close enough to see that it was a stage cylinder, a strategically placed source of air that could be used to decompress or facilitate an escape in the event of an emergency. Under normal circumstances, it should have been tied into a baseline, a permanent guide that could be extended as the exploration of the cave system advanced, but the only sign that there had been one, were long thin impressions in the silt. Mike reasoned that if the exploration had been abandoned at some point, the stage cylinder ought to have been removed along with the baseline. The fact that it had been abandoned, suggested that someone had left in a hurry.

Deep in thought, Mike opened the neck valve and saw from the gauge that the cylinder was still full. He shut it off again and examined the attached regulator. As he'd suspected, it carried the identifying stamp of CavePro. Now he knew that he was on the right track.

He wound his line around the cylinder valve and pushed on, entering a small cistern with two separate exits. After a moment of deliberation, he spotted the thin impressions left by the previous baseline and followed them towards the opening on the right. He soon found himself in a straight corridor, the walls of which were decorated with undulating layers of delicate white stalactites, like icicles on a frozen waterfall. Not a single one of them was broken and Mike revelled in their pristine beauty.

The passageway began to widen and Mike aimed his flashlight ahead. To his surprise it picked out a uniform flat square that appeared to have been carved directly into the right hand wall of the cave. Intrigued, he moved towards it, but the line from his reel suddenly pulled up tight. He looked down and cursed in frustration when he saw that the spool was empty. Mike knew that to abandon the lifeline, even temporarily, would be breaking a cardinal rule of cave diving and his dilemma was confounded when he read his gauges and found that he'd used a third of his gas supply, the point at which, in theory, he should turn back. A decision had to be made quickly and against his better nature Mike chose to bend the rules. He'd cheated death three times already today and what he was about to do was a walk in the park in comparison. With consummate care, he posed the reel onto a flat piece of rock close to the cave wall and placed his flashlight gently beside it. Adjusting his buoyancy with absolute precision, he rose a metre or so clear of the silted cave floor and executed two delicate kicks, his image reflected mirror-like in an air pocket which separated him from the ceiling above. The momentum took him further and further from the security of the reel and plunged him ever deeper into a mystery which defied logic. For there, exquisitely carved into the cave wall, was an image that had haunted him since the moment he'd first set eyes on it.

Condega, Nicaragua

The pneumatic brakes of the container truck hissed as it slowed to a halt before an isolated military roadblock. The driver, a chubby Mexican wearing filthy jogging bottoms and a threadbare Reebok tee-shirt, took a long pull on his cigarette and flicked it through the open window of his cab. It fell to the hot tarmac below, where it rolled to a halt and smouldered defiantly.

An official wearing a peaked cap, a white collared shirt with gold braided epaulettes and dark raybans glared at him from behind a wooden desk that was standing on bare earth, shaded by a large square of corrugated steel. The two soldiers flanking him picked up their semi-automatic rifles and sauntered over to their respective positions at either side of the barrier. The official twitched his moustache, spoke a few words into a VHF radio and walked towards the driver, a clipboard tucked under his arm.

'*Sus papeles* – your papers,' he ordered, his thin lips expressionless.

The chubby Mexican exchanged a few words with his co-driver and a handful of grubby documents appeared at the window. The official flicked through them while walking the length of the truck, making a point of inspecting the tyres and cables. He returned to the driver's window and made sucking sounds with his teeth.

'You are carrying refrigerators?' he asked, staring at the cargo manifest.

'That's what it says,' replied the Mexican.

'I know what it says,' said the official, pointedly. 'Open the doors. I want to make an inspection.'

The chubby Mexican was about to launch into a violent remonstration, but knowing the powers he was up against, he controlled his anger and yanked the ignition keys from the steering column.

'We already had a customs inspection at the border,' he protested.

'Then you have nothing to fear,' said the official flatly. He beckoned one of the guards over as the driver accompanied him to the rear of the truck, muttering under his breath. When the latch was released the metal doors swung open on their hinges, revealing a wall of cardboard boxes emblazoned with the blue Solaco logo.

'Take out the central row,' ordered the official.

'What? Are you crazy?' asked the driver insensed. 'Do you realise how much work that involves?'

'Well perhaps you would prefer to spend a few days in jail while we do it for you...and then strip your vehicle down until it's just a pile of nuts and bolts,' said the official icily.

The driver gritted his teeth and went to summon help from his co-driver. Fifteen minutes later, there was a row of boxes on the ground beside the truck and a narrow space inside the container which allowed the inspection of the entire cargo. A Toyota van pulled up behind the truck as the official was entering the hold and pulling apart random boxes. When the search drew a blank, the customs official stepped down and insisted on inspecting the cab in the presence of the two Mexicans. Despite a rigorous search he found nothing of interest and after filling in some exhaustive notes, he returned the driver's papers.

'Everything appears to be in order. You may go.'

The chubby Mexican said nothing. His eyes full of scathing, he glanced at his colleague and motioned towards the rear of the truck. As they were reloading their cargo, the official exchanged a few brief words with the driver of the waiting Toyota van and gave the signal for the barrier to be raised. The two Mexican's glared at him as the Toyota was allowed to overtake their truck and pass through the checkpoint unimpeded. A few minutes later there was a commotion when the chubby Mexican driver realised that something was wrong. There was space in the container for four more boxes and yet there were only three left on the ground. Enraged, he picked up a jack handle and walked towards the official, stopping only when the soldier flanking him raised his rifle and aimed it at his chest.

While the truck driver was pointing an accusing finger at the Nicaraguan official and risking a nervous trigger reaction from the young soldier, the driver of the Toyota van was pulling into an abandoned ranch, where a blacked out Mercedes had been awaiting his arrival. He sensed the occupants eyes on his back as he parked up, opened the rear hatch and slid a large cardboard box out onto the dusty ground before them. The doors of the Mercedes swung open and four men armed with semi-automatic weapons stepped out and walked towards him. A small, balding man paused before the large white cardboard box with the name Solaco emblazoned across it and pursed his lips.

'Did they find anything?'

The van driver shook his head.

'The Colonel said the truck was clean.'

Julio nodded, his face expressionless as he turned towards his men.

'Tear it apart,'

A six foot brute with long hair and a misshapen nose ripped open the

154

box and then with the help of his two colleagues began to strip off panels and tear out wires from the fridge. After half an hour of grunting, panting and sweating they had still not found what they were looking for.

'Are you sure about this boss?' asked one of the men.

'It has to be there somewhere,' said Julio, deep lines cutting into his forehead as he stared at the mangled fragments of metal and plastic which now littered the parched earth. He sifted through the debris, trying to spot dismembered parts of the fridge which might still have some form of cavity inside them. After a few minutes of close scrutiny, his eyes settled on the insulation panels. He stepped back and fired a couple of rounds into one of them. Beneath the pierced metal shell, there was a layer of material which had a plaster like consistency. Julio broke away a piece, crumbled it between his fingers and tasted it with the tip of his tongue. The tension in his expression melted away and his lips curled into a smile.'

'I think we found it. Let's get this to a laboratory.'

* * * *

Mike hovered inside the mouth of the cave for a moment. When he saw nothing besides the refracted greenery of the surrounding forest, he left the protection of the shadows and lifted his head above the surface of the pool. All appeared calm. He pulled off his fins and made his way up the rocky incline, stirring Fabrizio who immediately emerged from the surrounding bushes.

'Did you find anything?'

Mike slipped off his gear and quickly began to dismantle it.

'Frank was here,' he said, keeping a level voice. 'And he found more than just a cave.'

'What did you see in there?' asked Fabrizio.

'I'd prefer to talk about it later if you don't mind. Right now I just want to get out of here before anyone sees us.'

'OK with me. I don't want to stay here one second longer,' said Fabrizio, slinging the backpack which he'd just repaired with vines over his shoulder.

'Good. Let's make tracks.'

Mike quickly packed away his equipment and followed Fabrizio back through the forest. They walked in silence, their eyes sweeping the surrounding trees and their ears alert to any sudden noise or movement. They passed the small cassava plot without a backward glance and pushed on into thick jungle, retracing the route which Fabrizio had cleared that morning. When they finally reached the place where they'd left the car, Fabrizio pulled up short.

'*Che cazzo*?' he cried, throwing his arms up in frustration.

Mike was about to ask what was wrong when he saw it too; the Landcruiser had gone. Fabrizio sunk to the floor holding his head in his hands.

'What are we going to do now?' he said wearily.

Mike walked over to the place where the Landcruiser had been parked.

'Walk, I guess,' he said, staring at the tyre marks which clearly indicated that Fabrizio's car had been driven away.

'Walk all the way to the coast?'

'No. Just as far as the main road. We'll have to try and hitch a ride from there.'

'But it could be dark by the time we arrive.'

'Maybe, but I'd much prefer to spend the night by the roadside than here in this place. Wouldn't you?'

Fabrizio sighed and rose to his feet.

'If there's no better choice.' He threw his backpack over one shoulder and glanced at the equipment that Mike was carrying. 'Aren't you going to leave some of that stuff behind now?'

Mike shook his head emphatically.

'I don't want anyone to know what I've been doing here,' he said. 'In fact I don't want anyone to know that I'm alive at all at this present moment.'

156

'Please yourself,' said Fabrizio with a disinterested shrug. He wiped the sweat from his brow, picked a small huano palm leaf to use as a fan and set off walking along the unsurfaced track.

An hour later, just as the sun was about to drop below the horizon, they reached the main road. The driver of a petroleum tanker returning from a delivery to the interior stopped when he saw their frantic signals and offered to take them to the outskirts of Akumal. Mike and Fabrizio gladly joined him and it was not long before they were being safely deposited at the side of the highway. Fabrizio insisted on giving the driver 100 pesos for his trouble and after some over dramatic gestures of refusal, their unlikely saviour finally accepted his reward with a toothless grin and drove off into the sunset honking his horn.

A short taxi ride took them to the centre and the *estación de policia*, where Fabrizio intended to report the theft of the Landcruiser. Mike went along with him, keen to ensure that he didn't divulge the full details of their ordeal.

The police station was an informal concrete structure lit by humming fluorescent tubes which at this late hour were alive with the fluttering wings of night insects. Mike watched a gravity defying gecko sprint from the shadows and bite a chunk from the wing of a confused moth, which escaped only to spiral down to the ground like a stricken aircraft.

Inside there was a row of benches placed in front of a glass encased reception booth. Mike and Fabrizio sat next to a smartly dressed man and a glum faced young girl whose eyes remained firmly fixed to the floor. A plump middle-aged man was leaning against the kiosk and pleading his case to a bored looking police receptionist seated behind the glass screen. He was waved away, but not before angrily brandishing what appeared to be a parking fine, his eyes burning with injustice. Mike and Fabrizio exchanged amused glances as his protestations continued unabated outside the police station. The receptionist shook his head wearily and motioned to the man and the young girl, who rose to their feet and approached the booth. Fabrizio leaned in towards Mike.

'Are you going to tell me what you saw inside that cave now?'

Mike frowned and bit his lip.

'What I saw defies all logic,' he replied after a pause.

Fabrizio's determined stare prompted him to explain.

'You remember I told you that Frank made a drawing...a sketch?'

'Yes, you asked me if I know about it, but I never saw it,' replied Fabrizio.

'Well I did...and I've just seen the original. It was in that cave, carved into solid rock below the waterline.'

'Beneath the water?' asked Fabrizio, his eyes widening in surprise.

'Yes. Beneath the water.'

'But what is it? What does it show?'

'An upturned figure, like a Mayan god or king.'

'Maya?' asked Fabrizio, astonished. 'You think it has been there for a long time?'

'Yes,' said Mike nodding. 'From the deposition on it, I'd say it's been there for centuries.'

'So, could it perhaps be the work of ancient Maya?'

'I'm no expert, but it looks pretty damned genuine to me.'

'But how could it get there?'

'Well that's what I find most perplexing. Sure, these caves were formed when the sea level was lower, otherwise there'd be no stalactite and stalagmite formation, but over 500 to 1000 years, we're talking about maybe a metre rise at most...and my average depth during the dive was 5·4 metres.'

Fabrizio frowned reflectively.

'Could they have hold their breath and maybe swim there?'

'If they did, it would have made them world apnea champions well before their time,' said Mike, shaking his head, 'and even if they *had* developed such abilities, they wouldn't have got very far without a source of light and those caves are as black as a coal miner's boot laces.'

'Then perhaps there is another entrance.'

'It's a possibility, I suppose. I guess the only way I can find out for sure is to go back and explore the system properly.'

'You want to go back there?' asked Fabrizio astonished. 'After all that happened today?'

'It's the only way I'm going to find out what happened to Frank,' replied Mike with a shrug.

'Why don't you just tell the police what you know and let them deal with it?'

'If I felt confident they'd listen to me and put together a serious expedition, I'd do it...but frankly I think that's about as likely as asking them to go on duty wearing clown suits.'

They looked up in unison as the police receptionist stamped a document belonging to the smartly dressed man and returned it to him with a few words of instruction. The man nodded solemnly, hooked his arm around the young girl and quietly led her out of the building. After scribbling a few notes in his ledger, the receptionist glanced over at Mike and Fabrizio and beckoned them over with a curt nod.

'Remember; no mention of the caves,' cautioned Mike as they rose to their feet.

'*D'accordo.*'

Fabrizio approached the kiosk, greeted the receptionist in fluent Spanish and began to explain the reason for his visit. Mike found the exchange a little too swift for his comfort and let his eyes drift around the walls of the grimy, green and white interior, absently tracing the cracks in the aging plasterwork. To the left of the kiosk a door marked *Jefe de la Policía* opened and Mike saw an official, who he presumed to be the Chief of Police, emerge laughing and shaking hands with a man in a black business suit. The two men exchanged parting pleasantries and as the man in the suit turned to leave he glanced briefly in Mike's direction. Mike watched him begin to walk away and then pause and frown as if trying to remember something. There was something oddly familiar about him and Mike was just trying to think why that was when the man suddenly turned on his heel and fixed him with a stare of utter disbelief. It was then that Mike spotted the gold cross at his neck and the ugly red scar beneath his jaw.

*   *   *   *

'There are three villagers headed your way carrying sacks of freshly harvested cassava plants,' said Dan, speaking urgently into the satellite phone.

'What? How in God's name did that happen?' said Rafael.

'It all went nuts down here about a half hour ago. Those two white guys turned up again and we were just following them out of the forest when the remote camera picked up movement at the cassava field.'

'Hang on, I thought you said those two were pushed into the cenoté.'

'That was an assumption. We saw two white guys, we heard two splashes. We put two and two together.'

'Well are they connected to our investigation or not?'

'I'm not sure Rod. We followed them to a clearing, they started aruguing over something and then they set off walking towards the main road. We abandoned our pursuit when the alarm triggered on the remote.'

'OK,' said Rafael with a sigh. 'Forget about them for now. What's the deal with the three villagers?'

'They stripped the plot bare a few minutes ago and then set off in the direction of the village. We're tracking them through the jungle as I speak.'

'How long before they reach us?'

'We're about a half click away.'

'Is Spicer with you?'

'He's on their tails up ahead.'

'You'd better go catch up with him and make sure he doesn't do anything rash. As soon as you reach the village boundaries ease back, stay out of sight and await orders.'

'Will do.'

Rafael keyed off and slipped the satellite phone into his pocket.

'You get any of that Zach?'

'Some. Sounds like they's playin cowboys and Indians again.'

'That's not too far from the truth. There are three villagers headed this way carrying sacks of those hybrid cassava plants. They should be making an appearance any moment, so you'd better keep on your toes.'

'I'm on it,' said Zach, peering intently through a pair of night vision binoculars. 'Say Rod.'

'Yeah?'

'You really think someone from this backward little village could be holding the whole of Europe to ransom?'

'I have to admit that I have my reservations. Most of the villagers here look like they'd be happy with a new car, a few more chickens and the latest flat screen TV.'

'Hell, I'd be happy with that,' said Zach. 'Swap the chickens for pizza and a fridge full of beer and you got yourself a contented man.' He thought for a second and then added, 'presuming there's plenty of hot bitches in the deal.'

'I admit it sounds tempting Zach, but sooner or later you'd want more. These people are no different to you and me. Chances are they're being manipulated.'

Zach's brow tightened in sudden concentration.

'Well this might be your opportunity to find out. Your three enchanted gardeners just turned up. Come take a look.'

Rafael drew closer, snatching up a pair of binoculars. He watched three men dressed in loincloths and tattered tee-shirts entering the village square below, each carrying a bulging fertilizer sack over his shoulder. The men squeezed between two closely parked trucks, climbed the fluted steps of the whitewashed church and rapped on the studded oak doors. Almost immediately one of doors was drawn aside and the three men disappeared into the dark interior.

'Something tells me they aint going to confession,' said Zach, watching the door closing shut behind them.

'I'd like to be the priest in the stalls if they did.'

'Can we risk going in?'

Rafael pursed his lips.

'Not without causing a major disturbance. We have nothing concrete to go on and we're operating out on a limb here. It could all blow up in our faces if we act too soon. I think we need to try something a little more discreet. We can't do a great deal tonight, but tomorrow might be a good opportunity for me to go and pay my respects.'

* * * *

The National Security Adviser glanced uneasily at the General Secretary, the Commander in Chief of the Armed Forces and the Foreign Secretary as they sank into leather seats around a polished walnut conference table. At the head of the table, seated beneath a gilt framed nude by the hand of Goya, the Prime Minister rolled his Mont Blanc pen through his long, nimble fingers while scanning the details of a brief. It was clear from the dark half moons beneath his eyes and the grey pallor of his skin that he was close to exhaustion.

'Can we take these threats seriously?' he asked, turning towards the security adviser.

'With all due respect Señor Presidente, I think that it would be foolish to ignore them. The deadline expires at midnight tonight and all attempts to defer it have fallen on deaf ears. Their message is as simple as it is ominous. If the money is not paid in full within the next fifteen hours, there will be grave consequences.'

'But we are close to exposing them now are we not?' asked the Prime Minister, turning his attention towards the Commander in Chief of the Armed Forces.

'Our counterparts in America claim to have made significant progress and are confident that their investigations will lead to arrests within the next 72 hours. Naturally, they cannot divulge the details of their operations, but given the resources which they have at their disposal, I think we can safely assume that they have good reason to make such a claim.'

The Prime Minister nodded and jotted down some notes.

'How long can we hold out before our present situation becomes untenable?'

'The Minister of the Interior judges that we have a week, maybe two before we're likely to face any serious civil unrest,' said the General Secretary. 'The death toll has officially passed the one hundred mark now and with major hospitals operating at full capacity, we can expect that figure to rise significantly. Public opinion is generally favourable to our strict policy of non-compliance, but there have been some violent clashes with protesters. Several minority groups are claiming that we are not doing enough to support the victims and their families.'

'I fail to see what else we can do,' sighed the Prime Minister, his silver eyebrows coming together to form a deep frown. 'We've released emergency funds to hospitals to help them deal with the extra strain on their services, we've drafted paramedics in from our security forces and we've allocated supplementary personnel to our drug enforcement and customs agencies. Besides, I fail to see how we can be held responsible for the actions of individuals who choose to break the law. Of course we want to protect the interests of our citizens, but that protection comes at a cost. Yes, we could pay the ransom demand and drug users would be able to continue their illegal activities with renewed peace of mind, but that would neither eliminate the weakness in our society nor strengthen our position against terrorism and extortion.'

There were nods of approval around the table.

'I think we're all agreed that we should continue to hold out against the threats,' said the General Secretary. 'In fact it may be to our advantage.'

'Why do you say that?' asked the Prime Minister, his eyes probing.

'Because it will force the enemy to show their hand.'

'That's a fair assumption,' agreed the Commander. 'Their frustration will push them to act and that is when they will be at their most vulnerable.'

The Prime Minister frowned, resting his chin on his interlaced fingers.

'Well Gentlemen. I sincerely hope that you are right, because if we don't get to the bottom of this soon, we may find ourselves in the unenviable position of defending ourselves against our own people.

* * * *

The look of surprise soon turned to one of irritation. The man in the dark suit turned and strode stiffly away out into the darkness of the street. Almost immediately afterwards the Chief of Police re-emerged from his office with a telephone clasped to his ear. His face was rigid with concentration as he scanned the room, his jaw tightening when his dark eyes settled on Mike.

Sensing that he'd run into trouble, Mike walked towards the exit, only to be called back by a booming authoritative voice. His stomach in knots, he turned and was met by the steely regard of the Chief of Police, who with a flick of the finger ordered him to return to the kiosk. Fabrizio was left staring from one person to another as the Chief of Police conferred with the receptionist and ushered them into an adjoining room.

'What's going on here Mike? Are you in some kind of trouble?'

'Be quiet,' bellowed the Chief of Police, his voice belying his small stature. Mike noticed the tattoos on his bulky arms, exposed by a short sleeved uniform shirt. It looked as if he was more than capable of handling himself.

'Sit down,' the Police Chief ordered, pointing to two well-worn plastic seats, placed before a rudimentary table. Finding that his seat was broken, Fabrizio perched on the edge of it while the Police Chief leafed through his soaked and battered passport.

'What are you doing in Mexico Mr....Germini?'

'I'm a researcher...for a Pharmaceutical company. You can see that my permits are in order.'

'That is for me to decide,' barked the Police Chief. 'What is your relationship with this man?' he demanded, pointing towards Mike. Fabrizio hesitated and stole a glance at Mike before he replied.

'We met only a few days ago. He spoke to me because he's interested in my research work.'

Mike breathed an inward sigh of relief.

'You expect me to believe that?' spat the Police Chief. 'What were you doing today?'

'We were out exploring an area of forest just south of Yalché.'

'Why were you exploring that particular area?'

'It's a place that I know,' replied Fabrizio with a shrug. 'It's not a restricted area as far as I know, and the conditions are ideal for the growth of many different types of plant.'

'Including the coca plant?'

'The coca plant?' asked Fabrizio, taken aback. 'No, the conditions are not ideal for the coca plant and besides its properties are already well researched and documented. Ees not of any interest to either me or my company.'

'Then perhaps it is of greater interest to Mr. Summers,' said the Police Chief, turning his attention towards Mike.

'Look, I really don't know what you're trying to imply,' began Mike, 'but_'

'Silence!' interrupted the Police Chief. After a carefully measured pause he switched his attention back to Fabrizio. 'Mr. Germini, is your missing vehicle a Toyota Landcruiser with the registration plate UVL 4678?'

'It's a Landcruiser, but I'm not sure of the number,' replied Fabrizio, 'it's a hire vehicle. I don't have the documents with me. They were in the car when it was stolen.'

'It *is* your car Mr. Germini, and a call to the hire company will soon confirm that.'

'Perhaps,' replied Fabrizio, with a shrug. 'But is it so important? I just want to get my car back.'

'I'm sure that you do Mr. Germini,' said the Police Chief with a sneer. He called in a guard and ordered Mike and Fabrizio to empty their bags and turn out their pockets. When he saw the contents of Mike's backpack, he confined them to the interview room and stepped outside, leaving the guard watching over them.

'What's going on here Mike?' Fabrizio asked anxiously.

'I think it has something to do with me,' admitted Mike. 'I saw a man talking to the Police Chief while you were making your report. I'm not sure who he is, but he seems to wield some kind of power here. He approached me just before we met this morning and in a roundabout way told me to keep my nose out of other people's business, which I took to mean Frank's disappearance.'

'What? And you ignored him and got me involved,' said Fabrizio, a flicker of resentment in his eyes.

'Yes, but...' Mike noticed that the guard was straining to hear their conversation and lowered his voice.

'You were involved before I met you Fabrizio. I think you've just been lucky up until now...and if I were you I'd be very careful about what I say from now on. There are people watching and listening...and that probably includes the guy who's guarding us.'

'Nonsense,' scoffed Fabrizio. He glanced at the guard only to see him look away when their eyes met.

'So what do you think will happen now?' he asked.

'I've no idea, but I guess we'll soon find out,' said Mike with a shrug of resignation.

Fabrizio sighed and rested his head in his hands.

For a while they sat in silence, staring at the peeling paintwork, the cigarette burns on the table top and the dead insects littering the covers of the flickering fluorescent tubes. Forty minutes later the Police Chief returned accompanied by an armed officer. Mike and Fabrizio were led out of the police station and taken towards a vehicle yard at the rear, where to their surprise they found Fabrizio's Landcruiser parked between two patrol cars.'

'Is this your vehicle?' asked the Police Chief.

'Yes,' replied Fabrizio, 'but where did you find it?'

'It was found without fuel on the outskirts of Akumal. You must now check to see that nothing has been stolen before you sign the release papers.'

The Police Chief handed Fabrizio the envelope which contained his personal effects. Fabrizio retrieved the keys and began his inspection, starting with the equipment in the rear. When he came to open the door on the driver's side, he paused, seeing an unfamiliar package in the side pocket. The Police Chief appeared at his side.

'What is that you have Mr. Germini?' he asked, an eyebrow raised.

'I-I've never seen it before,' said Fabrizio, bemused.

Mike closed his eyes and lowered his head, knowing only too well what was coming next.

'Open it!' ordered the Police Chief.

Fabrizio untied the coarse string that was holding the package together and removed the waxed paper beneath to reveal a large cake of cocaine, sealed in plastic film.

'It is surprising what one can find in the Yucatan forest isn't it?' said the Police Chief, with a self-satisfied grin.

GUATEMALA CITY, GUATEMALA

The navy blue Daimler left the Spanish embassy in zone 9 and motored through the concrete towers of the central business district into the chaotic throng of the sprawling suburbs.

In the air conditioned comfort of the leather upholstered rear seat, the Spanish Ambassador was cushioned from the harsh reality of life in the outskirts of the Guatemalan capital, where slums housed thousands of unfortunates drawn by the promise of a better life.

It was not that he was impervious to their plight, it was just that there seemed little that anyone could do about it. Guatemala was way behind its Mexican neighbour in terms of economic development. There was simply not enough industry to sustain economic growth and too little money to go around. Of course, Spain would always do whatever it could to help a former colony, but through investment rather than charity. A developing country must learn to stand on its own two feet.

Soon they were climbing the foothills to the north, where modern apartment blocks housed the city's lawyers, bankers and government officials. The new developments crept like tendrils along river valleys and across hillsides, threatening to engulf and digest the fragile forest which surrounded them. The Daimler finally left the sprawling commuter belt behind and entered the small, rural town of Sacojito, nearly eight miles from the centre. The Ambassador closed a dossier and placed it in his briefcase as the Chauffeur turned into a quiet, leafy drive and approached a magnificent wrought iron entrance gate. It swung open at a touch of the Chauffeur's remote control and the Daimler's engine hummed as if in contentment as its tyres crunched along a cinder drive bordered by an immaculately tended lawn. The Chauffeur brought the car smoothly to a halt outside an imposing modern dwelling, its shaded, over-elaborate entranceway supported by neo-classical colonnades. The Ambassador alighted and sent the driver away with instructions for the morning then strode up a flight of white sandstone steps to a solid beech door. He slipped his key into the gleaming brass security lock and let himself in.

'*Mariana, ya lleugué!* – Mariana, I'm here!' he shouted, posing his briefcase on a polished walnut chest of drawers. He caught his reflection in the mirror and pushed a wayward lock of his grey flecked hair behind his ear. He noticed that his eyes were a little drawn and his moustache needed clipping again. Not too short though, because it helped to draw attention away from his large nose. He frowned, wondering why there was no noise in the house.

'Mariana!' he shouted again. He paused to listen and was surprised to hear a low murmur; a gentle sobbing coming from the direction of the salon. He hurried towards the swinging double doors which separated him from the salon and pushed them wide open. There, sitting on the tiled floor, eyes wide with fear and mascara streaming down her face he found his wife clutching their sobbing daughter to her chest. The Ambassador was about to speak when two masked figures emerged from behind the swinging doors and pointed the muzzles of their sub machine guns at his face. It looked as if his worst nightmare had just become reality.

If the curious looks of the villagers were anything to go by, they didn't get too many visits from tourists. The tiny settlement wasn't exactly on the way to anywhere of note and its points of interest could be counted on the fingers of one hand. There was the carefully tended village square, the whitewashed colonial church, a few of the original stucco walled town dwellings and the crumbling remnants of a long dead plantation owner's house, set back into the hillside. In fairness, khaki pants, combat boots and a white tee-shirt were probably not the sort of thing that a tourist would normally wear, but Rafael was gambling on there still being enough oddball travellers of the Hemingway type wandering around Mexico for him to be able to pull it off.

He paused at the perimeter of the village square and looked around as he imagined a curious visitor might do. The stables of the abandoned plantation house were visible over the plane trees which bordered the square to his right and although he couldn't see him, he knew that Zach would be watching his every move from one of its shuttered openings.

He walked towards the colonial church, admiring the finely carved arches, ornate window frames and Madonna figurine set back into a sheltered recess above the porch. The fluted stairway led to the entrance which the three villagers had used the previous evening, weighed down with their hoard of toxic plants. Rafael and Zach had watched them leave empty handed shortly afterwards, so it was fair to assume that unless someone inside the church had a huge appetite for roasted cassava, the plants had to be inside there still.

The weathered oak doors creaked open on heavy iron hinges when Rafael pushed against them and he peered into a gloomy interior lit by the ghostly shafts of natural light which filtered in through the surrounding window frames. He entered and walked into the centre of the nave, admiring the gold threaded tapestries that were mounted between the towering stone columns forming the structural ribs of the building. His eye was drawn towards a particularly gruesome painting of the crucifixion above the main altar, flanked by golden crosses that were raised on wrought iron stands. In the darkness it appeared as if they were floating in thin air.

He looked up, tracing the graceful curves of the vaulted ceiling high above the rows of wooden pews to see a small section of roof covered by a dark tarpaulin. As he was pondering over its presence, a voice pierced the shadows. Rafael swung round, stifling the impulse to reach down and draw the snub nosed Colt that was strapped to his ankle.

'Padre, you gave me such a fright,' he said, recognising the priests flowing black gown. 'I didn't hear you approaching.'

He inwardly cursed himself for his lack of vigilance.

'I'm sorry if I startled you,' said the priest, his childlike features breaking into a wide smile. 'I was praying in the chapel.'

'I hope I didn't disturb you Padre.'

'Not in the least; I was just drawing to a close,' said the priest, examining Rafael's attire. 'Might I ask what brings you to visit our humble village?'

'I'm hiking. Slowly making my way up towards Coba. I saw this place on the map and thought I'd come take a look. This is quite a place you have here.'

'Yes, it is a site of worship much treasured by the community.'

'It looks pretty old. What's the history of it?'

'The church was founded in 1547 by Francisco de Quevedo, a wealthy Spanish landowner. The ruins of his family home can still be seen from the village square.'

'Yes, I think I saw them as I came in. What happened to him?'

'I'm afraid that fortune did not smile upon the members of the de Quevedo family. Francisco de Quevedo died in a freak hunting accident, bitten by a poisonous snake. The following year, his daughter and two sons fell victim to a fever and when they passed away their mother returned heartbroken to Spain.'

'That's quite a run of bad luck.'

'God giveth, and God taketh away,' said the priest, reflectively.

Amen, thought Rafael.

'Do you mind if I take a look around?'

'Please feel free,' said the priest, opening his arms. 'This is the house of God.'

Rafael inclined his head and began to stroll around the perimeter of the church. Most of it was bare limestone blocks, with the occasional carved wooden panel and velvet drape. The chapel from which the priest had appeared was accessible by a narrow doorway. It was a small rectangular room with a raised altar at the far end, a statue of the Madonna standing imposingly above it, illuminated by the light of several thin white candles. The last place that he saw on his tour of the building was a small room behind the chancel, furnished with a bookshelf, a rudimentary desk and a mattress, propped up against the wall. There was no sign of the cassava plants.

'Do you ever store or prepare food in here?' asked Rafael, 'for special occasions or anything like that?'

'Food?' questioned the priest, frowning. 'No. Why do you ask?'

'Oh, I just wondered. You know; being on the church on your own and everything.'

'I rarely take meals here,' replied the priest, his patience slowly thinning.

Rafael nodded, walked a few steps and then let his eyes drift up towards the dark canvas once more.

'Are you having some restoration work done up there?'

The priest followed his line of sight.

'There is some falling plasterwork. It needs a little attention, but we are short of funds at the moment. We are only a small congregation as you can imagine.'

Rafael pursed his lips, nodding. He glanced down at the black and white chequered marble tiles covering the floor and his eyes were drawn towards a large circular motif with a sunburst design set into the floor before the altar. He approached it, squatted down and crossed himself while discreetly tracing the edge of the circumference with the back of his hand. There was a thin draught of cool air rising from it.

'Were any of the de Quevedo family buried here?' he asked, straightening up.

The priest took a moment to answer.

'It is believed that members of the family were laid to rest beneath the chapel.'

'And is there perhaps a crypt beneath the main building?'

Rafael noticed a miniscule widening of the priest's eyes.

'Not to my knowledge,' he replied. 'Why? Is it of some importance to you?'

'No, not really' replied Rafael, with a shrug. 'I'm just the inquisitive type.'

The priest nodded, uncertainly.

'Well Padre, it was very kind of you to show me around your church, but time is pressing and I really ought to be on my way.'

'Of course. It was a pleasure to meet you Mr...,' prompted the priest.

'Rod,' replied Rafael as he was guided towards the exit.

'Please come and visit us again...Rod.'

'Thank you, I'll see what I can arrange,' said Rafael, grinning as he stepped out into the glare of the morning sun.

'May God guide you,' said the priest, his mouth twitching into a smile.

Rafael walked a few paces and then looked back over his shoulder. The church door was slightly ajar and he could just see the shine of the priest's eye, staring out after him. He waved mischievously and then marched swiftly out of the square in the direction of the main road.

* * * *

There seemed to be no obvious way out of the cave. The flashlight beam revealed numerous identical exits which radiated away from it like the spokes of a wheel. Only one of them led back to the surface and safety, but which one? There was no lifeline to guide him. Why in God's name had he entered the system without a reel? He looked at the needle of his pressure gauge and saw that it had slipped into the red. It was now or never. He turned and chose an exit at random, placing his life in the hands of the gods. Now he was moving through it; pushing through liquid darkness, not knowing when his last breath would come. The flashlight beam disappeared into a straight corridor. Was this the way he'd come in? Impossible! He changed direction and started back towards the cave. It suddenly became hard to breathe, the needle of the pressure gauge was touching zero. In desperation, he crossed the cave and entered another passageway at random. His lungs were cramping. There was nothing to replace the stale air which burned within them. Would death be swift or linger agonisingly? Suddenly a bright light burst through the darkness and Mike sat bolt upright gasping for breath.

'Wake up you stinking cockroaches,' yelled the guard, shining his flashlight into the eyes of Mike and Fabrizio and rattling the metal grill of the cell in which were being held.

'*Che cazzo vuoi?*' swore Fabrizio, throwing his arm across his face. The guard flicked on the overhead lights sending shiny brown bodies scuttling away into cracks and holes in the wall. Mike was once more confronted with the heat and squalor of the small cell in which they were being held. The floors were stained with blood and vomit, the crumbling walls were covered in graffiti and the acrid smell of stale urine seemed to invade their every breath.

'What do you want from us now?' Mike asked wearily.

'I want you both to stay here and rot,' said the guard, 'but unfortunately there are people with other ideas. Señor Germini has a visitor.'

Fabrizio rose to his feet, shading his eyes when he noticed the short, well dressed man standing beside the guard.

'Señor Germini, my name is Alfredo Martinez, I am a lawyer and I have been assigned to represent you by the Italian Consulate,' said the man, his English as impeccable as his dress. 'I am here to secure your release.'

'I can go?' asked Fabrizio, astonished.

'Bail has been arranged Mr. Germini, you are free to leave.'

'*Grazie a Dio*,' sighed Fabrizio, shaking his head. After a pause he frowned and glanced at Mike. 'What about my friend here?'

'Regretfully, I have no authority to secure your friend's release,' said the lawyer.

'Then I stay here,' said Fabrizio, firmly 'We are both innocent and there is no reason why any of us should stay in this stinking jail any longer.'

'Perhaps we could try to get him freed later today Mr. Germini, I'm sure that the_'

'No!' shouted Fabrizio. 'We have been through far worse than this together. Mike helped me when I most needed it and the least I can do is return his favour. Either you release us together or we both stay here.'

The lawyer sighed and shook his head.

'This will be difficult Mr. Germini; it is very early in the morning and people will be sleeping. But if that is your wish, I will try my best.'

'Good,' said Fabrizio. 'And I would like my car back too.'

'Your car?'

'It's in the parking lot. They're holding it as evidence.'

'I see...then I will try to arrange for it to be returned to you.'

'Thank you.'

The lawyer inclined his head and turned to leave. The guard, shrugged, grinned and shook his keys at Mike and Fabrizio.

'Have a nice night lover boys,' he said, kissing the air.

A switch was flicked and they were plunged into darkness once more.

'There was no need for you to do that Fabrizio,' said Mike. 'You should have taken your chance to get out of this place.'

'Would you prefer that I leave you alone here?'

'Well no, I'd be lying if I said that I would; but you're injured and you must be exhausted after all that's happened.'

'I am, but I would feel much worse if I was still stuck at the bottom of that cenoté. Here at least I know that help isn't far away.'

'You obviously have friends in important places,' said Mike, flicking his hand away as something crawled over it.

'I'm as surprised as you. Of course, my company has connections all over the world, but any problem with illegal drugs would normally make them run.'

'Maybe you're worth more to them than you think.'

'I never really thought about that.'

'You should. It's useful when you need to ask for a pay rise,'

'I would have more chance of discovering the cure for Alzheimer's disease,' chuckled Fabrizio.

'From what I've seen, I wouldn't put it past you.'

'Well right now, I'll settle for getting out of here.'

'You and me both.'

They talked for a while in the darkness until exhaustion got the better of them and they drifted into a fitful sleep. A few hours later they were awoken by the sound of a key turning in a heavy lock and the sudden illumination of the windowless cell. Through splayed fingers they saw the guard appear before the metal grill, accompanied once more by Señor Martinez.'

'Stand up prisoners!' shouted the guard, his face stony as he pushed open the door of the cell.

'Señor Germini, Señor Summers, I now have the authority from your respective embassies to secure your release on bail,' said the lawyer. 'Although this does not absolve you of the crimes of which you have been accused, it will give us the necessary time to prepare your_'

'Out, out!' shouted the guard, hurrying Mike and Fabrizio through the cell door before Señor Martinez had time to finish speaking.

They were marched up a flight of concrete steps which emerged into a corridor at the rear of the police station. From there they were led to the interview room and under the watchful eye of Señor Martinez, their belongings were returned to them. After signing the necessary release papers, they were cleared to leave.

'Fresh air at last,' said Fabrizio as they stepped outside and walked towards the vehicle yard. 'You forget how wonderful it is until it is taken away from you.'

'I hope that you'll enjoy it for some time to come,' said Señor Martinez.

'Do you think the charges brought against us will stick?' asked Mike.

'Before I answer that question, I'll need some information from you,' said Señor Martinez, slowing to a halt. 'I saw from the statements you gave the police that your car was stolen yesterday sometime before 4pm.'

'Yes, that's correct.'

'And at what time did the police find the package of drugs?'

'About seven when they asked us to check the Landcruiser,' said Mike. 'The drugs were inside. They'd been planted on us.'

'I'm afraid that would be difficult to prove,' said Señor Martinez, 'but tell me, was that the first time you'd seen the vehicle since it went missing?'

'Yes,' replied Fabrizio. 'The police told us that it was found abandoned outside the town.'

'Well, drugs traffickers would not normally leave such a valuable cargo behind, but the most important thing from our point of view is that the car was not in your possession just prior to the cocaine being found. In my professional opinion that puts you in the clear. You have been implicated by association and where there is doubt there is no foundation for a conviction. Having said that, I will of course be happy to represent you should the police be determined to press charges. Here are my details in case you need to get in touch with me.'

Mike and Fabrizio took Señor Martinez's business card and shook his hand profusely.

'Do we need to contact our embassies now?' asked Fabrizio.

'No, I will inform them of your release when I return to my office.'

'Excellent. Thank you for all your help Señor Martinez,' said Mike.

'It has been my pleasure. Please enjoy the rest of your stay in Mexico.'

'We hope to. Goodbye.'

Fabrizio climbed behind the wheel of the Toyota and started the engine. The fuel gauge hovered just above zero.

'They used up all the fuel,' he complained as Mike jumped in beside him.

'Consider yourself lucky they didn't torch the lot.'

Fabrizio cursed and let out the clutch.

On the way to the gas station, Mike opened up his phone, removed the chip and transferred it to one which Fabrizio kept in the glove compartment of the car. When he switched the power on, the log indicated that there had been several unexpected calls from Beth. He frowned, hit the dial button and waited for a connection.

'Beth Draper.'

'Hey Beth, you been trying to get hold of me?'

'You betcha. I've been trying to call you since I left Roatan. Where've you been in the last 24 hours?'

'It's a long and very unpleasant story. Where are you now?'

'Well, you remember you said that if I ever came to the Yucatan you'd show me a yellow mouthed toadfish?...promised me actually!'

'Er...yeah.'

'Well I'm taking you up on it. I'm in Cancun at this very moment and as soon as I've had a shower and eaten one of the hotel's delicious fruit cocktails, I'm going to hire a car and start driving down the coast.'

'Um, this is not really the best time Beth. There are some odd things going on down this way.'

'Is that some kind of lame excuse?' said Beth, her voice clipped.

'No...no it's not Beth. I'd love to see you, but I'm in some kind of trouble right now.'

'So what's new? Trouble's your middle name.'

'No but this is serious. It could...well it could get someone killed.'

'So could diving with Humbolt squid in the Sea of Cortez. Never stopped me though.'

Mike sighed in exasperation.

'OK, I'm too tired to fight with you Beth. You can come on down if you wish, but on one condition; I want you to promise me that you'll do exactly as I tell you if things start to get out of hand.'

'OK, I guess I can live with that. So where are you staying? I only have the address of CavePro.'

'Just give me a call when you're close to Akumal and I'll come and meet you.'

'OK. See you for sundowners then?'

'It's a deal.'

Mike slipped his phone into his pocket and sank back into his seat with a sigh.

'You have a friend coming to see you?' asked Fabrizio.

'Yeah...Beth. She's a great girl, but boy is she stubborn!'

'I admire women with spirit. Much better than the one's who just want to spend their lives shopping.'

'True, but I'm a little afraid for her safety. Beth's too curious for her own good sometimes and the way things are going that can only spell trouble.'

'Maybe you should take a rest and just enjoy your time together. Those caves have been there for thousands of years and they'll still be around in a couple of days.'

'Yeah, maybe you're right. We could both do with a few days break.'

'I feel like I could sleep for a week,' said Fabrizio, but right now, more than anything, I need food.'

'Me too, I'm starving.'

'Then let's go eat.'

Once the Landcruiser had been refuelled, Fabrizio took Mike to the Dolce Vita where they gorged themselves on a feast of freshly baked bread, gorgonzola and prosciutto. After savouring the last drop of his foaming cappuccino, Mike left Fabrizio to recount his adventures to Claudio and went over to CavePro to return the cylinders. Ken was behind the counter as he breezed through the door.

'Hey Ken. How's it going?'

'*How's it going*?' said Ken, scowling. 'It couldn't be worse frankly.'

'Why? What's the problem?'

'You're the problem Mike. I don't know what you've been getting up to, but you've stirred up some shit somewhere and it's landed right here on my doorstep.'

'I don't understand. What's been happening?'

'I had the police around here early this morning. They told me that you've been involved in drugs trafficking and that your work permit has been cancelled. I've got advanced cave courses booked for two days time and I can't run them because I no longer have a qualified instructor. The bottom line is that you no longer work here Mike and there isn't a damned thing I can do about it. If I employ you illegally, they'll shut me down.'

'Jesus Ken, I'm so sorry. Everything seems to be getting way out of hand. Believe me, I'm not in any way involved in drugs trafficking, that's just an excuse which the police are using to keep me away from Yalché.'

'Yalché? What the hell's that got to do with anything?'

Mike glanced around to make certain that no one was in earshot of them.

'Ken, the cave system which Frank discovered wasn't the one which you saw in Chalchén. I don't even know what he was doing there to be honest. He found a much bigger and far more extensive system close to Yalché.'

180

'How do you know that?'

'Because I've been there. I discovered some notes which Frank left in my locker and used them to help me find the caves. I explored part of the system yesterday.'

'OK,' said Ken, tugging at his goatee. 'So even if that's true. What does this have to do with the police?'

'I've stumbled into something which goes very deep Ken. I'm not entirely sure what it is yet, but I do know that it was enough to get Frank killed.'

'You think Frank was murdered just because he discovered some caves?'

'No, I think he was murdered because of what he discovered *inside* the caves. Believe me, it's not idle speculation. I narrowly avoided being killed there myself.'

'Are there drugs inside the cave Mike?'

'Not to my knowledge.'

'Then what?'

'Look, I don't have all the answers Ken. I've no idea who wanted Frank dead or why. The only way that I'll be able to make any sense of this at all is to go further into the cave system and find out for myself.'

'If I was you I'd let it drop Mike. Whatever Frank was into, it's too late to bring him back now.'

'Yeah, I could walk away. We could all walk away. But if everyone did that the whole world would be corrupt.'

'You can pay a pretty high price for principles like that Mike. Sometimes you've just got to admit that you're out of your league.'

'I'm too close to let it drop now Ken.'

'Well, that's up to you Mike. I'm afraid that there's not much I can do to help you.'

'There's still something you could do.'

'Yeah? And what's that?'

'Rent me some cylinders.'

MADRID, SPAIN

The Prime Minister removed his reading glasses and pinched the bridge of his nose as the Foreign Secretary relayed the devastating news from Guatemala. The National Security Adviser sat rigid in his chair, his shifting eyes communicating the outrage that was silently burning behind them. Across the table, the General Secretary rubbed his hands nervously over the two day old stubble which had surreptitiously invaded his jowls.

'We've been given forty eight hours to comply with the kidnapper's demands,' continued the Foreign Secretary, 'after which time Ambassador Perez will, they claim, be executed.'

'Good God! Who the hell are we dealing with here,' blurted the Prime Minister, in frustration. 'Doesn't anyone have any idea who these savages are?'

'I'm afraid that the extortionists have so far revealed neither their aims nor their identity,' said the National Security Adviser, 'and therefore we have very little to go on. All we can say for sure at the moment is that they are a major player in the illegal traffic of narcotics, they are well organised and have one or more points of contact in the Americas.'

'But surely they must have political ambitions. This cannot be just a question of money. A hundred million euros is a small fortune, certainly, but for a drugs cartel?' said the Prime Minister, spreading his hands in supplication. 'And if they have no political agenda, then why are they specifically targeting Spain? Has anyone considered the involvement of our traditional antagonists? ETA for instance?'

'With all due respect *Señor Presidente*, these attacks bear no similarity to those of the Basque separatist movement,' said the Commander in Chief of the Armed Forces. 'At one time their attacks may have been ruthless, but they now take great pains to avoid loss of life for fear of alienating themselves from the Spanish public and damaging their international reputation. Their principal objective is to cause disruption and draw attention to their plight...and therefore, in my opinion, they stand to gain nothing from hiding their involvement in outside terrorist activities.'

'And ETA has no history of links with extremist groups in the Americas,' added the Foreign Secretary.

'Well then if we are not dealing with ETA, which other extremist groups could have an interest in attacking us?' asked the Prime Minister. 'Al Qaida?'

'It's very unlikely that Al Qaida has infiltrated the cocaine smuggling industry' said the National Security Adviser. 'There are simply not enough Islamic sympathisers in that part of the world to make it viable. If they tried to muscle in on a share of the market, they would be quickly identified and targeted by rival gangs.'

'So we are probably looking at terrorist groups already operating in that part of the world,' surmised the Prime Minister. 'Who do we know of?'

'The first one that springs to mind is *Sendero Luminoso*, the Peruvian Maoist group who have confirmed associations with the traffic of narcotics, specifically cocaine.'

'The Shining Path?' nodded the Prime Minister, 'but haven't they faded into obscurity?'

'They certainly went into decline in 1992 when their leader Abimael Guzmán was imprisoned, but there is recent evidence to suggest that they are quietly gaining support in the mountains of Peru and once again financing themselves through coca production.'

'And extortion?' questioned the Prime Minister.

'It's not beyond them. Traditionally their target is the ruling power in Peru, but it's possible that they have became frustrated with the government's heavy handed measures and chosen to pursue a softer target.'

'But why us?'

'Apart from the obvious language connection, as former colonists we may be seen by some as the cause of their present plight. In fact another Peruvian resistance movement, the *Movimiento Revolucionario Tupac Amaru*, is named after a rebel leader who fought Spanish colonial control in the eighteenth century, which perhaps demonstrates the resentment which still lingers in the collective subconscious. The MRTA themselves can be discounted of course. They faded into oblivion after a failed attempt to occupy the Japanese Embassy in Lima.

'Yes I remember that hostage situation well. Still, I'm not convinced that the Shining Path would attempt a potentially damaging attack on Spain, however convenient it appears. It's not as if we've openly attacked them.'

'Well, the only other active guerrilla movement of any significance in South America is the FARC, *Fuerzas Armadas Revolucionarias de Colombia*. Of course, the FARC finance their activities through coca production as well, but they are presently restricted by military operations being directed against them by the Colombian and US governments.'

'It still makes no sense to me why any of these groups would purposely compromise a major source of funding for their political aims,' said the Foreign Secretary. 'Or why they would go to such trouble to source an exotic poison from thousands of miles away.'

'Yes, I'm inclined to agree with you there,' said the Prime Minister nodding. 'Isn't there any guerrilla activity closer to Mexico?'

'Actually, there *is* a well known separatist group based in Mexico; Southern Mexico to be exact,' said the Foreign Secretary.

'Of course!' said the National Security Adviser, nodding enthusiastically. 'The *Ejército Zapatista de Liberación Nacional* - the EZLN. The Zapatistas are based in the state of Chiapas, close to the borders of Guatemala. It's one of the most deprived areas in Mexico.'

'That's quite correct,' said the Foreign Secretary. The primarily Mayan population of Chiapas have been engaged in a long standing battle to gain independence from the Mexican authorities. Their grievances stretch back as far as the Mexican Revolution when their hero Emiliano Zapata fought for agrarian reform.'

'The Zapatistas!' said the prime Minister, pensively. 'Now that is interesting. And is there perhaps a Maya presence in the place where these toxic plants were found?'

'Very much so,' said the Foreign Secretary. 'I had the pleasure of visiting the Yucatan a few years ago with my wife. The Maya Indians are very prevalent there, particularly in the south where those plant samples originate from. In fact the whole coastline is known as the *Riviera Maya*.'

'And is it conceivable that these Zapatistas have a strong hatred of Spain.'

'To the point of attacking the Spanish public? I very much doubt it,' said the National Security Adviser. 'I think they understand that European expansionism would eventually have changed their way of life even if our country had not been the first to conquer them. What they may find harder to accept is that in modern times they continue to be treated with prejudice by their own authorities. Even so, they rarely resort to violence and when they do their actions are primarily defensive.'

'Then could it be possible that there is a breakaway group, an extremist minority who do not share the same humanitarian values?'

'If there is, then our intelligence services have no knowledge of them,' said the National Security Adviser.

'Well given the lack of concrete information we have to go on, I think it might be prudent to find out,' said the Prime Minister. 'Contact your counterparts in the Mexican Security Services and find out everything you can about the EZLN, their aims, capabilities, funding, sympathisers and former leaders. We have very little time left and we need to use it wisely.'

'I will give it my immediate attention *Presidente*.'

* * * *

Plaza Ukana was already undergoing its late afternoon transition by the time that Mike arrived. Market stall holders were clearing away their wares, café owners were putting the last touches to their evening menu boards and tourists were searching for a quiet spot to sip margaritas under the glow of the setting sun. A slender arm was raised at a nearby terrace attracting Mike's attention and he beamed when he saw Beth, smiling coolly at him from behind a pair of dark 1950's style shades. She was wearing long flower print beach shorts, flip-flops and a short sleeved cotton top.

'Hey stranger,' she trilled as Mike approached.

'My pretty little scientist. It's good to see you,' said Mike, leaning over to greet her with a kiss. He pulled up a chair and sat facing her. 'Did you miss me?'

'Sundowners at the lodge just weren't the same without you.'

'I'm sure the manager thought so. His profits must have taken quite a hit. Can I get you a drink?' he asked, drawing the attention of a passing waiter.

'I think another Piña Colada might be in order...but let me buy. After all I'm now officially on holiday.'

'Actually, as from this morning, so am I.'

'Uh? How come?'

Mike placed an order for a Piña Colada and a Corona beer.

'I can't work here anymore. They cancelled my permit.'

'They cancelled your work permit? But why?'

'Like I told you Beth, there have been some very nasty things happening here over the last week or so and I seem to be caught right in the thick of it.'

'What kind of things?'

'You don't want to know.'

'Try me.'

Mike waited for the drinks to be served.

'You remember I told you my friend Frank was killed?'

'Sure I do. It was the reason you left Utila as I recall.'

'Yeah, but the problem is he wasn't just killed; he was murdered.'

'Murdered? Do you know why?'

'I don't have the full facts Beth, but I do know that the official version of events is a complete fabrication.'

'Perhaps you should explain this to me from the beginning.'

Mike took a long slug from his Corona and spent the next half hour recounting everything which had happened to him since his return to Mexico. By the time that he'd finished speaking, Beth had removed her sunglasses and was staring at him in wide eyed astonishment.

'Now do you understand why I was reluctant to have you around?' said Mike, gravely.

Beth nodded and took his hand in hers.

'I guess I didn't take you too seriously,' she admitted. 'I thought you were exaggerating...or maybe trying to find some excuse to keep me out of the way.'

'Put those ideas out of your head,' said Mike, stroking a loose strand of hair behind her ear.

Beth flashed him a smile

'I guess all that makes my life seem a little boring.'

'Boring? Chasing whale sharks around the Caribbean is not exactly what I'd call boring Beth.'

'Yeah, provided you can find them.'

'What do you mean?'

'It all went quiet after you left. Sure, we got a couple more sightings, but we had to work damned hard for them. Bill was great, but even he says that there are fewer and fewer seen each year.'

'That must be very frustrating for you.'

'It is...but hey, let's forget all that depressing stuff for a while. I'm on holiday now and I just want to enjoy being here with you.'

'That suits me. With all that's been going on recently I could do with a bit of distraction myself.'

'Glad we agree. So what exciting things have you got planned for me?'

'Well, tomorrow morning we're booked for a dive on the reef and in the afternoon I thought we could go see the temples in Tulúm. After that it's up to you. We can do as much or as little as you like.'

'OK. And tonight?'

'You like lobster?'

'Sure I like lobster.'

'Good, cause someone gave me a couple of big ones. We can stick them on the barbecue at my place, throw together a salad, and watch everything sizzle while we slowly empty the nice bottle of wine that I have chilling in the fridge.'

'That sounds absolutely perfect.'

* * * *

It was hard to breathe through the hessian sack that was covering his head, the more so because he was being pushed at a relentless pace. He'd been on the move now for two maybe three days. There'd been a long drive in the back of a van, a strenuous hike through mountains, a night river crossing and now he was trekking through thick forest.

Tired, hungry and exhausted, he felt absolutely wretched, but the pain of the frequent headlong falls was nothing compared to the agony in his mind. The Ambassador had no knowledge of what had become of his family, no idea why he'd been abducted and only vague notions of what his captor's intentions were. The fact that he was still alive led him to think that they were seeking a ransom or some kind of political concession, although neither prospect gave him much cause for optimism. His family was comfortable, but by no means wealthy and his value to Spain was nominal at best. Despite what status he enjoyed in Guatemala, he knew that in the grand scheme of things he was merely a minor diplomat. Why they'd chosen to target him in the first place he couldn't imagine. It wasn't as if he'd been outspoken or negligent in his duties. He might have turned a blind eye to certain corrupt business transactions in the past, but that was to be expected. Compared to many diplomats he knew, his hands were positively clean. But then the lawless monsters who'd abducted him probably didn't care one way or the other. To them he was in all probability just a pawn; a means to apply pressure on someone in order to force them to comply with their selfish demands.

As they marched along a stone flagged causeway, the Ambassador tried to get some idea of where he was being taken. All around him was the chirrup of insects, the hooting of exotic birds and the deep booming call of some fearsome sounding creature. Through the tiny holes in the hessian sack he sought to locate the position of the sun. The tiny shafts of light filtering through to his eyes told him that it was now directly above him, which meant that it was close to midday, but beyond that there was not much that he could determine. Over the next hour he tried to track its movement across the sky and he was still gazing upwards when everything suddenly went black and the temperature dropped sharply. All around was the echo of footsteps and the sound of dripping water.

The party came to a sudden halt and the Ambassador was shoved forwards. His heart lurched as the ground fell from beneath his feet, but hands were there to support him when he set foot on an unstable surface. The rocking motion, the sharp odour of fuel and the gentle lapping of water told him that he was now in a boat. He was unceremoniously pushed to a seating position and there was a whining rumble as an outboard engine stuttered into life. The boat rocked when others stepped aboard and the noise of the outboard reverberated deafeningly around the underground chamber as they began to move away. After a few minutes the engine was throttled back and there was a gentle bump as they came to a halt. The Ambassador was dragged to his feet, pulled from the boat and forced to walk over rocky ground. He was brought to a halt and heard the creaking squeal of metal hinges before being thrown forward, stumbling onto a cold hard floor. His hands were untied while he lay groaning on the ground and the sound of a key being turned in a lock was followed by footsteps receding into the distance. He clawed at the bindings of the hood until he'd pulled it free only to find himself in a cell hewn from solid rock and sealed by a heavy steel grill. By the yellow glow of a single light bulb, he inspected the meagre comfort of his surrounds. There was a simple wooden bed covered by a coarse blanket, a bowl of bananas, a bottle of water and a rudimentary latrine - a large clay pot standing in one corner. The Ambassador sat wearily on the side of the wooden bed, mumbled a short prayer, then put his head in his hands and sobbed.

YAL KU LAGOON, AKUMAL

Just a short ride north of the bay was Yal Ku lagoon and the shallow reefs which fed on the nutrient rich water that flowed from it on the falling tide. Owing to their favourable location, the reefs of Yal Ku were vibrant, diverse and well preserved, which made them one of the most popular dive sites in Akumal.

The CavePro launch slowed as it approached the mooring buoy and while the guests were busying themselves with their equipment, Mike leaned over the bow to secure the lines. That done, he turned to see the beaming face of Soon Yi, the pretty Japanese Divemaster who was guiding CavePro's guests that morning.

'Thank you Mike,' she trilled.

'Any time,' replied Mike.

'You diving with your friend?' she asked, glancing at Beth.

'Yeah. Don't worry about us. Me and Beth will be doing our own thing.'

'OK. No problem, you can go when you like. I don't think you need to hear my briefing.'

'I always enjoy them Soon Yi, but I think I'll pass just this once.'

'OK then,' she said smiling. 'Have a nice dive.'

'Thank you,' Beth said. 'You too.'

'Perfect,' said Mike. 'Let's kit up then.'

They donned their diving equipment and slipped into the warm Caribbean water, drifting gently down through shimmering ribbons of light towards the forest of fawn Elkhorn corals which lay below. The twisting, velvet limbs were patrolled by banded sergeant majors, yellow tangs, blue striped grunts and the ever-present butterfly fish, their delicate disc-like bodies painted with striking designs of silver, black and gold.

Tubular vase sponges, sprouting like organ pipes made perfect homes for spidery arrow crabs and slender trumpet fish hid motionless amongst finger-like sea rods. A honeycombed cowfish ambled into view, its bright markings, box-like shape and protruding horns giving it an inescapably comic appearance.

A queen angelfish made a sudden majestic appearance, displaying the vibrant blues, yellows and greens of its elegant disc-shaped body before turning and flitting haughtily away. There was a crunching sound as the powerful beak of a stoplight parrotfish scraped the surface of a beachball sized brain coral, filtering out the delicate polyps before evacuating the inedible limestone understructure through its gills. The powdery substance would eventually make its way to shore to help form the stunning white beaches for which the Yucatan is famous.

After making a circuit of the elongated reef, Mike led Beth into its interior, through the maze of natural vents which had formed beneath. The antennae of scores of spiny lobster twitched nervously as they backed into their lairs, sensing the presence of a potential predator, while in the shade of dark recesses, orange striped squirrelfish huddled together, waiting for the fall of night when they would come out to reclaim the reef for their own.

A small moray eel peeped out from a hole in the coral, its jaws opening and closing as it fed oxygenated water over its gills. Mike glided gently past it and Beth followed him into a small channel which cut through the centre of the reef. About half way along it, resting on a bed of sand was a solitary 5 foot nurse shark which Mike gleefully pointed out to Beth. They slowly advanced to draw level with it and studied its striking golden eyes, much like those of a cat. Its body tensed as if to move away and sensing that it felt threatened, Beth and Mike decided to move on and leave it in peace.

They spent the rest of the dive searching the reef for shrimp, brightly coloured fireworms and the perfectly disguised and elusive seahorse. When their eyes tired of scouring the multitude of nooks, crevices, folds and fronds, which the living reef provided, they watched blue runner, silvery permit and pompano flash through the open water in tight formation.

With the cares of the world temporarily forgotten, Mike was in mischievous mood. He pulled off Beth's fins and swam away, refusing to let her have them back. When he finally relented, Beth tried to take her revenge by flooding his mask, but Mike saw it coming and gripped her wrist, pulling her sharply towards him. He wrapped his legs around her thighs, took the regulator from his mouth and offered to share it with her. When she accepted and pulled her own regulator free of her mouth, he kissed her full on the lips. It was a scintillating experience, heightened by the knowledge that there was an element of risk. Beth regained her regulator, drew Mike towards her, and pressed her hips against him, a mischievous look in her eyes. She was wearing only a rash vest and swimsuit and Mike a neoprene top and board shorts. The look which they exchanged, communicated their mutual desire. Mike glanced at his watch, checked both his and Beth's air supplies and then slowly swivelled around. They were completely alone in the water. He led her towards a reef which had a sandy depression in its centre and laid her down upon it. Working quickly, he deflated his buoyancy jacket, slipped it off and took up Beth's secondary regulator as he cast his SCUBA unit aside. Their eyes were feverish. Mike slipped off Beth's bikini bottom, stuffed it into a pocket and his board shorts soon followed. The first contact of their joining was electric. They trembled with a desire heightened by the risk of discovery, their movements urgent and unrelenting. For a second Mike caught sight of a grey angel fish staring at him in curiosity. He nursed a brief desire to laugh, but it passed as Beth began to flex her hips with greater urgency and soon his conscience of the outside world was blotted out. The fever within them approached its crescendo and their bodies began to stiffen. They pulled themselves deeper into an all consuming union, their heads swimming with the sensory ecstasy of a thousand glowing nerve impulses.

As the euphoria began to subside, Beth gradually released the powerful grip in which she held Mike's hands. Her eyes opened and her jaw relaxed, her lips slowly curling into a contented smile. Mike grinned back at her, his panting breath escaping from the vents of his regulator to form huge columns of rising bubbles. He reached for Beth's air gauge and saw that the needle had dipped into the red caution zone. Hardly surprising after the extra workload which they'd put on it. He showed it to Beth with a shrug and then quickly retrieved his cylinder. They executed a less than elegant underwater dance while dressing themselves and then hurried back to the boat. The skipper was waiting for them impatiently, the other guests having returned to the boat some time ago. He fired up the outboard and headed for shore at full speed.

'Did you have a good dive?' asked Soon Yi.

'Yes, it was quite...eventful,' said Mike, grinning.

'We saw a nurse shark,' said Beth flatly, firing a warning glance in Mike's direction.

'A nurse shark? Oh, that was lucky! Where you see it?'

'Just a little to the north, lying in a channel in the reef,' said Mike. 'She was a five footer I'd guess.'

'I went the other way,' sighed Soon Yi. 'No shark but we see nice eagle ray.' Her enthusiasm was reflected in the smiles of the other divers. 'Mike is always lucky with sharks,' she said with a resigned shrug.

'That's because he's very closely related to them,' said Beth.

Soon Yi and the other guests laughed.

When they reached the shore, Mike and Beth dropped their equipment off at the dive centre, grabbed a bite to eat and then jumped in Beth's hired Jeep.

Soon they were making their way south towards Tulúm with a salsa track pulsing through the speakers of the music system. Mike spotted a car on their tail, an old blue Buick with two grim faced passengers in the front, but tried not to pay it too much attention. He wasn't doing anything which might attract unwanted attention and if he was to give the impression that he'd abandoned his enquiries into Frank's death, he could do a lot worse than playing tourist for a few days.

By mid-afternoon they arrived on the outskirts of Tulúm and followed the signs for the ruined temple complex which gave the small town its name. As they skirted the coast, they caught glimpses of bone-white sand and limpid turquoise shallows between the palm thatched bars and cabañas which lined the beach head. The ruins were now up ahead of them, towering majestically above white limestone cliffs and Beth, who'd never set eyes on a Mayan temple before, was tense with excitement.

'What an awesome setting. The Maya sure knew how to make an impression. How old are those temples?'

'I think most of the Mayan structures are not much more than a thousand years old, but I'm no expert. To be honest, I've been living in the area for close to a year now and I've never actually visited this place.'

'You've never been here before?' asked Beth, astonished, 'but this place is unique.'

'Yeah, but only because of its location. By all accounts the temple complex itself is pretty tame compared with places like Uxmal, Palenque or Chichen Itza.'

'Well I'm a temple virgin, so it all looks pretty good to me.'

'I don't think you have quite the necessary credentials for that title,' teased Mike.

Beth elbowed him in the ribs.

'If you're not careful, you might get the credentials to become a temple Eunuch.'

They pulled into a parking lot, purchased tickets at a small booth and followed a footpath which led to the site entrance; a narrow gateway and tunnel which penetrated the five metre thick boundary wall. They emerged from the dark seclusion of the passageway into the brightness of a vast plateau, walled on three sides, with the cliff edge forming the fourth side of a rectangle. Beyond the cliff was a backdrop of shimmering blue and towering majestically above it, reaching towards the sky was *El Castillo*, the largest and most prominent of the temples in Tulúm.

'Oh wow!' said Beth awestruck.

'Oh wow indeed,' said Mike nodding. 'I guess that's *El Castillo* - The Castle, said Mike, looking at a site plan. 'Half temple, half fortress, it was once painted red and is believed to have acted as a marker for trading boats, helping them to locate a break in the shallow reef. It is now a hotel and casino with rooms for forty guests.'

'You're kidding me?' said Beth. She studied his face for a second and her eyes narrowed when she saw his lips curl into a smile.

'Wise guy!'

'Almost had you,' said Mike smugly.

Beth's attention turned towards an official guide who was about to address a small group of tourists.

'Hey come on; let's go and listen in,' she said.

'Do we have to?' protested Mike.

'Yes, I'd like a more reliable source of information.'

Mike rolled his eyes and followed reluctantly.

'The word Tulúm comes from the Yucatec Mayan word for wall or enclosure, but many scholars believe that the city's original name was

Zama, or Dawn,' the guide was saying. 'The city was established around 1200 A.D. to act as a sea port for Coba and by the fourteenth century it controlled coastal commerce from as far down the coast as Honduras. The site was chosen for its vantage point, its proximity to a natural break in the reef along with a small beach for landing and perhaps most importantly, a supply of fresh water from a small cenoté to the north. At the height of Tulúm's success there were around 600 people living here, but their houses were located outside the city walls since the interior was reserved for ceremonies and public functions. When the Spanish colonists arrived at the beginning of the sixteenth century the site was still occupied, but for reasons that we have yet to discover it was completely abandoned around seventy years later. Tulúm, like Coba was an important place of worship for the Mayan Descending God, or Diving God and we will see him depicted in several murals around the site, along with the more familiar rain god Chaac...'

'Did I hear correctly there?' said Mike, turning to Beth. 'Did he just say Diving God?'

'That's what it sounded like to me. What kind of diving do you think he does?'

'I dunno, but I doubt it's the kind I'm thinking of. I like the idea of a diving god though. I think I might be a convert.'

'Well perhaps you'll get a chance to worship him later.'

'...and now we will visit the Temple of the Frescoes,' the guide's voice continued in the background, 'once an important place of pilgrimage for Mayan women.'

'I think we'll pass on that until it's a bit quieter,' said Beth. 'Where next?'

'How about we climb *El Castillo* and check out the view from the top?'

'OK, let's do it. I could do with a workout.'

They crossed the main plaza and climbed the seven metre high stepped pyramid which supported the temple and altar above. When they reached the high platform, they turned to admire the view of the complex below.

'Wow. Just imagine what this place must have looked like when it was still occupied,' said Beth.

'Pretty amazing I would've thought. Especially with all those buildings painted in their original colours.'

'They were all painted?'

'Apparently so.'

Beth walked towards a small altar and ran the tips of her fingers over it.

'I wonder what went on up here back then. Do you think they might have sacrificed anyone on this thing?'

'Without a shadow of a doubt,' replied Mike. 'Human sacrifice was a way of life for them. I would imagine that hundreds of people, men, women and children died on that altar over the years.'

Beth winced and pulled her hand away.

'It's hard to believe that a race so advanced and intelligent could resort to such pointless butchery.'

'For them it wasn't pointless. They were offering up something of value in order to win the favour of their gods. It not exactly a unique idea. After all Abraham was prepared to sacrifice his son to demonstrate his faith. There are examples of sacrifice in all religions, it just that we don't see it as such. Monks sacrifice their freedom, ascetics deprive themselves of basic comfort, puritans forego luxuries and of course there are events like Lent and Ramadan.'

'You can't really compare human sacrifice to Lent Mike.'

'It's an extreme, sure, but the same principle applies. Besides, if you want to talk about butchery, were we Europeans really any better when we first arrived here, slaying the Indians and justifying it by claiming they had no soul?'

'I don't know. But can we talk about something else now?'

'Of course we can,' said Mike, breaking into a smile. He wrapped his arm around her and let his eyes trace the surf washed shoreline to the south.

'Great views of the coast from up here.'

'Yeah, it's stunning isn't it? If this place really was converted into a hotel, it would make a killing.'

Mike gave her a sideways glance.

'Hopefully, not in the literal sense,' he said.

Beth rolled her eyes. She pushed away from him and stepped back to admire the temple portico, supported by four stone pillars.

'I think this entrance would be a bit too Las Vegas though, don't you think?'

Mike followed her gaze towards the pillared portico and for the first time noticed the three niches that were cut into the stone fascia above it. Each of them housed a striking carving and when Mike's eyes fell on the central panel, he suddenly went rigid.

'Holy shit!' he said, his eyes widening.

'What's wrong?'

Mike shook his finger at the central panel, his mind racing.

'This image. I've seen it before,' he said, his eyes glued to the bas-relief carving of an upturned deity with its arms looping down below its head. 'Do you think it could be the Diving God?'

'I've no idea,' replied Beth. 'Why? Is it important?'

'Very!'

Bewildered, Beth pulled out the information she'd been given at the ticket office and began to leaf through it. After a moment she shook her head.

'There are no illustrations in here Mike, but the Temple of the Descending God is just over there if you want to check,' she said pointing.

'OK, let's go!'

Beth was left speechless as Mike strode towards the edge of the platform and began to scamper down the steep flight of steps.

'You could at least wait!' she called after him.

Mike slowed, but didn't turn around until he reached the foot of the pyramid.

'What's the rush?' asked Beth, struggling to catch her breath.

'I'll tell you when we get there.'

He grabbed Beth by the arm and took off in the direction of a small temple built on a raised platform, almost a miniature version of *El Castillo*. The approach took them past a series of stone pillars and ended in a short flight of steps that had been carved directly into the plinth. Before they reached the foot of the steps they could clearly see the sculpted niche that adorned the stone fascia above the temple entrance. It housed the same inverted figure.

'It's the Diving God alright,' said Mike, biting his thumb nail.

'So are you going to share the relevance of this life-changing discovery with me? Or do I just continue to stare at you like some dumb understudy?'

'It's the image which I saw carved into the wall of the submerged cave system Beth; the one that Frank made a sketch of.'

'Are you sure?' said Beth, frowning.

'I'm absolutely certain.'

'Do you think it dates from the same period? I mean, there was obviously some kind of theme going on in the area back then.'

'I can only say what I think... and for me it's genuine. How it got there, I have no idea. It's a mystery, like everything else surrounding those caves.'

'Well maybe we can at least find out a little more about this skinny-dipping god. Look, there's an information plaque right here. How's your Spanish coming along?'

'I can read the first bit. *Templo del Dios Descendente* – Temple of the Descending God.'

'Outstanding!' said Beth, raising her eyebrows. 'It's just as well I spent several months studying whale migration patterns in Baja California. Let's see now...it says that the Descending God or Diving God appears to have been an important figure of worship in Tulúm and is associated with *Zenial* passages – what are those?'

'Something to do with the position of the sun I think.'

'OK...and he is the primordial god of Maize who watches over the harvest. He is often pictured sailing his maize canoe along the Milky Way on his trip to...Xibalba, the underworld, realm of the rain god Chaac.'

'Is that all it says?'

'I'm afraid so.'

'Hmm, that doesn't advance me a great deal. If he was the primordial god of the coca plant there might be some sense in it, but apart from the fact that he seems to like diving and hanging out with rain gods in the underworld, I can't see any connection to what happened to Frank.'

'Maybe, but it does tell us that the cave system he found is extraordinary and if I know one thing about you Mike, it's that you won't be able to rest until you've explored it properly.'

'You're not wrong Beth, but I can certainly hold back until you've left.'

'I'm not sure I want that. I'm pretty curious myself now...and besides, do you think I could possibly enjoy the rest of my holiday when I know that each time you put your arms around me, you'll be thinking more about those damned caves than you are about me?'

Mike scratched his chin and stared up at *El Castillo*.

'I guess I could go there early in the morning, then at least we'd have the afternoon together.'

Beth stared at him blankly.

'I wasn't suggesting you go alone Mike.'

'What? You mean you want to come along? After all that I've told you?'

'I can look after myself. Besides, you need a car and you need someone to help you; someone who's familiar with diving equipment.'

'No way Beth. I can't put you through that. I couldn't live with myself if anything happened to you.'

'Judging by what you've told me, if anything did happen to me, you wouldn't have too long to live anyway.'

Mike breathed a sigh of exasperation.

'Look, even if I agreed, there's no way I could leave you alone in the jungle while I'm exploring the cave. I wouldn't be able to concentrate properly with that weight of responsibility on my mind.'

'Then bring someone else along.'

'That's not so easy Beth. You have to understand that anyone who gets involved in this business runs the risk of being persecuted, and perhaps even killed.'

'So why don't you get your professor to come along since he's already involved up to his neck.'

'Fabrizio?' snorted Mike. 'He'd *never* agree to it. Not after what he went through the last time.'

'And if he did, would you go along with it?'

Mike tried to read Beth's eyes through the dark lenses of her shades.

'He wouldn't.'

'Then you've nothing to lose.'

'Christ you're stubborn!'

'So do we have a deal?'

'I-I suppose so.'

'Right. Where can we find him?'

* * * *

'You're never going to believe this, but it looks as if the whole damn church has been relocated at some point.'

'How'd you figure that?' said Rafael.

'I checked the aerial photographs after examining the ruins outside,' said Dan. 'There's a piece of land beside what used to be the plantation owner's house which bears the marks of foundations. Seen from above the size and layout of them are identical to those of the church.'

'So what does that prove? Only that there was once a similar sized building there.'

202

'A building with empty tombs inside it?' countered Dan.

'Empty tombs?' Rafael said, his eyes narrowing. 'What kind of tombs?'

'The kind that someone might have buried a wealthy Spanish family in.'

'You sure you didn't just stumble across an abandoned graveyard?'

'Don't listen to him Rod,' said Zach. 'He's been smoking them funky Indian herbs again. Next minute he'll be telling you we've consecrated a sacred burial ground and the undead are gonna come eat our brains out.'

'That wouldn't surprise me,' added Spicer. 'This place spooks me out plenty.'

'It's not a graveyard,' said Dan, ignoring their comments. 'The tombs were carefully positioned in relation to the original perimeter of the building and besides, none of them have headstones.'

'So are there any names or inscriptions on these tombs?'

'Yeah, a curse on those who disturb the sleep of the undead,' sniggered Zach.

'Quiet Zach!' hissed Rafael.

Zach muttered under his breath.

'There was wording on a few of the stone fragments,' said Dan, 'but the letters were badly weathered and close to being unreadable.'

'So the church must have been moved some time ago.'

'Oh yeah, we're talking centuries; probably not too long after the house was abandoned.'

'But why would anyone go to such pains to take the church down brick by brick and rebuild it just a few hundred yards away?'

'Who knows? Maybe the villagers converted to Christianity, but couldn't stand the idea of sharing their church with a family who'd exploited them.'

'I don't buy it,' said Rafael, shaking his head. 'The only reason I can see for moving a church is that the new site offers some kind of advantage over the old one.'

'Such as?'

'Well, it might have been of some spiritual significance, or maybe it offered a physical advantage of some sort.'

'Like the concealed chamber you think lies beneath it?'

'It's not such a far fetched idea Dan. In the past monks built underground passageways beneath churches and cathedrals in order to escape capture and persecution by their enemies. Maybe these guys did the same.'

'Yeah, but the difference is that monks built them beneath existing churches. It would make no sense to build the passageway before the church.'

'What if it was already in place,' countered Rafael.

'Then that would make a little more sense,' agreed Dan, 'but the advantages would have to be huge to convince me that it would merit the resiting of an existing church over it.'

'As were going for unlikely scenarios, can I offer an opinion?' asked Zach.

'No!' said Rafael, with a withering stare.

'OK,' said Zach with a shrug. 'Have it your way...but if you'd seen that movie about space ants you'd...'

'Just shut it!' said Rafael, his eyes burning with a dangerous calm. He turned, staring pensively at the crumbling walls and then suddenly noticed that the secure satellite phone had begun to flash. He reached over to answer it and with a warning glare aimed at Zach and Spicer, switched to speaking in clipped professional tones. The message he received was short, to the point, and when it ended left him with a deep frown of concern.

'What is it Rod?' asked Dan, sensing his unease.

'Intelligence. This has just turned into a hostage crisis. The terrorists are holding a Spanish diplomat under threat of execution.'

'No shit!' blurted Spicer.

'What are our orders?' asked Dan.

'They want us to go in.'

* * * *

Mike entered the Dolce Vita arm in arm with Beth, amused to see covetous male eyes admiring her figure beneath a stunning black chiffon dress before giving Mike, dressed in the smartest surf pants and collared shirt he owned, a cursory and somewhat bemused glance.

They paused in the foyer until Claudio, noticing their arrival, rushed over to greet them, arms outstretched and beaming from ear to ear.

'Mike, it's so good to see you again...and with such exquisite company,' he said with an admiring glance at Beth. 'May I ask your name *senorina*?'

'Beth Draper,' said Beth, stretching out a hand. Claudio clasped it and kept a gentle grip on it.

'It is a pleasure to have you in my restaurant Beth. My name is Claudio.'

'It's very nice to meet you Claudio,' said Beth, delicately prising her hand free.

'I presume you wish to dine?'

'If it's no trouble,' said Mike.

'Not at all,' said Claudio, shaking his head. 'The only problem is that I am a little short on tables. You would have to wait a while...unless of course, you don't mind to share with Fabrizio over there by the window?'

'Is he a friend of yours Mike?' Beth asked, her face a picture of innocence.

'Yes...at least he was the last time I spoke to him.'

'Good. Then I'd like to meet him.'

'*Perfetto.* I'll speak to him right away,' said Claudio.

'So far, so good, whispered Beth, as they watched Claudio pick his way through the crowded tables. Shortly afterwards Mike saw Fabrizio rise above a sea of heads and beckon them over. Claudio returned to guide them through the throng, fussing over Beth as if she was a dignitary. When they had all been introduced and seated, Fabrizio ordered a bottle of Prosecco and Claudio went to prepare it.

'So where did you meet such a beautiful lady?' asked Fabrizio, glancing at Beth, whose cheeks instantly flushed pink.

'Oh, we did a course in shark acupuncture together.'

'I'm sorry?'

'Ignore him. He's just trying to be smart,' said Beth. 'I was part of a team that was gathering information on the migratory patterns of whale sharks in the area. Mike joined up with us to help implant the tracking tags.'

'So you're a research scientist?' asked Fabrizio, impressed.

'I was a volunteer for that particular project. I'm actually a lecturer in marine biology at the Scripps Institute of Oceanography in San Diego.'

'Then we share a similar passion,' said Fabrizio beaming, 'although my field is perhaps not as exciting as yours.'

'Why? What do you study?'

'I'm a Botanist. I work for a pharmaceutical company, sourcing rare plants to help in the fight against disease.'

'That sounds very interesting...and I would imagine very rewarding too.'

'It is,' nodded Fabrizio, 'but it is also rather a solitary existence. To find plants which are not yet known to medical science, it is necessary to travel to remote and sometimes inhospitable places.'

'I can vouch for that,' said Mike, raising his eyebrows.

'I suppose that's the price we scientists must pay for our insatiable curiosity,' said Beth.

'Yes, you're probably right,' agreed Fabrizio, with a wry smile.

Claudio arrived with an ice bucket at that moment and filled their tall glasses with sparkling *Prosecco*. Beth restricted herself to a half glass.

'*Salute!* Good health!' said Fabrizio.

'*Salute!*' echoed Mike and Beth, raising their glasses. They took a sip and gave the *Prosecco* their full approval.

'So have you found anything interesting here in the Yucatan Fabrizio?' asked Beth.

'Ees a little early to tell right now,' Fabrizio replied, rolling the stem of the glass between his fingers. 'Once an active chemical has been identified and extracted from a plant source, it can take weeks, months or even years to develop and find a commercial use for it. And if the following drug trials are inconclusive, it might still be dropped altogether.'

'Gosh. It's no wonder these new drugs can be so expensive.'

'Yes, there are sometimes considerable development costs involved,' agreed Fabrizio, 'but of course there are also enormous profits to be made when things go well.'

'Yes I'm sure there are.'

'Actually, now I think about it, there was one unusual plant I found on this trip,' said Fabrizio, 'although I'm almost certain that it has no medicinal properties. Mike saw it too. It's a type of *Manihot Esculenta*; a hybrid cassava plant that contains very high levels of toxins.'

'Yeah, I wouldn't count on that earning you the Nobel prize,' chuckled Mike.

'Don't be so sure Mike. Toxins can have beneficial properties too,' said Beth. 'After all, digitalis is a deadly poison found in the common foxglove and yet for many years it has been successfully used in the treatment of heart failure.'

'That's absolutely true,' said Fabrizio beaming. 'And remember the curare Mike.'

'OK, I'm obviously out of my depth here,' said Mike, crossing his arms sulkily. 'You two just carry on your intellectual conversation in private and I'll sit here and read the menu or something.'

'Don't be so touchy Mike,' said Beth, squeezing his knee affectionately. 'You're very smart and your contribution is much appreciated.'

'Absolutely!' agreed Fabrizio.

Claudio arrived at that moment, his face flushed from the heat of the kitchen. He carefully placed a dark chocolate torte in front of Fabrizio and then turned to face Mike and Beth.

'So, are you ready to order?' he asked, clasping his hands together.

'Oh! I'm afraid I haven't had time to look at the menu yet,' said Beth, biting her lip. 'Could you perhaps recommend something?'

'Well, tonight's special is *Pollo Vesuvio*; breast of chicken topped with a garlic and tomato sauce, mozzarella and asparagus tips,' said Claudio, with purring enthusiasm.

'Sounds wonderful. I'll have that.'

'Very good. Mike?'

'I'll go for something simple...a seafood pizza.'

'*Una pizza ai frutti di mare. Perfetto!*'

'And a bottle of Pinot Grigio,' Mike added.

'Of course,' said Claudio, inclining his head graciously before taking his leave.

Fabrizio stared at his dessert and spread his hands apologetically.

'I'm sorry, I ordered this before you arrived.'

'Please go ahead and eat,' said Beth. 'I know I wouldn't hesitate if someone placed that before me.'

'Would you like to try?' he asked.

'No thank you, but it's a very kind offer.'

Fabrizio nodded and self-consciously dipped his spoon into the light chocolate fondant.

'How long have you been here in Mexico Beth?' he asked.

'Oh, I flew in just a couple of days ago, but I've been to Mexico many times before; mostly the west coast. I live in San Diego, which is just a stone's throw from Tijuana on the border.'

'Yes, I know the area well. I spent some time collecting succulents in the Sonoran Desert, but I much prefer to be here in the Yucatan.'

'I can understand why,' said Beth. 'At least you get some shade down this way.'

'And good food,' said Fabrizio, savouring the last spoonful of his torte.

'If you like good food, you'd love San Diego. We have hundreds of different restaurants from all over the world and some of the best seafood on the coast.'

'Then perhaps I should come and visit sometime.'

'You won't regret it.'

'All this talk of food is making me hungry,' said Mike, reaching for a breadstick.

'Don't spoil your appetite,' teased Beth.

Claudio appeared with the Pinot Grigio, pulled the cork and poured a measure into Beth's glass. She took a sip and declared it delicious, much to Claudio's satisfaction.

'Your order will be ready in just a couple of minutes,' he announced while filling all three glasses.

'*Grazie Claudio,*' said Mike, pleased with his new found command of the Italian language.

'*Si, grazie mille,*' added Beth, not to be outdone.

'*Prego,*' replied Claudio, inclining his head before excusing himself and returning to the kitchen.

'So what are your plans for the next few days?' asked Fabrizio, staring between Mike and Beth.

'Well, we haven't quite decided yet,' said Beth. 'We did a dive on the reef in Akumal today and then Mike took me to see the ruins of the temple in Tulúm.'

'Oh yes, it's a beautiful place isn't it?'

'It certainly is,' agreed Beth. 'Tulúm is the first Mayan temple complex I've seen and I thought it was incredible, but Mike tells me the ones in Uxmal are even better.'

'Yes, there are some magnificent Mayan temples here in the Yucatan,' agreed Fabrizio, 'and also in Guatemala and Honduras.'

'So much to see and so little time,' sighed Beth.

'Very true,' agreed Fabrizio, with a shrug.

'But tomorrow should be incredibly exciting too because Mike has promised to take me to a very special place; one that very few people have seen.'

'Oh? Where is that?'

'What's the name of the place again Mike?'

Mike glanced at Beth and steeled himself.

'We're going to Yalché...to dive the cave.'

'W-What?' spluttered Fabrizio, nearly choking on his wine. *'Che cazzo vuoi Mike? Sei scemo?'* he shouted, unable to contain his anger. You want to get her killed? You must be crazy! Kill yourself if you have to, but don't take other people with you.'

'Actually, it was my idea,' said Beth calmly. 'Mike tried to talk me out of it, but I insisted.'

Fabrizio stared from one to the other as if he was sharing his table with a pair of lunatics.

'Did Mike tell you what happened to us when we were there the last time?'

'Yes, and I imagine it must have been very harrowing for you. Obviously there's a risk involved. This is not something I would enter into lightly, but I have good reason to believe that Mike is on the verge of discovering something extraordinary and I'd like to be a part of it.'

'And you would risk your life for that?' asked Fabrizio, exasperated.

'Today we found out that the carving which Mike discovered in the submerged cave is a representation of the Descending God,' explained Beth, 'a deity which has been revered in this area for centuries. If the image in the cave dates from the same time as those decorating the temples in Tulúm, as the evidence suggests, then we are talking about a major historical find and in my opinion, that's worth a risk or two. As for my own safety, a lot of my field work involves an element of danger, but I know from experience that when proper precautions are taken, it becomes manageable.'

'Manageable!' shouted Fabrizio, almost beside himself. 'Our friend

Frank was killed there...tortured and butchered. Mike and I were thrown into a pit and left for dead. What do you think they will do to you?'

'I don't know, but if you're so concerned for my safety, why don't you come along with us?'

'Come with you! Not in a thousand years!' he said shaking his head. He scowled, turning suddenly towards Mike. 'Is this your idea of a joke?'

'Steady on,' said Mike, raising his hands in an attempt to bring calm.

'I hate to admit this Mike, but you were right' said Beth. 'He's obviously too afraid to go back. Let's do this alone.'

Mike watched Fabrizio's reddened face contort as anger, shame, guilt and exasperation fought simultaneously for expression.

'Hey, why all the noise?' demanded Claudio, arriving at the table with Mike and Beth's order. 'Are you trying to scare away all my clients?'

'We're really sorry about this Claudio,' said Beth. 'We had a slight difference of opinion.'

'You know what these two lunatics want to do?' said Fabrizio, throwing up his arms in exasperation.

'No,' replied Claudio, 'but whatever it is, I hope they do it away from my restaurant.'

Fabrizio's jaw muscles trembled as he glanced in turn at Mike and Beth. He beckoned Claudio over and launched into a staccato tirade of Italian. When he'd finally purged all the anger which had welled up inside him, he slumped back into his chair, slowly shaking his head. Claudio nodded, whistled and studied Mike and Beth carefully.

'I'm afraid that in this case I have to agree with Fabrizio. You're obviously both very courageous, no doubt about that, but Mike, surely you must realise that you cannot leave Beth out there in the jungle on her own, especially after all that has happened.'

'It was never my intention. In fact I'd feel a lot more comfortable if Beth wasn't coming at all...but she insists.'

'Damned right I do!'

'As you see,' said Mike, spreading his hands. 'I only agreed to go along with this on the condition that Beth could convince Fabrizio to come along with us.'

'So this was all planned!' said Fabrizio, outraged.

'Wait...wait!' said Claudio, holding up his hand. 'Why Fabrizio? Why not someone else?'

'Because Fabrizio knows the area...and right at this moment, present company excepted, he's about the only person I can trust.'

Claudio nodded pensively and then turned towards Fabrizio. There was a rapid exchange between them, accompanied by flapping arms and red faces. Finally Fabrizio sighed and rested his head in his hands.'

'*D'accordo!*' said Claudio, calmly turning towards Mike and Beth. 'So Fabrizio has agreed to go with you on one small condition.'

'Seriously?' said Mike, amazed.

'What's the condition?' asked Beth, her eyes narrowing.

Claudio shrugged and broke into a smile.

'I come along too.'

SEVILLE, SPAIN

The Prime Minister swirled the ruby red Rioja around the Bordeaux Glass that was engraved with his initials, a gift from the President of France. It was a Gran Reserva, one of his favourites and although it was to his entire satisfaction, it did little to lift the melancholic mood which had settled over him.

He leaned back into a rattan armchair on the first floor balcony of his private residence and studied the neat parallel lines which had been expertly mown into the lawn below. The sound of the gentle trickle of water drifted to his ears from the ornamental fountain that lay at its centre, the arcing jets glowing gold under the rays of a setting sun. He lifted the Bordeaux glass from his rotund stomach and let out a curse when he saw a ruby red stain, spreading into the white cotton of his shirt.

'Oh Jorge! What is wrong with you tonight?' scalded his wife. 'You've been in a strange mood ever since you came home.'

The Prime Minister posed his glass on a small marble topped table, patted his shirt with a napkin and let out a heavy sigh.

'There are problems at work,' he replied, evasively.

'There are always problems at work, but you don't have to bring them home with you.'

'I don't always have people dying in the streets.'

'Oh that again!' said his wife wearily. 'Well it's not exactly your fault is it...and I'm sure that you've done everything that can possibly be expected of you.'

'Have I?'

'Well, what else could you do?'

'In reality there's nothing I can do; my hands are tied, but if I could, I would order the ransom to be paid.'

'So that those murdering thieves can live a life of luxury while they plan their next attack?'

'No, so that I could save the lives of innocent people.'

'But they're not innocent people. They broke the law.'

'Drug use is not an offence which merits capital punishment...and besides, I wasn't thinking about those people.'

'Who then?'

'The Ambassador and his family.'

'Do you know him?

'If you remember, we were introduced to Señor Perez and his wife at the international trade convention we attended last year.'

'Oh yes, now let me see. Wasn't his wife that charming lady from Barcelona who wore the beautiful gold and emerald necklace?'

'Yes...I believe she was. Charming couple. Excellent credentials. You may remember that they have a young daughter who was just starting school.'

The Prime Ministers wife frowned and shook her head.

'The poor woman. Can you imagine what she must be going through?'

'Yes. Unfortunately I can.'

'Isn't there anything that you can do to help Jorge?'

'Apart from paying the ransom?'

'I don't know. Can't you broker some kind of deal?'

'I wish I could, but we have no way of contacting these people. In fact we still don't have any clear idea who they are.'

'Didn't you say the Americans were working on it?'

'Their Intelligence services are closing in,' the Prime Minister said nodding, 'but, it will be a miracle if there's a breakthrough before tomorrow's deadline.'

'Do you think there's any chance that the kidnappers will see reason and release the Ambassador unharmed?'

The Prime Minister frowned and shook his head sadly.

'I'm afraid that the people we're dealing with do not share the same moral values as us.'

'Then all we can do is pray.'

*　*　*　*

Mike groaned, lifted an eyelid and reached over to silence his alarm clock. Beth's arm hooked around his chest and drew him back towards her. He turned and kissed her forehead, tempted to melt into the warmth of her embrace, but there was a busy day ahead. He yawned, propped himself up on an elbow and peeled back the curtains. Streaks of crimson were creeping across the sinuous morning clouds. He stretched and threw back the sheets.

'Time to get up,' he said, shaking Beth's shoulder.

'Already?' Beth replied, yawning and rubbing her eyes, 'so much for the relaxing holiday.'

'You can still back out if you want to. No one's forcing you to come along.'

'Let's not start that again. I'm on the team. End of story.'

'OK,' said Mike. 'So lets not keep *the team* waiting.'

In the cramped confines of the small room, they quickly dressed in sweaters and jeans, pulled on training shoes and were soon stepping out into the cool morning air. Beth drove Mike to within a few hundred yards of CavePro, dropped him off and then parked at the rear as they'd agreed the night before. Chicho was waiting in the dive shop when Mike stepped through the door.

'Hey Chicho, sorry to get you up early buddy, but I've got a special expedition planned.'

'Did you OK this with Ken?'

'Yeah, of course. He said it was fine as long as you were OK with it.'

'No Problem Mike,' said Chicho with a shrug. 'Where's your car?'

'Er, it's out back. I'm going over the wall again.'

'Why don't you just go out the front like everyone else?'

'I could tell you, but then I'd have to kill you.'

Chicho gave him a strange look.

'It's just a joke Chicho. It was meant to be anyway. Look, just give me a hand to get my equipment and three cylinders over the wall and then you'll be forty pesos richer and I'll be out of your hair. OK?'

'OK Mike, go get your gear. The cylinders are ready.'

Mike filled a sturdy canvas holdall from his locker, threaded his arms through the straps then went to the compressor room to collect the cylinders. When he was ready to leave, Chicho opened the back door and helped him to lift the equipment over the wall.'

'Thanks bud. Don't spend this all on junk,' said Mike, slipping Chicho two twenty peso notes.

'I won't,' replied Chicho, watching Mike disappear from view.

After a short pause, he pulled out a mobile phone, dialled the number which he'd been given and began to speak in rapid, hushed tones of Mayat'an.

* * * *

'So far, so good,' said Mike, staring out of the rear window of Beth's Jeep.

'Where are we supposed to be meeting the others?' asked Beth.

"Not too far away. Just keep going straight and I'll tell you when to turn.'

Mike stared out of the window as a blood red sun crept above the eastern horizon, its reflection like a fiery path reaching towards him across the sea. As he watched it, he thought of Tulúm, City of Light, City of the Dawn, where that same spectacular sight had been observed for centuries. The Descending God, he now understood, represented the rays of the sun, falling to earth and powering the cycle of life and death, driving forward the weather and the ocean currents and marking the changes of the seasons. To the ancient Maya it was the manifestation of an untouchable and incomprehensible power that existed in a world oblivious to the passage of time.

Mike pulled his eyes away when a familiar gas station cum diner flashed past.

'Slow down Beth, our turning is just ahead on the left,' he said. 'We're looking for a sign directing us towards the Hotel Palmeira.'

Beth squinted, peering into the distance.

'Is that it?' she asked, as a grey and white panel came into view.

'Yeah, that's the one,' said Mike, spinning around to check the road behind.

Beth slowed and turned into the hotel drive. After a few hundred yards, Mike directed her onto a track which forked off to the right and soon afterwards they arrived at a maintenance area where a black Dodge truck was waiting for them. Inside it, the faces of Claudio and Fabrizio stared back at them.

'*Buongiorno!* You're right on time,' said Claudio, leaning out of the

217

window and glancing at his wristwatch. 'Did anyone follow you?'

'No, I was checking all the way. The road behind was clear.'

'Good. Throw your equipment in the back and climb in.'

'OK.'

Mike transferred the bags to the Dodge while Beth parked the Jeep out of the way. When she returned, they installed themselves behind Claudio and Fabrizio.

'Everyone ready?' asked Claudio.

'We were born ready,' said Beth.

'Good. Then let's go and have some fun.'

Mike and Beth exchanged nervous glances. Fabrizio shook his head wearily.

'So how long were you in the army for Claudio?' asked Beth.

'Too long. About seven years in all.'

'Where were you based?'

'Most of the time we were in Northern Italy, training in the mountains, but we also did some jungle training in the Congo and a few desert operations in Sudan.'

'That's where the sun sent him a little crazy,' said Fabrizio, tapping his temple with his forefinger.

'Oh no!' said Claudio, shaking his head. 'It happened long before then.'

They all laughed.

'Were you involved in any serious conflicts?' asked Mike.

We were sent to Kosovo for a while, but all we did was show our faces and keep our heads low. Nobody wanted to get mixed up in that madness; not even me!'

'I can imagine,' said Mike. 'Well it's still reassuring to know that we have a man of your experience along with us.'

'It's been a long time,' said Claudio with a shrug, 'but I still remember one or two things.'

'Let's hope you don't have to put those skills into practice,' said Beth.

'Yes, let's hope that,' agreed Fabrizio.

They entered the highway and joined the heavy traffic moving south. Mike and Beth swapped amused glances as they listened to the constant bickering and animated conversation of Claudio and Fabrizio in the front.

Once they'd they left the highway and turned north towards Coba, Mike began to notice familiar features in the passing landscape. Small hamlets and farming communities flashed past in a whirr of shapes and colours that broke the monotony of the dull grey-green of the dry forest. After a while Mike spotted the place from which they'd hitched a ride back to Akumal and heard Fabrizio instructing Claudio to slow down and make the turn. The Dodge bounced as it pulled over onto the dirt track, clouds of dust spewing from the wheels as it plunged into the forest. Mike noticed that Fabrizio had gone quiet and it was not long before he began to share his unease. Beth slipped her hand into his and he held it firmly, hiding his misgivings behind a reassuring smile.

The track continued to rise and fall, the engine whining as the wide tyres of the Dodge climbed over rutted earth, rocks and roots. Finally they caught glimpses of the escarpment through the trees and entered the clearing which Mike and Fabrizio had used as a base during their previous visit. After scrutinising the area carefully, Claudio instructed everyone to get out of the car and unload the gear. When they'd done so, he drove the Dodge straight into a clump of giant ferns, threw a camouflage net over it and chained the rear axle to the trunk of a large dogwood tree. To make absolutely certain that it was going nowhere, he removed the starter leads and hid them inside the car.

'That should make things difficult for anyone who thinks of stealing it,' he said, satisfied with his work.

'Yes, we should have no problem now,' said Fabrizio, 'unless you lose your keys again,'

Claudio rolled his eyes.

'Who needs a wife when you have someone like Fabrizio huh?' he said,

219

to Mike and Beth's amusement. 'OK, time for a little talk. I don't think anybody saw us coming here, but we should behave as if they did. We'll keep talking to a minimum, move carefully and try to stay out of sight. Mike, do you remember the way to the caves?'

'Yes, I can find them.'

'Good. So this is how we'll do it. We'll be advancing as a unit, five to ten metres apart keeping low to the ground. I'll be scouting ahead and you'll be behind me giving directions Mike. Beth will be next and then Fabrizio will take up the rear. No voices; hand signals only. Left or right for turns, hand raised for ahead, flat palm for wait. 'OK?'

'What about my gear?'

'We'll transport it between us. I'm afraid you'll have to take most of it yourself though Mike because Fabrizio and I need to stay light. Can you carry the cylinders on your back?'

'I think I can handle them, if you could take the sling Beth?'

'No problem,' she replied.

'Good,' said Claudio, 'then we should make a start.'

Mike and Beth drank their fill of water, strapped on their equipment and followed Claudio and Fabrizio towards the start of the trail. They fell into formation and cautiously entered the cool humidity of the jungle, Claudio forging ahead under Mike's guidance, hunched over and advancing a few metres at a time. Moving in absolute silence, every whoop, chirrup, whistle and squeal that reached their ears seemed to be amplified a hundred times. The sweat was soon trickling down Mike's face and soaking into his shirt collar attracting the attention of a cloud of buzzing insects. He turned at regular intervals, checking on Beth to make sure that she was keeping pace. He could see that she was struggling with the extra weight of the equipment, but she never fell far behind and Mike felt a glowing admiration for her resilience.

After a while they approached the site of the cassava plot and as Mike drew level with it he was surprised to see that it had been stripped bare.

The square of tilled earth looked like an open wound set amongst such lush surroundings, but tender green shoots pushing through the soil were a sign that the jungle had already moved in to reclaim it.

He looked up when he felt Claudio's eyes on him and when he was urged to keep moving, he steeled himself against the dull ache in his thighs. A few hundred yards further down the trail they came within sight of the base of the escarpment and Claudio permitted them a brief reprieve behind the shelter of a fallen ceiba. Once they'd quenched their thirsts, Fabrizio pointed Claudio in the direction of the submerged cave and after a brief consultation they were moving again, following the sinuous trail like foraging ants.

Nerves were tense as they drew closer to their objective and when a startled pig-like peccary left its refuge and shot away across the leaf litter, Mike was surprised to see that Claudio had drawn a gun. Instinctively, he turned to check on Beth and as he did so he saw that Fabrizio was similarly armed. The sight might have been reassuring under the circumstances, but Mike's only thought was of what would happen if he and Beth were caught in an exchange of fire, unprotected and hopelessly exposed. When his and Beth's eyes locked, he tried to play down the danger with a show of bravado, shrugging and winking as if it was all just an amusing escapade.

With a last searching inspection of the surrounding vegetation, Claudio holstered the gun and gave the signal to move on. They followed the game trail diagonally towards the base of the escarpment and finally caught sight of the waterhole which marked the entrance to the cave. To avoid exposing their presence, Claudio led them away into the cover of trees where he searched for a place to set up a hideout. He found a hollow in the centre of a large patch of garabato and while he and Fabrizio scouted the surrounding area, Mike used its cover to set up his equipment. With Beth's help it went quickly and Mike was soon pulling on a short wetsuit and running through his pre-dive checks. Once he'd satisfied himself that everything was functioning perfectly, he strapped himself into the cylinder harness and rose to his feet. With a flashlight and two dive computers strapped to his wrists, a small emergency nitrox cylinder attached to his thigh and a back up light, compass and cave reel clipped to his harness, Mike felt ready to face every eventuality. Claudio and Fabrizio returned just as Beth was handing him his mask and fins.

'It's all clear,' said Claudio, keeping his voice low. 'Are you ready?'

'As ready as I'll ever be.'

Claudio nodded pensively.

'I wish I was going in there with you.'

'Are you cave certified?' asked Mike.

'Not really. I did some diving in caves in Sicily with my brother when I was young. It was a lot of fun, but I suppose that we didn't really know what we were doing.'

'Sounds like a good way to get yourself killed.'

'There were no rules then. I guess it was dangerous, but we survived.'

'Well I'm afraid that luck won't get you very far in these caves Claudio. One mistake in there and you won't get a second chance.'

'Well maybe one day you can teach me the right way to do it.'

'Sure, but it will cost you a lot of pasta.'

Claudio grinned.

'I'm sure that could be arranged.'

'Can you both stop talking now?' interrupted Fabrizio. 'I'd like to get this over with as quickly as possible so we can get out of here.'

'Where's your sense of adventure?' teased Claudio.

'Adventure? I left it in the bottom of a damned cenoté!'

'It's OK Fabrizio,' said Mike, reassuringly, 'I'm going.'

Beth gave Mike a peck on the cheek.

'You take care in there.'

'And you take care out here. Stay close to these guys and keep your head down OK?'

'I will,' nodded Beth. She squeezed Mike's hand and watched him turn and walk through the trees towards the waterhole without a backward glance.

He entered until the water reached his chest, put on his fins and then slipped quietly beneath the surface. As Beth watched the last ripples roll towards the edge of the pool she was acutely aware that they were now separated by a physical barrier. Whatever happened now, she was as powerless to help him as he was to help her.

* * * *

In the crystalline clarity of the fresh water, the penetrating natural light was enough to guide Mike through the first twelve metres of the subterranean passageway. The ceiling was at first swathed in sinuous tree roots that had wormed their way down through metres of rock fissures to tap into the source of fresh water below, but as Mike went deeper into the system, they became scarcer and gave way to a covering of delicate mineral formations.

There were tall ivory columns, fingers of dripping wax, shining, angular crystals and opposing rows of spikes and daggers, their translucent tips turning blood red as Mike's light shone through them. It was a place of beauty, isolated and eerily calm; an underwater cathedral, untouched by human hands. The only signs of the thriving world above were specks of detritus and the occasional dead leaf that had been drawn in by the current, bringing tiny amounts of nutrients to a place that was practically starved of them.

Mike's concentration sharpened as the beam of his flashlight picked out the staged cylinder which he'd stumbled across on his previous exploration. He checked the pressure once more and made a mental note of the position of the regulator before following the lifeline into the cistern with double exits. The line led him into the right hand passage and after a few carefully executed kicks, he came across the reel which he'd abandoned on his first visit. He clipped a fresh line onto it and extended it until he was level with the carved image of the Diving God.

Now he could study it at his leisure. It was beautifully worked and having been protected from any form of weathering, it was in an exceptional state of preservation. Only after examining it in minute detail could Mike be absolutely certain that it was genuine and not someone's idea of a practical joke. Frank certainly had an odd sense of humour, but even by his standards this would have been taking it to extremes. The real puzzle was trying to work out how it could have been done without the use of diving equipment. It seemed an almost impossible feat. There was an air pocket above which could undoubtedly sustain life for a while, but it would first have to be reached and that was no light endeavour.

Mike was aware that pioneering cave explorers in the Pyrenees had discovered some of the worlds most astonishing primitive cave paintings by plunging blindly into dark sumps with matches and candles tucked into rubber bonnets, but whether the Mayans had been capable of such feats of daring was impossible to say. The route that Mike had taken was certainly beyond the capabilities of all but the finest breath hold divers, although as Fabrizio had rightly pointed out, there might yet be an alternative entrance. Determined to explore as much of the system as possible before he was obliged to turn back, Mike shone his flashlight into the passageway ahead, checked his air gauge and pushed on.

The ceiling began to slope downwards as he advanced and soon the air pocket above his head had disappeared altogether. The natural corridor became elongated, the walls gradually narrowing to form a slit that was wider at its base. Mike was forced to drop deeper and soon found himself advancing uncomfortably close to the cave floor. He detached and staged his front mounted sling tank in an attempt to gain space, but when the gap became tighter still he knew that he was pushing the limits of prudence. The fine silt was now just inches from his body and risked being whipped into suspension at the slightest movement. With consummate care he rotated his body vertically, going head over heels in the narrow fissure so that his legs would come to rest on the opposite side. A milky suspension rained down from the rock above as his fins brushed against it, but Mike held his calm and was soon reeling his way back towards clear water. The tension eased as the passageway began to open up again, but frustration and disappointment remained. The only thing that Mike knew for sure was that no apneist could have entered the cave system from that direction and survived. It was close to being impossible for a diver breathing compressed air, especially one as well equipped and experienced as Mike. It looked as if the last remaining throw of the dice would be the left hand branch of the cistern with double exits, but Mike wasn't holding out much hope. Either the ancient Maya were far more ingenious than he'd thought possible, or he'd been fooled by a very elaborate hoax.

After retrieving his staged sling tank, Mike backtracked until he was level with the carving once more. Under the scrutiny of the flashlight beam, the face of the Diving God stared back at him as if challenging him to solve the riddle of its presence. As Mike thought about what he was doing, he suddenly realised that a vital clue to the authenticity of the carving might be found in the air pocket above. The pioneers who'd explored the caves in the Pyrenees didn't have the benefit of electric light. Their technique was to emerge blindly into air pockets, remove the candles and matches which they'd kept dry in their rubber bonnets and then light them in absolute darkness. Mike shone his flashlight into the air filled space above, reasoning that the Maya would have been faced with the same problem. To produce the light source required to carve the image they would have needed some form of aerobic combustion. Whether the fuel used was oil, wax or fat, there ought to be traces of soot on the ceiling of the air pocket above and maybe even the discarded remains of clay lamps or burnt out wicks.

Tense with anticipation, Mike slowly rose towards the surface and suddenly saw what he thought was a shelf positioned directly above the carving. As he drew level with it, his flashlight lit up the inside of a dome like opening and he found himself staring in astonishment at a series of shallow carved steps that disappeared into a narrow tunnel running perpendicular to the main passage. In a flash, it all became clear. The sculptors had not performed incredible feats of breath-hold diving. They'd simply discovered a dry cave system which fed directly into the aquifer. Using its support to create their work, the Diving God had been permanently placed in Xibalba, the Mayan underworld.

Mike's pulse was now racing as he placed his equipment on the ledge, freed himself from the cylinder harness and lifted himself clear of the water. Once he'd secured the floating rig to a sturdy stalagmite under the beam of his backup flashlight, he tied the line to it and began to reel away. Bent double, he climbed up the narrow tunnel and emerged into a small cistern, a dry antechamber about 20 feet in diameter. On the far side his flashlight picked out another carving, far larger and more impressive than that of the Diving God. He felt the hairs standing up on the back of his neck as he studied the distorted, angular features of the huge face which stood before him, watching him in silent scorn. He'd seen that same image just a day ago, carved into one of the temples at Tulúm. It was the rain god Chaac, one of the most venerated and bloodthirsty idols of the ancient Maya.

Yucatan Interior

It was a tough hike along the dry river bed, but the soldiers of the special ops units were no strangers to physical hardship. By daylight the trek would have been a walk in the park, but Dan had made it quite clear that the adversaries they were facing were far more experienced in jungle combat than they could ever hope to be. Every precaution had to be taken to prevent them from being seen. If they failed, they would know nothing about it until it was too late - and certainly much too late for the Spanish Ambassador.

The drop site had been chosen by Dan and Rafael the previous day, a bare peak just ten clicks to the north east. Once the logistics had been run past Washington, a unit was put together and a helicopter despatched from Beaufort. The bird arrived on schedule, just after two in the morning and Dan and Spicer were there to meet it. There was little in the way of ceremony as the Commander of the eight man unit presented himself, just a rapid, businesslike exchange as the throbbing heavy-lift engines of the

Chinook CH-47 roared away and receded into the distance.

Within a minute of touchdown they were on the move, following the trail which Dan had scouted before nightfall, following subtle indicators which only he could read. The soldiers of the special ops unit were physically fit, but they were also heavily armed and moving over difficult terrain. It was imperative that they approach the village while it was still dark. At daybreak the local hunters would be leaving their homes and ghosting through the forest, their keen senses alert to the sounds and smells being carried on the moist dawn air. Highly trained as they were, Dan knew that a group of ten men tramping through the forest after sunrise might as well be accompanied by a piper from the Scots Guards. When they began to fall behind schedule, he set a demanding pace to spur them on.

By five in the morning the most gruelling terrain was behind them and they began to make swift progress over level ground. Spicer was amused to see the commander of the unit consulting his compass and relating it to the position of the stars. Anyone who'd worked with Dan for more than a few hours tended to give up on traditional methods of navigation and follow him without question. He never got lost, rarely chose a poor route and wasted no time fixing his position on charts. If you asked him how he did it, he couldn't even tell you. It was something that was instinctive to him, like a migrating bird or a foraging insect. He didn't apply logic to the problem, he simply tapped into an unseen programme that had been locked into his head from an early age.

By six a blue haze was creeping above the horizon and the forest came alive with the calls of millions of waking creatures. It was a natural alarm call and it marked the progression of time more pertinently than the Marathon TSAR military issue watch which Dan wore on his wrist.

Over the last hour they'd picked up the pace considerably and they were slightly ahead of schedule as they approached to within a half click of the village. Dan spotted his marker up ahead, a thin twig he'd broken in the lower branches of a stout Mexican cedar. He led the small group along a narrow ridge towards a shallow cave that he'd discovered on a previous scouting mission. It was concealed behind a patch of fern and barossa saplings, far from the nearest hunting trails and large enough to accommodate the whole unit. He instructed the commander to set up a temporary camp there and wait for the order to advance. Once the men were installed, Dan checked the radio signal and briefed Spicer, who would act as the unit's guide. Before leaving, Dan collected some animal droppings from the cave floor and crushed them underfoot close to the entrance, adding a little water to release their pungent odour. Some of the soldiers exchanged irritable glances and wrinkled their noses, but none voiced a complaint.

After leaving the cave Dan backtracked for close to a kilometre, masking the most obvious signs of the men's passing. By seven thirty his mission was complete and he was back at the hideout, being congratulated by Rafael while wolfing down a double ration of tinned pork and beans. Everything had gone according to plan. All they had to do now was wait.

* * * *

There was no noise other than the gentle chirruping of a multitude of calling insects until a distant repetitive clanking sound reached their ears. They exchanged concerned glances as the metallic rhythm grew louder, accompanied by the crunching thud of heavy footfall on brittle dead leaves.

'That's someone wearing diving equipment,' whispered Beth with alarm in her eyes. 'Do you think it could be Mike?'

Claudio frowned and crept towards the edge of the clearing, parting some branches with a stick. Beth joined him as he peered out, scanning the trees to his left. A diver came into view, walking along the game trail and heading straight for the waterhole. He was a young man, dark skinned and athletic, sporting a thick crop of jet black hair which compensated for his small stature. He was wearing a light blue wetsuit with a single cylinder on his back and a canvas equipment bag slung casually over one shoulder.

'Oh my God, he's going to dive the waterhole,' whispered Beth, digging her nails into Claudio's shoulder. 'We've got to do something.'

Claudio thought for a moment, nodded and then rose to his feet. He left the protection of the garabato bushes and strode determinedly towards the stranger. Beth followed at a distance and Fabrizio joined her, keeping a firm grip on the pistol that was tucked into the pocket of his fatigue jacket.

'Hey! Excuse me, but can I ask where you're going?' challenged Claudio.

The diver casually turned towards him, seemingly unsurprised by his presence.

'I'm going to a fancy dress party. What do you think?' he sneered.

Claudio, jerked his head towards the waterhole.

'I'm sorry, but if you're planning to dive there, it's not possible right now.'

'Why? Are you in charge of it?' the diver mocked.

'No, of course I'm not,' replied Claudio testily, 'but someone is exploring the cave at the moment and I think its better you wait until he's finished.'

'And if I don't want to?' said the diver, slipping the kit bag from his shoulder.

Claudio turned towards Fabrizio and Beth, who'd now come to join him.

'Then we'll be forced to stop you.'

The diver laughed, shook his mane of black hair and continued towards the waterhole.

'Now just you listen here,' said Beth, marching towards him.

Without warning, the diver thrust his hand into his kit bag, swivelled around and pointed a gun at her, stopping her dead in her tracks.

Fabrizio was the first to react, drawing the pistol from his pocket, but before he'd had time to raise it, the diver adjusted his aim and a shot rang out. Fabrizio fell backwards clutching his chest, his eyes wide with shock.

Claudio's hand moved towards the stock of the Beretta tucked into his waistband, but it froze mid-air when he found himself staring down the barrel of the diver's pistol.

'Bastardo!' he snarled, baring his teeth.

'Go on, try to shoot me,' sneered the diver. 'You'll be dead before you pull the trigger.'

Claudio scowled, his eyes moving from left to right as long rifle barrels emerged from the surrounding bushes. He reluctantly let his hand drop to his side and turned to see Fabrizio lying on the ground with Beth crouched beside him.

'How bad is he hurt?' he asked, his voice taut with emotion.

'I don't know,' replied Beth, drawing close as Fabrizio tried to whisper something to her. 'It doesn't look good though.'

The dark haired diver uttered a brief command and five armed men emerged from the bushes to surround them. They were dressed in ragged tee-shirts and loincloths, their ebony eyes staring insect-like from their brown, leathery faces. Claudio's pistol was seized along with Fabrizio's and Beth was dragged roughly to her feet. When they reached for Fabrizio Beth kicked out at them only to be subdued with a blow to the stomach. Claudio lurched forward protectively, his eyes blazing with fury, but he was forced to hold back when rifles were cocked and levelled at his chest. He controlled his anger, knowing that he could only help his friends if he stayed alive. Beth winced and looked away as they pulled Fabrizio screaming to his feet, clutching his weakened left arm. There was a dark, wet stain on his chest that was slowly spreading into his jacket. Beth was brushed aside as one of the men pushed Claudio forward at gunpoint making it clear that he was to support Fabrizio during a forced march. As they prepared to move away Beth took a last anxious look at the waterhole, wondering if she would ever see Mike again. The odds looked cruelly thin when she saw the dark haired diver enter the pool and slip quietly below the surface with the sun glinting brightly from the barbed tip of a speargun.

* * * *

It was eerie staring into those mocking eyes, standing alone in a cold, dark place, far from the safety of the familiar world above. Perhaps the more so because he knew that the idol had been nurtured with human blood. The air in the chamber seemed to be charged with a suffocating malevolence and although it was probably just his heightened state of mind, he couldn't help the feeling that he was being watched.

Mike checked his watch and saw that he had just twelve minutes to explore the dry section of the cave system before he would have to return to the water and make his way back to the entrance. If he overran the schedule, Beth and the others would think that something had gone seriously wrong.

Determined to make the most of the time available, he swung the flashlight around in an arc and discovered a second exit; a narrow trapezoid passageway which led away from the dry antechamber. He entered and walked up a gently sloping gradient, having to stoop to avoid striking his head on the low ceiling. After a few yards the passageway emerged into a much larger chamber, so vast in fact that the flashlight could not illuminate the far side.

The constant dripping of percolating water filled his ears, the sound reverberating around towering walls that remained unseen in the darkness. He turned around, sweeping the flashlight back the way he'd come and was astonished to find that he'd emerged from an intricately carved gateway, cut into the lowest of a series of pillared galleries that were decorated with yet more images of the rain god Chaac. Directly above the passage entrance was a keystone carved with a striking image of the Descending God, diving towards the earth like the ones depicted in the temples of Tulúm. Beneath his feet, stone flags formed a broad causeway that led deeper into the chamber and Mike began to follow it, paying out line as he went. After a while the dripping water started to sound like rain and Mike shone the flashlight to his left to reveal a vast underground lake, its dark surface alive with circles of ever widening ripples. When the causeway skirted a raised bank at the edge of the lake, Mike shone his flashlight into the transparent water and saw that the bottom was sculpted with beautiful terrace like formations which shelved down towards a dark fissure in the middle. From its size and orientation, he guessed that it was the uppermost part of the narrow passageway which he'd been attempting to follow earlier. It almost certainly served as the outflow for the lake.

Mike checked his watch and saw that he'd already used up five of the six minutes available for the outward leg of his exploration. He was also running out of line. Knowing that it was time to think about retracing his steps, he decided to make one last circular sweep of the area with the flashlight. The yellow beam played across random piles of fallen boulders dotted at intervals on either side of the causeway and then to Mike's astonishment, it suddenly illuminated the carved frame of a doorway. Gripped with curiosity, Mike approached as far as the reel would allow and found himself staring at the remains of a small dwelling. A quick search to either side of the ruin revealed that it was one amongst many. He was standing at the site of an ancient underground settlement.

With his heart pounding at the implications of the discovery, Mike began to reel his way back towards the causeway keen to return and share his find with his friends, but just as he was picking his way through the last of the fallen masonry, a flame burst into life in the distance, spitting tongues of yellow light into the darkness. He turned in stunned surprise, unable to comprehend what he was seeing. Another flame flared up beside the first and then another, until the vast cavern was lit by a row of blazing torches, revealing the full extent of the ruined underground city which lay within the confines of its smooth marble-like walls. The dwellings close to where Mike was standing were rudimentary, but further along the causeway they gave way to more refined structures; temples of worship, elaborate civil buildings and the residences of the privileged. They were all worthy of attention and yet Mike barely gave them a second glance, for eclipsing them all and rising majestically from the flat expanse of a central plaza until it terminated just short of the cavern ceiling, was a sublime pyramid, capped by a golden dome of electrum that captured the light of the torch flames and threw them out in a huge shimmering halo. Mike rubbed his eyes, questioning whether he'd completely lost his hold on reality. He looked down and studied one of his wrist mounted computers in an attempt to bring his mind into focus, but when he looked up again the impossible vision remained.

The flaming torches were drawing closer now and their flickering light began to reveal their bearers. They were bronze skinned Maya Indians, wearing little more than loincloths and sandals, with intricate tattoos and brightly coloured paint marks decorating their skin. Some wore sleeveless shirts or cloaks of iridescent plumage and had amulets of shining metal in their ears and noses. They were as resplendent as they were terrifying and as they rounded the lake and converged on Mike, he saw no smile of welcome on their faces. In his struggle to reach an understanding, Mike's thoughts went back to Frank, the fate of whom had first drawn him to these caves in the first place and he suddenly realised that his life was in danger. The incredible subterranean city which lay before him was unknown to the outside world because the people who were its custodians had taken great pains to conceal its presence. And since Mike, like Frank before him had now compromised those efforts, he had almost certainly sentenced himself to death.

Sick with fear, Mike immediately dropped the reel and bolted back the way he'd come, using the abandoned white line as a guide. The sound of running feet filled the huge cavern with a noise like rolling thunder, the most terrifying sound which Mike had ever heard. His heart felt like it would explode as he ran semi-blind through the cavern, the smooth wet rock threatening to take his feet from under him at any second. Finally the tiered gateway came into view and grotesque carvings of the rain god Chaac bared their fangs as he raced towards them. The trapezoid passageway which led to the underground river was now just a short sprint ahead, but as Mike was bowing his head in readiness to charge into it, he was suddenly blinded by a powerful flashlight. Sliding to a stop just short of the entrance, he shaded his eyes and saw a man in a wetsuit step out from the dark passageway carrying a loaded speargun that was aimed at his chest. The full weight of his betrayal was cruelly revealed when a chillingly familiar voice said, 'going somewhere Mike?'

* * * *

Dan stripped down to his boxer shorts and put on the army issue tee-shirt which he'd just ripped and rubbed into the dirt outside.

'This had damn well better work,' he said, with an accusative glance in Rafael's direction.

'It'll work a hell of a lot better than if you go down there wearing your combat fatigues.'

'I don't know why you even think I look remotely like the Maya. I'm too tall for one thing.'

'You could pass for a Mestizo,' said Rafael. 'They're half Mexican, half Mayan and they come in all shapes and sizes.'

'Is that supposed to reassure me?'

'Hey, I'd willingly go in your place, you know that,' said Zach, in his most earnest voice. 'But check out the colour of my skin. I'd stick out like a zebra in a snow field.'

Dan ignored him.

'What if someone challenges me? I don't speak a word of Spanish.'

'Then you'll just have to act dumb,' suggested Rafael.

'Should come naturally,' Zach mumbled.

'And if they don't buy it?'

'Look, I don't have all the answers Dan, but the special ops unit is going

235

to be here any minute and I need eyes on the ground. All I ask is that you do your best. If the worst comes to the worst, play for time and I'll send a team in to pull you out.'

'How many favours do you owe me now?' asked Dan, as he tucked a satellite phone and a throwing knife into a harness below his armpit.

'More than I can ever hope to repay,' admitted Rafael, 'but for the record, you're unquestionably the best soldier I've ever had on my team.'

Dan studied him in silence for a moment, then dropped his head, padded across the room and slipped quietly through the door.

'Whoo! That was emotional,' declared Zach, when he and Rafael were alone. 'I thought you two were gonna start huggin and kissin one another.'

'Dan's one helluva soldier Zach and you wanna count yourself lucky we have someone like him along with us. It could just as easily be *you* out there putting your ass on the line.'

'Yeah. I reckon it must be hard for you to have to make those kinds of decisions,' said Zach, staring out of the open window. 'I mean, if I got my ass shot in the call of duty, you'd have to live with the consequence of breaking the hearts of thousands of beautiful women.'

Rafael snorted.

'I'd happily live with that responsibility.'

Zach was still chuckling to himself when he noticed movement down in the village square. He frowned and reached for the binoculars.

'What is it?' asked Rafael.

'You'd better come see. Looks like the whole village is out and heading towards the church.'

Keeping low to the ground, Rafael picked up his binoculars and joined Zach by the open window.

'What the hell is going on down there?'

'Beats me,' said Zach, shrugging. 'Maybe it's a fancy dress ball.'

'That's traditional Maya costume they're wearing,' said Rafael, seeing a half naked man with an elaborate feather head-dress enter the church.

236

'There must be some kind of ceremony going on inside. I need Dan down there now.'

He picked up the satellite phone and keyed in a number.

'Hey Dan, you seeing what we're seeing?'

'Affirmative. I'm holed in right at this moment. It's like Times Square down here.'

'I really need to know what's going on inside that church Dan. Do you think there's any chance you could...er... infiltrate?'

'Tell me you're joking Rod.'

'I'm out on a limb here.'

'It would be suicidal. I stick out like a sore thumb as it is, and these people are all known to one another.'

'OK, point taken. I guess we'll just have to stick with plan 'A' then. Report back as soon as you're in position.'

'That's Copied.'

Dan replaced the satellite phone in his shoulder harness and from the protection of the scrub at the boundary of the plantation house, watched the last of the villagers converging on the church. When the square had emptied, he began to move again, leaving the protection of the foliage and using his memory of the satellite imagery to follow the layout of the surrounding buildings until he reached the back of the church. Now hidden from view, he scaled a buttress wall to reach one of the slender windows and then leaned across to peer inside. To his surprise the whole building appeared to be empty. He reached into his shoulder holster and pulled out the satellite phone to make his report.

'I'm in position Rod, but you're not going to like what I see,' he said, keeping his voice low. 'The church is empty.'

'Empty? But that's impossible!'

'Well I've looked from two different angles and I can't see a single person. Either they're all hiding behind the curtains or they've moved on.'

'This is crazy,' said Rafael in frustration, 'They can't have just disappeared into thin air.'

'Wish I could tell you different. What do you want me to do?'

Dan heard Rafael conferring with Zach.

'Stay where you are and keep the line open. Looks like we got a latecomer approaching the church. Just hang tight and watch where he goes.'

With his arms and legs aching from the effort, Dan clung to his tenuous holds until the entrance doors swung open.

'OK I have a visual. The guy's just come in and he's now crossing the main hall...looks like he's about to enter the chapel...yep, he's definitely heading that way.'

'He's going to the chapel?'

'Affirmative. I'm going to have to move Rod or I'll lose him.'

'OK, make it quick.'

Dan shimmied to the ground, ran to the chapel wall and climbed to an overlooking window.

'Damn it!' he said panting into the speaker of the satellite phone. 'I've switched position, but there's no sign of him now.'

'You sure he didn't backtrack?'

'I don't think so. I can see right into the main building.'

'Can you see anything unusual in there, like a trapdoor or something?'

'Negative. It all looks perfectly normal from here.'

Rafael breathed a long reflective sigh.

'It doesn't make sense. There has to be some kind of hidden passageway in there.'

'You want me to try to take a look inside?'

'Negative. Spicer's just this second arrived with the cavalry so we'll go in as a unit. Let's rendezvous at the main entrance in....seven minutes.'

'OK, seven minutes it is Rod. Ready to synchronise?'

'Ready. Five, four, three, two, one, mark!'

Dan activated his stopwatch, shimmied down to the ground and skirted around the outside of the church. He crouched behind a fence which afforded him a view of the main square and when he'd counted off six minutes, he stuck out his head to see Rafael leading Zach, Spicer and the special ops unit around the perimeter. With ten seconds remaining to rendezvous, he made his presence known with a bird cry and hurried towards the church entrance. He arrived just ahead of Rafael, followed closely by the Commander of the ops unit who immediately imposed his authority by gently brushing the two of them aside. On his order the doors were flung open and the small unit of Marines stormed in with rifles raised. While they were fanning out and securing the interior, Rafael took Dan aside.

'Look at that!' he said pointing excitedly at a perfectly circular opening in the roof.'

'Unusual,' remarked Dan. What's its purpose?'

'I don't know, but the last time I came here it was concealed by a sheet of tarpaulin. When I asked the Pastor why it was there, he told me that there were some roof repairs taking place. He clearly lied to me. Why would he do that?'

Dan frowned, looking from the aperture to the circle of sunlight which it projected onto the church floor almost directly beneath. It was illuminating another circle of the exact same dimensions.

'Is that the sunburst design that you were talking about?' he asked, pointing to the motif that was set into the marble tiled floor.

'Yeah, that's the one,' said Rafael.

Dan nodded.

'If you look carefully, you'll see that it has the exact same diameter and circumference as the circle of sunlight which is being projected from the opening in the roof...and it looks as if they're about to coincide. What's the time now?'

'11.55,' said Rafael, puzzled. 'Why?'

'I think that a zenial passage is about to take place and if I'm not mistaken, in exactly five minutes time, the sun, the aperture and this circular motif will all be perfectly aligned.'

'And what does that signify?'

'To you and me, probably not very much, but to someone who considers exceptional positions of the sun to have profound spiritual significance, a great deal. It would be a time for celebration, feasting and perhaps even sacrifice.'

'Sacrifice!' said Rafael, his eyes widening.

Dan nodded.

'The date and time of the Ambassador's execution may not have been chosen entirely at random.'

They broke eye contact when Spicer came running towards them.

'Hey Rod, we found something over in the chapel, come take a look.'

Dan and Rod hurried after Spicer, following him to the rear of the chapel where they found Zach standing behind the altar, surrounded by a group of Marines and grinning from ear to ear.

'Would you like a drink gentlemen? Bloody Mary's on the house!'

Rafael and Dan looked on in amazement as Zach pulled back the small statue of the Madonna, activating a lever which caused the top of the altar to pivot and rise up on one end. Beneath it, a stone staircase was revealed, descending into a dark passageway that was illuminated by flickering candles, sprouting from the crowns of human skulls.

'Well I'll be damned,' said Rafael, shaking his head. 'I guess that explains where the congregation went.' He pursed his lips and then looked up sharply. 'Commander, prepare your men to make an assault. It's time to flush out the nasties.'

The Commander of the ops unit nodded, called his men together and was distributing final orders when a low grating rumble was heard in the nave. Rafael and Dan hurried over to investigate and found to their astonishment that the sunburst motif had completely disappeared, leaving a huge circular opening in the floor. They dropped onto their bellies, cautiously crawled towards it and peeked over the rim. Nothing could have prepared them for what they saw.

'Holy shit. I knew there had to be something down there,' whispered Rafael, as they retreated to a safe distance, 'but I never in my wildest dreams thought it would be anything like that.'

'We've gotta hope those steps lead down there,' said Dan, checking his watch, 'cause midday is now only thirty seconds away.'

* * * *

Claudio continued to support Fabrizio as they moved through the forest, following a narrow hunting trail that snaked back and forth through the dense undergrowth. He took the time to study his captors, noticing that they hardly broke sweat as they marched in the humid heat. They were lithe, lean and alert to every movement, perfectly in tune with their surroundings. He'd hoped to spot some sign of weakness that he could exploit when the opportunity arose, but it soon became apparent that these men were the apex hunters of the forest and outwitting them would be no easy task.

After a couple of kilometres the trail opened into a small clearing and hoods were placed loosely over their heads. Claudio and Beth had their hands tied behind their backs.

They began to march again, their progress hampered by buttress tree roots and exposed rocks which threatened to send them crashing to their knees at each step. After a stiff hike the hard ground eventually gave way to soft sand and mud and they were marched through thick foliage where darkness suddenly descended on them. The sound of dripping water and the echo of their footsteps told them that they'd been led into a cave. They were brought to a halt and lined up in silence, listening to the sound of lapping water followed by the hollow bump of a boat at their feet. Under the glow of overhead lights they were bundled into a narrow craft and forced to sit on damp wooden thwarts while an outboard engine was coaxed into life.

As the boat began to move away and pick up speed in the dimly lit subterranean channel, Claudio teased a small flat bladed knife from the heel of his boot. Huddled over, he held it between thumb and forefinger and discreetly began to saw away at the coarse twine that was binding his wrists.

The sharp blade made short work of the thin fibres and soon he felt his fingers throbbing as the circulation was restored to them. Through the tiny holes in the hessian hood he could see the back of Fabrizio's head, and the outline of Beth's dark hair beyond. He nudged Fabrizio in the back with his forehead and when he was sure that he had his full attention, he discreetly slipped the knife blade into the gap below his armpit. Gentle twisting movements persuaded Fabrizio to investigate and when the knife was pulled from Claudio's hand, he gave two brief words of instruction over the echoing throb of the outboard.

'*Libera Beth* – free Beth.'

The next few seconds were unbearably tense. Claudio had no idea how long the boat journey would last and he needed to act fast. He began to count to twenty, hoping that it would give Fabrizio enough time to cut through Beth's bindings, but he'd only reached fifteen when there was a sudden flash of light and the boat was rocked by an ear-splitting detonation.

Xibalba, Realm of Chaac

'Pablo! I expected a lot of things from you, but I never thought that it would come to this.'

The diver holding the speargun inclined his head and shrugged.

'There's nothing personal in it Mike,' he said soberly. 'My people have to protect their culture in whatever way they can.'

'Even if that involves murder?' spat Mike in disgust. He heard a shuffle of feet behind him and turned to see a semi-circle of obsidian tipped spears pointing at his back.

'I can't deny that life has been taken,' said Pablo, 'but it was not done out of hatred. We consider death to be a transformation; a celebration of the cycle of life.'

'So let me guess. You managed to convince Frank to convert to your twisted ideology and accept his death willingly.' said Mike, his eyes shining with outrage. 'He was your friend Pablo. He trusted you!'

'I tried to prevent him from coming here, but he wouldn't listen. What did you expect me to do? Betray my people and let him reveal what he'd seen to the rest of the world? Have this most sacred of places visited by thousands of ignorant tourists so that the Mexican government can line their pockets at our expense?'

'You were responsible for his murder Pablo. I don't care what type of spin you want to put on it. You're a murderous traitor and I hope you rot in whatever hell your culture believes in.'

'We've already lived through hell and we continue to live in it, but you'll never understand that. Your country once had a religion like ours, but it was taken from you when you were defeated by a foreign power. Now you have lost all knowledge of that culture and the significance of the rites and ceremonies which you once performed. You no longer understand your place in the universe and you have lost touch with the world of nature. We have seen this and we are determined not to let the same thing happen to us.'

'Perhaps we have lost something of ourselves, but at least we know fantasy from fact. The world has moved on and there's no longer any need for us to perform pointless ceremonies to try to control our destiny. You are living in the past here and you are living a lie. And if you think it's worth killing innocent people to protect your secret world then you're no better than the gold hungry colonists who brought your culture to an end.'

Mike heard someone clapping behind him.

'Bravo Mr. Summers; a very courageous speech for someone who is about to die.'

Mike turned to see an elaborately dressed man step forward, his face illuminated by the flaming torch which he held aloft in one hand. In the flickering light Mike studied the dark eyes that were glinting icily at him from the sunken orbits of a thin angular face. At first Mike didn't recognise him, but then he noticed the gold cross at the man's neck and the dark mark of an angry scar below his jawline.

'You again!' he said scowling. 'Who the hell are you anyway?'

244

The man laughed, curling his lip and raising his head imperiously.

'My official identity is of no consequence. Here, amongst my people I am known as Pacal.'

'How do you know so much about me?' asked Mike, narrowing his eyes, 'in fact, come to think of it, how did you know that I was coming here in the first place?'

'Mr. Summers,' Pacal replied in a condescending tone. 'Do you not realise that you are in the country of the Maya? We are everywhere. In government, security, banking, communications. We speak the same language, we share a common ancestry and more importantly, we are united in the fight to preserve our culture.'

'And yet you wear the symbol of Christianity around your neck.'

'This?' said Pacal, fingering the golden cross. He began to laugh. 'Your arrogance is as insulting as your ignorance. The cross was a symbol of the Maya long before you Christians came to our lands. It represents a cosmic conjunction, the significance of which you would not begin to understand. You foreigners treated us as ignorant savages when you came here and yet we were in advance of you on many fronts. We could predict solstices and eclipses and accurately calculate the orbits of stars when in Europe you still believed that the sun revolved around the earth. We had a calendar, a system of writing and an understanding of complex mathematics. While you rotted in the filth and disease of medieval slums, we built magnificent cities with proper sanitation, law courts and a vast system of communications.'

'I don't deny that. I have great respect for many of your achievements,' said Mike. 'What I don't understand is why you can't accept what happened in the past and move on. I've met a lot of Maya in my time here and on the whole I've found them to be kind, decent and friendly people. Up until now I've never had any bitterness or resentment shown towards me, so what makes your people so different?'

'The people you speak of are only Maya in name. They have no knowledge of what it truly means to be Maya. They have been downtrodden, exploited, stripped of their dignity and forced to become slaves to the modern world. But with our help, they will one day rediscover the ways of our ancestors and then they will bow down to no one.'

'Yeah? Well personally I much prefer the modern Maya. At least they don't go around murdering people.'

There was a flash of anger in Pacal's eyes. He spat instructions to his followers and they immediately closed in on Mike. His was grabbed by the arms and a noose with a long tail was placed over his head. It pulled tight like a dog's leash when he was dragged forwards, forcing him to fight for every breath. Like a farmyard animal, he was dragged along the causeway by the side of the lake, next to the abandoned lifeline which now lay useless on the muddy ground. They passed the ruins of the city perimeter along routes of finely carved stone, each interlocked with precision to form a perfectly flat surface. The grandeur and complexity of the buildings accrued as they approached the main plaza, with dazzling stucco walls and intricately sculpted stonework decorating every inch. But to Mike it was merely an extravagantly decorated hell, and one from which he would gladly have escaped given the slightest opportunity.

In his desperation Mike's thoughts turned to Beth, Fabrizio and Claudio who were waiting for him at the cave entrance and it suddenly struck him that if his visit had been expected then he'd almost certainly led them into a trap. Tortured by recriminations, he tried desperately to think of a way to escape so that he could find some way to warn them, if it wasn't already too late.

As his eyes searched the unfamiliar surrounds, he spotted a building which looked like a warehouse, from which a flue extended, sending vapours rising high towards the cavern roof. Inside there were steaming vats, rotating glass jars and coiled condensing tubes of shining chrome; a modern laboratory at striking odds with the slow decay of the ancient city in which it nestled. It had the sordid looks of an illegal drugs factory and probably was for all he cared at that moment, but then something unusual caught his eye. There was a pile of leafy plants with thick tubers lying on a workbench to one side, clearly the raw material of some chemical extraction process and Mike suddenly realised that he'd seen those distinctive leaves before. As he was led across the central plaza, where a small, bloodthirsty crowd was gathering in anticipation of the ghoulish spectacle in which he would play a leading role, the pieces of the puzzle slowly started to fall into place and Mike began to understand that there was considerably more at stake here than the preservation of his own life.

Now the great pyramid stood before him, towering up towards the cave roof some 70 feet above. There were shouts of excitement from the gathering crowd as he was dragged up the steep steps, his eyes bulging and his face discoloured from the tightness of the noose around his neck. At the head of the procession was Pacal, wearing a head-dress of jade and scarlet plumage with a cloak of jaguar pelts hanging from his shoulders. Beyond him, Mike could see the ceremonial platform from where a winged serpent stared down at him, its snout and fangs black with dried blood. Like the altar beside it, it was alive with the flickering light of a huge fire burning fiercely in the bowl of a large beacon. When Mike felt the heat radiating from it, an idea began to take root in his mind. It would be a long shot, but time was running out and in the absence of a better plan, he quickly resolved to give it a try. He eased his head forwards to fill his lungs with air and when he was within two steps of the platform he pulled his arms in towards his chest and quickly rotated them backwards, breaking the hold of the men on either side. Now he rushed forwards, throwing his shoulder into the knees of the person holding the noose and forcing him to stumble to the ground. After wrenching the cord free, he ran towards the blazing beacon before anyone had a chance to stop him. The searing heat was unbearable, but Mike endured it, passing to the blind side and working quickly before his captors hands were on him again. He tried to escape them by launching himself down the steep steps, but strong arms held him and he was dragged back towards the winged serpent, where Pacal was waiting for him, his lips curled into a smile.

'Did you really think that you could escape?' he sneered, watching Mike's wrists being bound tightly together. 'Even if you managed to stay on your feet and reach the bottom of the pyramid alive, you would then have had to fight your way through the crowd and find an exit in total darkness. I'm disappointed Mr. Summers. I credited you with more intelligence.'

'What do you plan to do with me?' Mike demanded.

'Oh, I think you already know that,' said Pacal, stroking his hand across the top of the altar. 'This happens to be a very special day in our calendar and it has been quite some time since the great Chaac feasted on the blood of so many captured enemies.'

'How many?' asked Mike, steeling himself in readiness for the answer.

'Five in total,' said Pacal nonchalantly. 'Three of which are your incompetent friends.'

Mike bared his teeth and tried to charge forwards, but he was quickly restrained.

'You sick bastard,' he screamed as he was forced to his knees. 'What have they done to harm you?'

'If you are looking for someone to blame, you should start with yourself,' said Pacal, his eyes unblinking. 'It's an inconvenience to have to take the lives of your friends, but by bringing them here you left me with no choice.'

The words ate into Mike's heart like acid.

'You'll never get away with this,' he said, his voice choked with remorse. 'People will come looking for us.'

'Perhaps, but that will no longer be your concern,' replied Pacal.

Mike frowned and stared in silence at the cold rock platform beneath him. It seemed to harbour the promise of death.

'Where are they? Can I at least speak to them?'

'By the time they arrive it will be too late, you'll already be in the next world. The moment we have been waiting for is drawing near.'

There were cheers from the crowd as a small group of warriors climbed to the ceremonial platform, dragging another captive along with them. They advanced towards the altar and threw a middle-aged man to the floor at Pacal's feet. He was taller and lighter skinned than the Maya and although his clothes were filthy, Mike could see that he was a person used to privilege. As the man rose to his knees, his sagging bloodshot eyes lifted towards Pacal and then slowly turned in Mike's direction. There was a look of weary resignation in them and Mike wished that he could offer him more than the empathy of a man similarly condemned.

Pacal hissed something to the middle-aged man at his feet in scathing tones of Spanish. Trembling, the man glanced at Mike once more, crossed himself and began to pray. Strong hands lifted Mike from the floor and dragged him kicking towards the altar. The coarse twine binding his hands was cut through with a knife and he was forced to lie on the cold, hard surface, flat on his back with his arms and legs pulled wide apart. As he was struggling against the hold of the four men restraining him, Mike saw Pablo standing at the edge of the platform.

'Traitor!' he shouted with all the venom he could muster, but Pablo's expression was distant and unflinching, as if they'd never met.

A chorus of rhythmic chanting filled the air when a high priest appeared from the entrance of the pillared temple beyond the platform. He wore an elaborate head-dress, a cloak of iridescent feathers and jade skulls in each ear. The chanting intensified as the priest approached the altar and when a ceremonial knife was lifted high above his chest, Mike tensed in anticipation of the searing pain that would end his life. He gasped and drew shuddering breaths when his wetsuit was slit open along the left side of his breastbone, barely registering the stinging pain as the blade nicked his skin.

Pacal barked orders and there were suddenly people moving in all directions. There followed a low rumbling sound accompanied by a piercing light from above; a crescent of blinding silver which steadily grew until it formed a perfect circle, like an accelerated solar eclipse. The vertical shaft of sunlight which poured in from above, struck the dome of electrum at the apex of the pyramid and was reflected outwards, sending shimmering light cascading in every direction, illuminating the cavern walls, the furthest reaches of the subterranean city and its elaborately carved temples, some rising magnificently from the lake itself.

Mike struggled to keep his hold on reality as Pacal ushered a beautiful girl, naked from the waist upwards, towards the altar. She wore an intricate necklace of jade, coral and gold and a fine head-dress of red and green plumage. She stared ahead, visibly trembling and as Mike studied the rawness around her bright almond eyes, he suddenly realised who it was.

'Gabriela?'

Gabriela's lower lip quivered as she tried to bite back the tears that were welling in the corners of her eyes. Seeing this, Pacal stepped forward and intervened, his face snarling. He hissed something into her ear which prompted her to draw a knife and hold it clasped in both hands above Mike's chest.

'Don't do this Gabriela,' Mike whispered, his eyes darting between her face and the trembling blade. 'In your heart you know it's wrong.'

'Silence!' barked Pacal.

Gabriela's expression hardened and Mike saw her tighten her grip on the knife. It was time to throw in his wild card.

'They know about the poisoned cocaine Pacal,' he shouted, tearing his eyes from the glinting point of the blade to watch the uncertainty creep into Pacal's scowling face.

Gabriela hesitated, her hands shaking once more.

'What are you talking about?' spat Pacal, his eyes glinting with fury.

'You know exactly what I'm talking about. You're behind the contaminated cocaine shipments which have been circulating in Europe. You import the cocaine, poison it with lethal toxins extracted from the cassava plant and then ship it across the Atlantic.'

Pacal laughed uneasily.

'You have a very vivid imagination Mr. Summers. Cassava plants are grown all over the world.'

'Not these ones,' said Mike, shaking his head. 'They're a hybrid; specially bred for their toxic qualities...and they're grown and harvested within walking distance of this cave.'

'Who told you this?' demanded Pacal, surging towards the altar once more.

'If you kill me you'll never find out,' said Mike.

Pacal sneered

'What do I care? No one will ever find us here.'

'Are you certain?' challenged Mike. 'Frank found you, I found you...and if you kill me or any of my friends, others will come looking too. This has become too big. Even you must realise that. Whatever did you hope to achieve by holding the Spanish authorities to ransom?'

'What do I hope to achieve?' said Pacal, his nostrils flaring. 'Justice...and vengeance! The Spanish came here claiming that they wanted to trade with us, to share their knowledge and convert us to the Christian faith, but all they ever did was steal from us and bring us death, pestilence and misery. My people were slaughtered, robbed, humiliated and turned into slaves. We lost our lands, our identity, our knowledge, our religion and our way of life. And worst of all, that situation continues because our country is still run by a government of colonial half-breeds. We have waited hundreds of years for the chance to regain control of our lands and now at last that dream is within our reach. When the taste of victory is at last on our lips it will be that much sweeter for knowing that it was won through the suffering and humiliation of the nation which once tried to wipe us from the face of the earth.'

'That all happened hundreds of years ago Pacal. Can't you see that the people who you're targeting now are innocent? You can't hold them responsible for what their ancestors did.'

'Innocent? Cocaine is a vice of the rich. They couldn't give a damn about the poverty and corruption it brings to the third world. It is just another form of colonialist oppression. Besides, they are fortunate that they have been given a choice. What choice did my people have when they were exposed to the deadly smallpox brought here by you Europeans?'

'You have a very twisted logic Pacal.'

'Enough! We are wasting time,' said Pacal, staring up at the shaft of sunlight that was slowly beginning to lose its intensity. 'You can take what knowledge you have with you to the afterlife.'

He nodded to the high priest, who stepped forwards, snatched the knife from Gabriela's hand and shoved her to the floor. Mike knew that there was no further hope of reprise as the knife was raised above his chest, the high priest began to mumble a rapid incantation and the hands gripping his wrists and ankles pulled so tight that he could barely breathe.

* * * *

It was now or never. He had to make his move while they were all distracted. The timing was far from being ideal, but then a great deal of the plan had been based on guesswork. In a flash, he reached out, grabbed Fabrizio by the shoulder and threw his weight to one side. The boat rolled and there were shouts of alarm as everyone was flung into the water. The cold contact of the underground river made Claudio want to gasp, but he held out and kicked away below the waterline, dragging Fabrizio along with him.

After a few seconds he surfaced, pulled off the wet hood and helped Fabrizio to do the same. Flashes of light and the sound of gunfire came from the further reaches of the cave. Claudio looked around and saw to his satisfaction that the boat they were being transported in had capsized completely. The small outboard was swamped with the prop clear of the water and four anxious Maya were clinging in desperation to the upturned hull, their weapons now lying harmlessly at the bottom of the river. Seeing the fear in their eyes, Claudio knew that he'd guessed correctly. The Maya were undoubtedly masters in their natural environment, but water didn't play a part of it and in the dry forests of the Yucatan there'd been no need for them to learn to swim.

In the dim light Claudio spotted a dark shape jerking back and forth at the surface of the river and he realised that it was Beth, fighting to breathe through the wet hood, her hands still tied behind her back. She was treading water close to the boat and one of the Maya had seen her and was reaching over to grab her. Leaving Fabrizio to fend for himself, Claudio raced over to help and arrived as Beth's head was being forced under the water. He grabbed her attacker's wrist and rolled like a crocodile, twisting the man's arm until he lost his grip on the boat. Without its support, the man found himself struggling to stay above the surface of the water and he began to choke, his eyes growing wide with terror. Claudio watched him claw his way back to the submerged boat and then he turned to help Beth only to find that she had disappeared. Fearing the worst he took a couple of rapid breaths and was just preparing to dive down into the dark water when he heard Fabrizio's voice calling out to her.

'Beth, stay where you are! I'm coming!'

Peering into the distance, Claudio finally spotted her a short distance away, still struggling to breathe through the wet hessian hood. He bolted towards her and arrived just as Fabrizio was pulling it from her head.

'Oh thank God it's you Fabrizio,' he heard her say between rasping breaths. 'Someone just tried to drown me.'

'Don't worry, he won't trouble you any more,' said Claudio, panting.

'Thank you, both of you,' said Beth, looking between them.

'Let's get your hands free,' said Claudio. 'Do you still have the knife Fabrizio?'

'No. I lost it when I fell in the water.'

'OK, just try to support her then.'

Claudio reached down and working by feel, set about freeing the twine that was binding Beth's wrists.

'Where did you go back there?' he asked as he worked. 'For a moment I thought you'd drowned.'

'Oh...I was being held under the water, so I blew out some air, let myself sink and then kicked away.'

Claudio stared at her in admiration for a moment, shaking his head.

'You're quite an amazing woman.'

'Oh, er thanks, but it was really just an act of desperation.'

'More like an act of intelligence and courage,' said Claudio, pulling the last loop of twine from her wrists.'

'Well I don't feel particularly courageous,' said Beth.

'That's usually a sign that you are.'

'Do you think we're safe now?' asked Fabrizio, staring at the four men who were clinging resolutely to the upturned boat.

'We are for the moment,' replied Claudio. 'We can swim and they can't, but we need to get away from here before they get a chance to raise the alarm.'

'Which way did we come in?' asked Beth.

'Back that way,' said Claudio, turning his head, 'but I'm afraid it's going to be a long swim.'

'There seems to be some kind of battle going on in the other direction.'

'Yes. I've no idea what's happening there, but I think it would be best for us to keep away.'

'Yes, I agree with you there,' said Beth. 'What about you Fabrizio?

'Do you think you'll be able to swim all the way back?'

'I don't know. I'll try, but my ribs are very sore. I think there's a bullet in there somewhere.'

He fished out a soggy, bloodstained, leather bound note book from his breast pocket.

'Fortunately it had to go through this first,' he said smiling.

Claudio, shook his head.

'He's never without his notebook,' he explained to Beth with a shrug. 'I think he even sleeps with it under his pillow at night.'

'Who can blame him?' replied Beth. 'It probably just saved his life.'

'Perhaps, but we're still not out of this mess yet,' said Claudio, seeing the four Maya attempting to paddle the upturned boat with cupped hands. 'Let's start swimming and see if we can help Fabrizio along.'

'OK,' agreed Beth.

They got into position on either side of Fabrizio and were just about to move away when the overhead lights failed and they were suddenly plunged into almost total darkness.

'Damn it!' said Beth. 'Got any other ideas?'

*　*　*　*

The knife was just inches away from his chest when it happened. There was a huge ball of flames, a wave of searing heat that instantly charred the skin of those who stood closest and a deafening blast that blew people over like skittles. It had come terrifyingly late, but the cylinder of nitrox which Mike had slipped into the beacon had finally ruptured, the high oxygen content fuelling a deadly explosion and a violent shock wave which shook the huge pyramid to its foundations. Lying flat, Mike had been protected from the worst of the blast and better still, there was no longer anyone holding him down. Huge stalactites began to break free and rain down from the ceiling of the cavern, impaling those who were unfortunate enough to be caught beneath them.

Mike rolled from the altar a fraction of a second before a sizeable one came hurtling down towards him, shattering into thousands of pieces when it struck the flat stone surface. He landed on a body and tried to scramble to his feet, but a hand suddenly seized him and pulled him back. Twisting around, he found himself face to face with the high priest, his scorched eyes blazing with hatred from behind the charred flesh of his cheekbones. Before Mike could break his hold, the priest snatched up the ceremonial dagger and tried to plunge it into his face. Mike's forearm swung upwards to block the attack and he grabbed the high priest's wrist as he was rolled onto his back. Bright flashes of light, detonations and clouds of white smoke were billowing up into the air as Mike struggled to stop the point of the dagger advancing towards his throat. Suddenly there was a dull crack and Mike was surprised to see the high priest's head fly sideways, a bloody tooth falling from his open mouth. He pushed the limp body away from him to find Gabriela standing over him with a piece of shattered stalactite held firmly in her hands.

'Thank you Gabriela,' he said, gasping for breath.

Gabriela held out a hand and pulled him to his feet.

'You must go before they kill us both,' she warned. 'You'll find a way out at the far side of the pyramid.'

'Come with me,' he implored her.

'It's too late for that,' said Gabriela, shaking her head. 'Go now, while you still can.'

There was a burst of automatic gunfire followed by a desperate cry from someone lying on the floor nearby.

'*Ayuda me!* – Help!'

Through the smoke Mike spotted the Spanish speaking prisoner struggling to his knees, his tailored white cotton shirt now ripped to shreds. He grabbed the knife from the limp hand of the high priest and rushed over to cut through the rope that was binding his wrists.

'*Muchas gracias, Señor. Que Dios le bendiga* – Thank you sir. May God bless you,' he said, his eyes moist with emotion.

'*De nada* – Think nothing of it,' replied Mike. '*Venga, debemos partir!* – Come, we must leave!'

As Mike was helping him to his feet, Pacal emerged phantom like from the swirling white smoke to his left, flanked on either side by surly warriors. On Pacal's command the two warriors charged forward, their spears held aloft and ready to strike. Mike stood his ground grasping the knife in his raised fist, but at the last moment, he squatted down, tripping his attacker and sending him stumbling over the edge of the platform and down the steep stone steps to his death. In the blink of an eye Mike was on his feet again, rushing to the aid of his fellow captive. To his surprise, he found him lying flat on his back, his shirt smeared with blood and the warrior lying motionless on top of him. When the prisoner rolled the lifeless body from him, Mike was surprised to see dark blood oozing from a wound in the warrior's head.

Spitting a curse, Pacal bared his teeth and drew a knife, ready to charge forward, but he was forced to stop short when a stocky man in combat fatigues stepped from a doorway, aiming a semi-automatic rifle at his chest. The gun barrel swung between Pacal, Mike and Gabriela.

'Nobody moves, understand?' the soldier ordered.

Mike and Gabriela nodded. Pacal slowly eased back.

The soldier kicked the dead warrior and then flicked his eyes towards the light skinned man crouching beside him. He frowned, put a finger to his ear and spoke into a helmet mounted microphone.

'Hostage located! Get Rodriguez over here.'

The sound of automatic gunfire intensified. Mike saw small groups of armed warriors running up the sides of the pyramid only to be mown down in their tracks before they reached the platform.

'Area secured!' someone shouted close by.

Another man in combat fatigues emerged from the smoke with an automatic pistol held in front of him. He wore his hair in a long ponytail that swung loosely from the back of his combat helmet. When he drew level with his colleague, he squatted down and addressed the light skinned man in urgent, authoritative tones.

'Señor Perez?'

The light skinned man nervously nodded his head.

'*Estamos aqui para liberarte* – We're here to free you.'

A trembling smile appeared on the Ambassador's face and tears sprang from the corners of his eyes.

'Good work Commander,' said the man with the pony tail, tapping his colleague on the shoulder.

'My pleasure,' replied the Commander. 'But tell me something. There's just the one hostage here right?'

'Yeah, as far as I know.'

'Then who the fuck are these people?' he asked, jerking his head towards Mike and Gabriela.

The man with the pony tail turned around and stared dumbfounded at Mike. Mike stared back.

'Rod?'

'Mike! What in hell's name are you doing here?'

Mike shrugged.

'I guess I was just in the wrong place at the wrong time.'

'It couldn't have been more wrong,' said Rafael, his face rigid.

'I think you've already met Gabriela,' said Mike, motioning with his head.

Rafael's jaw dropped as his eyes swung towards her. Gabriela self-consciously folded her arms across her breasts as Dan, Spicer, Zach and two of the Special Ops soldiers arrived at the scene.

'You got any more surprises for me?' Rafael asked.

'Yup, I saved the best for last,' said Mike, turning his head, 'I've found the guy you're...'

He stopped short when he saw an empty space where Pacal had been standing just seconds before.

'Where did he go?' he demanded, staring at Gabriela.

'I-I don't know,' she replied.

'Shit!'

Mike jumped to his feet and sprinted towards the edge of the platform.

'Hey, Mike, come back!' shouted Rafael. But Mike was already gone.

'Would someone like to tell me what the hell's going on here?' asked the Commander.

'Ask her,' said Rafael, getting to his feet. 'She's going to give you all the answers you need. Just make damned sure you don't let any of the other prisoners get near her.'

He turned to address his own men.

'Right, Dan, Zach, you come with me. Spicer, I want you to help the Commander and his men evacuate our two guests.'

'Yes sir,' replied Spicer.

'Can I swap with Spicer,' asked Zach, his eyes glued to Gabriela.

'Not a chance Romeo. Let's go.'

*   *   *   *

Pacal had a head start, but Mike was not about to let him get away without a fight. He was Frank's murderer - and perhaps more importantly, he was the only person who knew where Beth, Fabrizio and Claudio were being held.

The steps of the pyramid were perilously steep, but Tulúm had given Mike some useful practice and he attacked them with skill and daring. There were several bodies littering the foot of the steps and when Mike passed one that was wearing a ripped and bloodied wetsuit, he didn't give it a second glance.

By the rapidly diminishing light of the reflected sun he saw Pacal crossing the by now deserted plaza and heading towards the main causeway, a flaming torch held aloft to light his path. Mike followed, leaping the last few steps of the pyramid and stooping to pick up a piece of burning timber mid-stride. Smoke and flames began to balloon up from a building ahead and when Mike drew level with it, he saw that it was the laboratory, no doubt set alight by the fleeing Pacal. As the flames reached higher, the dull red glow pushed back the darkness and Mike saw the slight figure of Pacal, discarding what remained of his jaguar skin cloak while making his escape along the causeway. The black sheen of the lake was now visible in the distance and the Mayan chief was surging towards it, steadily increasing his advance. Mike could not hope to match his pace and only thoughts of Beth and his friends kept him going when his lungs felt fit to burst. Finally he saw Pacal slow to a trot in the distance and head towards the shore of the lake where a jetty protruded into the darkness. In the dim light, he watched him walk along it and then step down. A second later an outboard engine burst into life. Cursing, Mike grit his teeth and ran the last 50 yards at a sprint, arriving beside the rickety wooden jetty in a state of near collapse.

'Pacal!' he managed to shout between breaths, bent almost double with exhaustion.

Pacal, who was busily untying the mooring lines of a small red power boat, turned in surprise, snatching up a pistol. When he saw that Mike was alone, he lowered it again, laughing.

'You never give up do you?' he said shaking his head. 'I suppose that you've come here to try and talk me into giving myself up?'

'No, I'm not here to waste my words,' said Mike, fighting for breath. 'I just want to know what you've done with my friends.'

'Your friends? By now they're already dead,' he said callously.

'You're lying,' countered Mike.

Pacal shook his head, an evil smile playing across his lips.

'I ordered them to be killed when you and your military friends chose to attack us. It was your own fault, but rest assured that they were going to die anyway.'

'You coward,' shouted Mike. 'I had nothing to do with the attack. You made yourself a target when you attempted to hold a country to ransom.'

'That is an accusation which you cannot prove,' said Pacal stepping back onto the jetty. 'Now I don't know who you work for Mr. Summers nor how you knew where to find us, but I do know that you are the only person who can identify me, and right now that makes you a problem; a problem that can easily be resolved.'

Pacal raised the pistol and Mike's fear turned to surprise when he saw a shadow rise up out of the water close to the jetty.

'Don't you want to know how we found you?' asked Mike, stalling for time.

'The reason why you found me is that I didn't kill you when I had the chance,' said Pacal, taking aim. 'How you found me is of no further consequence.'

Mike saw the shadow transform into that of a man, creeping up behind Pacal with a stick held aloft like a baseball bat.

'They know your real name,' Mike lied, holding his breath as the shadow drew closer.

Pacal's eyes narrowed, his senses suddenly alert to the sound of dripping water. When a board creaked behind him, he crouched, spun around and fired instinctively. The stick dropped from the hand of the man hovering in the shadows and there was a groan as he collapsed backwards onto the jetty. At the same moment there was a muffled scream from the darkness. Unsettled, Pacal's raven eyes searched the shore of the lake. He looked down at the wounded man, hesitated and then swung around to point the gun at Mike once more. Scowling, he pulled the trigger, but Mike anticipated the attack and dived for cover behind a large boulder. The echo of the gun blast was followed by the sound of approaching feet.

'Mike, stay down!' someone shouted.

The outboard engine of the red power boat roared into life and Mike peered from behind the boulder to see Pacal accelerating away from the jetty.

At the same moment Rod and two other soldiers came sliding to a halt nearby, their rifles shouldered and spitting bullets at the fleeing vessel. A couple of hits sent splinters flying from the stern before it melted into the darkness.

'You OK Mike?' asked Rafael, without turning his head.

'I'm fine Rod, but there's someone wounded over there on the jetty.'

'A friendly?'

'Yeah, I think so. He was trying to help me.'

Rafael went over to investigate, closely followed by Mike, curious to find out who'd risked their life in an attempt to protect him. Under the glow of Rafael's flashlight, he was astonished to see the face of Claudio staring back at him, his hand sealing a bloody wound to his chest.

'Claudio! Christ, are you OK?' he asked anxiously.

'A hole in the lung,' replied Claudio wheezing, 'I'll live.'

'A friend of yours?' asked Rafael.

'Most definitely,' replied Mike.

'Spicer, get your med kit over here.'

'How'd you get here?' Mike asked.

'We were brought in by boat,' replied Claudio. 'We escaped and then swam here.'

'Is Beth with you?'

'Yes, she's with Fabrizio. They're hiding nearby. Call them. They'll come.'

'Do you mean to say that there's a river exit?' Rafael asked as Mike was peering into the darkness.

'There's a tunnel at the other side of this lake,' said Claudio, wincing. 'It leads outside...to the forest.'

'Beth, Fabrizio. Are you there?' Mike shouted.

'We're here Mike!' Beth's voice called back. 'Over here!' she said, rising to her feet and waving her arm. 'Thank God you're alive.'

'Are you OK?'

'We're fine Mike. What about Claudio? Is he badly hurt?' she asked anxiously.

'Don't worry, he's going to be OK.'

Rafael used his flashlight to guide Beth and Fabrizio as they picked their way around the boulders at the edge of the lake.

'Thank God they all made it,' said Mike, breathing a sigh.

'So who's the guy in the boat?' asked Rafael.

'He calls himself Pacal. He's the local Maya chieftain; the head honcho, the crazy bastard behind all of this madness.'

Rafael narrowed his eyes and glanced at a row of jetskis that were moored alongside the jetty.

'Zach, Dan, radio for support!' he said decisively. 'We need a stretcher and we need to get these people escorted out of here.'

'I'm on it,' replied Dan.

'Take care of your friends Mike, I'm going after him,' Rafael announced, holstering his guns.

'Wait. I'll come with you.'

'No time,' said Rafael, breaking into a sprint.

'We'll see about that.'

As Beth approached the jetty Mike ran towards her, embraced her and then held her at arms length.

'Beth, I'm sorry, but I've got to go. I've got some unfinished business to attend to.'

Beth began to protest, but Mike pressed his finger to her lips.

'Don't worry; I'll be back as soon as I can,'

Silencing her with a kiss, he turned and ran back along the jetty. Rafael was already powering away into the darkness, but Mike quickly slipped the lines of a jetski and gave chase. He flicked the switch of the specially installed headlamp and picked out Rafael as he sped towards the far side of the lake. The cavern entrance was easy to find, its huge mouth spanned by glowing limestone columns and huge stalactites which reached down towards the dark water, like the teeth of some nightmarish sea creature. It swallowed up Rafael and Mike was quick to follow, plunging deep into the folds of its cavernous entrails. Waves slapped against the passage walls and crashed back in on themselves, churning the water into a maelstrom that threw Mike around as if he was on a white-knuckle ride. He grit his teeth and put caution to the wind, flying through the air and crashing into foaming troughs, advancing until he was just a few metres behind Rafael.

'You can't get rid of me that easily,' he shouted as he drew closer.

Rafael merely laughed, shook his head and gunned away.

They reached a fork in the river and seeing the agitated water in the left hand channel, Rafael entered it with Mike hot on his heels. A sharp bend took them into a straight corridor where they were rewarded by the sight of a distant glow up ahead. They surged forward with renewed determination, their hair whipping behind them and the bare rock rushing by just a few feet to either side. The passageway started to widen and they saw more and more of the red power boat's stern as they closed in on it, relentlessly gnawing away at Pacal's lead. There was a sudden, sharp echoing crack and a metallic ping as a bullet ricocheted off the cavern wall close by. Two more shots rang out, a jet of water sprayed into the air and there was a heavy thud as the front of Mike's jetski took a hit. The headlamp blew out and shards of glass and plastic flew up, stinging his face as he fought to regain control. He swerved frighteningly close to Rafael, dropping off the throttle in time to avoid a dangerous, high speed collision. Rafael, unflinching, continued at full speed, crouched low with his pistol drawn, firing a sustained volley of rounds. Pacal replied with three more shots, fired quickly and inaccurately, merely spraying them with powdered rock. The power boat turned around sharply and Rafael saw it pause for a second before it came racing back up the tunnel towards them. He shouted a warning to Mike as it approached, bouncing off the cavern walls, careering out of control and slicing across their path with no one at the helm. Rafael swerved, narrowly avoiding a collision, but with no lights, Mike's reaction was late. Anticipating the impact, he lifted his leg a fraction of a second before the powerboat scythed into him and scraped along the jetski's flank. The deflection pushed him towards the cavern wall where he narrowly avoided striking a solitary stalagmite that rose threateningly from the dark water. He held his nerve and recovered quickly, easing the jetski back towards the middle of the channel. Ahead of him, Rafael was entering a domed cavern where the underground river terminated in a circular bank of mud and rock. Mike watched him leap from the moving jetski onto a stone embankment which ran along one side of the channel, his gun raised and his eyes scanning the darkness in all directions. Determined to maintain the pace, Mike crash-stopped into the embankment and stumbled after him, following the beam of Rafael's wavering flashlight as he hurried towards the far end of the cavern.

'There's an exit over here,' Mike heard him shout, before seeing his flashlight disappear behind a solid wall of rock. Chasing after the diminishing glow, Mike found himself in a narrow passageway that was partially lit by penetrating fingers of greyish daylight. At the far end of it, he caught up with Rafael, who'd been stopped by a padlocked metal gate, separating him from the wall of foliage beyond. A car engine burst into life and Rafael stepped back, pushing Mike aside and raising his gun. Two rounds were enough to separate the arm from the casing of the padlock and Rafael's boot did the rest. They crashed through the undergrowth and emerged onto a dirt track which skirted the entrance to the cave before plunging deep into the forest. Rafael began to sprint along it, following the sound of the retreating vehicle to catch a fleeting glimpse of the back of a white truck before it picked up speed and left him choking in a cloud of dust. Mike caught up with him and fell to his knees gasping for breath.

'I guess that's that then,' he said resignedly.

'We're not beaten yet,' said Rafael, pulling out his satellite phone. He made a call, pacing back and forth until it was answered.

'PIC. Enter your security code.'

Rafael tapped a number into the keypad.

'Rodriguez! Where the hell are you?'

'Nice to hear from you too Kruger. At this moment I'm unsure of my exact position. I need you to get a fix on me.'

'Got ourselves lost have we?'

'Look Kruger this isn't a courtesy call,' he snapped. 'I'm in pursuit of a dangerous terrorist and right now I need your assistance.'

'At your service...*sir*,' Kruger said, his voice heavy with sarcasm. 'What do you need?'

'Do you still have the coordinates of my car?'

'Yeah, I'm sure we have that logged somewhere.'

'Good, I need you to lead me to it by the most advantageous route. There's a dirt track right in front of me, heading north-east which would be a good place to start...and somewhere along it you'll find a fleeing white Dodge Ram which I want you to track.'

'The system isn't designed to be in two places at once Rodriguez. The best I can do is to give you the coordinates of your assigned vehicle and a rough heading to follow while we concentrate on finding the truck.'

'OK, I guess that will have to do.'

'You got a pen?'

'Fire away.'

Rafael entered the coordinates directly into a handheld GPS, rang off and then turned to face Mike.

'Do you keep yourself fit?'

'I'm reasonably fit, but I'm no athlete.'

'Can you run steady for two miles? Cause it's either that or go back the way you came.'

'I'm coming with you,' said Mike determinedly.

'Then you might want to ditch that wetsuit.'

'Yeah, don't think it will be much use to me now anyway,' said Mike, pulling at the slash that the high priest's knife had made. He quickly stripped down to his swim shorts and fell in beside Rafael as they set off into the forest. They ran hard along the dirt track for a mile or so and then veered off into the cover of trees. Rafael climbed a hill to get a better look at the terrain and then led them northwards along a patch of dry grassland

and scrub. Within sixteen minutes of exiting the cave, they were standing beside Rafael's Chevrolet.

'Strap yourself in, this isn't going to be comfortable,' Rafael said as he climbed in behind the wheel. Mike attached his seatbelt and braced himself as Rafael let out the clutch and gunned the Chevrolet out of the forest and along a rutted track.

'You still got all your teeth?' asked Rafael as they screeched out onto the main highway a few minutes later.

'I think so,' replied Mike.

'Good, take the steering wheel a second.'

Mike reached over to steady the Chevrolet as Rafael put on a wireless headset that linked to his satellite phone. After he'd hit the redial button, he floored the gas pedal and took the wheel again, much to Mike's relief.

'Hey Kruger, you got a fix on that truck yet?' he bawled into the microphone.

'Affirmative. The target is heading south-east towards the coast, approximately 15 miles from the junction with the main highway.'

'OK, I need you to let me know the moment he joins it.'

'Will do.'

Mike felt himself shrinking back into his seat as the needle of the Chevrolet's speedometer touched 125 miles an hour. He involuntarily pressed his foot to the floor as they overtook slower moving vehicles, swerving into the path of the oncoming traffic and risking a fatal head on collision. A police patrol vehicle came out from a siding and attempted to follow them, but it was no match for Rafael's supercharged Chevrolet and quickly became a tiny speck in the rear view mirror. An update came in from the PIC.

'The truck just made the turn Rodriguez, heading north on Highway 307.'

'Copy that. I'm ten minutes behind and closing,' said Rafael. 'Inform me if he attempts to leave it.'

'Evidently.'

Rafael kept his foot firmly on the gas pedal until he reached the junction with the highway. There was a truck waiting to pull out at the stop which Rafael chose to pass in the opposing lane, bursting out in front of a crossing car with his tyres screeching on the hot tarmac. Mike stared from behind splayed fingers as Rafael corrected the counter swerve and began to accelerate in and out of the fast moving traffic. After a series of heart-stopping manoeuvres Rafael finally caught sight of the rear of the white Dodge Ram. He eased off the power and crept forward until he was just one car behind it, but before he had time to figure out his next move, the Dodge's indicator light signalled that he would leave at the next junction. Rafael followed when it drifted onto the exit lane, but he realised that he'd been duped when it swerved back onto the highway at the last second and accelerated away. With all pretence at subtlety now abandoned, Rafael jammed his foot on the gas pedal and gave chase. The rear window of the Dodge exploded as a stream of automatic machine gun fire was directed towards them. Rafael returned fire, trying to blow out the Dodge's tyres, but he was shooting left handed, his arm thrust awkwardly out of the window.

'Shit!' he swore as the Dodge picked up speed, weaving erratically through the traffic. 'You know how to use one of these things?' he asked, holding out his Beretta.

'No, I haven't a clue,' replied Mike, tentatively taking the gun and turning it over in his hand.

'It's loaded. Just point and shoot. Tyres get you bonus points.'

Rafael floored the accelerator and the finely tuned engine of the Chevrolet began to whine as they closed in on the Dodge. Mike leaned out of the open window, holding the Beretta at arms length with his finger poised on the trigger. A burst of machine gun fire struck the nearside wing of the Chevrolet and Rafael was forced to swerve and brake. He fell back several car lengths and had to work hard to regain his position, edging closer through fast moving traffic. Pacal moved to the outside lane, shielding himself in front of a freight truck and Rafael made an approach along its flank. Mike caught sight of the front tyres of the dodge as they moved closer and he took aim, waiting until he had a clear shot. The dodge edged closer to the central reservation as an intersection approached and then with a screech of tyres, it suddenly turned sharply and was gone. Hemmed in by the truck, Rafael was powerless to follow and overshot the junction. In frustration, he swerved towards the inner lane, slowed and when there was a gap in the traffic he cut straight across both lanes and bounced over the central reservation onto the other side of the road. There was a blaring of horns as he swerved out in front of the oncoming cars, blue smoke screaming from the tyres as he corrected the slide and floored the gas pedal.

'That's one sneaky sonofabitch,' he said scowling.

Mike sat in stunned silence, his face ashen and his wet palms planted firmly against the dashboard.

The satellite phone began to ring and Rafael tapped a button on his headset.

'Yeah?'

'Looks like you're getting your ass whipped Rodriguez,' Kruger said smugly. 'In case you're still interested, your target just left the highway.'

'Thanks for your enlightened observations. Where's he heading?'

'Well now, remember that hidden passageway you found on the coast last week?'

'Yeah. What about it?'

'Looks like he's headed in that direction.'

'You sure about that?'

'It's either that or he's planning to ditch the car and make a run for it. It's a dead end.'

'OK, keep the line open, I'll need instructions.'

'From what I just saw, you need all the help you can get. Take the next exit on your left.'

Rafael kept his foot down hard on the accelerator and drifted towards the inside lane. When he spotted the turn he braked sharply, dropped down a couple of gears and threw the wheel hard over. Mike was thrown against the passenger door as the Chevrolet skidded across loose grit, the wheels momentarily drifting onto the sun baked mud at the side of the road.

'There's a right turn coming up approximately four hundred yards ahead,' said Kruger's voice. 'Two hundred now. One hundred and closing.'

Rafael slammed on the brakes, sending Mike flying forwards and then sideways as he powered through the turn, narrowly missing a tree.

'Where is he now?' asked Rafael, wincing as they crashed and bounced over rutted ground.

'The target is just approaching the tunnel entrance, approximately a quarter of a mile ahead of you.'

'That puts me about a minute behind,' said Rafael.

'Thank God for that,' muttered Mike, nursing a bump on the side of his head.

The Chevrolet squealed and shuddered as it bounced over the baked earth, sending dust and grit shooting out from its underside. Beyond a small ridge they finally saw a flash of white and Rafael floored the accelerator for the last few yards before skidding to a halt behind the stationary Dodge.

'Pass me the gun,' he said, holding out his hand insistently.

Mike handed over the Beretta and stayed put while Rafael jumped out of the Chevrolet and ran hunched over towards the Dodge. After a rapid peek inside Rafael scanned the surrounding trees and then studied the ground intently. Within seconds he'd located the camouflaged hatch and Mike joined him as he was wrenching it open.

'You still there Kruger?' Rafael said into his microphone.

'Affirmative.'

'The target entered the tunnel. I'm going in after him so

communications will be temporarily suspended. Maintain close surveillance on the seaward exit and get a helicopter on standby in case our target tries to make an escape.'

'We have it covered.'

Rafael threw a flash grenade down the shaft and then quickly followed, dropping down to the wooden steps below. He squatted down, swinging the gun in a sweeping arc. Pacal was nowhere to be seen. The sound of a distant jetski told him that he was making his advantage count.

'Hurry, let's go,' Rafael shouted, leaping to the cave floor as Mike's feet touched the wooden planking behind. There were two jetskis drifting free from their moorings and Rafael placed his gun on the quayside before diving straight into the water and swimming hard until he reached the nearest of them. He climbed onto it, started up the engine, whipped around tightly and then returned to pick up Mike.

'Grab the gun and jump on,' he said as he neared the edge of the pool.

Mike reacted quickly, and within seconds Rafael was transferring him to the other jetski. Rafael went on ahead, gunning the jetski for all he was worth, but Mike was soon hurtling down the tunnel after him. As they reached the halfway point the overhead lights suddenly went out and two powerful lamps at the end of the tunnel were all that remained to light their way. Mike realised that that the lamps were submersible when they dimmed to a faint greenish glow and then melted into the darkness. Under the limited beam of Rafael's flashlight, they continued until they reached the quayside at the end of the tunnel. There was no sign of Pacal. Mike dismounted and ran along the quayside towards the white control box. He threw the main light switch and then checked the winch control.

'The sea gate is open,' he shouted in alarm. 'He must have escaped using the sled.'

'That's what I figured,' sighed Rafael. 'There's probably a boat waiting for him outside. The PIC will have to take it from here.'

Mike wrenched open the locker doors and pulled out two SCUBA sets and a speargun.

'Come on, we can't give up just yet,' he said.

Rafael eyed the equipment warily.

'I guess it won't hurt to try,' he said with a shrug.

Spurred into action, Mike strapped weighted buoyancy jackets onto two cylinders, attached regulators to them and turned on the air supply.

'Just jump straight in with the gear,' he said.

'What?'

'Like this.'

Rafael watched Mike pull a mask over his head, slip on a pair of fins and tuck one of the cylinders under his arm. With the regulator held in his mouth, he picked up the speargun and jumped straight into the water. When Rafael realised that Mike was not coming back, he quickly donned the remaining gear and leapt in after him.

He plunged into darkness, the dim artificial light from above enough to orient him until he could see the dazzling blue window which marked the cave's seaward exit. In the centre of it, he could see Mike's grainy shadow, slowly melting into the vastness of the liquid world beyond. With the current behind him, Rafael moved swiftly along the passageway, slipping his arms into the buoyancy jacket as he went. He passed under the raised barrier without a backward glance and a few firm scissor kicks sent him shooting out into the open sea. Mike was already some distance ahead of him, following the guide chain along the seabed in the hope that Pacal had done the same. Rafael caught up with him as he was reaching the end of it. After a brief exchange of signals they rose towards the surface, turning in all directions.

'Did you see anything?' asked Rafael, his eyes scanning the empty horizon.

'Not a damned thing,' answered Mike.

'He must be out here somewhere. I heard the whine of the electric motors when I jumped in.'

272

'Yeah, so did I...and if there was a boat out here waiting for him, we should've heard her engines too.'

'You think maybe he's trying to make his escape underwater?'

'It's possible,' replied Mike with a shrug. 'He's obviously determined enough.'

'What kind of range do those things have?'

'A couple of miles I'd guess.'

'Then the PIC guys should still be able to spot him when he surfaces.'

'Unless he's lying low on the seabed somewhere, waiting to return to the cave.'

'That's a good point,' agreed Rafael, 'but if we close the gate, he'll have no choice but to surface somewhere around here within the next couple of hours, right?'

'I suppose so.'

'And even if he's crazy enough to try digging underneath it like you did, he'd still have to exit through the hatch right?'

'I prefer to use the word daring,' said Mike, 'but yes; that would seem logical.'

'Good, because I'd much prefer to wait this out in the comfort of my car, where I have access to a satellite phone, a half bottle of tequila and a cigar.'

'You really are a credit to your profession,' said Mike.

'Yeah. I'm sure my boss would agree with you.'

They slipped back into the water, followed the chain back to the cave entrance and used it to pull themselves back against the current. Once inside, Mike threw his equipment onto the quayside and went to close the gate. Rafael retrieved his gun and flashlight from behind one of the lockers and then they jumped on their jetskis and headed back down the tunnel in the sure knowledge that they'd done all that was possible to prevent Pacal's escape. However, there was a nasty surprise waiting for them when they reached the bowl shaped cavern. For there, abandoned and floating ominously beside the quayside was an all too familiar craft. When Mike found the will to speak, his words seemed to resonate from the pit of his stomach.

'I don't believe it. The devious bastard never left the cave. He turned off the lights and used the sled to pass beneath us.'

AKUMAL

Gabriela picked up a handful of sand and watched the tiny white grains flow through the gaps in her fingers.

'Pacal is your uncle?' said Mike, astonished.

'His real name is Luis. He adopted the name Pacal from an ancient Maya king...and yes he's my uncle, not that it ever won me any favours. I think maybe I remind him of my mother, who he once loved...and my father, who he murdered.'

'He killed your father? But why?'

'Jealousy,' she said with a shrug. 'My Grandfather was the Chieftain of the village back then and my father, being the eldest of his two sons was in line to succeed him. That was hard enough for Luis to accept, but when my mother rejected his advances and chose to marry my father instead, he lost all sense of reason.'

Gabriela drew her knees towards her chest and wrapped her arms tightly around them.

'My father's body was discovered at the bottom of a cenoté shortly after my Grandfather's death. Everyone knew that Luis had killed him, but no one could speak against him because with my father out of the way he'd become the new Chieftain.'

Mike shook his head.

'You must really hate him.'

'I do, but not for those reasons. I was too young to know my father...and my mother...well I've never known her to be happy. I hate him more than anything because he forced the other villagers to turn against us. We were treated like outcasts and forced to move away from our home.'

Mike watched her staring fixedly out to sea.

'That must have been hard for you all.'

'It wasn't easy, but we survived. My mother's a tough lady.'

'Her daughter too,' said Mike, raising an eyebrow.

'I'm not sure whether I should take that as a compliment,' said Gabriella aiming a sideways glance at Mike.

'You should - and it is.'

Mike leant back and propped himself up on his elbows. 'So did everybody in the village know that Pacal was using the cave to process drugs?'

'No, it came as a surprise to most of us. Only a few of Pacal's most trusted men really knew what was happening down there and the rest of us were never allowed to visit the City of Darkness alone. I suppose he counted on the fact that no one from Yalché would ever expose the existence of the caves. They were a link to our past; a secret that was entrusted to us by our ancestors.'

'And without Pacal, it might have stayed that way.'

'No,' replied Gabriela, shaking her head solemnly. 'We all knew that it was just a matter of time before they were discovered. Tourism draws attention to an area and when adventurous people like you and Frank come along...'

Mike shuffled uncomfortably.

'Yeah, I see what you mean.'

'So how *did* you find out about the caves anyway?' asked Gabriela, eying him enquiringly.

'By accident really. I found a rough sketch of the caves that Frank made and then by asking around I tracked down the person who first introduced him to them.'

'So it wasn't Frank who discovered the caves?' asked Gabriela, surprised. 'I assumed that it was because I knew that Pablo would never have told anyone.'

'No, Frank didn't find them...and the person who did isn't a diver so he had no particular interest in them. Frank realised their potential and I presume he trusted Pablo enough to ask his help in exploring the system. They worked together after all.'

'What bad luck,' said Gabriela frowning, 'Frank was so young and full of life. If only he'd given me some idea of what he was planning, I could have warned him before it was too late.'

'Don't beat yourself up about it. If I know Frank, he wouldn't have told another living soul, but I appreciate the fact that you tried to warn me.'

'Tried, but obviously didn't succeed,' said Gabriela, pursing her lips.

'That's just me. I'm far too stubborn for my own good.'

'I've noticed!'

Mike smiled and traced a circle in the sand with his finger.

'I take it you weren't there when Frank was killed?'

'No,' replied Gabriela, shaking her head vigorously.

'So how come you took part in the ceremony when I was up on the altar?'

Gabriela winced.

'Pacal was growing bolder and I think he wanted to use the Ceremony of the Descending God to demonstrate his power to the whole of Yalché. He obviously didn't trust me after what happened that night on the beach and I think he wanted to make an example of me; to show what would happen to anyone who stepped out of line.'

'Yeah? Well, I'm very grateful that you didn't give him that satisfaction.'

'Me too,' said Gabriela, her mascara rimmed eyes sparkling as her lips curled into a smile.

Mike watched her brush a strand of hair behind her ear, nursing a strong desire to kiss her.

'So what will you do now?' he asked.

'I'm not sure. I'm thinking about maybe going to work in Cancun for a while. My brother is the manager of a hotel up there.'

'Sounds good,' said Mike. 'Cancun's not too far away. Maybe I could come and visit you there.'

'I would like that,' said Gabriela, smiling, 'but not while you still have a girlfriend.'

'You mean Beth? Sure she's a great girl and everything, but we're not going steady. Her life's in San Diego and mine is...well, anywhere where the seas are warm and the skies are blue.'

'Is that why she's been staring at us for the past fifteen minutes?'

'What?'

Mike turned to see Beth standing outside the *Buena Onda* bar with her arms crossed and her lips pulled tight. He smiled and waved sheepishly, nodding as she pointed to her watch.'

'Nice try,' said Gabriela, with a knowing smile.

Before Mike had a chance to speak, she pressed a piece of paper into his hand and kissed him on the cheek.

'Here's my phone number for when you learn to be a true gentleman.'

'No wait, I just...can't we talk about this?' pleaded Mike as Gabriela stood up and shook the sand from her skirt.

Gabriela's response was to smile, fan her hand in salute and saunter away without a backward glance. Mike rose to his feet, biting back his disappointment as he watched her pad barefoot along the shoreline, the graceful movement of her hips in perfect harmony with the glistening waves that were sliding back and forth across the bone white beach. He stood rooted to the spot until he felt Beth's eyes burning into the back of his head, then with a sigh of resignation he pocketed the piece of paper, turned and strolled back along the beach towards her.

'What was that all about,' she asked as he approached.

'Oh, no big deal; there were just one or two questions that I needed answering,' he said, ignoring Rafael's mischievous smile.

'Such as?' pressed Beth.

'Just a few details about Frank's death.'

Beth's frown softened.

'She's very pretty,' she said, somewhat accusingly.

Mike looked her dead in the eye and marked a pause.

'Not as pretty as you Beth.'

Beth sucked in her cheeks and made a low grunting sound. Over her shoulder Mike could see Rafael miming applause.

'I'll have a strawberry daiquiri,' Beth said finally.

'My pleasure,' replied Mike, breathing an inward sigh of relief. He strolled over to the bar and was quickly joined by Rafael.

'Congratulations! You really have quite a talent for this subterfuge stuff Mike. Have you ever thought about doing it as a profession?'

'Doing what?'

'You know. Intelligence work,' said Rafael, lowering his voice. 'That's all there is to it really. A bit of casual observation, telling people what they want to hear, making them believe what you want them to believe, you know what I'm saying?'

'You're talking about doing what *you* do for a living right?'

Rafael shrugged.

'Why not? It's exciting and the money's good.'

'Do you get to dive?' asked Mike

Rafael, pulled a face and sucked air through his teeth.

'Not very often.'

'Do you get to choose where you go?'

Rafael replied by frowning and rocking his hand from side to side.

'More importantly,' asked Mike. 'Is there a chance you'll get killed far from home in some godforsaken shithole?'

Rafael thought about this one carefully.

'So tell me. How much can you earn as a diving instructor?'

They both burst into laughter.

'I'm ordering a beer. You want one?' said Mike, drawing the attention of a slightly built waiter.

'Sure. I'll have a Sol.'

'A strawberry daiquiri, a Tecate and a Sol, *por favour*,' Mike said to the waiter.

Beth came over to join them.

'So, did Rafael tell you about our invitation?' she asked.

'No,' said Mike, turning towards Rafael.

'Oh yeah. The Spanish consulate and the Mexican authorities want to fly us to Mexico City to thank us for our help in freeing Ambassador Perez and putting an end to Meléndez's terrorist organisation.'

'That sounds like a blast,' said Mike. 'Will it be an official function?'

'These kind of things usually are,' said Rafael. 'Chances are it'll be covered by the media too. Everyone will be there to milk the publicity.'

'No such thing as a free lunch eh? I guess that means I'll have to splash out on a suit and tie then.'

'That might be wise,' said Beth. 'Dignitaries have a tendency to frown upon ripped tee shirts and beach pants.'

'Hmmm, Pacal has got a lot to answer for,' said Mike, tetchily. He glanced at Rafael, who for some reason was edging his way along the bar.

'Hey Rod, did you know that Pacal was Gabriela's uncle?' His real name is Luis. Uncle Luis; can you believe that?'

'Yeah, I know. His full name is Luis Meléndez,' said Rafael, staring across the room. 'A respectable and influential businessman if you believe what the official records say. I guess that no one outside of Yalché ever knew that his alter-ego was a drug-dealing, murdering megalomaniac.'

'And that was on his good days,' said Mike.

'Have there been any sightings of him?' asked Beth.

'Not a thing. He seems to have disappeared off the face of the earth. His house was abandoned by the time we got there and the Dodge was left on the drive with the keys still in the ignition. There were signs that he'd been there and left in a hurry, but no clues as to where he was going. We informed all the transport networks and border controls of course, but I doubt if that will stop someone like Pacal. If he's escaped on foot through the jungle into Guatemala, the chances are that we'll never catch up with him again. The forested areas are so vast and isolated down that way he could travel for weeks on end without being seen.'

'So you think he's going to get away with it?' asked Mike.

'That's difficult to say. If he goes into hiding, it will certainly be a challenge to find him, but I've a feeling that a man with Pacal's ego won't be able to keep quiet for long.'

'What's the news from Fabrizio and Claudio?' asked Beth.

'I spoke to the chief medical officer at the military hospital in Fort Jackson this afternoon,' replied Rafael. 'They're both doing fine and it sounds like they'll be given the all clear to fly into Cancun tomorrow. From what I've been hearing the staff will probably be glad to see the back of them. The CMO says that Fabrizio hasn't stopped lecturing the doctors and nurses about the plant extracts used to form the basis of their drugs, while Claudio has spent most of his time shouting down the telephone at his restaurant staff and complaining about the food.'

'They're definitely on the mend then,' said Mike.

'Sure sounds like it,' agreed Beth.

The waiter arrived at that moment and placed their drinks on the bar. Mike was just about to pull out his wallet when Rafael reached over and grabbed the man's wrist, picking up one of the beers and holding it in front of his face.

'Drink it!' he ordered.

Beth and Mike stared at Rafael as if he'd gone mad.

'Please, you are hurting my wrist,' said the waiter, wincing.

'I'll break it if you don't take a drink.'

'I don't drink,' said the waiter. 'Help me, someone. Call the police.'

'Yes, please would someone call the police,' said Rafael to the frightened customers surrounding the bar, then I can explain to them that this man was trying to poison us.'

'Poison!' said Beth, staring in sudden horror at her untouched daiquiri.

'You're crazy,' said the waiter. 'Help me someone.'

'Hey, leave the guy alone,' said a stocky, shaven-headed tourist who was standing nearby.

'Sir, I promise you that I will release him, offer my apologies and compensate him with a hundred dollars if he just takes a drink from this bottle,' said Rafael, without diverting his eyes.

The waiter suddenly threw out his arm and sent the drinks flying from the serving counter, spraying the shaven headed tourist with strawberry daiquiri. The man looked down at the bright red stain on his shirt and slowly rose to his feet.

'Just hold him there one second,' he said, raising a precautionary finger. The man approached and without warning punched the waiter full in the face, sending him crashing to the floor.

'Nicely done sir,' said Rafael, letting go of the waiter's wrist.

From the corner of his eye Mike saw another waiter charging towards Rafael with a long steel blade protruding from his fist.

'Rafael!' he shouted, bolting forwards.

Beth screamed as Mike leapt onto the bar, thrusting his arm out in front of him and blocking the waiter's lunging attack. The man was momentarily knocked off his balance, but recovered quickly and tried to stab Mike in the ribs. Fortunately for Mike he was already sliding off the bar and the blade plunged harmlessly into the wooden counter. Before the knifeman had time to pull it free, Rafael was upon him. He seized his wrist, broke his forearm with a sharp strike from his elbow and taking no chances, slammed his head against the solid wood counter until he was out cold. Mike dragged himself to his feet, pulling a shard of glass from his arm and wincing from a heavy fall on his knee. Beth came over to help him, her face a mask of terror.

'Mike! Are you okay?'

'I'll live,' said Mike, brushing himself down. 'Just another few bruises to add to the collection.'

'It goes with the territory,' said Rafael, wiping his hands on the back of the waiter's waistcoat. He turned to see the other customers staring nervously at him from behind the protection of their seats. A mischievous smile lit up his face as he spread his arms wide.

'Well ladies and Gentlemen, I'm afraid that wraps up the entertainment for the evening. Due to an unforeseeable staff shortage the bar will be closing early tonight, but in the meantime, please feel free to help yourself to complimentary drinks. I wish you a pleasant evening.'

He chuckled to himself and then casually lifted the knife wielding waiter's head up by his lank, greasy hair.

'You remember this guy Mike?'

Mike peeled away from Beth's embrace and stared at the bloodied face of his unconscious attacker. It was the same flat-nosed barman who'd confronted him the night he first met Gabriela.

'Oh yeah, I remember him all right!' he said, narrowing his eyes. 'I'll bet it was his idea to poison us.'

'More than likely,' agreed Rafael. 'I noticed him lurking behind the partition when we arrived and I've been watching him since. I knew that something was going down when the waiter who took your order went to fetch the drinks from the other side of the bar. He served everyone else from this side. Once I'd guessed their little ruse, it was easy enough to spot our friend here adding a little spice to the drinks before the waiter brought them over.'

'You're damned good Rod,' said Mike, slipping his arm around Beth's waist and pulling her towards him.

'Thank God you were here,' added Beth, 'I don't know what would've happened if we'd been here alone.'

'It was no big deal,' said Rafael. 'I was just doing my job. Mike's the one who should get the accolades. If it wasn't for his quick reactions I'd have a wooden handle sticking out of my back right now and I'd have more than strawberry daiquiri staining my shirt.'

Mike shrugged.

'I just did what anyone would do.'

'No. You did what anyone *could* do, but probably wouldn't if push came to shove. That's what makes the difference.'

Rafael opened a fridge, pulled out three beers and popped their caps.

Mike glanced at Beth, who smiled proudly and kissed him.

'Anyhow, I think we can all take this as a warning,' he said, pushing the bottles across the counter towards them. 'Pacal may no longer be around, but his cronies are and I can't see them inviting us round for a hog roast anytime soon. If I was you Mike, I'd go right home, pack my belongings and get the hell out of here without a backward glance. That's what I intend to do just as soon as I've finished this beer.'

'He's right Mike,' said Beth. 'You've no reason to stick around here any longer. Let's just pack our things, jump in the car and head north.'

'Where to?

'I'm heading up to Playa del Carmen, if you want to join me,' said Rafael. 'I still have a week's rental left on a twin bedroom beachfront villa. Seems a shame to waste it.'

'Well that sounds absolutely perfect,' said Beth, 'and it's just a short hop on the ferry to Cozumel from there.'

'Cozumel?' said Rafael. 'What's the attraction there?'

'It's the only place in the world where you can find yellow-mouthed toadfish.'

Puzzled, Rafael looked to Mike for an explanation.

'Don't ever make vague promises to a Marine Biologist,' he said wearily.

EPILOGUE

SOMEWHERE IN THE CARIBBEAN SEA

The small power boat tore across the glistening sea like a razor blade slicing through silk. On the horizon a gleaming white motor yacht was waiting, its sleek lines, polished chrome and darkened windows marking it as a luxury vessel, built for speed. The smaller vessel approached and throttled back, shaping its course to come gently alongside. Cables were lowered from a lifting gantry aboard the motor yacht and connected to eyes in the smaller vessel's bow and stern. With a whirr of machinery, it was lifted clear of the water, swung inboard, and lowered onto a purpose built cradle.

A man in a beige linen suit, open-necked shirt and alligator skin shoes emerged from the smoked glass doors which separated the main salon from the spacious teak afterdeck. There was a flash of gold from the Rolex that hung from his wrist as he lifted his hand to pull on a long Cuban cigar. Everything about his appearance spoke of sophistication, but his skin bore the scars of an earlier life spent fighting for survival in the slums of a tough city.

He watched in silence as three men stepped from the power boat dragging a heavy canvas sack along with them. A grunt was heard as it slipped over the rail and slumped to the deck. The three men stood aside, waiting for instructions. There was a moment of distraction as a slim, dark haired girl wearing a white bikini and towel robe appeared at the salon doors. The man in the linen suit cursed and pushed her back inside, closing the sliding doors behind her. He sighed, took a pull on his cigar and stared at the three men in turn.

'So are you going to open it, or do we need to wait for Christmas?'

A small balding man with a neat moustache pulled out a flick-knife and sliced open the canvas bag along its length. Inside, a man wriggled free, like a caterpillar shedding its skin. With his hands and feet bound, he lay prostrate until he was dragged to his knees before the man in the linen suit.

'So this is the infamous Señor Pacal,' said Ángel Batista, spitting a strand of tobacco from the side of his mouth. 'Or should we call you Señor Meléndez, now that there is no longer any need for pretence?'

Pacal's eyes narrowed. He stared in defiance at his captor, muttering curses from behind the surgical band that was taped across his mouth.

'You've never seen me before have you Señor Meléndez? And if that doesn't worry you - it should. You see it doesn't make sense to reveal one's true identity when you are in the kind of business that I am in, as many of my competitors have found to their cost. Discretion is absolutely fundamental to the continued success of an organisation like mine...and naturally I expect my clients to display a similar level of discipline. Of course, if your presence here was simply the result of a matter of personal indiscretion, a sharp reminder of your obligations might be in order. But never in my wildest dreams, Señor Meléndez, did I think it possible that one of my own clients could do something so devastatingly idiotic, that it would plunge the whole industry into crisis. Now you can imagine that I might simply have had my men dispose of you and that would be the end of the affair, but to ensure that I never have to deal with this situation again, I'm prepared to spare you your life Señor Meléndez if you can explain to me just what it was that drove you to commit this act of lunacy.'

A brief nod from his brother-in-law was Julio's cue to rip the surgical band from Pacal's mouth in a single movement. Pacal grimaced and spat an angry crimson splash of blood onto the bone white deck. Ángel stared at it in disgust, knowing that it would stain, leaving an indelible reminder of the incident.

'I paid for the merchandise in full,' Pacal said sullenly. 'There was no mention of what I could or could not do with it...and besides, there was never any risk of it being traced back to you.'

Ángel picked at his teeth with his thumb nail.

'You're an amateur Señor Meléndez. The capabilities of the DEA and the CIA should never be underestimated. You have compromised the security and sustainability of my operation through your arrogance and ignorance. Whether you intended to do so or not is irrelevant.'

Pacal thrust out his jaw and stared at his captor from the depths of his brow.

'You're Colombian aren't you?'

'What of it?'

'The Spanish colonists destroyed your people too. They killed your men, raped your women and took your children into slavery. How can you sit back and watch their bastard sons run your nation?'

'My people?' said Ángel, frowning and pointing to his chest. 'My people?' he repeated, now laughing out loud. 'I don't even know who my parents are!'

Julio and the other men joined in his laughter.

Pacal's face darkened.

'If you have lost all knowledge of your culture then I pity you,' he said, his eye's unwavering, 'for it is the most important thing a man can have. I am and always have been Maya, my people are Maya and our fight to save our way of life is as important today as it was when the Spaniards first soiled our land with their presence.'

'And that's why you decided to poison them?' asked Ángel, shaking his head.

'They stole from us and never offered compensation,' spat Pacal. 'They murdered us and never uttered a word of regret. For centuries we have been forced to live in the shadow of their passing, but now all that will change. The Sun Jaguar has at last returned to guide us from the darkness of the underworld and in his name we shall seek our vengeance.'

Ángel watched in open-mouthed astonishment as Pacal threw back his head, his feverish eyes gazing fixedly towards the skies.

'*Está loco* – He's crazy,' said Julio, shaking his head. What you wanna do with him?'

Ángel sighed, blowing out his cheeks.

'Julio, don't you ever bring a crazy sonofabitch like him anywhere near my business again; otherwise you're going to be wearing your balls like a necklace... *¿me entiendes?*'

'I hear you,' replied Julio.

'Good. Let him go for a swim.'

Julio nodded to the tattooed man standing on his left whose face cracked into a toothless grin. He unsheathed a machete, tossed it from one hand to the other and then brought it down on the back of Pacal's heels. A torrent of curses flew like poisoned darts from Pacal's mouth as the razor sharp blade was dragged across them, slicing clean through his Achilles tendons. Ángel had to admit a grudging admiration for his unrelenting defiance.

'I said that I would spare your life and despite what you may think, I am a man of my word,' he said, as Pacal was dragged towards the stern of the motor launch. 'But whether or not you survive the next 24 hours is an entirely different matter.'

The ropes binding Pacal's hands and feet were severed and he was unceremoniously kicked into the water. Julio shouted to the helmsman and the twin screws of the motor yacht burst into life, instantly churning the water white and sending Pacal tumbling in the roiling outflow. With his feet now next to useless, Pacal had to thrash his arms to keep his head above the surface of the water. He watched in growing desperation as the sleek motor yacht receded towards the horizon, taking with it all hope of reprieve. He turned in all directions, hoping to sight land, but all he could see was a featureless oily sheen, the sea almost indistinguishable from the sky. How long had it been since they'd left the shore? One hour? Two hours? He couldn't say for sure. He shaded his eyes and looked up at the sun through splayed fingers trying to orient himself towards the west, but it was nearly twenty four hours since he'd fled the city of darkness and the sun was once again reaching its zenith, dead centre in the sky. How could the god's betray him in such an hour of need? He cried out in anger and frustration, furiously beating the water with his fists. And deep below the surface, the low resonance of the rhythmic pounding stimulated a predatory impulse that was compounded by the scent of blood.

Lightning Source UK Ltd.
Milton Keynes UK
UKOW052153100112

185117UK00002B/37/P

9 781906 628406